DEAD RECKONING

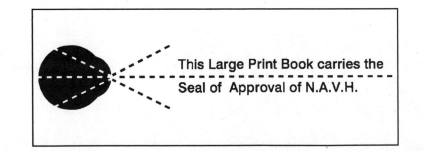

DEAD RECKONING

CHARLAINE HARRIS

WHEELER PUBLISHING
A part of Gale, Cengage Learning

GALE
CENGAGE Learning·

Detroit • New York • San Francisco • New Haven, Conn • Waterville, Maine • London

Copyright © 2011 by Charlaine Harris, Inc.
A Sookie Stackhouse Novel.
Wheeler Publishing, a part of Gale, Cengage Learning.

Wheeler Publishing Large Print Hardcover.
The text of this Large Print edition is unabridged.
Other aspects of the book may vary from the original edition.
Set in 16 pt. Plantin.

LIBRARY OF CONGRESS CATALOGING-IN-PUBLICATION DATA
Harris, Charlaine.
Dead reckoning / by Charlaine Harris.
p. cm.
"A Sookie Stackhouse novel."
ISBN-13: 978-1-4104-3508-8 (hardcover)
ISBN-10: 1-4104-3508-3 (hardcover)
1. Stackhouse, Sookie (Fictitious character)—Fiction. 2. Vampires—Fiction. 3. Werewolves—Fiction. 4. Large type books. I. Title.
PS3558.A6427D433 2011b
813'.54—dc22   2011011659

Published in 2011 by arrangement with The Berkley Publishing Group, a member of Penguin Group (USA) Inc.

Printed in the United States of America
1 2 3 4 5 6 7 15 14 13 12 11

I have to dedicate this book to
the memory of my mother.

She would not have thought it strange
to have an urban fantasy novel
dedicated to her.
She was my biggest fan and my most
faithful reader.
There was so much to admire
about my mother.
I miss her every day.

ACKNOWLEDGMENTS

I am afraid I'll skip someone this time around, because I am fortunate enough to have a lot of great help as I work on these books. Let me thank my assistant and best friend, Paula Woldan, first and foremost, for allowing me the peace of mind to work without worry; my friends and readers Toni L. P. Kelner and Dana Cameron, who help me focus on the important aspects of the work at hand; Victoria Koski, who tries to keep the huge world of Sookie in order; and my agent, Joshua Bilmes, and my editor, Ginjer Buchanan, who work so hard to keep my professional train on the tracks. For this book, I had the excellent advice of Ellen Dugan, writer, mother, and witch.

CHAPTER 1

The attic had been kept locked until the day after my grandmother died. I'd found her key and opened it that awful day to look for her wedding dress, having the crazy idea she should be buried in it. I'd taken one step inside and then turned and walked out, leaving the door unsecured behind me.

Now, two years later, I pushed that door open again. The hinges creaked as ominously as if it were midnight on Halloween instead of a sunny Wednesday morning in late May. The broad floorboards protested under my feet as I stepped over the threshold. There were dark shapes all around me, and a very faint musty odor — the smell of old things long forgotten.

When the second story had been added to the original Stackhouse home decades before, the new floor had been divided into bedrooms, but perhaps a third of it had been relegated to storage space after the

largest generation of Stackhouses had
thinned out. Since Jason and I had come to
live with my grandparents after our parents
had died, the attic door had been kept
locked. Gran hadn't wanted to clean up
after us if we decided the attic was a great
place to play.

Now I owned the house, and the key was
on a ribbon around my neck. There were
only three Stackhouse descendants — Jason, me, and my deceased cousin Hadley's
son, a little boy named Hunter.

I waved my hand around in the shadowy
gloom to find the hanging chain, grasped it,
and pulled. An overhead bulb illuminated
decades of family castoffs.

Cousin Claude and Great-Uncle Dermot
stepped in behind me. Dermot exhaled so
loudly it was almost a snort. Claude looked
grim. I was sure he was regretting his offer
to help me clean out the attic. But I wasn't
going to let my cousin off the hook, not
when there was another able-bodied male
available to help. For now, Dermot went
where Claude went, so I had two for the
price of one. I couldn't predict how long
the situation would hold. I'd suddenly realized that morning that soon it would be
too hot to spend time in the upstairs room.
The window unit my friend Amelia had

installed in one of the bedrooms kept the living spaces tolerable, but of course we'd never wasted money putting one in the attic.

"How shall we go about this?" Dermot asked. He was blond and Claude was dark; they looked like gorgeous bookends. I'd asked Claude once how old he was, to find he had only the vaguest idea. The fae don't keep track of time the same way we do, but Claude was at least a century older than me. He was a kid compared to Dermot; my great-uncle thought he was seven hundred years my senior. Not a wrinkle, not a gray hair, not a droop anywhere, on either of them.

Since they were much more fairy than me — I was only one-eighth — we all seemed to be about the same age, our late twenties. But that would change in a few years. I would look older than my ancient kin. Though Dermot looked very like my brother, Jason, I'd realized the day before that Jason had crow's-feet at the corners of his eyes. Dermot might not ever show even that token of aging.

Pulling myself back into the here and now, I said, "I suggest we carry things down to the living room. It's so much brighter down there; it'll be easier to see what's worth keeping and what isn't. After we get everything out of the attic, I can clean it up after you two leave for work." Claude owned a strip club in Monroe and drove over every day, and Dermot went where Claude went. As always . . .

"We've got three hours," Claude said.

"Let's get to work," I said, my lips curving upward in a bright and cheerful smile. That's my fallback expression.

About an hour later, I was having second thoughts, but it was too late to back out of the task. (Getting to watch Claude and Dermot shirtless made the work a lot more interesting.) My family has lived in this house since there have been Stackhouses in Renard Parish. And that's been well over a hundred and fifty years. We've saved things.

The living room began to fill up in a hurry. There were boxes of books, trunks full of clothes, furniture, vases. The Stackhouse family had never been rich, and apparently we'd always thought we could find a use for anything, no matter how battered or broken, if we kept it long enough. Even the two fairies wanted to take a break after maneuvering an incredibly heavy wooden desk down the narrow staircase. We all sat on the front porch. The guys sat on the railing, and I slumped down on the swing.

"We could just pile it all in the yard and burn it," Claude suggested. He wasn't joking. Claude's sense of humor was quirky at best, minuscule the rest of the time.

"No!" I tried not to sound as irritated as I felt. "I know this stuff is not valuable, but if other Stackhouses thought it ought to be stored up there, I at least owe them the courtesy of having a look at all of it."

"Dearest great-niece," Dermot said, "I'm afraid Claude has a point. Saying this debris is 'not valuable' is being kind." Once you heard Dermot talk, you knew his resemblance to Jason was strictly superficial.

I glowered at the fairies. "Of course to you two most of this would be trash, but to humans it might have some value," I said. "I may call the theater group in Shreveport to see if they want any of the clothes or furniture."

Claude shrugged. "That'll get rid of some of it," he said. "But most of the fabric isn't even good for rags." We'd put some boxes out on the porch when the living room began to be impassable, and he poked one with his toe. The label said the contents were curtains, but I could only guess what they'd originally looked like.

"You're right," I admitted. I pushed with my feet, not too energetically, and swung for a minute. Dermot went in the house and returned with a glass of peach tea with lots of ice in it. He handed it to me silently. I thanked him and stared dismally at all the old things someone had once treasured. "Okay, we'll start a burn pile," I said, bowing to common sense. "Round back, where I usually burn the leaves?"

Dermot and Claude glared at me.

"Okay, right here on the gravel is fine," I said. The last time my driveway had been graveled, the parking area in front of the house, outlined with landscape timbers, had gotten a fresh load, too. "It's not like I get a lot of visitors."

By the time Dermot and Claude knocked off to shower and change for work, the parking area contained a substantial mound of useless items waiting for the torch. Stackhouse wives had stored extra sheets and coverlets, and most of them were in the same ragged condition as the curtains. To my deeper regret, many of the books were mildewed and mouse-chewed. I sighed and added them to the pile, though the very idea of burning books made me queasy. But broken furniture, rotted umbrellas, spotted place mats, an ancient leather suitcase with big holes in it . . . no one would ever need these items again.

The pictures we'd uncovered — framed, in albums, or loose — we placed in a box in the living room. Documents were sorted into another box. I'd found some old dolls, too. I knew from television that people collected dolls, and perhaps these were worth something. There were some old guns, too, and a sword. Where was *Antiques Roadshow* when you needed it?

Later that evening at Merlotte's, I told my boss Sam about my day. Sam, a compact man who was actually immensely strong, was dusting the bottles behind the bar. We weren't very busy that night. In fact, business hadn't been good for the past few weeks. I didn't know if the slump was due to the chicken processing plant closing or the fact that some people objected to Sam being a shapeshifter. (The two-natured had tried to emulate the successful transition of the vampires, but it hadn't gone so well.) And there was a new bar, Vic's Redneck Roadhouse, about ten miles west off the interstate. I'd heard the Redneck Roadhouse held all kinds of wet T-shirt contests, beer pong tournaments, and a promotion called "Bring in a Bubba Night" — crap like that.

Popular crap. Crap that raked in the customers.

Whatever the reasons, Sam and I had time

to talk about attics and antiques.

"There's a store called Splendide in Shreveport," Sam said. "Both the owners are appraisers. You could give them a call."

"How'd you know that?" Okay, maybe that wasn't so tactful.

"Well, I do know a few things besides tending bar," Sam said, giving me a sideways look.

I had to refill a pitcher of beer for one of my tables. When I returned, I said, "Of course you know all kinds of stuff. I just didn't know you were into antiques."

"I'm not. But Jannalynn is. Splendide's her favorite place to shop."

I blinked, trying not to look as disconcerted as I felt. Jannalynn Hopper, who'd been dating Sam for a few weeks now, was so ferocious she'd been named the Long Tooth pack enforcer — though she was only twenty-one and about as big as a seventh grader. It was hard to imagine Jannalynn restoring a vintage picture frame or planning to fit a plantation sideboard into her place in Shreveport. (Come to think of it, I had no idea where she lived. Did Jannalynn actually have a house?)

"I sure wouldn't have guessed that," I said, making myself smile at Sam. It was my personal opinion that Jannalynn was not

16

good enough for Sam.

Of course, I kept that to myself. Glass houses, stones, right? I was dating a vampire whose kill list would top Jannalynn's for sure, since Eric was over a thousand years old. In one of those awful moments you have at random, I realized that everyone I'd ever dated — though, granted, that was a short list — was a killer.

And so was I.

I had to shake this off in a hurry, or I'd be in a melancholy funk all evening.

"You have a name and phone number for this shop?" I hoped the antiques dealers would agree to come to Bon Temps. I'd have to rent a U-Haul to get all the attic contents to Shreveport.

"Yeah, I got it in my office," Sam said. "I was talking to Brenda, the female half of the partnership, about getting Jannalynn something special for her birthday. It's coming right up. Brenda — Brenda Hesterman — called this morning to tell me she had a few things for me to look at."

"Maybe we could go see her tomorrow?" I suggested. "I have things piled all over the living room and some out on the front porch, and the good weather won't last forever."

"Would Jason want any of it?" Sam asked

diffidently. "I'm just saying, family stuff."

"He got a piecrust table around a month ago," I said. "But I guess I should ask him." I thought about it. The house and its contents were mine, since Gran had left it to me. Hmmmm. Well, first things first. "Let's ask Ms. Hesterman if she'll come give a look. If there's pieces that are worth anything, I can think about it."

"Okay," Sam said. "Sounds good. Pick you up tomorrow at ten?"

That was a little early for me to be up and dressed since I was working the late shift, but I agreed.

Sam sounded pleased. "You can tell me what you think about whatever Brenda shows me. It'll be good to have a woman's opinion." He ran a hand over his hair, which (as usual) was a mess. A few weeks ago he'd cut it real short, and now it was in an awkward stage of growing back. Sam's hair is a pretty color, sort of strawberry blond; but since it's naturally curly, now that it was growing out it couldn't seem to pick a direction. I suppressed an urge to whip out a brush and make sense out of it. That was not something an employee should do to her boss's head.

Kennedy Keyes and Danny Prideaux, who worked for Sam part-time as substitute bartender and bouncer, respectively, came in to climb on two of the empty barstools. Kennedy is beautiful. She was first runner-up to Miss Louisiana a few years ago, and she still looks like a beauty pageant queen. Her chestnut hair's all glossy and thick, and the ends wouldn't dare to split. Her makeup is meticulous. She has manicures and pedicures on a regular basis. She wouldn't buy a garment at Wal-Mart if her life depended on it.

A few years ago her future, which should have included a country club marriage in the next parish and a big inheritance from her daddy, had been derailed from its path when she'd served time for manslaughter.

Along with pretty nearly everyone I knew, I figured her boyfriend had had it coming, after I saw the pictures of her face swelling black-and-blue in her mug shots. But she'd confessed to shooting him when she called 911, and his family had a little clout, so there was no way Kennedy could walk. She'd gotten a light sentence and time off for good behavior, since she'd taught deportment and grooming to the other inmates. Eventually, Kennedy had done her time. When she'd gotten out, she'd rented a little apartment in Bon Temps, where she had an aunt, Marcia Albanese. Sam had offered her a job pretty much right after he met her, and she'd accepted on the spot.

"Hey, man," Danny said to Sam. "Fix us two mojitos?"

Sam got the mint out of the refrigerator and set to work. I handed him the sliced limes when he was almost through with the drinks.

"What are you all up to tonight?" I asked. "You look mighty pretty, Kennedy."

"I finally lost ten pounds!" she said, and when Sam deposited her glass in front of her, she lifted it to toast with Danny. "To my former figure! May I be on the road to getting it back!"

Danny shook his head. He said, "Hey! You don't need to do anything to look beautiful." I had to turn away so I wouldn't say, *Awwww.* Danny was one tough guy who couldn't have grown up in a more different environment than Kennedy — the only experience they'd had in common was jail — but boy, he was carrying a big torch for her. I could feel the heat from where I stood. You didn't have to be telepathic to see Danny's devotion.

We hadn't drawn the curtains on the front window yet, and when I realized it was dark outside, I started forward. Though I was looking out from the bright bar to the dark parking lot, there were lights out there, and something was moving . . . moving fast. Toward the bar. I had a slice of a second to think *Odd,* and then caught the flicker of flame.

"Down!" I yelled, but the word hadn't even gotten all the way out of my mouth when the window shattered and the bottle with its fiery head landed on a table where no one was sitting, breaking the napkin holder and scattering the salt and pepper shakers. Burning napkins flared out from the point of impact to drift down to the floor and the chairs and the people. The table itself was a mass of fire almost instantly.

Danny moved faster than I'd ever seen a human move. He swept Kennedy off her stool, flipped up the pass-through, and shoved her down behind the bar. There was a brief logjam as Sam, moving even faster, grabbed the fire extinguisher from the wall and tried to leap through the pass-through to start spraying.

I felt heat on my thighs and looked down to see that my apron had been ignited by one of the napkins. I'm ashamed to say that I screamed. Sam swiveled around to spray me and then turned back to the flames. The customers were yelling, dodging flames, running into the passage that led past the bathrooms and Sam's office through to the back parking lot. One of our perpetual customers, Jane Bodehouse, was bleeding heavily, her hand clapped to her lacerated scalp. She'd been sitting by the window, not her usual place at the bar, so I figured she'd been cut by flying glass. Jane staggered and would have fallen if I hadn't grabbed her arm.

"Go that way," I yelled in her ear, and shoved her in the right direction. Sam was spraying the biggest flame, aiming at the base of it in the approved manner, but the napkins that had floated away were causing lots of little fires. I grabbed the pitcher of water and the pitcher of tea off the bar and began methodically tracking the flames on the floor. The pitchers were full, and I managed to be pretty effective.

One of the window curtains was on fire, and I took three steps, aimed carefully, and tossed the remaining tea. The flame didn't quite die out. I grabbed a glass of water from a table and got much closer to the fire than I wanted to. Flinching the whole time, I poured the liquid down the steaming curtain. I felt an odd flicker of warmth behind me and smelled something disgusting. A powerful gust of chemicals made a strange sensation against my back. I turned to try to figure out what had happened and saw Sam whirling away with the extinguisher.

I found myself looking through the serving hatch into the kitchen. Antoine, the cook, was shutting down all the appliances. Smart. I could hear the fire engine in the distance, but I was too busy looking for yellow flickers to feel much relief. My eyes, streaming with tears from the smoke and the chemicals, were darting around like pinballs as I tried to spot flames, and I was coughing like crazy. Sam had run to retrieve the second extinguisher from his office, and he returned holding it ready. We rocked from side to side on our feet, ready to leap into action to extinguish the next flicker.

Neither of us spotted anything else.

Sam aimed one more blast at the bottle that had caused the fire, and then he put down the extinguisher. He leaned over to plant his hands on his thighs and inhaled raggedly. He began coughing. After a second, he bent down to the bottle.

"Don't touch it," I said urgently, and his hand stopped halfway down.

"Of course not," he said, chiding himself, and he straightened up. "Did you see who threw it?"

"No," I said. We were the only people left in the bar. I could hear the fire engine getting closer and closer, so I knew we had only a minute more to talk to each other alone. "Coulda been the same people who've been demonstrating out in the parking lot. I don't know that the church members are into firebombs, though." Not everyone in the area was pleased to know there were such creatures as werewolves and shapeshifters following the Great Reveal, and the Holy Word Tabernacle in Clarice had been sending its members to demonstrate at Merlotte's from time to time.

"Sookie," Sam said, "sorry about your hair."

"What about it?" I said, lifting my hand to my head. The shock was setting in now. I had a hard time making my hand mind my directions.

"The end of your ponytail got singed," Sam said. And he sat down very suddenly. That seemed like a good idea.

"So that's what smells so bad," I said, and collapsed on the floor beside him. We had our backs against the base of the bar, since the stools had gotten scattered in the melee of the rush out the back door. My *hair* was burned off. I felt tears run down my cheeks. I knew it was stupid, but I couldn't help it.

Sam took my hand and gripped it, and we were still sitting like that when the firefighters rushed in. Even though Merlotte's is outside the city limits, we got the official town firefighters, not the volunteers.

"I don't think you need the hose," Sam called. "I think it's out." He was anxious to prevent any more damage to the bar.

Truman La Salle, the fire chief, said, "You two need first aid?" But his eyes were busy, and his words were almost absentminded.

"I'm okay," I said, after a glance at Sam. "But Jane's out back with a cut on her head, from the glass. Sam?"

"Maybe my right hand got a little burned," he said, and his mouth compressed as if he was just now feeling the pain. He released my hand to rub his left over his right, and he definitely winced this time.

"You need to take care of that," I advised him. "Burns hurt like the devil."

"Yeah, I'm figuring that out," he said, his eyes squeezing shut.

Bud Dearborn came in as soon as Truman yelled, "Okay!" The sheriff must have been in bed, because he had a thrown-together look and was minus his hat, a reliable part of his wardrobe. Sheriff Dearborn was probably in his late fifties by now, and he showed every minute of it. He'd always looked like a Pekinese. Now he looked like a gray one. He spent a few minutes going around the bar, watching where his feet went, almost sniffing the disarray. Finally he was satisfied and came up to stand in front of me.

"What you been up to now?" he asked.

"Someone threw a firebomb in the window," I said. "None of my doing." I was too shocked to sound angry.

"Sam, they aiming for you?" the sheriff asked. He wandered off without waiting for an answer.

Sam got up slowly and turned to reach his left hand to me. I gripped it and he pulled. Since Sam's much stronger than he looks, I was on my feet in a jiffy.

Time stood still for a few minutes. I had to think that I was maybe a bit in shock.

As Sheriff Dearborn completed his slow and careful circuit of the bar, he arrived back at Sam and me.

By then we had another sheriff to deal with.

Eric Northman, my boyfriend and the vampire sheriff of Area Five, which included Bon Temps, came through the door so quickly that when Bud and Truman realized he was there, they jumped, and I thought Bud was going to draw his weapon. Eric gripped my shoulders and bent to peer into my face. "Are you hurt?" he demanded.

It was like his concern gave me permission to drop my bravery. I felt a tear run down my cheek. Just one. "My apron caught fire, but I think my legs are okay," I said, making a huge effort to sound calm. "I only lost a little hair. So I didn't come out of it too bad. Bud, Truman, I can't remember if you've met my boyfriend, Eric Northman from Shreveport." There were several iffy facts in that sentence.

"How'd you know there was trouble here, Mr. Northman?" Truman asked.

"Sookie called me on her cell phone," Eric said. That was a lie, but I didn't exactly want to explain our blood bond to our fire chief and our sheriff, and Eric would never volunteer any information to humans.

One of the most wonderful, and the most appalling, things about Eric loving me was that he didn't give a shit about anyone else. He ignored the damaged bar, Sam's burns, and the police and firefighters (who were keeping track of him from the corners of their eyes) still inspecting the building.

Eric circled me to evaluate the hair situation. After a long moment, he said, "I'm going to look at your legs. Then we'll find a doctor and a beautician." His voice was absolutely cold and steady, but I knew he

27

was volcanically angry. It rolled through the bond between us, just as my fear and shock had alerted him to my danger.

"Honey, we have other things to think about," I said, forcing myself to smile, forcing myself to sound calm. One corner of my brain pictured a pink ambulance screeching to a halt outside to disgorge emergency beauticians with cases of scissors, combs, and hair spray. "Dealing with a little hair damage can wait until tomorrow. It's a lot more important to find out who did this and why."

Eric glared at Sam as if the attack were Sam's responsibility. "Yes, his bar is far more important than your safety and well-being," he said. Sam looked astonished at this rebuke, and the beginnings of anger flickered across his face.

"If Sam hadn't been so quick with the fire extinguisher, we'd all have been in bad shape," I said, keeping up with the calm and the smiling. "In fact, both the bar and the people in it would have been in a lot more trouble." I was running out of faux serenity, and of course Eric realized it.

"I'm taking you home," he said.

"Not until I talk to her." Bud showed considerable courage in asserting himself. Eric was scary enough when he was in a *good* mood, much less when his fangs ran out as they did now. Strong emotion does that to a vamp.

"Honey," I said, holding on to my own temper with an effort. I put my arm around Eric's waist, and tried again. "Honey, Bud and Truman are in charge here, and they have their rules to follow. I'm okay." Though I was trembling, which of course he could feel.

"You were frightened," Eric said. I felt his own rage that something had happened to me that he had not been able to prevent. I suppressed a sigh at having to babysit Eric's emotions when I wanted to be free to have my own nervous breakdown. Vampires are nothing if not possessive when they've claimed someone as theirs, but they're also usually anxious to blend into the human population, not cause any unnecessary waves. This was an overreaction.

Eric was mad, sure, but normally he was also quite pragmatic. He knew I wasn't seriously hurt. I looked up at him, puzzled. My big Viking hadn't been himself in a week or two. Something other than the death of his maker was bothering him, but I hadn't built up enough courage to ask him what was wrong. I'd cut myself some slack. I'd simply wanted to enjoy the peace we'd shared for a few weeks.

Maybe that had been a mistake. Something big was pressing on him, and all this anger was a by-product.

"How'd you get here so quick?" Bud asked Eric.

"I flew," Eric said casually, and Bud and Truman gave each other a wide-eyed look. Eric had had the ability for (give or take) a thousand years, so he disregarded their amazement. He was focused on me, his fangs still out.

They couldn't know that Eric had felt the swell of my terror the minute I'd seen the running figure. I hadn't had to call him when the incident was over. "The sooner we get all this settled," I said, baring my teeth right back at him in a terrible smile, "the sooner we can leave." I was trying, not so subtly, to send Eric a message. He finally calmed down enough to get my subtext.

"Of course, my darling," he said. "You're absolutely right." But his hand took mine and squeezed too hard, and his eyes were so brilliant they looked like little blue lanterns.

Bud and Truman looked mighty relieved. The tension ratcheted down a few notches. Vampires = drama.

While Sam was getting his hand treated and Truman was taking pictures of what remained of the bottle, Bud asked me what I'd seen.

"I caught a glimpse of someone out in the parking lot running toward the building, and then the bottle came through the window," I said. "I don't know who threw it. After the window broke and the fire spread from all the lit napkins, I didn't notice anything but the people trying to leave and Sam trying to put it out."

Bud asked me the same thing several times in several different ways, but I couldn't help him any more than I already had.

"Why do you think someone would do this to Merlotte's, to Sam?" Bud asked.

"I don't understand it," I said. "You know, we had those demonstrators from the church in the parking lot a few weeks ago. They've only come back once since then. I can't imagine any of them making a — was that a Molotov cocktail?"

"How do you know about those, Sookie?"

"Well, one, I read books. Two, Terry doesn't talk about the war much, but every now and then he does talk about weapons." Terry Bellefleur, Detective Andy Bellefleur's cousin, was a decorated and damaged Vietnam veteran. He cleaned the bar when everyone was gone and came in occasionally to substitute for Sam. Sometimes he just hung at the bar watching people come in and out. Terry did not have much of a social life.

As soon as Bud declared himself satisfied, Eric and I went to my car. He took the keys from my shaking hand. I got in the passenger side. He was right. I shouldn't drive until I'd recovered from the shock.

Eric had been busy on his cell phone while I was talking to Bud, and I wasn't totally surprised to see a car parked in front of my house. It was Pam's, and she had a passenger.

Eric pulled around back where I always park, and I scrambled out of the car to hurry through the house to unlock the front door. Eric followed me at a leisurely pace. We hadn't exchanged a word on the short drive. He was preoccupied and still dealing with his temper. I was shocked by the whole incident. Now I felt a little more like myself as I went out on the porch to call, "Come in!"

Pam and her passenger got out. He was a young human, maybe twenty-one, and thin to the point of emaciation. His hair was dyed blue and cut in an extremely geometric way, rather as if he'd put a box on his head, knocked it sideways, then trimmed around the edges. What didn't fit inside the lines had been shaved.

It was eye-catching, I'll say that.

Pam smiled at the expression on my face, which I hastily transformed into something more welcoming. Pam has been a vampire since Victoria was on the English throne, and she's been Eric's right hand since he called her in from her wanderings in northern America. He's her maker.

"Hello," I said to the young man as he entered the front door. He was extremely nervous. His eyes darted to me, away from me, took in Eric, and then kind of strafed the room to absorb it. A flicker of contempt crossed his clean-shaven face as he took in the cluttered living room, which was never more than homey even when it was clean.

Pam thumped him on the back of his head. "Speak when you're spoken to, Immanuel!" she growled. She was standing slightly behind him, so he couldn't see her when she winked at me.

"Hello, ma'am," he said to me, taking a step forward. His nose twitched.

Pam said, "You smell, Sookie."

"It was the fire," I explained.

"You can tell me about it in a moment," she said, her pale eyebrows shooting up. "Sookie, this man is Immanuel Earnest," she said. "He cuts hair at Death by Fashion in Shreveport. He's brother to my lover, Miriam."

That was a lot of information in three sentences. I scrambled to absorb it.

Eric was eyeing Immanuel's coiffure with fascinated disgust. "*This* is the one you brought to correct Sookie's hair?" he said to Pam. His lips were pressed together in a very tight line. I could feel his skepticism pulsing along the line that bound us.

"Miriam says he is the best," Pam said, shrugging. "I haven't had a haircut in a hundred fifty years. How would I know?"

"Look at him!"

I began to be a little worried. Even for the circumstances, Eric was in a foul mood. "I like his tattoos," I said. "The colors are real pretty."

Aside from his extreme haircut, Immanuel was covered with very sophisticated tattoos. No "MOM" or "BETTY SUE" or naked ladies; elaborate and colorful designs extended from wrists to shoulders. He'd look dressed even when he was naked. The hairdresser had a flat leather case tucked under one of his skinny arms.

"So, you're going to cut off the bad parts?" I said brightly.

"Of your hair," he said carefully. (I wasn't

34

sure I'd needed that particular reassurance.) He glanced at me, then back down at the floor. "Do you have a high stool?"

"Yes, in the kitchen," I said. When I'd rebuilt my burned-out kitchen, custom had made me buy a high stool like the one my gran had perched on while she talked on the old telephone. The new phone was cordless, and I didn't need to stay in the kitchen when I used it, but the counter simply hadn't looked right without a stool beside it.

My three guests trailed behind me, and I dragged the stool into the middle of the floor. There was just enough room for everyone when Pam and Eric sat on the other side of the table. Eric was glowering at Immanuel in an ominous way, and Pam was simply waiting to be entertained by our emotional upheavals.

I clambered up on the stool and made myself sit with a straight back. My legs were smarting, my eyes were prickly, and my throat was scratchy. But I forced myself to smile at the hairstylist. Immanuel was real nervous. You don't want that in a person with sharp scissors.

Immanuel took the elastic band off my ponytail. There was a long silence while he regarded the damage. He wasn't thinking good thoughts. My vanity got hold of me. "Is it very bad?" I asked, trying to keep my voice from quavering. Reaction was definitely getting the upper hand, now that I was safe at home.

"I'm going to have to take off about three inches," he said quietly, as if he were telling me a relative was terminally ill.

To my shame, I reacted much the same way as if that had been the news. I could feel tears well up in my eyes, and my lips were quivering. *Ridiculous!* I told myself. My eyes slewed left when Immanuel set his leather case on the kitchen table. He unzipped it and took out a comb. There were also several pairs of scissors in special loops and an electric trimmer with its cord neatly coiled. Have hair care, will travel.

Pam was texting with incredible speed. She was smiling as though her message were pretty damn funny. Eric stared at me, thinking many dark thoughts. I couldn't read 'em, but I could sure tell he was unhappy in a major way.

I sighed and returned my gaze to straight ahead. I loved Eric, but at the moment I wanted him to take his broodiness and shove it. I felt Immanuel's touch on my hair as he began combing. It felt strange when he reached the end of its length, and a little tug and a funny sound let me know that some of my burned hair had fallen to the floor.

"It's damaged beyond repair," Immanuel murmured. "I'll cut. Then you wash. Then I cut again."

"You must quit this job," Eric said abruptly, and Immanuel's comb stopped moving until he realized Eric was talking to me.

I wanted to throw something heavy at my honeybun. And I wanted it to smack him right in his stubborn, handsome head. "We'll talk later," I said, not looking at him.

"What will happen next? You're too vulnerable!"

"We'll talk *later.*"

Out of the corner of my eye, I saw Pam look away so Eric wouldn't see her smirk.

"Doesn't she need something around her?" Eric snarled at Immanuel. "Covering her clothes?"

"Eric," I said, "since I'm all smelly and smoky and covered with fire extinguisher stuff, I don't think keeping my clothes free of burned hair is a big deal."

Eric didn't snort, but he came close. However, he did seem to pick up on my feeling that he was being a total pain, and he shut up and got a hold on himself.

The relief was tremendous.

Immanuel, whose hands were surprisingly steady for someone cooped up in a kitchen with two vampires (one remarkably irritable) and a charred barmaid, combed until my hair was as smooth as it could be. Then he picked up his scissors. I could feel the hairdresser focusing completely on his task. Immanuel was a champion at concentration, I discovered, since his mind lay open to me.

It really didn't take long. The burned bits drifted to the floor like sad snowflakes.

"You need to go shower now and come back with clean, wet hair," Immanuel said. "After that, I'll even it up. Where's your broom, your dustpan?"

I told him where to find them, and then I went into my bedroom, passing through it to my own bathroom. I wondered if Eric would join me, since I knew from past experience that he liked my shower. The way I felt, it would be far better if he stayed in the kitchen.

I pulled off my smelly clothes and ran the water as hot as I could stand it. It was a relief to step into the tub and let the heat and wetness flow over me. When the warm water hit my legs, it stung. For a few moments I wasn't appreciative or happy about anything. I just remembered how scared I'd been. But after I'd dealt with that, I had something on my mind.

The figure I'd spotted running toward the bar, bottle in hand — I couldn't be completely sure, but I suspected it had not been human.

CHAPTER 2

I stuffed my grimy, reeking clothes into the hamper in my bathroom. I'd have to presoak them in some Clorox 2 before I even tried to wash them, but of course I couldn't just toss them out before they were clean and I could assess the damage. I wasn't feeling too optimistic about the future of the black pants. I hadn't noticed they were a little scorched until I pulled them down over my tender thighs and found that my skin was pink. Only then did I remember looking down to see my apron on fire.

As I examined my legs, I realized it could have been much worse. The sparks had caught my apron, not my pants, and Sam had been very quick with the extinguisher. Now I appreciated his checking the extinguishers every year; I appreciated his going down to the fire station to get them refilled; I appreciated the smoke alarms. I had a flash of what might have been.

Deep breath, I told myself as I patted my legs dry. *Deep breath. Think of how good it feels to be clean.* It had felt wonderful to wash away the smell, to lather up my hair, to rinse out all the smell along with the shampoo.

I couldn't stop worrying about what I'd seen when I'd looked out Merlotte's window: a short figure running toward the building, holding something in one hand. I hadn't been able to tell if the runner was a man or a woman, but one thing I was sure of: The runner was a supe, and I suspected he — or she — was a twoey. This suspicion gained more weight when I added in the speed and agility of the runner and the strength and accuracy of the throw — the bottle had come at the window harder than a human could have hurled it, with enough velocity to shatter the window.

I couldn't be 100 percent sure. But vampires don't like to handle fire. Something about the vampire condition causes them to be extra flammable. It would take a very confident, or very reckless, fanger to use a Molotov cocktail as a weapon.

For that reason alone, I was inclined to put my money on the bomber being a twoey — a shapeshifter or Were of some variety. Of course, there were other sorts of supernatural creatures like elves and fairies and goblins, and they were all quicker than humans. To my regret, the whole incident had happened too swiftly for me to scope out the bomber's mind. That would have been decisive, because vampires are a big blank to me, a hole in the aether, and I also can't read fairies, though they register differently. Some twoeys I can read with fair accuracy, some I can't, but I see their brains as warm and busy.

Normally, I'm not an indecisive person. But as I patted myself dry and combed through my wet hair (feeling how strange it was that my comb completed its passage much more quickly), I worried about sharing my suspicions with Eric. When a vampire loves you — even when he simply feels proprietary toward you — his notion of protection can be pretty drastic. Eric loved going into battle; often he had to struggle to balance the political savvy of a move with his instinct to leap in with a swinging sword. Though I didn't think he'd go charging off at the two-natured community, in his present mood it seemed wiser to keep my ideas to myself until I had some evidence one way or another.

I pulled on sleep pants and a Bon Temps Lady Falcons T-shirt. I looked at my bed with longing before I left my room to rejoin the strange crowd in the kitchen. Eric and Pam were drinking some bottled synthetic blood I'd had in the refrigerator, and Immanuel was sipping on a Coke. I was stricken because I hadn't thought of offering them refreshment, but Pam caught my eye and gave me a level look. She'd taken care of it. I nodded gratefully and told Immanuel, "I'm ready now." He unfolded his skinny frame from the chair and gestured to the stool.

This time my new hairdresser unfolded a thin, shoulders-only plastic capelet and tied it around my neck. He combed through my hair himself, eyeing it intently. I tried to smile at Eric to show this wasn't so bad, but my heart wasn't in it. Pam scowled at her cell phone. A text had displeased her.

Apparently Immanuel had passed the time by combing Pam's hair. The pale golden mane, straight and fine, was pushed off her face with a blue headband. You just couldn't get any more Alice-like. She wasn't wearing a full-skirted blue dress and a white pinafore, but she *was* wearing pale blue: a sheath dress, perhaps from the sixties, and pumps with three-inch heels. And pearls.

"What's up, Pam?" I asked, simply because the silence in my kitchen was getting oppressive. "Someone sending you a nasty text?"

"Nothing's up," she snarled, and I tried not to flinch. "Absolutely nothing is happening. Victor is still our leader. Our position doesn't improve. Our requests go unanswered. Where is Felipe? We need him."

Eric glared at her. Whoa, trouble in paradise. I'd never seen them seriously at odds.

Pam was the only "child" of Eric's I'd ever met. She'd gone off on her own after spending her first few years as a vampire with him. She'd done well, but she'd told me she was glad enough to return to Eric after he'd called her to help him out in Area Five when the former queen had appointed him to the position of sheriff.

The tense atmosphere was getting to Immanuel, who was wavering in and out of his focus on his job . . . which was cutting *my hair.*

"Chill out, guys," I said sharply.

"And what is it with all the crap sitting out in your driveway?" Pam asked, her original British accent peeking through. "To say nothing of your living room and your porch. Are you having a garage sale?" You could tell she was proud of getting her terminology correct.

"Almost finished," Immanuel muttered,

his scissors snicking at a frantic rate in response to the growing tension.

"Pam, that all came out of my attic," I said, glad to talk about something so mundane and (I hoped) calming. "Claude and Dermot are helping me clean it out. I'm going to go see an antiques dealer with Sam in the morning — well, we were going to go. I don't know if Sam'll be able to make it, now."

"There, see!" Pam said to Eric. "She lives with other men. She goes shopping with other men. What kind of husband are you?"

And Eric launched himself across the table, hands extended toward Pam's throat.

The next second the two were rolling on the floor in a serious attempt to damage each other. I didn't know if Pam could actually initiate the moves to hurt Eric, since she was his child, but she was defending herself vigorously; there's a fine line there.

I couldn't scramble down from the stool fast enough to escape some collateral damage. It seemed inevitable that they would slam into the stool, and of course they did in a second. Over I went to join them on the floor, banging my shoulder against the counter in the process. Immanuel very intelligently leaped backward, and he didn't drop his scissors, a blessing to all of us. One of the vampires might have grabbed them as a weapon, or the gleaming scissors might have become embedded in some part of me.

Immanuel's hand gripped my arm with surprising strength, and he yanked me up and away. We scuttled out of the kitchen and into the living room. We stood, panting, in the middle of the cluttered room, staring down the hall in case the fight followed us.

I could hear crashing and banging, and a persistent snarly noise I finally identified as growling.

"Sounds like two pit bulls going at each other," Immanuel said. He was handling this with amazing calm. I was glad to have some human company.

"I don't know what's wrong with them," I said. "I've never seen them act like this."

"Pam's frustrated," he said with a familiarity that surprised me. "She wants to make her own child, but there's some vampire reason she can't."

I couldn't curb my surprise. "And you know all this — how? I'm sorry, that sounds rude, but I hang around with Pam and Eric a fair bit, and I haven't seen you before."

"Pam's been dating my sister." Immanuel didn't seem offended by my frankness, thank goodness. "My sister Miriam. My mom's religious," he explained. "And kind of crazy. The situation is, my sister is sick and getting sicker, and Pam really wants to bring her over before Mir gets any worse. She'll be skin and bones forever if Pam doesn't hurry."

I hardly knew what to say. "What illness does your sister have?" I said.

"She has leukemia," Immanuel said. Though he maintained his casual facade, I could read the pain underneath, and the fear and worry.

"So that's how Pam knows you."

"Yeah. But she was right. I am the best hairstylist in Shreveport."

"I believe you," I said. "And I'm sorry about your sister. I don't guess they told you why Pam wasn't able to bring Miriam over?"

"Nope, but I don't think the roadblock is Eric."

"Probably not." There was a shriek and a clatter from the kitchen. "I wonder if I ought to intervene."

"If I were you, I'd leave them to it."

"I hope they plan on paying to have my kitchen set to rights," I said, doing my best to sound angry rather than frightened.

"You know, he could order her to be still and she'd have to do it." Immanuel sounded almost casual.

He was absolutely right. As Eric's child, Pam had to obey a direct order. But for whatever reasons, Eric wasn't saying the magic word. In the meantime, my kitchen was getting wiped out. When I realized he could make the whole thing stop at any time he chose, I lost my own temper.

Though Immanuel made an ineffective grab at my arm, I stomped on my bare feet into the hall bathroom, got the handled pitcher Claude used when he cleaned the bathtub, filled it with cold water, and went into the kitchen. (I was walking a little wonky after the fall from the stool, but I managed.) Eric was on top of Pam, punching away at her. His own face was bloody. Pam's hands were on his shoulders, keeping him from getting any closer. Maybe she feared he would bite.

I stepped into position, estimating trajectory. When I was sure I had it right, I pitched cold water on the battling vampires.

I was putting out a different kind of fire, this time.

Pam shrieked like a teakettle as the cold water drenched her face, and Eric said something that sounded vile in a language I didn't know. For a split second, I thought they'd both launch themselves at me. Standing with my feet braced, empty pitcher in my hand, I gave them glare for glare. Then I turned on my heel and walked away.

Immanuel was surprised to see me return in one piece. He shook his head. Obviously, he didn't know whether to admire me or think me an idiot.

"You're nuts, woman," he said, "but at least I got your hair looking good. You should come in and get some highlights. I'll give you a break on the price. I charge more than anybody else in Shreveport." He added that in a matter-of-fact way.

"Oh. Thanks. I'll think about it." Exhausted by my long day and my burst of anger — anger and fear, they wear you out — I perched on an empty corner of my couch and waved Immanuel to my recliner, the only other chair in the room that wasn't covered with attic fallout.

We were silent, listening for renewed combat in the kitchen. To my relief, the noise didn't resume. After a few seconds Immanuel said, "I'd leave, if Pam wasn't my ride." He looked apologetic.

"No problem," I answered, stifling a yawn. "I'm just sorry I can't get into the kitchen. I could offer you more to drink or something to eat if they'd get out of there."

He shook his head. "The Coke was enough, thanks. I'm not a big eater. What do you think they're doing? Fucking?"

I hoped I didn't look as shocked as I felt. It was true that Pam and Eric had been lovers right after he turned her. In fact, she'd told me how much she'd enjoyed that phase of their relationship, though over the decades she'd found she preferred women. So there was that; also, Eric was married to me now, in a sort of nonbinding vampire way, and I was pretty sure that even a vampire-human marriage precluded the having of sex with another partner in the wife's kitchen?

On the other hand . . .

"Pam usually prefers the ladies," I said, trying to sound more certain than I actually was. When I thought of Eric with someone else, I wanted to rip out all his beautiful blond hair. By the roots. In clumps.

"She's sort of omnisexual," Immanuel offered. "My sister and Pam have had another man in the bed with them."

"Ah, okay." I held up a hand in a "stop" gesture. Some things I didn't want to imagine.

"You're a little prudish for someone who goes with a vampire," Immanuel observed.

"Yes. Yes, I am." I'd never applied that adjective to myself, but compared to Immanuel — and Pam — I was definitely straightlaced.

I preferred to think of it as having a more evolved sense of privacy.

Finally, Pam and Eric came into the living room, and Immanuel and I sat forward on the edge of our seats, not knowing what to expect. Though the two vampires were expressionless, their defensive body language let me know that they were ashamed of their loss of control.

They'd begun healing already, I noticed with some envy. Eric's hair was disheveled and one shirt sleeve was torn off. Pam's dress was ripped, and she was carrying her shoes because she'd broken a heel.

Eric opened his mouth to speak, but I jumped in first.

"I don't know what that was about," I said, "but I'm too tired to care. You two are liable for anything you broke, and I want you to leave this house right now. I'll rescind your invitation, if I have to."

Eric looked rebellious. I was sure he'd planned on spending the night at my place. This night, though, that was not gonna happen.

I'd seen headlights coming up the drive, and I was sure Claude and Dermot were here. I couldn't have fairies and vampires in the same house at the same time. Both were strong and ferocious, but vampires literally found fairies irresistible, like cats and catnip. I wasn't up to another struggle.

"Out the front door," I said, when they didn't move immediately. "Shoo! Thanks for the haircut, Immanuel. Eric, I appreciate your thinking about my *hair care needs.*" (I might have said this with more than a touch of sarcasm.) "It would have been nice if you had thought a little longer before you trashed my kitchen."

Without more ado, Pam beckoned to Immanuel, and they went out the door together, Immanuel looking very faintly amused. Pam gave me a long look as she passed me. I knew it was meant to be significant, but for the life of me I couldn't figure out what she was trying to tell me.

Eric said, "I would hold you while you sleep. Were you hurt? I'm sorry." He seemed oddly nonplussed.

At another time I would have accepted this rare apology, but not tonight. "You need to go home now, Eric. We'll talk when you can control yourself."

That was a huge rebuke to a vampire, and his back stiffened. For a moment I thought I'd have another fight on my hands. But Eric stepped out the front door, finally. When he was on the porch, he said, "I'll talk to you soon, my wife." I shrugged. Whatever. I was too tired and too aggravated to summon up any kind of loving expression.

I think Eric got in the car with Pam and the hairdresser for the drive back to Shreveport. Possibly he was too battered to fly. What the hell was up with Pam and Eric?

I tried to tell myself it was not my problem, but I had a sinking feeling that it really, really was.

Claude and Dermot came in the back a moment later, ostentatiously sniffing the air.

"The smell of smoke and vampires," Claude said, with a pronounced rolling of the eyes. "And your kitchen looks like a bear came in search of honey."

"I don't know how you stand it," Dermot said. "They smell bitter and sweet at the same time. I don't know if I like it or hate it." He held his hand over his nose dramatically. "And do I detect a trace of burned hair?"

"Fellas, chill," I said wearily. I gave them the condensed version of the firebombing at Merlotte's and the fighting in my kitchen. "So just give me a hug and let me go to bed without any more vampire comments," I said.

"Do you want us to sleep with you,

Niece?" Dermot asked, in the flowery way of the old fae, the ones who didn't spend that much time with humans. The nearness of one fairy to another is both healing and soothing. Even with as little fairy blood as I had, I found the proximity of both Claude and Dermot comforting. I hadn't realized that when I'd first met Claude and his sister Claudine, but the longer I'd known them and the more they'd touched me, the better I'd felt when they were near. When my great-grandfather Niall had embraced me, I'd felt sheer love. And no matter what Niall had done, or how dubious his decisions were, I felt that love all over again when I was near him. I had a moment's regret that I might not ever see Niall again, but I just didn't have any remaining emotional energy. "Thanks, Dermot. But I think I better fall into bed by myself tonight. You guys sleep well."

"And you, too, Sookie," Claude told me. Dermot's courtesy was rubbing off on my grumpy cousin.

I woke in the morning to the sound of knocking at the door. Rumple-headed and bleary, I dragged myself through the living room and looked through the peephole. Sam.

I opened the door and yawned in his face.

"Sam, what can I do for you? Come on in."

His glance flickered over the crowded living room, and I could see him struggling with a smile. "Aren't we still going to Shreveport?" he asked.

"Oh my gosh!" Suddenly I felt more awake. "My last thought when I fell asleep last night was that you wouldn't be able to go because of the fire at the bar. You can? You want to?"

"Yep. The fire marshal talked to my insurance company, and they've started the paperwork. In the meantime, Danny and I hauled out the burned table and the chairs, Terry's been working on the floor, and Antoine's been checking that the kitchen's in good shape. I've already made sure we've got more fire extinguishers ready to go." For a long moment, his smile faltered. "If I have any customers to serve. People aren't likely to want to come to Merlotte's if they think they might get incinerated."

I didn't exactly blame folks for worrying about that. We hadn't needed the incident of the night before, not at all. It might hasten the decline of Sam's business.

"So they need to catch whoever did it," I said, trying to sound positive. "Then people will know it's safe to come back, and we'll be busy again."

Claude came downstairs then, giving us Surly. "Noisy down here," he muttered as he passed on his way to the hall bathroom. Even slouching around in rumpled jeans, Claude walked with a grace that drew attention to his beauty. Sam gave an unconscious sigh and shook his head slightly as his eyes followed Claude, gliding down the hall as though he had ball bearings in his hip joints.

"Hey," I said, after I heard the bathroom door shut. "Sam! He doesn't have anything on you."

"Some guys," Sam began, looking abashed, and then he stopped. "Aw, forget it."

I couldn't, of course, not when I could tell directly from Sam's brain that he was — not exactly envious, but rueful, about Claude's physical attraction, though Sam knew as well as anyone that Claude was a pain in the butt.

I've been reading men's minds for years, and they're more like women than you would think, really, unless you're talking trucks. I started to tell Sam that he was plenty attractive, that women in the bar mooned over him more than he thought; but in the end, I kept my mouth shut. I had to let Sam have the privacy of his own thoughts. Because of his shifter nature, most of what was in Sam's head remained in Sam's head . . . more or less. I could get the odd thought, the general mood, but seldom anything more specific.

"Here, I'll make some coffee," I said, and when I stepped into the kitchen, Sam close on my heels, I stopped dead. I'd forgotten all about the fight the night before.

"What happened?" Sam said. "Did Claude do this?" He looked around with dismay.

"No, Eric and Pam," I said. "Oh, *zombies.*" Sam looked at me oddly, and I laughed and began to pick things up. I was abbreviating one of Pam's curses, because I wasn't *that* horrified.

I couldn't help reflecting that it would have been really, really nice if Claude and Dermot had straightened the room up before they turned in the night before. Just as lagniappe.

Then again, it wasn't their kitchen.

I set a chair on its legs, and Sam dragged the table back into position. I got the broom and dustpan, and swept up the salt, pepper, and sugar that crunched under my feet, and made a mental note to go to Wal-Mart to replace my toaster if Eric didn't send one today. My napkin holder was broken, too, and it had survived the fire of a year and a half ago. I double-sighed.

"At least the table is okay," I said.

"And only one broken leg on one of the chairs," Sam said. "Eric going to get this stuff fixed or replaced?"

"I expect he will," I said, and found that the coffeepot was intact, as were the mugs that had been hanging on a mug tree next to it; no, wait, one of them had broken. Well, five good ones. That was plenty.

I made some coffee. While Sam was carrying the garbage bag outside, I ducked into my room to get ready. I'd showered the evening before, so I only needed to brush my hair and my teeth and pull on some jeans and a "Fight Like a Girl" T-shirt. I didn't fool with makeup. Sam had seen me under all sorts of conditions.

"How's the hair?" he asked, when I emerged. Dermot was in the kitchen, too. Apparently, he'd made a quick run into town, since he and Sam were sharing some fresh doughnuts. Judging from the sound of running water, Claude was in the shower.

I eyed the bakery box longingly, but I was all too aware that my jeans were feeling tight. I felt like a martyr as I poured a bowl of Special K and sprinkled Equal on the cereal and added some 2 percent milk. When Sam looked as though he wanted to make a comment, I narrowed my eyes at him. He grinned at me, chewing a mouthful of jelly-filled.

"Dermot, we're off to Shreveport in a few minutes. If you need my bathroom . . ." I offered, since Claude was terrible about hogging the one in the hall. I rinsed my bowl in the sink.

"Thanks, Niece," Dermot said, kissing my hand. "And your hair still looks glorious, though shorter. I think Eric was right to bring someone to cut it last night."

Sam shook his head as we were getting into his truck. "Sook, that guy treats you like a queen."

"Which guy do you mean? Eric or Dermot?"

"Not Eric," Sam said, trying his best to look neutral. "Dermot."

"Yeah, too bad he's related! And also, he looks way too much like Jason."

"That's no obstacle to a fairy," Sam said seriously.

"You've got to be joking." I felt serious in a hurry. From Sam's expression, he wasn't joking one little bit. "Listen, Sam, Dermot has never even looked at me like I was a woman, and Claude is gay. We're strictly family." We'd all slept in the same bed, and there'd never been anything but the comfort

59

of their presence in that, though of course I'd felt a little weird about it the first time. I'd been sure that was just my human hang-up. Due to Sam's words, now I was second-guessing myself like crazy, wondering if I'd picked up on a vibe. After all, Claude did like to run around nude, and he'd told me he'd actually had sex with a female before. (I figured there'd been another man involved, frankly.)

"And I'm saying again, weird things happen in fae families." Sam glanced over at me.

"I don't mean to sound rude, but how would you know?" If Sam had spent a lot of time with fairies, he had kept it a close secret.

"I read up on it after I met your great-grandfather."

"Read up on it? Where?" It would be great to learn more about my dab of fairy heritage. Dermot and Claude, having decided to live apart from their fairy kin (though I wasn't sure how voluntary those decisions had been), remained closemouthed about fairy beliefs and customs. Aside from making derogatory comments from time to time about trolls and sprites, they didn't talk about their race at all . . . at least, around me.

"Ah . . . the shifters have a library. We have records of our history and what we've observed about other supes. Keeping track has helped us survive. There's always been a place we could go on each continent to read and study about the other races. Now it's all electronic. I'm sworn not to show it to anyone. If I could, I'd let you read it all."

"So it's not okay for me to read it, but it's okay for you to tell me about it?" I wasn't trying to be snarky; I was genuinely curious.

"Within limits." Sam flushed.

I didn't want to press him. I could tell that Sam had already stretched those limits for me.

We were each preoccupied with our own thoughts for the rest of the drive. While Eric was dead for the day, I felt alone in my skin, and usually I enjoyed that feeling. It wasn't that being bonded to Eric made me feel I was possessed, or anything like that. It was more like during the dark hours, I could feel his life continuing parallel to mine — I knew he was working or arguing or content or absorbed in what he was doing. A little trickle of awareness, rather than a book of knowledge.

"So, the bomber yesterday," Sam said abruptly.

61

"Yeah," I said. "I think maybe a twoey of some kind, right?"

He nodded without looking at me.

"Not a hate crime," I said, trying to sound matter-of-fact.

"Not a human hate crime," Sam said. "But I'm sure it's some kind of hatred."

"Economic?"

"I can't think of any economic reason," he said. "I'm insured, but I'm the only beneficiary if the bar burns down. Of course, I'd be out of business for a while, and I'm sure the other bars in the area would take up the slack, but I can't see that as an incentive. Much of an incentive," he corrected himself. "Merlotte's has always been kind of a family bar, not a wild place. Not like Vic's Redneck Roadhouse," he added, a little bitterly.

That was true. "Maybe someone doesn't like you personally, Sam," I said, though it came out sounding harsher than I'd intended. "I mean," I added quickly, "maybe someone wants to hurt you through damaging your business. Not you as a shapeshifter, but you as a person."

"I don't recall anything that personal," he said, genuinely bewildered.

"Ah . . . Jannalynn have a vengeful ex, anything like that?"

Sam was startled by the idea. "I really

haven't heard of anyone who resented me dating her," he said. "And Jannalynn's more than capable of speaking her mind. It's not like I could coerce her into going out with me."

I had a hard time repressing a snort of laughter. "Just trying to think of all possibilities," I said apologetically.

"That's okay," he said. He shrugged. "Bottom line is, I can't remember when I've made anyone really mad."

I couldn't remember any such incident myself, and I'd known Sam for years.

Pretty soon we were pulling up to the antiques shop, which was located in a former paint store in a down-sliding older business street in Shreveport.

The big front windows were sparkling clean, and the pieces that had been positioned there were beautiful. The largest was what my grandmother had called a hunt sideboard. It was heavy and ornate and just about as tall as my chest. The other window featured a collection of jardinières, or vases, I wasn't sure which to call them. The one in the center, positioned to show that it was the cream of the crop, was sea green and blue and had cherubs stuck on it. I thought it was hideous, but it definitely had style.

Sam and I looked at the display for a moment in thoughtful silence before we went in. A bell — a real bell, not an electronic chime — jangled as we pushed open the door. A woman sitting on a stool behind a counter to the right looked up. She pushed her glasses up on her nose.

"Nice to see you again, Mr. Merlotte," she said, smiling with just the right intensity. *I remember you, I'm glad you came back, but I'm not personally interested in you as a man.* She was good.

"Thanks, Ms. Hesterman," Sam said. "This is my friend, Sookie Stackhouse."

"Welcome to Splendide," Ms. Hesterman said. "Please call me Brenda. What can I do for you today?"

"We've got two errands," Sam said. "I'm here to look at the pieces you called me about. . . ."

"And I've just cleaned out my attic and I have some things I wondered if you could take a look at," I said. "I need to get rid of some of the odds and ends I brought down. I don't want to put it all back." I smiled, to show general goodwill.

"So you've had a family place a long time?" she asked, encouraging me to give her a clue about what sort of possessions my family might have accumulated.

"We've lived in the same house for about a hundred and seventy years," I told her, and she brightened. "But it's an old farm, not a mansion. Might be some things you'd be interested in, though."

"I'd love to come take a look," she said, though clearly "love" was overstating it a little. "We'll set up a time as soon as I help Sam pick out a gift for Jannalynn. She's so modern, who would have thought she'd be interested in antiques? She's such a little cutie!"

I had a hard time keeping my mouth from dropping open. Did we know the same Jannalynn Hopper?

Sam poked me in the ribs when Brenda turned her back to fetch a ring of small keys. He made a significant face, and I smoothed out my expression and batted my eyelashes at him. He looked away, but not before I caught a reluctant grin.

"Sam, I've put together some things Jannalynn might like," Brenda said, and led us over to a display case, keys jingling in her hand. The case was full of little things, pretty things. I couldn't identify most of them. I leaned over the glass top to look down.

"What are those?" I pointed at some lethal sharp-pointed objects with ornate heads. I wondered if you could kill a vampire with one

"Hat pins and stickpins, for scarves and cravats."

There were also earrings and rings and brooches, plus enamel boxes, beaded boxes, painted boxes. All these little containers were carefully arranged. Were they snuff-boxes? I read the price tag discreetly peeking out from under a tortoiseshell and silver oval box, and had to clamp my lips together to restrain my gasp.

While I was still wondering about the items I was examining, Brenda and Sam were comparing the merits of art deco pearl earrings versus a Victorian pressed-glass hair receiver with an enameled brass lid. Whatever the hell that was.

"What do you think, Sookie?" he asked, looking from one item to another.

I examined the art deco earrings, pearl drops dangling from a rose gold setting. The hair receiver was pretty, too, though I couldn't imagine what it was for or what Jannalynn would do with it. Did anyone need to receive hair anymore?

"She'll wear the earrings to show them off," I said. "It's harder to brag about getting a hair receiver." Brenda gave me a veiled look, and I understood from her thoughts that this opinion branded me as a philistine. So be it.

"The hair receiver's older," Sam said, wavering.

"But less personal. Unless you're Victorian."

While Sam compared the two smaller items to the beauties of a seventy-year-old New Bedford police badge, I wandered around the store, looking at the furniture. I discovered I was not an antiques appreciator. This was just one more flaw in my mundane character, I decided. Or maybe it was because I was surrounded by antiques all the day long? Nothing in my house was new except the kitchen, and that only because the old one had been destroyed by fire. I'd still be using Gran's ancient refrigerator if the flames hadn't eaten it up. (That refrigerator was one antique I didn't miss, for sure.)

I slid open a long, narrow drawer on what the tag described as a "map chest." There was a sliver of paper left in it.

"Look at that," Brenda Hesterman's voice said from behind me. "I'd thought I'd gotten that thoroughly clean. Let that be a lesson, Miss Stackhouse. Before we come to look at your things, be sure to go through them and remove all papers and other objects. You don't want to sell us something you didn't intend to part with."

I turned around to see that Sam was holding a wrapped package. While I'd been lost in exploration, he'd made his purchase (the earrings, to my relief; the hair receiver was back in its spot in the case).

"She'll love the earrings. They're beautiful," I said honestly, and for a second Sam's thoughts got snarled, almost . . . purple. Strange, that I would think of colors. Lingering effect of the shaman drug I'd taken for the Weres? I hoped to hell not.

"I'll be sure to look over everything real carefully, Brenda," I said to the antiques dealer.

We made an appointment for two days later. She assured me that she could find my isolated house with her GPS, and I warned her about the long driveway through the woods, which had led several visitors to believe they'd become lost. "I don't know if I'll come, or my partner, Donald," Brenda said. "Maybe both of us."

"I'll be glad to see you," I said. "If you run into any trouble or need to change the date, please let me know."

"Do you really think she'll like them?" Sam asked when we were in the truck and buckled up. We'd reverted to the topic of

Jannalynn.

"Sure," I said, surprised. "Why wouldn't she?"

"I can't shake the feeling I'm on the wrong track with Jannalynn," Sam said. "You want to stop and get something to eat at the Ruby Tuesday's on Youree?"

"Sure," I said. "Sam, why do you think that?"

"She likes me," he said. "I mean, I can tell. But she's always thinking about the pack."

"You think maybe she's more focused on Alcide than on you?" That was what I was getting from Sam's head. Maybe I was being too blunt, though. Sam flushed.

"Yeah, maybe," he admitted.

"She's a great enforcer, and she was real excited to get the job," I said. I wondered if that had come out neutral enough.

"She was," he said.

"You seem to like strong women."

He smiled. "I do like strong women, and I'm not afraid of the different ones. Run-of-the-mill just doesn't cut it with me."

I smiled back at him. "I can tell. I don't know what to say about Jannalynn, Sam. She'd be an idiot not to appreciate you. Single, self-supporting, good looking? And you don't even pick your teeth at the table!

What's not to love?" I took a deep breath, because I was about to change the subject and I didn't want to offend my boss. "Hey, Sam, about that website you visit? You think you could find out about why I'm feeling more fairy after hanging out with my fairy relatives? I mean, I couldn't actually be changing into more of a fairy, right?"

"I'll see what I can find," Sam said, after a fraught moment. "But let's try asking your bunk buddies. They ought to cough up any information that would help you. Or I could beat it out of them."

He was serious.

"They'll tell me." I sounded more sure of that than I felt.

"Where are they now?" he asked.

"By this time, they've gone to the club," I said, after a glance at my watch. "They get all their business done before the club opens."

"Then that's where we'll go," Sam said. "Kennedy was opening for me today, and you're not on until tonight, right?"

"Right," I said, discarding my plans for the afternoon, which hadn't been very urgent to start with. If we ate lunch at Ruby Tuesday's, we couldn't reach Monroe until one thirty, but I could make it home in time to change for work. After I'd ordered, I excused myself. While I was in the ladies' room, my cell phone rang. I don't answer my phone while I'm in a bathroom. I wouldn't like to be talking to someone and hear a toilet flush, right? Since the restaurant was noisy, I stepped outside to return the call after a wave at Sam. The number seemed faintly familiar.

"Hey, Sookie," said Remy Savoy. "How you doing?"

"Good. How's my favorite little boy?" Remy had been married to my cousin Hadley, and they'd had a son, Hunter, who would be starting kindergarten in the fall. After Katrina, Remy and Hunter had moved to the little town of Red Ditch, where Remy had gotten a job working at a lumberyard through the good services of a cousin.

"He's doing good. He's trying hard to follow your rules. I wonder if I could ask a favor?"

"Let's hear it," I said.

"I've started dating a lady here name of Erin. We were thinking about going to the bass fishing tournament outside Baton Rouge this weekend. We, ah, we were kind of hoping you could keep Hunter? He gets bored if I fish more than an hour."

Hmmm. Remy moved pretty fast. Kristen hadn't been too long ago, and she'd already

71

been replaced. I could kind of see it. Remy was not bad-looking, he was a skilled carpenter, and he had only one child — plus, Hunter's mom was dead, so there weren't any custody issues. Not too shabby a prospect in the town of Red Ditch. "Remy, I'm on the road right now," I said. "Let me call you back in a little while. I gotta check my work schedule."

"Great, thanks a lot, Sookie. Talk to you later."

I went back inside to find that our food had been served.

"That was Hunter's dad calling," I told my boss after the server left. "Remy's got a new girlfriend, and he wanted to know if I could keep Hunter this weekend."

I got the impression that Sam believed Remy was trying to take advantage of me — but Sam also felt he could hardly tell me what to do about it. "If I remember the schedule right, you're working this Saturday night," he pointed out.

And Saturday night was when I made my biggest tips.

I nodded, both to Sam and myself. While we ate, we talked about Terry's negotiations with a breeder of Catahoulas in Ruston. Terry's Annie had gotten out of her pen last time she'd been in heat. This time, Terry had a more planned pregnancy in mind, and the talks between the two men had nearly reached prenup status. A question rose to my mind, and I wasn't quite sure how to phrase it to Sam. My curiosity got the better of me.

"You remember Bob the cat?" I asked.

"Sure. That guy Amelia turned into a cat by accident? Her friend Octavia turned him back."

"Yeah. Well, the thing is, while he was a cat, he was black and white. He was a really cute cat. But Amelia found a female cat in the woods with a litter, and there were some black-and-white kittens among 'em, so she got — okay, I know this is weird — she got pissed off at Bob because she thought he'd, you know, become a dad. Sort of."

"So your question is, is that a common thing?" Sam looked disgusted. "Naw, Sookie. We can't do that, and we don't want to. None of the two-natured. Even if there were a sexual encounter, there wouldn't be a pregnancy. I think Amelia was accusing Bob falsely. On the other hand, he isn't — wasn't — really two-natured. He was completely transformed by magic." Sam shrugged. He looked very embarrassed.

"Sorry," I said, feeling mortified. "That was tacky of me."

"It's a natural thing to wonder about, I guess," Sam said dubiously. "But when I'm in my other skin, I'm not out making puppies."

Now I was *horribly* embarrassed. "Please, accept my apology," I said.

He relaxed when he saw how uncomfortable I was. He patted me on the shoulder. "Don't worry about it." Then he asked me what plans I had for the attic now that I'd emptied it, and we talked of trivial things until we were back to feeling okay with each other.

I called Remy back when we were on the interstate. "Remy, this weekend won't work for me. Sorry!" I explained that I had to work.

"Don't worry about it," Remy said. He sounded calm about my refusal. "It was just a thought. Listen, here's the thing. I hate to ask for another favor. But Hunter has to visit the kindergarten next week, just a thing the school does every year so the kids will have a mental picture of the place they're going in the fall. They tour the classrooms, meet the teachers, and see the lunchroom and the bathrooms. Hunter asked me if you could go with us."

My mouth fell open. I was glad Remy couldn't see me. "This is during the day,

I'm assuming," I said. "What day of the week?"

"Next Tuesday, two o'clock."

Unless I was on for the lunch shift, I could do it. "Again, let me check my work schedule, but I think that's going to be doable," I said. "I'll call you back tonight." I snapped my phone shut and told Sam about Remy's second request.

"Seems like he waited to ask you the more important thing second, so you'd be more likely to come," Sam asked.

I laughed. "I didn't think of that until you said it. My brain is wired in a straighter line than that. But now that it's crossed my mind, that seems . . . not unlikely." I shrugged. "It's not like I object, exactly. I want Hunter to be happy. And I've spent time with him, though not as much as I should have." Hunter and I were alike in a hidden way; we were both telepathic. But that was our secret because I feared Hunter might be in danger if his ability was known. It sure hadn't improved *my* life any.

"So why are you worried? Because I can tell you are," Sam said.

"Just . . . it'll look funny. People in Red Ditch will think Remy and I are dating. That I'm sort of — close to being Hunter's mom. And Remy just told me he's seeing a woman named Erin, and she may not like it. . . ." My voice trailed off. This visit seemed like a mildly bad idea. But if it would make Hunter happy, I supposed I ought to do it.

"You have that sucked-in feeling?" Sam's smile was wry. It was our day to talk about awkward things.

"Yeah," I admitted. "I do. When I got involved in Hunter's life, I didn't ever imagine he'd really depend on me for anything. I guess I've never been around kids that much. Remy's got a great-aunt and great-uncle in Red Ditch. That's why he moved there after Katrina. They had an empty rental house. But the aunt and uncle are too old to want to keep a kid Hunter's age for more than an hour or two, and the one cousin is too busy to be much help."

"Hunter a good kid?"

"Yes, I think he is." I smiled. "You know what's weird? When Hunter stayed with me, he and Claude got along great. That was a big surprise."

Sam glanced over at me. "But you wouldn't want to leave him with Claude for hours, would you?"

After a moment's thought, I said, "No."

Sam nodded, as if I'd confirmed something he'd been wondering about. "Cause after all, Claude's a fairy?" He put enough question into his voice to ensure that I knew he was genuinely asking me.

The words sounded very unpleasant said out loud. But they were the truth. "Yes, because Claude's a fairy. But not because he's a different race from us." I struggled with how to express what I wanted to say. "Fairies, they love kids. But they don't have the same frame of reference as most humans. Fairies'll do what they think will make the child happy, or will benefit the child, rather than what a Christian adult would do." It made me feel small and provincial to admit all this, but those were my true feelings. I felt like adding a series of disclaimers — *Not that I think I'm such a great Christian, far from it. Not that non-Christians are bad people. Not that I think Claude would hurt Hunter.* But Sam and I had known each other long enough that I was sure he'd understand all that.

"I'm glad we're on the same page," Sam said, and I felt relieved. But I was far from comfortable. We might be on the same page, but I wasn't happy about reading it.

Spring was verging on summer, and the day was beautiful. I tried to enjoy it all the way east to Monroe, but my success was limited.

My cousin Claude owned Hooligans, a

strip club off the interstate outside Monroe. On five nights a week, it featured the conventional entertainment offered at strip clubs. The club was closed on Mondays. But Thursday night was Ladies Only, and that was when Claude stripped. Of course, he wasn't the only male who performed. At least three other male strippers came in on a rotating basis pretty regularly, and there was usually a guest stripper, too. There was a male strip circuit, my cousin had told me.

"You ever come here to watch him?" Sam asked as we pulled up to the back door.

He was not the first person to ask me that. I was beginning to think there was something wrong with me, that I hadn't felt the need to rush over to Monroe to watch guys take off their clothes.

"No. I've seen Claude naked. I've never come over to watch him do his thing professionally. I hear he's good."

"He's naked? *At your house?*"

"Modesty is not one of Claude's priorities," I said.

Sam looked both displeased and startled, despite his own earlier warning about the fae not thinking kin were off-limits sexually. "What about Dermot?" he said.

"Dermot? I don't think he strips," I said, confused.

"I mean, he doesn't go around the house naked, does he?"

"No," I said. "That seems to be a Claude thing. It would be really icky if Dermot did that, since he looks so much like Jason."

"That's just not right," Sam muttered. "Claude needs to keep his pants on."

"I dealt with it," I said, the edge in my voice reminding Sam that the situation was not his to worry about.

It was a weekday, so the place didn't open until four in the afternoon. I hadn't ever been to Hooligans before, but it looked like any other small club; set apart in a fair-sized parking lot, electric-blue siding, a jazzy shocking-pink sign. Places for selling alcohol or flesh always look a little sad in the daytime, don't they? The only other business close to Hooligans, now that I was looking, was a liquor store.

Claude had told me what to do in case I ever dropped in. The secret signal was knocking four times, keeping the raps evenly spaced. After that was done, I gazed out across the fields. The sun beat down on the parking lot with just a hint of the heat to come. Sam shifted uneasily from foot to foot. After a few seconds, the door opened.

I smiled and said hello automatically, and began to step into the hall. It was a shock to realize the doorman wasn't human. I froze.

I'd assumed that Claude and Dermot were the only fairies left in modern-day America since my great-grandfather had pulled all the fairies into their own dimension, or world, or whatever they called it, and closed the door. Though I'd *also* known that Niall and Claude communicated at least occasionally, because Niall had sent me a letter via Claude's hands. But I'd deliberately refrained from asking a lot of questions. My experiences with my fairy kin, with all the fae, had been both delightful and horrible . . . but toward the end, those experiences had come down far heavier on the horrible side of the scale.

The doorman was just as startled to see me as I was to see him. He wasn't a fairy — but he was fae. I'd met fairies who'd filed their teeth to look the way this creature's did naturally: an inch long, pointed, curved slightly inward. The doorman's ears weren't pointed, but I didn't think it was surgical alteration that had made them flatter and rounder than human ears. The alien effect was lessened by his thick, fine hair, which was a rich auburn color and lay smooth, about three inches long, all over his head. The effect was not that of a hairstyle, but of an animal's coat.

"What are you?" we asked each other simultaneously.

It would have been funny . . . in another universe.

"What's happening?" Sam said behind me, and I jumped. I stepped all the way inside the club with Sam right on my heels, and the heavy metal door clanged shut behind us. After the dazzling sunlight, the long fluorescent bulbs that lit the hall looked doubly bleak.

"I'm Sookie," I said, to break the awkward silence.

"What are you?" the creature asked again. We were still standing awkwardly in the narrow hallway.

Dermot's head popped out of a doorway. "Hey, Sookie," he said. "I see you've met Bellenos." He stepped out into the hall and took in my expression. "Haven't you ever seen an elf before?"

"*I* haven't, thanks for asking," muttered Sam. Since he was much more knowledgeable about the supe world than I was, I realized that elves must be pretty rare.

I had a lot of questions about Bellenos's presence, but I wasn't sure if I had any right to ask them, especially after my faux pas with Sam. "Sorry, Bellenos. I did meet a half elf once with teeth like yours. Mostly, though, I know fairies who file their teeth to look that way. Pleased to meet you," I said with a huge effort. "This is my friend Sam."

Sam shook hands with Bellenos. The two were much the same height and build, but I noticed that Bellenos's slanted eyes were dark brown, matching the freckles on his milky skin. Those eyes were curiously far apart, or perhaps his face was broader across the cheekbones than normal? The elf smiled at Sam, and I caught a glimpse of the teeth again. I shuddered and looked away.

Through an open door I glimpsed a large dressing room. There was a long counter running along one wall, which was lined with a brightly lit mirror. The counter was strewn with cosmetics, makeup brushes, blow-dryers, hair curlers and hair straighteners, bits of costume, razors, a magazine or two, wigs, cell phones . . . the assorted debris of people whose jobs depended on their appearance. Some high stools were set haphazardly around the room, and there were tote bags and shoes everywhere.

From farther down the hall Dermot called, "Come into the office."

We went down the hall and crowded into a small room. Somewhat to my disappointment, the exotic and gorgeous Claude had a completely prosaic office — cramped, cluttered, and windowless. Claude had a secretary, a woman dressed in a JCPenney women's business suit. She could not have looked more incongruous in a strip club. Dermot, who was evidently the master of ceremonies today, said, "Nella Jean, this is our dear cousin Sookie."

Nella Jean was dark and round, and her bitter-chocolate eyes were almost a match for Bellenos's, though her teeth were reassuringly normal. Her little cubbyhole was right next door to Claude's office; in fact, I conjectured that it had been converted from a storage closet. After a disparaging look at Sam and me, Nella Jean seemed more than ready to retreat to her own space. She shut her office door with an air of finality, as if she knew we were going to do something unsavory and she wanted nothing to do with us.

Bellenos shut Claude's office door, too, closing us in a room that would have been crowded with two of us, much less five. I could hear music coming from the club proper (or rather, the club improper), and I wondered what was happening out there. Did strippers rehearse? What did they make of Bellenos?

83

"Why the surprise visit?" Claude asked. "Not that I'm not delighted to see you."

He wasn't delighted to see me at all, though he'd invited me to drop by Hooligans more than once. It was clear from his sulky mouth that he'd never believed I'd come to see him at the club unless he was onstage stripping. *Of course, Claude's sure everyone in the world wants to see him take off his clothes,* I thought. Did he just not enjoy visitors, or was there something he didn't want me to know?

"You need to tell us why Sookie's feeling more and more fae," Sam said abruptly.

The three fae males turned to look at Sam simultaneously.

Claude said, "Why do we need to tell her that? And why are you concerning yourself with our family affairs?"

"Because Sookie wants to know why, and she's my friend," Sam said. His face was hard, his voice very level. "You should be educating her about her mixed blood instead of living in her house and leeching off her."

I didn't know where to look. I hadn't known Sam was so opposed to my cousin and my great-uncle staying with me, and he really didn't need to give his opinion. And Claude and Dermot weren't leeching off me; they bought groceries, too, and they cleaned up after themselves very carefully. Sometimes. It was true that my water bill had jumped (and I had said something to Claude about that), but nothing else had cost me money.

"In fact," Sam said, when they continued to glare at him in silence, "you're staying with her to make sure she'll be more fae, right? You're encouraging that part of her to strengthen. I don't know how you're doing that, but I know you are. My question is: Are you doing this just for the warmth of it, the companionship, or do you have a plan in mind for Sookie? Some kind of secret fairy plot?"

The last words were more like an ominous rumble than Sam's normal voice.

"Claude's my cousin and Dermot's my great-uncle," I said automatically. "They wouldn't try to . . ." And I let the thought trail off dismally. If I'd learned anything over the past few years, it was not to make stupid assumptions. The idea that family would not harm you was a stupid assumption of the first order.

"Come see the rest of the club," Claude said suddenly. Before we could think about it, he'd hustled us out of the office and down the hall. He swung open the door to the club proper, and Sam and I went into it.

I guess all clubs and bars look basically the same — tables and chairs, some attempt at decor or theme, an actual bar, a stage with stripper poles, and some kind of booth for sound. In those respects, Hooligans was no different.

But all the creatures that turned to the door when we entered . . . all of them were fae. It came to me slowly and inevitably as I looked from face to face. No matter how human they looked (and most of them could "pass"), each one had a trace of fae blood of one kind or another. A beautiful female with flame red hair was part elf. She'd had her teeth filed down. A long, slim male was something I'd never encountered before.

"Welcome, Sister," said a short blond . . . something. I couldn't even be sure of the gender. "Have you come to join us here?"

I struggled to answer. "I hadn't planned on it," I said. I stepped back into the hall and let the door shut after me. I gripped Claude's arm. "What the hell is going on here?" When he didn't answer, I turned to my great-uncle. "Dermot?"

"Sookie, our dearest," Dermot said, after a moment's silence. "Tonight when we come home we'll tell you everything you need to know."

"What about him?" I said, nodding at Bellenos.

"He won't be with us," Claude said. "Bellenos sleeps here, as our night watchman."

You only needed a night watchman if you were afraid of an attack.

More trouble.

I could hardly stand the prospect of it.

CHAPTER 3

Okay, I've been stupid in the past. Not consistently stupid, but occasionally stupid. And I've made mistakes. You bet, I've made mistakes.

But during the ride back to Bon Temps, with my best guy friend driving and giving me the silence I needed, I thought hard. I felt a tear trickle from each eye. I looked away and blotted my face with a tissue from my purse, not wanting Sam to offer sympathy.

When I'd composed myself, I said, "I've been a fool."

To his credit, Sam looked startled. "What are you thinking of?" he said, so he wouldn't say, "Which time?"

"Do you think people really change, Sam?"

He took a moment to line up his thoughts. "That's a pretty big question, Sookie. People can turn themselves around to some extent, sure. Addicts can be strong enough to stop using whatever they're addicted to. People can go to therapy and learn how to manage behavior that's been out of control. But that's an external . . . system. A learned management technique imposed on the natural order of things, on what the person really is — an addict. Does that make sense?"

I nodded.

"So, on the whole," he continued, "I'd have to say no, people don't change, but they *can* learn to behave differently. I want to believe otherwise. If you have an argument that says I'm wrong, I'd be glad to hear it." We turned down my driveway and began to go through the woods.

"Children change as they grow up and adapt to society and their own circumstances," I said. "Sometimes in good ways, sometimes in bad. And I think if you love someone, you make an effort to suppress habits of yours that displease them, right? But those habits or inclinations are still there. Sam, you're right. Those are other cases of people imposing a learned reaction over the original."

He gave me worried eyes as we pulled up behind the house. "Sookie, what's wrong?"

I shook my head. "I'm such an idiot," I

told him. I couldn't look him square in the face. I scrambled out of the truck. "Are you taking the whole day off, or will I see you at the bar later?"

"I'm taking the whole day off. Listen, do you need me to stick around? I'm not real sure what you're worried about, but you know we can talk about it. I have no idea what is going on at Hooligans, but until the fairies feel like telling us . . . I'm here if you need me."

He was sincere in his offer, but I also knew he wanted to get home, call Jannalynn, make plans for the night so he could give her the gift he'd gone to such trouble to select. "No, I'm good," I said reassuringly, smiling up at him. "I've got a million things to do before I come to work, and a lot to think about." To put it mildly.

"Thanks for going to Shreveport with me, Sookie," Sam said. "But I guess I was wrong about getting your kinfolk to talk to you. Let me know if they don't come through tonight." I waved good-bye as he backed up to drive back to Hummingbird Road to return to his double-wide, situated right behind Merlotte's. Sam never completely got away from work — but on the other hand, it was a real short commute.

As I unlocked the back door, I was already

making plans.

I felt like having a shower — no, a bath. It was actually delightful to be alone, to have Claude and Dermot out of the house. I was full of new suspicion, but that was a sadly familiar feeling. I thought about calling Amelia, my witch friend who had returned to New Orleans to her rebuilt home and her reestablished job, to ask her advice about several things. In the end I didn't pick up the phone. I would have to explain so much. The prospect made my brain feel tired, and that was no way to start a conversation. An e-mail might be better. I could set everything down that way.

I filled the tub with bath oils, and I climbed into the hot water in a gingerly way, baring my teeth as I sank down. The front of my thighs still stung a bit. I shaved my legs and underarms. Grooming always makes you feel better. After I'd climbed out, the bath oil making me as slippery as a wrestler, I painted my toenails and brushed out my hair, startled all over again by how short it seemed. It was still past my shoulder blades, I reassured myself.

All buffed and polished, I put on my Merlotte's outfit, sorry to cover up my toenails with socks and sneakers. I was trying not to think, and I was doing a pretty good job of it.

I had about thirty minutes to spare, so I turned on the TV and clicked on my DVR button to view yesterday's *Jeopardy!* We'd started turning the bar TV to it every day, because the bar patrons got some enjoyment out of guessing the answers. Jane Bodehouse, our longest-lasting alcoholic, turned out to be an expert on old movies, and Terry Bellefleur surely knew his sports trivia. I could answer most of the questions about writers, since I read a lot, and Sam was pretty reliable on American history after 1900. I wasn't always at the bar when it was on, so I'd started recording it every day. I liked the happy world of *Jeopardy!* I liked getting the Daily Double, which I did today. When the show was finished, it was time to leave.

I enjoyed driving to work for the evening shift when it was still light outside. I turned up the radio and sang "Crazy" right along with Gnarls Barkley. I could identify.

Jason passed me driving in the opposite direction, maybe on his way to his girlfriend's house. Michele Schubert was still hanging in the relationship. Since Jason was finally growing up, she might make something permanent with him . . . if she wanted to. Michele's strongest suit was that she wasn't enthralled by Jason's (apparently) powerful bedroom mojo. If she was mooning over him and jealous of his attention, she was keeping it perfectly concealed. My hat was off to her. I waved at my brother, and he smiled back. He looked happy and unconflicted. I envied that from the bottom of my heart. There were big plusses to the way Jason approached life.

The crowd at Merlotte's was thin again. No surprise there; a firebombing is pretty bad publicity. What if Merlotte's couldn't survive? What if Vic's Redneck Roadhouse kept stealing customers? People liked Merlotte's because it was relatively quiet, because it was relaxed, because the food was good (if limited) and the drinks were generous. Sam had always been a popular guy until the wereanimals had made their own announcement. People who had handled the vampires with cautious acceptance seemed to regard twoeys as the straws that had broken the camel's back, so to speak.

I went into the storeroom to grab a clean apron and then into Sam's office to stuff my purse into the deep drawer of his desk. It sure would be nice to have a little locker. I could keep my purse in it and a change of clothes for nights when minor disasters struck, like spilled beer or a squirt of mustard.

I was taking over from Holly, who would marry Jason's best friend Hoyt in October. This would be Holly's second wedding, Hoyt's first. They'd decided to go all out and have a church ceremony and a reception in the church hall afterward. I knew more about it than I wanted to know. Though the wedding wasn't for months, Holly had already begun obsessing about details. Since her first wedding had been a justice-of-the-peace visit, this was (theoretically) her last chance to live the dream. I could imagine my grandmother's opinion about Holly's white wedding dress, since Holly had a little boy in school — but hey, whatever made the bride happy. White used to symbolize the virgin purity of the wearer. Now it just meant the bride had acquired an expensive and unusable dress to hang in her closet after the big day.

I waved at Holly to attract her attention. She was talking to the new Calgary Baptist preacher, Brother Carson. He came in from time to time but never ordered alcohol. Holly ended her conversation and strode over to tell me what was happening at our tables, which wasn't much. I shuddered when I looked at the scorched mark in the middle of the floor. One less table to serve.

"Hey, Sookie," Holly said, pausing on her way to the back to fetch her purse. "You'll be at the wedding, right?"

"Sure, wouldn't miss it."

"Would you mind serving the punch?"

This was an honor — not as big an honor as being a bridesmaid, but still significant. I'd never expected such a thing. "I'd be glad to," I said, smiling. "Let's talk again closer to time."

Holly looked pleased. "Okay, good. Well, let's hope business picks up here so we still have a job come September."

"Oh, you know we'll be okay," I said, but I was far from convinced that was so.

I stayed up waiting for Dermot and Claude for half an hour after I got home that night, but they didn't show, and I didn't feel like calling them. Their promised talk with me, the talk that was supposed to fill me in on my fairy heritage, would not take place tonight. Though I'd wanted to hear some answers, I found I was just as glad. The day had been too full. I told myself I was pissed off, and I tried to listen for the fairies to come in, but I didn't lie awake more than five minutes.

When I emerged the next morning a little after nine, I didn't see any of the usual signs

95

that indicated my houseguests had returned. The hall bathroom looked exactly as it had the day before, there weren't any dishes by the kitchen sink, and none of the lights had been left on. I went out on the enclosed back porch. Nope, no car.

Maybe they'd been too tired to make the drive back to Bon Temps, or maybe they'd both gotten lucky. When Claude had come to live with me, he'd told me that if he made a conquest, he'd spend the night at his house in Monroe with the lucky guy. I'd assumed Dermot would do the same — though come to think of it, I'd never seen Dermot with anyone, man *or* woman. I'd also assumed that Dermot would choose women over men, simply because he looked like Jason, who was all about the ladies. Assumptions. Dumb.

I fixed myself some eggs and toast and fruit, and read a library copy of one of Nora Roberts's books while I ate. I felt more like my former self than I had in weeks. Except for the visit to Hooligans, I'd had a nice time the day before, and the guys weren't trailing in and out of the kitchen, complaining about me being low on whole-wheat bread or hot water (Claude) or offering me flowery pleasantries when all I wanted to do was read (Dermot). Nice to discover that I could still enjoy being alone.

Singing to myself, I showered and made myself up . . . and by that time I had to leave for work again for the early shift. I glanced into the living room, tired of it looking like a junk store. I reminded myself that tomorrow the antiques dealers were supposed to come.

The bar was a little busier than it had been the night before, which made me even more cheerful. A little to my surprise, Kennedy was behind the bar. She looked as polished and perfect as the beauty queen she'd been, though she was wearing tight jeans and a white-and-gray-striped tank. We were quite the well-groomed women today.

"Where's Sam?" I asked. "I thought he would be working."

"He called me this morning, said he was still over in Shreveport," Kennedy said, giving me a sideways look. "I guess Jannalynn's birthday went real well. I need as many hours as I can get, so I was glad to roll out of bed and get my hiney over here."

"How's your mamma and your daddy?" I asked. "Have they visited lately?"

Kennedy smiled bitterly. "They're just rolling along, Sookie. They still wish I was Little Miss Beauty Pageant and taught Sunday school, but they did send me a good check when I got out of prison. I'm lucky to have 'em."

Her hands stilled in the middle of drying a glass. "I been wondering," she said, and paused. I waited. I knew what was coming. "I was wondering if it was a member of Casey's family who bombed the bar," she said, very quietly. "When I shot Casey, I was just saving my own life. I didn't think about his family, or my family, or anything but living."

Kennedy had never talked about it before, which I could understand completely. "Who would be thinking about anything else but surviving, Kennedy?" I said, quietly but with intensity. I wanted her to feel my absolute sincerity. "No one in her right mind would have done any different. I don't think God would ever want you to let yourself be beaten to death." Though I was not at all sure what God would want. I probably meant, *I think it would have been dumb as hell to let yourself be killed.*

"I wouldn't have gotten off so light if those other women hadn't come forward," Kennedy said. "His family, I guess they know he really did hit women . . . but I wonder if they still blame me. If maybe they knew I'd be in the bar, and they decided to kill me here."

"Are any of his family two-natured?" I asked.

Kennedy looked shocked. "Oh my gosh, no! They're Baptists!"

I tried not to smile, but I couldn't help it. After a second, Kennedy started laughing at herself. "Seriously," she said, "I don't think so. You think whoever threw that bomb was a Were?"

"Or some other kind of two-natured. Yeah, I think so, but don't tell this around anywhere. Sam's already feeling the backlash enough as it is."

Kennedy nodded in complete agreement, a customer called me to bring him a bottle of hot sauce, and I had new food for thought.

The server replacing me called in to say her car had a flat tire, and I stayed at Merlotte's two extra hours. Kennedy, who'd be there until closing, gave me a hard time about being indispensible, until I swatted her with a towel. Kennedy perked up quite a bit when Danny came in. He'd obviously gone home after work to shower and shave again, and he looked at Kennedy as if his world were now complete when he climbed onto the barstool. What he said was, "Give me a beer and be quick about it, woman."

"You want me to pour that beer on your

99

head, Danny?"

"Don't make no difference to me how I get it." And they grinned at each other.

Just after dark, my cell phone vibrated in my apron pocket. As soon as I could, I stepped into Sam's office. I'd gotten a text from Eric. "See U later," it said. And that was all. But I had a genuine smile on my face the rest of the evening, and when I drove home, I felt happy all over to see Eric sitting on my front porch, whether he'd wrecked my kitchen or not. And he had a new toaster with him, a red bow stuck to the box.

"To what do I owe the honor?" I asked tartly. It didn't do to let Eric know I'd been anticipating his visit. Of course, he probably had an idea that was so, through our blood bond.

"We haven't had any fun lately," he said. He handed over the toaster.

"Between me putting out a fire and you attacking Pam? Yeah, I'd say that was a fair statement. Thanks for the replacement toaster, though I wouldn't classify that as fun. What do you have in mind?"

"Later, of course, I have spectacular sex in mind," he said, standing up and walking over to me. "I've thought of a position we haven't tried yet."

I'm not as flexible as Eric, and the last time we'd tried something real adventurous, I'd had a sore hip for three days. But I was willing to experiment. "What do you have in mind before the spectacular sex?" I asked.

"We have to visit a new dance club," he said, but I caught the shade of worry in his voice. "That's what they're calling it, to try to bring in the young people who look pretty. Like you."

"Where is this dance club?" Since I'd been on my feet for hours, this plan was not the most tempting. But it *had* been a long time since we'd had fun as a couple — in public.

"It's between here and Shreveport," Eric said, and hesitated. "Victor just opened it."

"Oh. Is it smart for you to go there?" I said, dismayed. Eric's program had zero appeal now.

Victor and Eric were engaged in a silent struggle. Victor Madden was the Louisiana proxy for Felipe, King of Nevada, Arkansas, and Louisiana. Felipe was based in Las Vegas, and we wondered (Eric and Pam and I) if he'd given Victor this large bone simply to get the ambitious Victor out of Felipe's richest territory. In my heart of hearts, I wanted Victor to die. Victor had sent his two most trusted minions, Bruno and

Corinna, to kill Pam and me, simply in order to weaken Eric, whom Felipe had retained since he was the most productive sheriff in the state.

Pam and I had turned the tables. Bruno and Corinna were piles of dust by the interstate, and no one could prove we'd done it.

Victor had put out the word that he was offering a high bounty for anyone who could give him some information on his minions' whereabouts, but no one had come forward. Only Pam, Eric, and I knew what had happened. Victor could hardly accuse us outright, since that would be admitting that he'd sent them to kill us. Kind of a Mexican standoff.

Next time, Victor might send someone more cautious and careful. Bruno and Corinna had been overconfident.

"It's not smart to go to this club, but we don't have a choice," Eric said. "Victor has ordered me to make an appearance with my wife. He'll think I'm afraid of him if I don't bring you."

I thought this through while I was searching my closet, trying to think of anything I owned that would look good at a trendy dance club. Eric was lying on my bed, his hands behind his head. "There's something in my car, I forgot," he said suddenly, and was a blur going out the door. He was back in seconds, carrying a garment on a hanger enveloped in a clear plastic bag.

"What?" I said. "It's not my birthday."

"Can't a vampire give his lover a present?"

I had to smile back at him. "Well, yes he can," I said. I love presents. The toaster had been reparation. This was a surprise. I carefully removed the plastic bag. The garment on the hanger was a dress. Probably.

"This is — is this the whole thing?" I asked, holding it up. There was a black U-shaped neckband — a large U, both front and back — and the rest was bronze and shiny and pleated, like many broad bronze ribbons sewn together. Well, not so many. The saleswoman had left the price tag on. I tried not to look, failed, and felt my mouth fall open after I'd absorbed it. I could buy six or maybe ten pieces at Wal-Mart, or three at Dillard's, for the price of this dress.

"You will look wonderful," Eric said. He grinned fangily. "Everyone will envy me."

Who wouldn't feel good, hearing that?

I emerged from the bathroom to find that my new buddy Immanuel was back. He'd set up a hair and makeup station on my dressing table. It felt very odd to see yet another man in my bedroom. Immanuel seemed to be in a much happier mood tonight. Even his odd haircut looked perkier. While Eric watched as closely as if he suspected Immanuel of being an assassin, the skinny hairdresser poofed me and curled me and made me up. Since Tara and I had been little girls, I hadn't had such a fun time in front of a mirror. When Immanuel was through, I looked . . . glossy and confident.

"Thank you," I said, wondering where the real Sookie had gone.

"You're welcome," Immanuel said seriously. "You've got great skin. I like working on you."

No one had ever said that to me, and all I could come up with in response was, "Please leave a card." He fished one out and propped it against a china lady my grandmother had loved. The juxtaposition left me feeling a little sad. I'd come down a long road since her death.

"How's your sister?" I asked, since I was thinking of sad things.

"She had a good day today," Immanuel said. "Thanks for asking." Though he didn't look at Eric while he said this, I saw Eric glance away, his jaw tight. Irritated.

Immanuel departed after packing up all his paraphernalia, and I found a strapless bra and a thong — which I hated, but who

wants a pantyline under a dress like that? —
and began to assemble myself. Luckily, I
had good black heels. I knew strappy sandals
would suit the dress better, but the heels
would have to do.

Eric had really paid attention as I got
dressed. "So smooth," he said, running his
hand up my leg.

"Hey, you keep doing that, we won't get
to the club, and all this preparation will have
gone to waste." Call me pathetic, but I actually did want someone else besides Eric to
see the total effect of the new dress and the
new hair and the good makeup.

"Not entirely to waste," he said, but he
changed into his own party clothes. I
braided his hair so it would look neat and
tied the end with a black ribbon. Eric
looked like a buccaneer out on the town.

We should have been happy, excited about
our date, looking forward to dancing together at the club. I couldn't know what
Eric was thinking as we walked out to his
car, but I knew he wasn't happy with what
we were doing and where we were going.

That made two of us.

I decided to ease into a back-and-forth
with a little light conversation.

"How are the new vamps working out?" I
said.

"They come in when they're supposed to and put in their bar time," he said unenthusiastically. Three vampires who'd ended up in Eric's area after Katrina had asked Eric for permission to stay in Area Five, though they wanted to nest in Minden, not Shreveport itself.

"What's wrong with them?" I said. "You don't seem very excited about the addition to your ranks." I slid into my seat. Eric walked around the car.

"Palomino does well enough," he admitted grudgingly as he got in on the driver's side. "But Rubio is stupid, and Parker is weak."

I didn't know the three well enough to debate that. Palomino, who went by one name, was an attractive young vampire with freaky coloring — her skin was a natural tan tone, while her hair was pale blond. Rubio Hermosa was handsome, but — I had to agree with Eric — he was dim and never had much to say for himself. Parker was as nerdy in death as he had been in life, and though he'd improved the Fangtasia computer systems, he seemed scared of his own shadow.

"You want to talk to me about the argument between you and Pam?" I asked once I'd buckled up. Instead of his Corvette, Eric had brought Fangtasia's Lincoln Town Car. It was incredibly comfortable, and given the way he drove when he was in the Vette, I was always glad when we had an evening out in the Lincoln.

"No," said Eric. He was instantly brooding and emanating worry.

I waited for him to elaborate.

I waited some more.

"All right," I said, trying hard to regain my sense of pleasure in being out on a date with a gorgeous man. "Okeydokey. Have it your way. But I think the sex will be a few degrees less spectacular if I'm worried about you and Pam."

That bit of levity earned me a dark look.

"I know that Pam wants to make another vampire," I said. "I understand there's a time element involved."

"Immanuel shouldn't have talked," Eric said.

"It was nice to have someone actually share information with me, information directly pertaining to people I care about." Did I have to draw a picture?

"Sookie, Victor has said I can't give permission for Pam to make a child." Eric's jaw snapped shut like a steel trap.

Oh. "Kings have control over reproduction, I guess," I said cautiously.

"Yes. Absolute control. But you understand that Pam is giving me hell about this, and so is Victor."

"Victor isn't a king, really, is he? Maybe if you went directly to Felipe?"

"Every time I bypass Victor, he finds a way to punish me."

There was no point in talking about it. Eric was being pulled in two different directions as it was.

So on the way to Victor's club, which Eric said was called Vampire's Kiss, we talked about the visit of the antiques dealers the next day. There were lots of things I would have liked to discuss, but in view of Eric's overwhelmingly difficult position, I didn't want to bring up my own problems. Plus, I still had the feeling that I didn't know everything there was to know about Eric's situation.

"Eric," I said, and knew I was speaking too abruptly and with too much intensity. "You don't tell me everything about your business, am I right?"

"You're right," he said, without missing a beat. "But that's for many reasons, Sookie. Most important is that some of it you could only worry about, and the rest of it might put you in danger. Knowledge isn't always power." I pressed my lips together and refused to look at him. Childish, I know, but I didn't completely believe him.

After a moment of silence, he added, "There's also the fact that I'm not used to sharing my daily concerns with a human, and it's hard to break the habit after a thousand years."

Right. And none of those secrets involved my future. *Right.* Evidently, Eric read my stony self-possession as grudging acceptance, because he decided our tense moment was over.

"But you tell me everything, my lover, don't you?" he asked teasingly.

I glared at him and didn't answer.

That wasn't what Eric had expected. "You don't?" he asked, and I couldn't figure out everything that was in his voice. Disappointment, concern, a touch of anger . . . and a dash of excitement. That was a lot to pack into a couple of words, but I swear it was all there. "That's an unexpected twist," he murmured. "And yet, we say we love each other."

"We say we do." I agreed. "And I do love you, but I'm beginning to see that being in love doesn't mean sharing as much as I thought we would."

He had nothing to say to that.

We passed Vic's Redneck Roadhouse on

the way to the new dance club, and even from the interstate I could see that the parking lot was packed. "Crap," I said. "There sits all of Merlotte's business. What do they have that we haven't got?"

"Entertainment. The novelty of being the new place. Waitresses in hot pants and halter tops," Eric began.

"Oh, stop," I said, disgusted. "What with the trouble about Sam being a shapeshifter and all the other stuff, I don't know how much longer Merlotte's can hold out."

There was a surge of pleasure from Eric. "Oh, then you would have no job," he said, with faux sympathy. "You could work for me at Fangtasia."

"No thank you." I said it immediately. "I would hate to see the fangbangers come in night after night, always wanting what they shouldn't have. It's just sad and bad."

Eric glanced over at me, not at all happy with my quick response. "That's how I make my money, Sookie, on the perverse dreams and fantasies of humans. Most of those humans are tourists who visit Fangtasia once or twice and then go back to Minden or Emerson and tell their neighbors about their walk on the wild side. Or they're people from the Air Force base who like to show how tough they are by drinking at a vampire bar."

"I understand that. And I know if fang-bangers don't come to Fangtasia, they'll go somewhere else they can hang around with vampires. But I don't think I'd like the ambience on a day-to-day basis." I was kind of proud of myself for working in "ambience."

"What would you do, then? If Merlotte's closed?"

That was a good question, and one I was going to have to consider seriously. I said, "I'd try to get another waitressing job, maybe at the Crawdad Diner. The tips wouldn't be as good as at a bar, but the aggravation would be less. And maybe I'd try to take some online classes and get some kind of degree. That would be nice, to have more education."

There was a moment's silence. "You didn't mention contacting your great-grandfather," Eric said. "He could make sure you never wanted for anything."

"I'm not sure I could," I said, surprised. "Contact him, that is. I guess Claude would know how. In fact, I'm sure he would. But Niall made it pretty clear he thought staying in touch wouldn't be a good idea." It was my turn to think for a second. "Eric, do you think Claude has an ulterior motive for coming to live with me?"

"Of course he does; Dermot, too," Eric said, without missing a beat. "I only wonder that you need to ask."

Not for the first time, I felt inadequate for the task of coping with my life. I fought a wave of self-pity, of bitterness, while I forced myself to examine Eric's words. I'd suspected as much, of course, and that was why I'd asked Sam if people really changed. Claude had always been the master of selfishness, the duke of disinterest. Why would he change? Oh, sure, he missed being around other fairies, especially now that his sisters were dead. But why would he come live with someone who had as little fairy blood as I did (especially when I'd been indirectly responsible for Claudine's death) unless he had something else on his mind?

Dermot's motivation was just as opaque. It would be easy to assume Dermot's character was like Jason's because they looked so much alike, but I had learned (from bitter experience) what happened when I made assumptions. Dermot had been under a spell for a long time, a spell that had rendered him crazed, but even through the mental haze of the magic worked on him, Dermot had tried to do the right thing. At least, that was what he'd told me, and I had a little evidence that that was true.

I was still brooding over my gullibility when we took an exit ramp in the middle of nowhere. You could see the shine of the lights of Vampire's Kiss, which of course was the point.

"Aren't you afraid that people who would have driven on into Shreveport to go to Fangtasia are just going to pull off when they see this club?" I said.

"Yes."

I'd asked a dumb question, so I gave him some slack for being short with me. Eric must have been brooding over his financial downturn ever since Victor had bought the building. But I wasn't prepared to give Eric any more free passes. We were a couple, and he should either share his life completely with me or let me worry about my own concerns. It wasn't easy, being yoked to Eric. I glanced over at him, realizing how stupid that would sound to one of the Fang-tasia fangbangers. Eric was certainly one of the handsomest males I'd ever seen. He was strong, intelligent, and fantastic in bed.

Right now, there lay a frosty silence between that strong, intelligent, lusty man and me, and that silence lasted until we parked. It was hard to find a spot, which made Eric even more pissed off. *That* wasn't hard to tell.

Since Eric had been summoned, it would have been polite to have reserved him a parking spot by the front door . . . or given him the green light to come in by the back entrance. There was also the unavoidable lesson in pictures that Vampire's Kiss was so busy it was hard to find a parking spot.

Ouch.

I struggled to push aside my own worries. I needed to concentrate on the troubles we were about to face. Victor didn't like or trust Eric, and the feeling was mutual. Since Victor had been put in charge of Louisiana, Eric's position as the only holdover from the Sophie-Anne era had become increasingly precarious. I was pretty sure I'd gotten to continue my life unmolested only because Eric had hoodwinked me into marrying him in the eyes of the vampires.

Eric, his mouth pressed into a thin line, came around to open my door. I could tell he was using the maneuver as a way to scan the parking lot for danger. He stood in such a way that his body was between me and the club, and as I swung my legs out of the Town Car, he asked, "Who's in the parking lot, lover?"

I stood, slowly and carefully, my eyes

closed to concentrate. I put my hand over his where it rested on the door frame. In the warm night, with a light wind gently riffling my hair, I sent my extra sense out. "A couple having sex in a car two rows away," I whispered. "A man throwing up behind the black pickup on the other side of the parking lot. Two couples just pulling in, in an Escalade. One vampire by the door to the club. Another vampire closing *fast*."

When vamps go on alert, there's no mistaking it. Eric's fangs ran out, his body tensed, and he whirled to look outward.

Pam said, "Master." She stepped out of the shadow of a big SUV. Eric relaxed; and so, gradually, did I. Whatever had made the two fight at my house, it had been put aside for the evening.

"I came ahead as you bid me," she murmured, the night wind picking up her voice and tossing it. Her face looked oddly dark.

"Pam, step into the light," I said.

She did, though certainly she was not obliged to obey me.

The darkness under Pam's white skin was the result of a beating. Vampires don't bruise exactly like we do, and they heal quickly — but when they've been hit hard, you can tell it for a little while. "What happened to you?" Eric asked. His voice was completely empty, which I knew was an awfully bad thing.

"I told the door guards that I needed to come in to make sure Victor knew you were arriving. An excuse to make sure that the interior was secure."

"They prevented you."

"Yes."

A little breeze had sprung up, dancing the night air across the smelly parking lot. The breeze picked up my hair and blew it around my face. Eric had his tied at the nape of his neck, but Pam reached up to hold hers back. Eric had wished Victor dead for months, and I was sorry to say I felt the same. It wasn't only Eric's worry and anger that I was channeling; I myself understood how much better life would be for us if Victor was gone.

I'd come so far from what I'd been. At moments like this I was both sad and relieved that I could think about Victor's death not only without qualms, but with positive zeal. My determination to survive, and to ensure the survival of those I loved, was stronger than the religion I'd always held so dear.

"We have to go in, or they'll send someone after us," Eric said finally, and we walked to the main door in silence. All we needed was a badass theme song playing in the background: something ominous and cool, with a lot of drums, to indicate "The Visiting Vampires and Their Human Sidekick Walk into a Trap." However, the club's music was out of synch with our little drama — "Hips Don't Lie" was not exactly badass music.

We passed a bearded man hosing down the gravel close to the door. I could still spot dark patches of blood. Pam snorted. "Not mine," she muttered.

The vampire on duty at the door was a sturdy brunette wearing a studded leather collar and a leather bustier, with a tutu (I swear to God) and motorcycle boots. Only the frilly skirt looked out of character.

"Sheriff Eric," she said in heavily accented English. "I am Ana Lyudmila. I welcome you to Vampire's Kiss." She didn't even glance at Pam, much less me. I pretty much expected her to ignore me, but her disregard of Pam was an insult, especially since Pam had already had an encounter with the club personnel. This behavior was the kind of trigger that could send Pam over the edge, which I figured might be the plan. If Pam went ballistic, the new vamps would have a legitimate reason to kill her. The target on Eric's back would assume large proportions.

Naturally, I wouldn't even be a factor in

their thinking, because they couldn't imagine what a human could do against their vampire strength and speed. And since I wasn't Superwoman, they might be right. I wasn't sure how many of the vampires knew I wasn't wholly human, or how much they'd care even if they knew I was a fraction fairy. It wasn't like I'd ever exhibited any fairy powers. My value lay in my telepathic talent and my connection to Niall. Since Niall had left this world for the world of the fae, I had expected that value to decrease accordingly. But Niall might choose to return to the human world any moment, and I was Eric's wife by vampire rite. So Niall would side with Eric in an open conflict. At least that was my best bet. With fairies, who knew? It was time to assert myself.

I laid my hand on Pam's shoulder and patted her. It was like patting a rock. I smiled at Ana Lyudmila. "Hi," I said, perky as a cheerleader on uppers. "I'm Sookie. I'm married to Eric. I guess you didn't know that? And this is Pam, Eric's child and his strong right arm. I guess you didn't know that, either? Cause otherwise, not greeting us appropriately is just plain rude." I beamed at her.

Looking as though I were forcing her to swallow a live frog, Ana Lyudmila said,

"Welcome, human wife of Eric and revered fighter Pam. I apologize for failing to offer you a suitable greeting."

Pam was staring at Ana Lyudmila as if she were wondering how long it would take to pull Ana's eyelashes out one by one. I bumped Pam's shoulder with my fist, buddy-buddy. "We're cool, Ana Lyudmila," I said. "It's all good here." Pam switched her stare to me, and it was all I could do not to flinch. To add to the tension, Eric was doing a good imitation of a big white rock. I gave him a very laden look.

Ana Lyudmila couldn't have beaten Pam up. She didn't have the juice. Besides, she looked okay, and I was completely sure that if someone had laid a hand on Pam, that vampire would show the aftereffect.

After a second, Eric said, "I think your master is waiting for us." His tone was one of gentle chiding. He made sure his massive self-control was evident.

If Ana Lyudmila could have blushed, I think she would have. "Yes, of course," she said. "Luis! Antonio!" Two young men, dark-headed and brawny, materialized out of the crowd. They were wearing leather shorts and boots. Period. Okay, a different look for Vampire's Kiss workers. I'd assumed Ana Lyudmila was following her own fashion genie, but apparently all the vamps on duty had to wear sort of caveman–sex slave outfits. At least, I assumed that was the look they were going for.

Luis, the taller of the two, said, "Follow us, please," in accented English. His nipples were pierced, which was something I'd never seen before, and naturally I found myself wanting to take a closer look. But in my book, it was basically bad taste to stare at someone's assets, no matter how much on display they were.

Antonio couldn't hide the fact that Pam had made an impression on him, but that wouldn't stop him from killing us if Victor ordered him to do so. We followed the bondage Bobbsey Twins across the crowded dance floor. Those leather shorts were an adventure from behind, let me tell you. And the pictures of Elvis decorating the walls were an education, too. It wasn't often you ran into a bondage/Elvis/whorehouse-themed vampire club.

Pam was admiring the decor, too, but not with her normal sardonic amusement. There seemed to be a lot going on in Pam's head.

"How are your three friends?" she asked Antonio. "The ones who prevented me from entering."

He smiled in a tight sort of way, and I had

the feeling the injured vampires hadn't been his favorites. "They're taking blood from donors in the back," he said. "I think Pearl's arm has healed."

As he preceded me through the noisy room, Eric was evaluating the club in a series of casual glances. It was important to him that he seem at ease, as if he were quite sure that his boss meant him no harm. I could tell that through our bond. Since no one cared about me, I was free to look where I wished . . . though I hoped I was doing it with a suitably careless air.

There were at least twenty bloodsuckers in Vampire's Kiss, more than Eric ever had in Fangtasia at one time. There were also a lot of humans. I didn't know what the capacity of the building was, but I was pretty sure it had been exceeded. Eric reached behind him, and I took his cool hand. He tugged me forward, wrapped his left arm around my shoulders, and Pam closed in from the rear. We were at DEF-CON Four, Orange Alert, or whatever came right before the blowup. The tension vibrated through Eric like a plucked guitar string.

And then we spotted its source.

Victor was sitting at the back in a kind of corral for VIPs. It was lined with a huge, square red velvet banquette, before which was centered the usual low table. It was littered with little evening purses and half-empty drinks and dollar bills. Victor was definitely the centerpiece of the grouping, his arms around the young man and woman flanking him. The tableau was a poster of what conservative humans feared most: the corrupt vampire seducing the youth of America, inducting them into orgies of bisexuality and bloodsucking. I looked from one breather to the other. Though one was male and one female, they were otherwise startlingly the same. Dipping into their heads, I quickly learned both were using drugs, both were over twenty-one, and both were experienced sexually. I felt a little sad for them, but I knew I couldn't be responsible. Though they had yet to realize it, they were only props for Victor. Their position suited their vanity.

There was another human in the corral, a young woman seated by herself. She was wearing a white dress with a full skirt, and her brown eyes fixed on Pam with desperation. The woman was clearly horrified at the company she was keeping. A minute before I would have bet that Pam couldn't get any more angry or miserable than she'd been, but I would have been wrong.

"Miriam," Pam whispered.

Oh, Jesus Christ, Shepherd of Judea. This was the woman Pam wanted to turn, the woman she wanted to become her child. Miriam had to be the sickest woman I'd ever seen who wasn't in a hospital. But her light brown hair was puffed out in a party style, and she'd been made up, though the cosmetics stood out on a face so pale even her lips looked white.

Eric's face didn't show anything, but I could feel him scrambling, struggling to keep his face still and his thoughts clear.

Several points to Victor for an amazing ambush.

Luis and Antonio, having delivered us, positioned themselves at the opening to the VIP corral. I didn't know if they were there to keep us in or to keep other people out. We were further protected by stand-up cardboard figures of Elvis, at least life-size. I wasn't impressed. I'd met the real thing.

Victor greeted us with a wonderful smile, white and toothy, as brilliant as a game show host's. "Eric, how good to see you in my new enterprise! Do you like the decor?" He made his hand flow to indicate the whole crowded club. Though Victor was not a tall man, he was clearly the king of the castle, and he was devouring every minute of it. He leaned forward to pick up his drink from the low table.

Even the glass was dramatic — dark, smoky, fluted. It fit in with the "decor" that made Victor so proud. I would have called it (if I ever got a chance to describe it to someone else, which at this point seemed pretty unlikely) early bordello: lots of dark wood, flocked wallpaper, leather, and red velvet. It looked heavy and florid to me; possibly I was prejudiced. The people gyrating on the dance floor seemed to be enjoying Vampire's Kiss no matter how it was decorated. The band was a vampire band, so they were great. They'd play a current song, then they'd do a more bluesy rock number. Since the band members could have played with Robert Johnson and Memphis Minnie, they'd had several decades to practice.

"I'm amazed," Eric said in a completely uninflected voice.

"Pardon my bad manners! Please have a seat," Victor said. "My companions are . . . Your name, sweetness?" he asked the girl.

"I'm Mindy Simpson," she said with a coquettish smile. "This is my husband, Mark Simpson."

Eric acknowledged them with a flick of the eye. Pam and I hadn't even entered into the conversational game yet, so we didn't have to respond.

Victor didn't introduce the pale young woman. He was clearly saving the best for last.

"I see you have your dear wife with you," Victor said as we newcomers moved to sit on the long banquette to Victor's right. It wasn't as comfortable as I'd hoped it would be, and the depth of the seat didn't agree with the length of my legs. The life-size cutout of Elvis to my right was wearing the famous white jumpsuit. Classy.

"Yeah, I'm here," I said dismally.

"And your famous second, Pam Ravenscroft," Victor continued, as if he were identifying us for a hidden microphone.

I squeezed Eric's hand. He couldn't read my mind, which (just at this moment) I felt was a pity. There was a lot going on here we didn't know about. In vampire eyes, as Eric's human wife I pretty much ranked as his number one designated concubine. The "wife" title gave me status and protection, theoretically rendering me untouchable by other vampires and their servants. I wasn't exactly proud of being a second-class citizen, but once I'd understood why Eric had tricked me into the relationship, I'd gradually reconciled myself to the title. Now it was time to offer Eric a little support in return.

"How long has Vampire's Kiss been open?" I beamed at the loathsome Victor. I'd had years of experience in looking happy when I wasn't, and I was the queen of chitchat.

"You didn't see all my advance publicity? Only three weeks, but so far it's been quite the success," Victor said, his eyes barely brushing me. He was not interested in me as a person, not at all. He wasn't even interested in me sexually. Believe me, I know the signs. He was far more interested in me as a creature whose death would wound Eric. In other words, my absence would be more effective than my presence.

Since he was deigning to talk to me, I thought I'd take advantage of it.

"Do you spend a lot of time here? I'm surprised they don't need you in New Orleans more often." Snap! I waited for his answer, smiling steadily.

"Sophie-Anne saw fit to remain permanently based in New Orleans, but I see my rule as more of a floating government," Victor said genially. "I like to keep a firm hand on all that goes on in Louisiana, especially since I find I am simply a regent, holding the state for Felipe, my dear king." His grin became positively ferocious.

126

"My felicitations on becoming regent," Eric said, as though nothing could be more desirable.

There was a lot of pretending going on in this building. So many undercurrents, you could drown in them, and we just might.

"You're very welcome," Victor said savagely. "Yes, Felipe has decreed I should style myself 'regent.' It's so unusual for a king to have amassed as many territories as Felipe has, and he's taken his time deciding what to do. He has decided to keep all the titles for himself."

"And will you be regent of Arkansas, too?" Pam asked. At the sound of Pam's voice, Miriam Earnest began to cry. She was managing to be as quiet about it as a woman can be, but no weeping is silent. Pam did not look in Miriam's direction.

"No," Victor said, biting out the word. "Red Rita has been given that honor."

I didn't have any idea who Red Rita might be, but both Eric and Pam seemed impressed. "She's a great fighter," Eric told me. "A strong vampire. She's a good choice to rebuild Arkansas."

Great, maybe we could go live *there.*

Though I couldn't read vampire minds, I didn't have to. All you had to do was watch Victor's face to understand that Victor had wanted — yearned for — the title of king, that he had hoped to rule both of Felipe's new territories. His disappointment had made him angry, and he was focusing that anger on Eric, the biggest target within his reach. Provoking Eric and intruding on his territory would not be enough for Victor.

And that was why Miriam was sitting in the club tonight. I tried to get inside her head. When I carefully felt around the edges, I met with a sort of white fog. She was drugged, though I didn't know what sort of drug she'd taken or whether she'd been willing or coerced.

"Yes, of course," Victor said, and I pulled myself back into the here and now with a jerk. While I'd zoned out in Miriam's head, the vampires had stayed on the topic of Red Rita. "While she's settling in next door, I thought it would be appropriate to build up the area of Louisiana that abuts her territory. I opened the human place, and this one." Victor was practically purring.

"You own Vic's Redneck Roadhouse," I said numbly. Of course! I should have known. Was Victor *compiling* reasons for me to want him dead? Naturally, economics should have nothing to do with life and death, but all too often the two were definitely linked.

"Yes," Victor said, grinning at me. He was just as merry as a department store Santa. "You've been by?" He replaced his glass on the table.

"Nope, too busy," I said.

"But I heard business at Merlotte's has fallen off?" Victor tried a look of faux concern on for size, discarded it. "If you need a job, Sookie, I'll put in a good word with my manager at the Redneck Roadhouse . . . unless you'd prefer to work here? Wouldn't that be fun!"

I had to take a deep breath. There was a long moment's silence. For that moment, everything hung in the balance.

With an amazing control, Eric spackled his rage away behind a wall, at least temporarily. He said, "Sookie is well suited where she works now, Victor. If she were not, she would come to live with me and perhaps work at Fangtasia. She is a modern American woman and used to supporting herself." Eric said this as if he were proud of my independence, though I knew that wasn't the case. He really couldn't understand why I persisted in keeping my job. "While I'm discussing my female associates, Pam tells me that you disciplined her. It's not customary to discipline a sheriff's second. Surely that should be left for her master to do."

Eric allowed his voice to have a slight edge.

"You weren't here," Victor protested smoothly. "And she showed my doormen great disrespect by insisting she should come inside before you did for a security check, as if we would permit anything in our club to threaten our most powerful sheriff."

"Did you have business you wanted to discuss?" Eric said. "Not that it isn't wonderful seeing what you've done here. However . . ." He let his voice trail off, as if he were simply too polite to say, "I have better fish to fry."

"Of course, thanks for reminding me," Victor said. He leaned forward to pick up the smoky gray stemmed glass, refilled by a server so that it was brimming with dark red liquid. "I'm sorry, I haven't offered you a drink yet. Some blood for you, Eric, Pam?"

Pam had taken advantage of their conversation to glance at Miriam, who looked as though she were going to keel over any second . . . and maybe not get up again. Pam pulled her eyes away from the young woman and concentrated on Victor. She shook her head mutely.

"Thank you for the offer, Victor," Eric began, "but . . ."

"I know you'll raise a glass with me. The law prevents me from offering you a drink from Mindy or Mark since they're not registered donors, and I'm all about being law-abiding." He smiled at Mindy and Mark, who grinned back. Idiots. "Sookie, what will you have?"

Eric and Pam were obliged to accept the offer of synthetic blood, but because I was only a human, I was allowed to insist I wasn't thirsty. If he'd offered me country-fried steak and fried green tomatoes, I would've said I wasn't hungry.

Luis beckoned to one of the servers, and the man vanished to reappear with some TrueBlood. The bottles were on a large tray, along with the dark, fancy stemware matching Victor's. "I'm sure the bottles don't appeal to your aesthetic sense," Victor said. "They offend me."

Like all the servers, the man who brought the drinks was human, a handsome guy in a leather loincloth (even smaller than Luis's leather shorts) and high boots. A sort of rosette pinned to his loincloth read "Colton." His eyes were a startling gray. When he placed the tray on the table and unloaded it, he was thinking about someone named Chic, or Chico . . . and when he met my eyes directly, he thought, *Fairy blood on the*

131

glasses. Don't let your vamps drink.

I looked at him for a long moment. He knew about me. Now I knew something about him. He'd heard about my ability, common knowledge in the supernatural community, and he'd believed in it.

Colton cast his eyes down.

Eric twisted the cap to unseal the bottle, lifted it to pour the contents into the glass.

NO, I said to him. We couldn't communicate telepathically, but I sent a wave of negativity, and I prayed he'd pick up on it.

"I have nothing against American packaging, as you do," Eric said smoothly, raising the bottle directly to his lips. Pam followed suit.

A flicker of vexation crossed Victor's face so quickly I might have imagined it if I hadn't been watching him so intently. The gray-eyed server backed away.

"Have you seen your great-grandfather recently, Sookie?" Victor said, as if he were saying, "Gotcha!"

There was no point pretending ignorance about my fairy connection.

"Not in the past couple of weeks," I said cautiously.

"But you have two of your kind living in your house."

This was not classified information, and I

was pretty sure Eric's new vampire Heidi had told Victor. Heidi really didn't have a choice, which was the downside to having living human relatives whom you still loved. "Yes, my cousin and my great-uncle are staying with me for a while." I was proud that I managed to sound almost bored.

"I wondered if you might be able to give me some insight into the state of fairy politics," Victor said smoothly. Mindy Simpson, tired of conversations that didn't include her, began pouting. She was unwise.

"Not me. I stay away from politics," I told Victor.

"Truly? Even after your ordeal?"

"Yep, even after my ordeal," I said flatly. I really, really wanted to talk about my abduction and mutilation. Great party conversation. "I'm just not a political animal."

"But an animal," Victor said smoothly.

There was a moment's frozen silence. However, I was determined that if Eric died trying to kill this vampire, it wasn't going to be for an insult to me.

"That's me," I said, returning his smile with interest. "Hot-blooded, breathing. I could even lactate. The whole mammal package."

Victor's eyes narrowed. Maybe I'd gone too far.

"Did we have anything further to discuss, Regent?" Pam asked, rightly guessing Eric was too angry to speak. "I'll be glad to stay as late as you want, or as long as my words please you, but I am due to work at Fangtasia tonight, and my master Eric has a meeting to attend. And apparently my friend Miriam is the worse for wear tonight, and I'll take her home with me to sleep it off."

Victor looked at the pallid woman as if he were only just now noticing her. "Oh, do you know her?" he asked negligently. "Yes, I believe someone mentioned that. Eric, is this the woman you told me Pam wanted to bring over? I'm so sorry I had to say no, since by my reckoning she may not have too long to live."

Pam didn't move. She didn't even twitch.

"You may go," Victor said, overdoing the offhanded air. "Since I've given you the news about my regency, and you've seen my beautiful club. Oh, I'm thinking of opening a tattoo establishment and maybe a lawyer's office, though my man for that post has to study modern law. He received his law degree in Paris in the eighteen hundreds." Victor's indulgent smile faded completely. "You know that as regent, I have the right to open a business in anyone's sheriffdom? All the money from the new

134

clubs will come directly to me. I hope your revenues don't suffer too much, Eric."

"Not at all," Eric said. (I didn't think that actually had any meaning.) "We're all a part of your turf, Master." If his voice had been laundry, it would have flapped in the wind, it was so dry and empty.

We rose, more or less as one, and dipped our heads to Victor. He waved a dismissive hand at us and bent to kiss Mindy Simpson. Mark huddled closer on the vampire's other side to nuzzle Victor's shoulder. Pam went over to Miriam Earnest and bent over the girl to put her arm around her and help her to rise. Once on her feet and supported by Pam, Miriam focused on making it out the door. Her mind might be clouded, but her eyes were screaming.

We left the club in grim silence (at least as far as our own conversation went; the music just *never let up*), escorted by Luis and Antonio. The brothers bypassed sturdy Ana Lyudmila to follow us out into the parking lot, which surprised me.

When we had filed through the first row of cars, Eric turned to face them. Not coincidentally, the bulk of an Escalade blocked the view between Ana Lyudmila and our little party. "Do you two have something to say to me?" he asked very softly. As if she suddenly understood she was out of Vampire's Kiss, Miriam gasped and began crying, and Pam took her in her arms.

"It wasn't our idea, sheriff," said Antonio, the shorter of the two. His oiled abs gleamed under the parking lot lights.

Luis said, "We're loyal to Felipe, our true king, but Victor is not easy to serve. It was a bad night for us when we were dispatched to Louisiana to serve him. Now that Bruno and Corinna have disappeared, he hasn't found anyone to take their places. No strong lieutenant. He's traveling constantly, trying to keep his eye on every corner of Louisiana." Luis shook his head. "We're badly overextended. He needs to settle in New Orleans, building back up the vampire structure there. We don't need to be trailing around in leather scarcely covering our asses, draining the income from your club. Halving the available income is not good economics, and the startup costs were steep."

"If you're trying to lure me into betraying my new master, you've picked the wrong vampire," Eric said, and I tried not to let my mouth hang open. I'd thought it was Christmas in June when Luis and Antonio revealed their discontent, but obviously I hadn't been thinking deviously enough . . . again.

Pam said, "Leather shorts are attractive compared to the black synthetics *I* have to wear." She was holding up Miriam, but she didn't look at her or refer to her, as if she wanted everyone else to forget the girl was there.

Her costume complaint was not out of character, but it was irrelevant. Pam had always been nothing if not on task. Antonio gave her a look of disillusioned disgust. "You were supposed to be so fierce," he muttered. He looked at Eric. "And you were supposed to be so bold." He and Luis turned and strode back into the club.

After that, Pam and Eric began to move with speed, as if we had a deadline to get off the property.

Pam simply picked up Miriam and hurried to Eric's car. He opened the back door, and she got her girlfriend in and slid in after her. Seeing that haste was the order of the night, I climbed into the front passenger seat and buckled up in silence. I looked back to see that Miriam had passed out the minute she realized she was safe.

As the car left the parking lot, Pam began sniggering and Eric grinned broadly. I was too startled to ask them what was funny.

"Victor just can't restrain himself," Pam said. "Making the show of my poor Miriam."

"And then the priceless offer from the leather twins!"

"Did you see Antonio's face?" Pam demanded. "Honestly, I haven't had so much fun since I flashed my fangs at that old woman who complained about the color I painted my house!"

"That'll give them something to think about," Eric said. He glanced over at me, his fangs glistening. "That was a good moment. I can't believe he thought we'd fall for that."

"What if Antonio and Luis were sincere?" I asked. "What if Victor had taken Miriam's blood or brought her over himself?" I twisted in my seat to look back at Pam.

She was looking at me almost with pity, as if I were a hopeless romantic. "He couldn't," she said. "He had her in a public place, she has lots of human relatives, and he has to know I'd kill him if he did that."

"Not if you were dead first," I said. Eric and Pam didn't seem to have my own respect for Victor's lethal tactics. They seemed almost insanely cocky. "And why are you both so sure that Antonio and Luis were making all that up just to see how

138

you'd react?"

"If they meant what they said, they'll approach us again," Eric said bluntly. "They have no other recourse, if they've tried Felipe and he's turned them down. I suspect he has. Tell me, lover, what was the problem with the drinks?"

"The *problem* was that he'd rubbed the inside of the glasses with fairy blood," I said. "The human server, the guy with the gray eyes, gave me the tip-off."

And the smiles vanished as if they'd been turned off with a switch. I had a moment of unpleasant satisfaction.

Pure fairy blood is intoxicating to vampires. There's no telling what Pam or Eric would have done if they'd drunk from those glasses. And they'd have gulped it down as quickly as they could because the smell is just as entrancing as the actual substance.

As poisoning attempts went, this one was subtle.

"I don't think that amount could have caused us to behave in an uncontrollable way," Pam said. But she didn't sound so confident.

Eric raised his blond eyebrows. "It was a cautious experiment," he said thoughtfully. "We might have attacked anyone in the club, or we might have gone for Sookie, since she has that interesting streak of fairy. We would have made public fools of ourselves, in any case. We might have been arrested. It was an excellent thing that you stopped us, Sookie."

"I have my uses," I said, suppressing the jolt of fear that the idea of Eric and Pam going fairy-struck on me evinced.

"And you're Eric's *wife*," Pam observed quietly.

Eric glared at her in the rearview mirror.

The silence that fell was so thick I wished I'd had a knife. This Pam-and-Eric secret quarrel was both upsetting and frustrating. And that was the understatement of the year.

"Is there something you want to tell me?" I asked, frightened of the answer. But anything was better than not knowing.

"Eric got a letter —" Pam began, and before I could register that he'd moved, Eric had whipped around, reached over the seat, and seized her throat. Since he was still driving, I squawked in terror.

"Eyes ahead, Eric! Not with the fighting again," I said. "Look, just go on and tell me!"

With his right hand, Eric was still holding Pam in a grip that would have choked her if she'd been a breather. He was steering with his left hand, and we coasted to a stop on the side of the road. I couldn't see any oncoming traffic, and there were no lights behind us, either. I didn't know if the isolation made me feel good or bad. Eric looked back at his child, and his eyes were so bright they were practically throwing sparks. He said, "Pam, don't speak. That's an order. Sookie, *leave this be.*"

I could have said several things. I could have said, "I'm not your vassal, and I'll say what I want to say," or I could have said, "Fuck you, let me out," and called my brother to come get me.

But I sat in silence.

I am ashamed to say that at that moment I was scared of Eric, this desperate and determined vampire who was attacking his best friend because he didn't want me to know . . . something. Through the tie I felt with him, I got a confused bundle of negative emotions: fear, anger, grim resolve, frustration.

"Take me home," I said.

In an eerie echo, the limp Miriam whispered, "Take me home. . . ."

After a long moment, Eric let go of Pam, who collapsed in the backseat like a sack of rice. She hunched over Miriam protectively. In a frozen silence, Eric took me back to

141

my house. There was no further mention of the sex we'd been scheduled to have after this "fun" evening. At that point, I would rather have had sex with Luis and Antonio. Or Pam. I said good-bye to Pam and Miriam, got out, and walked into my house without a backward glance.

I guess Eric and Pam and Miriam drove back to Shreveport together, and I guess at some point he permitted Pam to speak again, but I don't know.

I couldn't sleep after I'd washed my face and hung up the pretty dress. I hoped I'd get to wear it on a happier evening, sometime in the future. I'd looked too good to be this miserable. I wondered if Eric would have handled the evening with such sangfroid if it had been me Victor had captured and drugged and put out there on that banquette for the entire world to gape at.

And there was another thing troubling me. Here's what I would have asked Eric if he hadn't been playing dictator. I would have said, "Where did Victor get the fairy blood?"

That's what I would have asked.

CHAPTER 4

I rose the next day feeling pretty grim in general, but I brightened when I saw that Claude and Dermot had returned to the house the night before. The evidence was clear. Claude's shirt was tossed over the back of a kitchen chair, and Dermot's shoes were at the foot of the stairs. Plus, after I'd had my coffee and my shower, and emerged from my room in shorts and a green T-shirt, the two were waiting for me in the living room.

"Good morning, guys," I said. Even to my own ears, I didn't sound too perky. "Did you remember that today was the day the antiques dealers come? They should be here in an hour or two." I braced myself for the talk we had to have.

"Good, then this room will not look like a junk shop," Claude said in his charming way.

I just nodded. Today, we had Obnoxious

Claude, as opposed to the more rarely seen Tolerable Claude.

"We did promise you a talk," Dermot said.

"And then you didn't come home that night." I sat back in an old rocker from the attic. I didn't feel particularly ready for this conversation, but I was also anxious for some answers.

"Things were happening at the club," Claude said evasively.

"Uh-huh. Let me guess, one of the fairies is missing."

That made them sit up and take notice. "What? How did you know?" Dermot recovered first.

"Victor has him. Or her," I added. I told them the story about last night.

"It's not enough that we have to handle our own race's problems," Claude said. "Now we're sucked into the fucking vampire struggles, too."

"No," I said, feeling I was walking uphill in this conversation. "You as a group weren't sucked into the vampire struggles. One of you was taken for a specific purpose. Different scenario. Let me point out that at the very least, that fairy who was taken has been bled, because that was what the vamps needed, the blood. I'm not saying your missing comrade couldn't be alive, but you know how the vamps lose control when a fairy is around, much less a bleeding fairy."

"She's right," Dermot told Claude. "Cait must be dead. Are any of the fairies at the club her kin? We need to ask if they've had a death vision."

"A female," Claude said. His handsome face was set in stone. "One we couldn't afford to lose. Yes, we have to find out."

For a second I was confused, because Claude didn't think that much about women in terms of his personal life. Then I remembered that there were fewer and fewer female fairies. I didn't know about the rest of the fae, but it seemed the fairies were on the wane. It wasn't that I lacked concern about the missing Cait (though I didn't think there was a snowball's chance in hell that she was alive), but I had other, selfish questions to ask, and I was not going to be diverted. As soon as Dermot had called Hooligans and asked Bellenos to call the fae together to ask about Cait's kin, I got back on my own track.

"While Bellenos is busy, you have some free time, and since the appraisers are coming soon, I really need you to answer my questions," I said.

Dermot and Claude looked at each other. Dermot seemed to lose the conversational

145

coin toss, because he took a deep breath and began, "You know when one of your Caucasians marries one of your Negroes, sometimes the babies turn out looking much more like one race than another, seemingly at random. That likeness can vary even between children of the same couple."

"Yes," I said. "I've heard that."

"When Jason was a baby, our great-grandfather Niall checked on him."

I felt my mouth drop open. "Wait," I said, and it came out in a hoarse croak. "Niall said he couldn't visit because his half-human son Fintan guarded us from him. That Fintan was actually our grandfather."

"This is *why* Fintan guarded you from the fae. He didn't want his father interfering in your lives the way he had interfered in his own. But Niall had his ways, and nonetheless, he found that the essential spark had passed Jason by. He became . . . uninterested," Claude said.

I waited.

He continued, "That's why he took so many years to make your acquaintance. He could have evaded Fintan, but he assumed you would be the same as Jason . . . attractive to humans and supernaturals, but other than that, essentially a normal human."

"But then he heard you weren't," Dermot said.

"Heard? From who? Whom?" My grandmother would have been proud.

"From Eric. They had a few business dealings together, and Niall thought to ask Eric to alert him to events in your life. Eric would tell Niall from time to time what you were up to. There came a time when Eric thought you needed the protection of your great-grandfather, and of course you were withering."

Huh?

"So Grandfather sent Claudine, and then when she grew worried she couldn't take care of you, he decided to meet you himself. Eric arranged that, too. I suppose he thought that he would get Niall's goodwill as kind of a finder's fee." Dermot shrugged. "That seems to have worked for Eric. Vampires are all venal and selfish."

The words "pot" and "kettle" popped into my mind.

I said, "So Niall appeared in my life and made himself known to me, via Eric's intervention. And that precipitated the fairy war, because the water fairies didn't want any more contact with humans, much less a minor royal who was only one-eighth fairy." Thanks, guys. I *loved* hearing that a whole war was my fault.

"Yes," Claude said judiciously. "That's a fair summary. And so the war came, and after many deaths Niall made the decision to seal off Faery." He sighed heavily. "I was left outside, and Dermot, too."

"And by the way, I'm not *withering,*" I pointed out with some sharpness. "I mean, do I look withered to you?" I knew I was ignoring the big picture, but I was getting angry. Or maybe, even angrier.

"You have only a little fae blood," Dermot said gently, as if that would be a crushing reminder. "You are aging."

I couldn't deny that. "So why am I feeling more and more like one of you, if I have such a little dab of fairy in me?"

"Our sum is more than our parts," Dermot said. "I'm half-human, but the longer I'm with Claude, the stronger my magic is. Claude, though a full-blooded fairy, has been in the human world for so long he was getting weak. Now he's stronger. You only have a dash of fae blood, but the longer you're with us, the more prominent an element it is in your nature."

"Like priming a pump?" I said doubtfully. "I don't get it."

"Like — like — washing a new red garment with the whites," said Dermot triumphantly, who had done that very thing the week before. Everyone in our house had pink socks now.

"But wouldn't that mean Claude was getting *less* red? I mean, less fae? If we're absorbing some of his?"

"No," Claude said, with some complacence. "I am redder than I was."

Dermot nodded. "Me, too."

"I haven't really noticed any difference," I said.

"Are you not stronger than you were?"

"Well . . . yeah. Some days." It wasn't like ingesting vampire blood, which would give you increased strength for an indeterminate period, if it didn't make you batshit crazy. It was more like I felt increased vigor. I felt, in fact . . . younger. And since I was only in my twenties, that was just unnerving.

"Don't you long to see Niall again?" Claude asked.

"Sometimes." Every day.

"Are you not happy when we sleep in the bed with you?"

"Yeah. But just so you know, I think it's kind of creepy, too."

"Humans," Claude said to Dermot, with a blend of exasperation and patronage in his voice. Dermot shrugged. After all, he was half-human.

149

"And yet you chose to stay here," I said.

"I wonder every day if I made a mistake."

"Why are you two still here, if you're so nuts about Niall and your life in Faery? How did you get the letter from Niall that you gave me a month ago, the one where he told me he'd used all his influence to make the FBI leave me alone?" I glared at them suspiciously. "Was that letter a forgery?"

"No, it was genuine," Dermot said. "And we're here because we both love and fear our prince."

"Okay," I said, ready to change subjects because I couldn't get into a debate about their feelings. "What's a portal, exactly?"

"It's a thin place in the membrane," Claude said. I looked at Claude blankly, and he elaborated. "There's a sort of magical membrane between our world — the supernatural world — and yours. At a thin place, that membrane is permeable. The fae world is accessible. As are the parts of your world that are normally invisible to you."

"Huh?"

Claude was on a roll. "Portals usually stay in the same vicinity, though they may shift a little. We use them to get from your world to ours. At the site of the portal in your woods, Niall left an aperture. The slit isn't big enough for one of us to pass through standing up, but objects can be transferred."

Like a mail slot in a door. "See? Was that so hard?" I said. "Can you think of some more honest things to tell me?"

"Like what?"

"Like why all those fae are at Hooligans, acting as strippers and bouncers and whatnot. They're not all fairies. I don't even know what they are. Why would they end up with you two?"

"Because they have nowhere else to go," Dermot said simply. "They were all shut out. Some on purpose, like Claude, and some not . . . like me."

"So Niall closed off access to Faery and left some of his people outside?"

"Yes. He was trying to keep all those fairies who still wanted to kill humans inside, and he was too hasty," Claude said. I noticed that Dermot, whom Niall had bespelled in a cruel way, looked dubious at this explanation.

"I understood that Niall had good reasons for closing the fae off," I said slowly. "He said experience had taught him that there's always trouble when fairies and humans mix. He didn't want the fairies to crossbreed with humans anymore because so many of the fae hate the consequence — halfbreeds." I looked apologetically at Dermot, who shrugged. He was used to it. "Niall never intended to see me again. Are you two really so anxious to go into the world of the fae and stay there?"

There was a pause that might be called "pregnant." It was clear that Dermot and Claude weren't going to respond. At least they weren't going to lie. "So explain why you're living with me and what you want from me," I said, hoping they'd answer that one.

"We're living with you because it seemed like a good idea to be with the kin we could find," Claude said. "We felt weak cut off from our homeland, and we had no notion that there were so many fae left out here. We were surprised when the other stranded fae in North America began to arrive at Hooligans, but we were happy. As we told you, we're stronger when we're together."

"Are you telling me the whole truth?" I got up and began pacing back and forth. "You could have told me all this before, and you didn't. Maybe you're lying." I held out my arms to either side, palms up. *Well?*

"What?" Claude looked affronted. Well, it was about time I served him up what he'd been dishing out. "Fairies don't lie. Everyone knows that."

Right. Sure. Common knowledge on the

street. "You may not lie, but you don't always tell the whole truth," I pointed out. "You certainly have that in common with vampires. Maybe you have some other reason for being here? Maybe you want to be around to see who comes through the portal."

Dermot shot to his feet.

Now we were all three angry, all three agitated. The room was full of accusation.

"I want to get back into Faery because I want to see Niall once more," Claude said, picking his words. "He's my grandfather. I'm tired of receiving the occasional message. I want to visit our sacred places, where I can be close to my sisters' spirits. I want to come and go between the worlds, as is my right. This is the closest portal. You're our closest relative. And there's something about this house. We belong here, for now."

Dermot went to look out the front window at the warm morning. There were butterflies outside and blooming things and lots of gorgeous sunshine. I felt a wave of intense longing to be outside with things I understood rather than in here, engaged in this bizarre conversation with relatives I didn't understand or wholly trust. If reading his body language was a reliable gauge, Dermot seemed to share the same mixed and unhappy feelings.

"I'll think about what you've said," I told Claude. Dermot's shoulders seemed to relax just a hair. "I have something else on my mind, too. I told you about the fire-bombing at the bar." Dermot turned around and leaned against the open window. Though his hair was longer than my brother's and his expression was more (sorry, Jason) intelligent, it was scary how much they looked alike. Not by any means identical, but they could certainly be mistaken for one another, at least briefly. But there were darker tones in Dermot than I'd ever seen in Jason.

Both the fairies nodded when I mentioned the firebombing. They looked interested, but uninvolved — a look I was used to seeing from vampires. They didn't really care a whole hell of a bunch about what happened to humans they didn't know. If they'd ever read John Donne, they would have disagreed with his idea that no man is an island. Most humans were on one big island, to the fairies, and that island was adrift on a sea called I Totally Don't Care.

"People talk in bars, so I'm sure they talk in strip clubs. Please let me know if you hear anything about who did it. This is important to me. If you could ask the staff at Hooligans

154

to listen for talk about the bombing, I'd sure appreciate it."

Dermot said, "Is business bad at Sam's, Sookie?"

"Yes," I said, not completely surprised at this turn of conversation. "And the new bar up off the highway is making inroads into our clientele. I don't know if it's the novelty of Vic's Redneck Roadhouse and Vampire's Kiss pulling people away, or if folks are turned off because Sam's a shifter, but it's not going so good at Merlotte's."

I was trying to decide how much I wanted to tell them about Victor and his evilness when Claude suddenly said, "You'd be out of a job," and closed his mouth, as if that had sparked a chain of thoughts.

Everyone was mighty interested in what I'd be doing if Merlotte's closed. "Sam would be out of his living," I pointed out, as I half turned to go to the kitchen to get another cup of coffee. "Which is way more important than my job. I can find another place to work."

"He could run a bar somewhere else," Claude said, shrugging.

"He'd have to leave Bon Temps," I said sharply.

"That wouldn't suit you, would it?" Claude looked thoughtful in a way that made me distinctly uneasy.

"He's my best friend," I said. "You know that." Maybe that was the first time I had said that aloud, but I guess I'd known it for quite a while. "Oh, by the way, if you want to know what happened to Cait, you might try contacting a human guy with gray eyes who works at Vampire's Kiss. The name on his uniform was Colton." I knew some places just handed out name tags every night, without any worries about who actually owned the name. But at least it was a start. I started back to the kitchen.

"Wait," Dermot said, so abruptly that I turned my head to look at him. "When are the antiques people coming to look at your junk?"

"Should be here in a couple hours."

Dermot said, "The attic is more or less empty. Didn't you plan to clean it?"

"That's what I was thinking of doing this morning."

"Do you want us to help?" Dermot asked.

Claude was clearly appalled. He glared at Dermot.

We were back on more familiar ground, and I, for one, was grateful. Until I'd had a chance to think all this new information through, I couldn't even guess at the right questions to ask. "Thanks," I said. "It would be great if you could carry up one of the big garbage cans. Then after I sweep and pick up all the bits and pieces, you could tote it down." Having relatives who are superhumanly strong can be very handy.

I went to the back porch to gather up my cleaning supplies, and when I trudged upstairs with laden arms, I saw that Claude's door was closed. My previous tenant, Amelia, had turned one upstairs bedroom into a pretty little boudoir with a cheap (but cute) dressing table, chest of drawers, and bed. Amelia had used another bedroom as her living room, complete with two comfortable chairs, a television, and a large desk, which now stood empty. The day we'd cleaned out the attic, I'd noticed that Dermot had set up a cot in the former living room.

Before I'd had time to say "Jack Robinson," Dermot appeared at the attic door carrying the garbage can. He set it down and looked around him. "I think it looked better with the family things in it," he said, and I had to agree. In the daylight streaming through the filthy windows, the attic looked sad and shabby.

"It'll be fine when it's clean," I said with determination, and I set to with the broom, sweeping down all the cobwebs, and then started in on the dust and debris on the planks of the floor. To my surprise, Dermot picked up a few rags and the glass cleaner, and began to work on the windows.

It seemed wiser not to comment. After Dermot finished the windows, he held the dustpan while I swept the accumulated dirt into it. When we'd completed that task and I'd brought up the vacuum to take care of the last of the dust, he said, "These walls need paint."

That was like saying the desert needs water. Maybe there had once been paint, but it had long ago chipped or worn away, and the indeterminate color remaining on the walls had been scuffed and stained by the many items leaning against them. "Well, yes. Sanding and painting. The floor needs it, too." I tapped with my foot. My forebears had gone crazy with whitewash when the second story had been added to the house.

"You'll only need part of this space for storage," Dermot said, out of the blue. "Assuming the antiques dealers buy the larger pieces and you don't move them back up here."

"That's true." Dermot seemed to have a point, but it was lost on me. "What are you saying?" I asked bluntly.

"You could make a third bedroom up here

if you only used that end as your storage,"
Dermot said. "See, that part?"

He was pointing to a place where the slope
of the roof formed a natural area, about
seven feet deep and the width of the house.
"It wouldn't be hard to partition that off,
hang some doors," my great-uncle said.

Dermot knew how to hang doors? I must
have looked astonished because he told me,
"I've been watching HGTV on Amelia's
television."

"Oh," I said, trying to think of a more
intelligent remark. I still felt at sea. "Well,
we could do that. But I don't think I need
another room. I mean, who's going to want
to live here?"

"Aren't more bedrooms always a good
thing? On the television, the hosts say they
are. And I could move into such a room.
Claude and I could share the television
room as a sitting room. We would each have
our own room."

I felt humiliated that I hadn't ever thought
of asking if Dermot minded sharing a room
with Claude. Obviously, he did. Sleeping on
a cot in the little sitting room . . . I'd been a
bad hostess. I looked at Dermot with more
attention than I'd given him before. He had
sounded . . . hopeful. Maybe my new tenant was underemployed. I realized that I

159

didn't know exactly what Dermot did at the club. I'd taken it for granted that he'd leave with Claude when Claude went to Monroe, but I'd never been curious enough to ask what Dermot did when he got there. What if being part fairy was the only thing he had in common with the self-centered Claude?

"If you think you have the time to do the work, I'd be glad to buy the materials," I said, not quite sure where the words came from. "In fact, if you could sand, prime, and paint the whole thing, and build the partition, I'd sure appreciate it. I'd be glad to pay you for the job. Why don't we go to the lumberyard in Clarice on my next day off? If you could figure out how much lumber and paint we need?"

Dermot lit up like a Christmas tree. "I can try, and I know how to rent a sander," he said. "You trust me to do this?"

"I do," I said, not sure I really meant that. But after all, what could make the attic look worse than it did now? I began to feel enthusiastic myself. "It would be great to have this room redone. You need to tell me what you think would be a fair wage."

"Absolutely not," he said. "You have given me a home and the reassurance of your presence. This is the least I can do for you."

I couldn't argue with Dermot when he

put it that way. There's such a thing as being too determined not to accept a gift, and I assessed this as just such a situation.

This had been a morning chock-full of information and surprises. As I was washing my hands and face to get rid of the attic dust, I heard a car coming up the driveway. The Splendide logo, in Gothic lettering, filled the side of a big white van.

Brenda Hesterman and her partner climbed out. The partner was a small, compact man wearing khakis and a blue polo shirt and polished loafers. His salt-and-pepper hair was clipped short.

I went out onto the front porch.

"Hello, Sookie," Brenda called, as if we were old friends. "This is Donald Callaway, the co-owner of the shop."

"Mr. Callaway," I said, nodding. "You two come on in. Can I get you all a drink?"

They both declined on their way up the steps. Once inside, they looked around the crowded room with an appreciation my fairy guests hadn't shown.

"Love the wooden ceiling," Brenda said. "And look at the plank walls!"

"It's an old one," Donald Callaway said. "Congratulations, Miss Stackhouse, on living in such a lovely historic home."

I tried not to look as astonished as I felt.

161

This was not the reaction I normally got. Most people tended to pity me for living in such an outdated structure. The floors weren't really true and the windows weren't standard. "Thanks," I said doubtfully. "Well, here's the stuff that was in the attic. You all see if there's anything you want. Just give me a yell if you need something."

There didn't seem to be any point in hanging around, and it seemed kind of tacky to watch them at work. I went into my room to dust and straighten, and I cleaned out a drawer or two while I was at it. Normally I would have listened to the radio, but I wanted to keep an ear out for the partners in case they needed to ask questions. They talked to each other quietly from time to time, and I found myself curious about what they were deciding. When I heard Claude coming down the stairs, I thought it was a good idea to go out to tell him and Dermot good-bye as they left.

Brenda gaped at the two beautiful men as the fairies passed through the living room. I made them slow down long enough to be introduced because that was only polite. I wasn't a bit surprised to notice that Donald was thinking of me in a different light after he'd met my "cousins."

I was scrubbing on the hall bathroom floor

when I heard Donald exclaim. I drifted into the living room, trying to look casually inquisitive.

He'd been examining my grandfather's desk, a very heavy and ugly object that had been the cause of much cursing and sweating on the part of the fairies when they carried it down to the living room.

The small man was crouched before it now, his head in the kneehole.

"You've got a secret compartment, Miss Stackhouse," he said, and he inched backward on his haunches. "Come, let me show you."

I squatted down beside him, feeling the excitement such a discovery naturally aroused. Secret compartment! Pirate treasure! Magic trick! They all trigger the happy anticipation of childhood.

With the help of Donald's flashlight I saw that at the back of the desk, in the area where your knees would fit, there was an extra panel. There were tiny hinges so high up a knee would never brush them; so the door would swing upward when it was open.

How to open it was the mystery.

After I'd had a good look, Donald said, "I'll try my pocketknife, Miss Stackhouse, if you have no objection."

"None at all," I said.

He retrieved the pocketknife, which was a businesslike size, from his pocket and opened the blade, sliding it gently into the seam. As I'd expected, in the middle of the seam he encountered a clasp of some kind. He pushed gently with the knife blade, first from one side and then another, but nothing happened.

Next, he began patting the woodwork all around the kneehole. There was a strip of wood at both points where the sides and top of the kneehole met. Donald pressed and pushed, and just when I was about to throw up my hands, there was a rusty click and the panel opened.

"Why don't you do the honors," Donald said. "Your desk."

That was both reasonable and true, and as he backed out, I took his place. I lifted the door and held it up while Donald held his flashlight steady, but since my body blocked a lot of the light, I had quite a time extracting the contents.

I gently gripped and pulled when I felt the contours of the bundle, and then I had it. I wriggled backward on my haunches, trying not to imagine what that must look like from Donald's viewpoint. As soon as I was clear of the desk, I rose and went over to the window with my dusty bundle. I examined what I held.

There was a small velvet bag with a drawstring top. The material had been wine red, I believed, once upon a time. There was a once-white envelope, about 6 × 8, with pictures on it, and as I carefully flattened it, I realized it had held a dress pattern. Immediately a flood of memory came undammed. I remembered the box that had held all the patterns, Vogue and Simplicity and Butterick. My grandmother had enjoyed sewing for many years until a broken finger in her right hand hadn't "set" well, and then it had become more and more painful for her to manage the tissue-thin patterns and the materials. From the picture, this particular envelope had held a pattern that was full-skirted and nipped in at the waist, and the three drawn models had fashionably hunched shoulders, thin faces, and short hair. One model was wearing the dress as midlength, one was wearing it as a wedding dress, and one was wearing it as a square-dance costume. The versatile full-skirted dress!

I opened the flap and peered in, expecting to see the familiar brown flimsy pattern paper printed with mysterious black directions. But instead, there was a letter inside, written on yellowed paper. I recognized the handwriting.

Suddenly I was as close to tears as I could be. I held my eyes wide so the liquid wouldn't trickle, and I left the living room very quickly. It wasn't possible to open that envelope with other people in the house, so I stowed it in my bedside table along with the little bag, and I returned to the living room after I'd blotted my eyes.

The two antiques dealers were too courteous to ask questions, and I brewed some coffee and brought it to them on a tray with some milk and sugar and some slices of pound cake, because I was grateful. And polite. As my grandmother had taught me . . . my dead grandmother, whose handwriting had been on the letter inside the pattern envelope.

CHAPTER 5

In the end, I didn't get to open the envelope until the next day.

Brenda and Donald finished going over all the attic contents an hour after he'd opened the hidden drawer. Then we sat down to discuss what they wanted from my miscellaneous clutter and how much they'd pay me for it. At first, I was minded to simply say, "Okay," but in the name of my family I felt obliged to try to get as much money as possible. To my impatience, the discussion went on for what seemed like forever.

What it boiled down to: They wanted four large pieces of furniture (including the desk), a couple of dress forms, a small chest, some spoons, and two horn snuffboxes. Some of the underwear was in good shape, and Brenda said she knew a method of washing that would remove stains and make the garments look almost new, though she wouldn't give me much for them. A nursing chair (too low and small for modern women) was added to the list, and Donald wanted a box of costume jewelry from the thirties and forties. My great-grandmother's quilt, made in the wagon wheel pattern, was obviously worth a lot to the dealers, and that had never been my favorite pattern so I was glad to let it go.

I was actually pleased that these items would be going to homes where they'd be enjoyed and cared for and cherished instead of being stowed in an attic.

I could tell that Donald really wanted to go through the big box of pictures and papers still awaiting my attention, but there was no way that was going to happen until I'd looked at all of them. I told him so in very polite terms, and we also shook on the agreement that if any more secret compartments of any kind were found in the furniture I was selling them, I would have first right to buy the contents back if the contents had any money value.

After they'd called their store to arrange pickup and written a check, the dealers departed with one or two of their smaller purchases. They seemed as satisfied as I was with the day's work.

Within an hour, a big Splendide truck

came up the driveway with two husky young men in the cab. Forty-five minutes after that, the furniture was padded and loaded into the back. After it was gone, it was time for me to get ready for work. I regretfully postponed examining the items in my night table drawer.

Though I had to hustle, I took a moment to enjoy having my house to myself as I put on my makeup and my uniform. It was warm enough to break out my shorts, I decided.

I'd gone to Wal-Mart and bought two new pair the week before. In honor of their debut, I'd made sure my legs were shaved extra smooth. My tan was already well established. I looked in the mirror, pleased with the look.

I got to Merlotte's about five. The first person I saw was the new waitress, India. India had smooth chocolate skin and cornrows and a stud in her nose, and she was the most cheerful human being I'd encountered in a month of Sundays. Today she gave me a smile as if I were exactly the person she'd been waiting to see . . . which was literally true. I was replacing India.

"You look out for trouble with that goober on five," she said. "He's tossing 'em back. He must've had a fight with his wife."

I would know if he had or not after a moment's "listening in." "Thanks, India. Anything else?"

"That couple on eleven, they want their tea unsweet with lots of lemon on the side. Their food should be up soon, the fried pickles and a burger each. Cheese on his."

"Okeydokey. Have a good evening."

"I'm planning on it. I got a date."

"Who with?" I asked, out of sheer idle curiosity.

"Lola Rushton," she said.

"I think I went to high school with Lola," I said, with only a short beat to indicate that India's dating women was any more than a daily occurrence.

"She remembers you," India said, and laughed.

I was sure that was so, since I'd been the weirdest person in my little high school class. "Everyone remembers me as Crazy Sookie," I said, trying to keep the rue from my voice.

"She had a crush on you for a while," India told me.

I felt oddly pleased. "I'm flattered to hear it," I said, and hustled off to start working.

I made a quick round of my tables to be sure everyone was okay, served the fried pickles and burgers, and watched in relief as Mr. Grumpy and Dumped downed his last drink and left the bar. He wasn't drunk, but he was spoiling for a fight, and it was good to see the last of him. We didn't need more trouble.

He wasn't the only grumpy guy in Merlotte's. Sam was filling out insurance forms that night, and because he hates filling out forms but has to do it all the time, his mood was not sunny. The paperwork was stacked on the bar, and in a lull between customers, I looked it over. If I read it carefully and slowly, it wasn't hard to figure out, no matter how convoluted the English got. I began checking boxes and filling in blanks, and I called the police station and told them we needed a copy of the police report on the firebombing. I gave them Sam's fax number, and Kevin promised he'd get it to me.

I looked up to find my boss standing there with an expression of total surprise on his face.

"I'm sorry!" I said instantly. "You seemed to be so stressed out about it, and I didn't mind taking a look. I'll hand 'em back over." I grabbed up the papers and thrust them at Sam.

"No," he said, backing away with his hands held up. "No, no. Sook, *thanks*. I never thought of asking for help." He

171

glanced down. "You called the police station?"

"Yeah, I got Kevin Pryor. He's gonna send over the report to attach."

"Thanks, Sook." Sam looked like Santa Claus had just appeared in the bar.

"I don't mind forms," I said, smiling. "They don't talk back. You better look it over to make sure I did it right."

Sam beamed at me without sparing a downward glance. "Good job, friend."

"No problem." It had been nice to have something to keep me busy, so I wouldn't think about the unexamined items in my night table drawer. I heard the front door open and looked around, relieved there was more business walking in the door. I had to work to hold the anticipation on my face when I saw that Jannalynn Hopper had arrived.

Sam is what you might call adventuresome in his dating, and Jannalynn was not the first strong (not to say scary) female he'd consorted with. Skinny and short, Jannalynn had an aggressive sense of fashion and a ferocious delight in her elevation to the job of pack enforcer for the Long Tooth pack, which was based in Shreveport.

Tonight Jannalynn was wearing abbreviated denim shorts, those sandals that lace up the calves, and a single blue tank top with no bra underneath. She was wearing the earrings Sam had bought her at Splendide, and about six silver chains of assorted lengths and pendants gleamed around her neck. Her short hair was platinum now, spiky and bright. She was like a suncatcher, I thought, remembering the brightly colored one Jason had given me to hang in the kitchen window.

"Hello, honey," she said to Sam as she bypassed me without a sideways glance. She took Sam in a ferocious embrace and kissed him for all she was worth.

He kissed her back, though I could tell from his brain signals that he was a little embarrassed. No such consideration bothered Jannalynn, of course. I hastily turned away to check the levels of salt and pepper in the shakers on the tables, though I knew quite well everything was fine.

In truth, I'd always found Jannalynn disturbing, almost frightening. She was very aware that Sam and I were friends, especially since I'd met Sam's family at his brother's wedding, and they were under the impression that I was Sam's girlfriend. I really didn't blame her for her suspicions; if I'd been her, I'd have felt the same way.

Jannalynn was a suspicious young woman

by both nature and profession. Part of her job was to assess threats and act on them before harm could come to Alcide and the pack. She also managed Hair of the Dog, a little bar that catered especially to the Long Tooth pack and other twoeys in the Shreveport area. It was a lot of responsibility for someone as young as Jannalynn, but she seemed born to meet the challenge.

By the time I'd exhausted all the busywork I could think of, Jannalynn and Sam were having a quiet conversation. She was perched on a barstool, her muscular legs crossed elegantly, and he was in his usual position behind the bar. Her face was intent, and so was his; whatever their topic was, it was a serious one. I kept my mind slammed shut.

The customers were doing their best not to gape at the young Were. The other waitress, Danielle, was glancing over at her from time to time while whispering with her boyfriend, who'd come in to nurse a drink all evening so he could watch Danielle as she moved from table to table.

Whatever Jannalynn's faults, you couldn't deny that she had real presence. When she was in a room, she had to be acknowledged. (I thought that was at least partially because she gave off such strong vibes that she was scary as hell.)

A couple came in and glanced around before heading to an empty table in my section. They looked a little familiar. After a moment, I recognized them: Jack and Lily Leeds, private detectives from somewhere in Arkansas. The last time I'd seen them, they'd come to Bon Temps to investigate Debbie Pelt's disappearance, having been hired by her parents. I'd answered their questions in what I now knew was sort of fairy-style — I'd stuck to the letter of the truth without its spirit. I myself had shot Debbie Pelt dead in self-defense, and I hadn't wanted to go to jail for it.

That had been over a year ago. Lily Bard Leeds was still pale, silent, and intense, and her husband was still attractive and vital. Her eyes had found me instantly, and it was impossible to pretend I hadn't noticed. Reluctantly, I went over to their table, feeling my smile growing more brittle with every step.

"Welcome back to Merlotte's," I said, grinning for all I was worth. "What can I get you two this evening? We put French-fried pickles on the menu, and our burgers Lafayette are real good."

Lily looked as if I'd suggested she eat breaded worms, though Jack looked a bit

175

regretful. He wouldn't have minded the pickles, I could tell.

"A hamburger Lafayette for me, I guess," Lily said unenthusiastically. As she turned to her companion, her T-shirt shifted and I caught a glimpse of a set of old scars that rivaled my own new ones.

Well, we had always had things in common.

"The hamburger for me, too," Jack said. "And if you have a moment to spare, we'd like to talk to you." He smiled at me, and the long, thin scar on his face flexed as his eyebrows rose. Was this personal-mutilation evening? I wondered if his light jacket, unnecessary on so warm a day, covered something even worse.

"We can have a talk. I figured you didn't come back to Merlotte's because of the great cuisine," I said, and took their drink order before I went over to the window to hand the slip to Antoine.

With their iced teas and a dish of lemon, I returned to the table. I looked around to make sure no one needed me before I sat down opposite Jack with Lily to my left. She was pretty to look at, but so controlled and muscular I felt like I could bounce a dime off her. Even her mind was sort of tidy and strict.

"What shall we talk about?" I asked, and opened up my mind to them. Jack was thinking about Lily, some concern about her health, no, her mother's health — a recurrence of breast cancer. Lily was thinking about me, puzzling over me, suspecting I was a killer.

That hurt.

But it was true.

"Sandra Pelt is out of jail," Jack Leeds said, and though I heard the words in his brain before he spoke them, I didn't have to fake a shocked face.

"She was in jail? So that's why I haven't seen her since her folks died." The older Pelts had promised to keep Sandra in check. After I'd heard about their deaths, I'd wondered when she'd show up. When I hadn't seen her right away, I'd relaxed. "You're telling me this because?" I managed to say.

"Because she hates your guts," Lily said calmly. "And you were never found guilty by any court of the disappearance of her sister. You weren't even arrested. I don't think you ever will be. You might even be innocent, though I don't think so. Sandra Pelt is simply crazy. And she's obsessed with you. I think you need to be careful. Real careful."

"Why was she in jail?"

"Assault and battery on one of her cousins. This cousin had gotten a cut of the money in Sandra's parents' will, and apparently Sandra took issue with that."

I was very, very worried. Sandra Pelt was a vicious and amoral young woman. I was sure she hadn't hit twenty yet, and she'd made a determined attempt to kill me more than once. There was no one now to call her to heel, and her mental status was therefore even more suspect, according to the private detectives.

"But why did you make a trip down here to tell me?" I said. "I mean, I do appreciate it, but you weren't obliged . . . and you could have picked up the phone. Private eyes work for money, last I heard. Is someone paying you to warn me?"

"The Pelt estate," Lily said, after a pause. "Their lawyer, who lives in New Orleans, is the court-appointed guardian for Sandra until she reaches twenty-one."

"His name?"

She pulled a piece of paper out of her pocket. "It's a sort of Baltic name," she said. "And I may not pronounce it correctly."

"Cataliades," I said, putting the emphasis on the second syllable where it belonged.

"Yes," said Jack, surprised. "That's him.

Big guy."

I nodded. Mr. Cataliades and I were friendly. He was mostly a demon, but the Leedses didn't seem to know that. In fact, they didn't seem to know much of anything about the other world, the one that lay beneath the human one. "So Mr. Cataliades sent you two down here to warn me? He's the executor?"

"Yeah. He was going to be away from his desk for some time, and he wanted to be sure you knew the girl was on the loose. He seemed to feel some obligation to you."

I pondered that. I only knew of one time I'd done the lawyer a good turn. I had helped him get out of the collapsing hotel in Rhodes. Nice to know that at least one person was serious when he said, "I owe you." It seemed pretty ironic that the Pelt estate was paying the Leedses to come warn me against the last living Pelt; not ironic as in "ha!" but ironic as in bitter.

"If you don't mind me asking, how come he contacted you two? I mean, I'm sure there are lots of private eyes in New Orleans, for example. You all are still based in the Little Rock area, right?"

Lily shrugged. "He called us; he asked if we were free; he sent the check. His instructions were very specific. Both of us, to the bar, today. In fact . . ." She glanced down at her watch. "To the minute."

They looked at me expectantly, waiting for me to explain this oddity on the part of the lawyer.

I was thinking furiously. If Mr. Cataliades had sent two tough people to the bar, instructing them to arrive at a given time, it must be because he knew they were going to be needed. For some reason, their presence was necessary and desirable. When would you need capable hardbodies?

When trouble was on its way.

Before I knew I was going to do it, I stood and turned toward the entrance. Naturally, the Leedses looked where I was looking, so we were all watching the door when trouble opened it.

Four tough guys came in. My grandmother would have said they were loaded for bear. They might as well have stenciled "Badass and Proud of It" on their foreheads. They were definitely high on something, full of themselves, brimming with aggression. And armed.

After a second's peek in their heads, I knew they'd taken vampire blood. That was the most unpredictable drug on the market — also the most expensive, because harvesting it was so dangerous. People who drank vampire blood were — for a length of time impossible to predict — incredibly strong and incredibly reckless . . . and sometimes batshit crazy.

Though her back was to the newcomers, Jannalynn seemed to smell them. She swung around on her stool and focused, just like someone had drawn a bow and aimed the arrow. I could feel the animal wafting off her. Something wild and savage filled the air, and I realized the smell was coming from Sam, too. Jack and Lily Leeds were on their feet. Jack had his hand under his jacket, and I knew he had a gun. Lily's hands were poised in a strange way, as if she were about to gesture and had frozen in midmove.

"Hidee-ho, jerkoffs!" said the tallest one, addressing the bar in general. He had a heavy beard and thick dark hair, but underneath it I saw how young he was. I thought he couldn't be more than nineteen. "We come to have some fun with you lizards."

"No lizards here," Sam said, his voice even and calm. "You fellas are welcome to have a drink, but after that I think you better leave. This is a quiet place, a local place, and we don't need trouble."

"Trouble's already here!" boasted the shortest asshole. His face was clean-shaven,

and his hair was only blond stubble, show-
ing scars on his scalp. He was built broad
and chunky. The third kid was thin and
dark, maybe Hispanic. His black hair was
slicked back, and his lips had a sensuous
pout to them that he tried to counteract by
sneering. The fourth guy had gotten off on
the vampire blood even more seriously than
the rest, and he couldn't speak because he
was lost in his own world. His eyes jerked
from side to side as if he were tracking
things the rest of us couldn't see. He was
big, too. I thought the first attack would
come from him, and though I was the least
of the combatants, I began to ease to my
right, planning to come at him from the
side.

"We can have peace here," Sam said. He
was still trying, though I knew he understood that there was no way we were going
to escape violence. He was buying time for
everyone in Merlotte's to understand what
was up.

That was a good idea. By the time a few
more seconds had passed, even the slowest
of the few patrons had moved as far from
the action as they could get, except for
Danny Prideaux, who'd been playing darts
with Andy Bellefleur, and Andy himself.
Danny was actually holding a dart. Andy

was off duty, but he was armed. I watched Jack Leeds's eyes and saw he'd realized, as I had, where the worst trouble would come from. The dazed hoodlum was actually rocking back and forth on his heels.

Since Jack Leeds had a gun and I did not, I carefully inched backward so I wouldn't interfere with his shot. Lily's cold eyes followed my small movement, and she nodded almost undetectably. I'd done a sensible thing.

"We don't want peace," snarled Bearded Leader. "We want the blonde." And he pointed in my direction with his left hand, while his right hand pulled a knife. It looked like it was two feet long, though maybe my fear was acting like a magnifying glass.

"We gonna take care of her," Blond Bristles said.

"And then maybe the resta you," Pouty Lips added.

Crazy Guy just smiled.

"I don't think so," Jack Leeds said. Jack pulled his gun in one smooth movement. Possibly he would have done it anyway out of sheer self-defense, but it didn't hurt that his wife, standing right by me, was a blonde. He couldn't be completely sure they meant me, the other white meat.

"I don't think so, either," said Andy Bellefleur. His arm was rock steady as he aimed his own Sig Sauer at the man with the knife. "You drop that pigsticker, and we'll work something out."

They might be high as kites, but at least three of the thugs retained enough sense to realize that facing guns was a bad idea. There was a lot of uncertain twitching and eye shifting as they flickered gazes at each other. The moment hung in the balance.

Unfortunately, Crazy Guy went over the edge and charged for Sam, so now we were all committed to stupidity. With Were swiftness, Pouty Lips whipped out his own gun, aimed, and fired. I'm not sure who he intended to hit, but he winged Jack Leeds, whose return shot went wild as he fell.

Watching Lily Leeds was a lesson in motion. She took two quick steps, pivoted on her left foot, and her right foot floated through the air to kick Pouty Lips in the head with the force of a mule. Almost before he hit the floor she was on him, pitching his gun toward the bar and breaking his arm in a flow of motion that was nearly hypnotic. As he screamed, Bearded Asshole and Blond Bristles gaped at her.

That second of inattention was all it took. Jannalynn took a flying leap off her barstool, describing an amazing arc through the air.

She landed on Crazy Guy as Sam tackled him, and though CG howled and snapped and tried to throw her off, Jannalynn reared back to punch him in the jaw. I distinctly heard the bone break, and then Jannalynn leaped to her feet and stomped on his femur. Another snap. Sam, still holding him down, yelled, "Stop!"

In those seconds, Andy Bellefleur rushed Bearded Asshole, who'd whirled to present his back to Andy when Lily attacked Pouty Lips. When the tall guy felt the gun in his back, he froze.

"Drop the knife," Andy said. He was in deadly earnest.

Blond Bristles cocked his arm back to strike a blow. Danny Prideaux threw his dart. It got Blond Bristles square in the meat of his arm, and he shrieked like a teakettle. Sam abandoned Crazy Guy to punch Blond Bristles right in his brisket. The guy went down like a sawn tree.

Bearded Asshole looked at his buddies, down and disabled, and then he dropped the knife. Sensible.

Finally.

In less than two minutes, it was all over.

I'd whipped my clean white apron off, and I bound Jack Leeds's wound while Lily held his arm out for me, her face white as a vampire's. She wanted to kill Pouty Lips in the worst possible way, because she loved her husband with an overwhelming passion. The strength of her feelings almost swamped me. Lily might be icy on the outside, but inside she was Vesuvius.

As soon as Jack's bleeding slowed, she turned to Pouty Lips, her face still absolutely calm. "You even move, I'll break your fucking neck," she said, her voice uninflected. The young thug probably didn't even hear her through his own groaning and moaning, but her tone came through and he tried to inch away from her.

Andy had already talked to the 911 dispatcher. In a moment I heard the siren, a disturbingly familiar sound. We might as well retain an ambulance to stay in the parking lot at this rate.

Crazy Guy was screaming weakly at the pain in his leg and jaw. Sam had saved his life: Jannalynn was actually panting, she was so close to changing after the excitement and stimulation of the violence. The bones had slid around underneath the skin of her face, which was looking long and lumpy.

It wouldn't be good if she became a wolf before law enforcement got here. I didn't try to spell out why to myself. I said, "Hey, Jannalynn." Her eyes met mine. Hers were changing shape and color. Her little figure began to twist and turn restlessly.

"You have to stop," I said. All around us there was yelling, and excitement, and the thick atmosphere of fear — not a good atmosphere for a young werewolf. "You can't change now." I kept my eyes fixed on hers. I didn't speak again but made sure she kept looking at me. "Breathe with me," I said, and she made the effort. Gradually her own breathing slowed, and even more gradually her face resumed its normal contours. Her body ceased its restless movement, and her eyes returned to their regular brown.

"All right," she said.

Sam put his hands on her thin shoulders. He gave her a tight hug. "Thanks, honey," he said. "Thanks. You're the greatest." I felt the faintest thrum of exasperation.

"Left your ass in the dust," she said, and laughed raggedly. "Was that a good jump, or what? Wait'll I tell Alcide."

"You're the quickest," Sam said, his voice gentle. "You're the best pack enforcer I ever met." You would have thought he'd told her she was as sexy as Heidi Klum, she was so proud.

And then the law enforcement people and the emergency people were there, and we had to go through the whole procedure again.

Lily and Jack Leeds took off to the hospital. She told the ambulance personnel she could take him herself in their car, and I understood from her thoughts that their insurance wouldn't cover the whole cost of the ambulance ride. Considering the emergency room was only a few blocks away and Jack was walking and talking, I could see her reasoning. They never did get their food, and I didn't get to thank them for the warning and for their promptness in obeying Mr. Cataliades's orders. I wondered more than ever how he'd managed to shunt them into the bar in such a timely manner.

Andy was pardonably proud of his part in the incident, and he got some pats on the back from his fellow officers. They all regarded Jannalynn with barely concealed mistrust and respect. All the bar patrons who'd tried to stay out of the way were falling all over themselves to describe Lily Leeds's great kick and Jannalynn's show-stopping leap onto Crazy Guy.

Somehow, the picture the police got was that these four strangers had announced their intention to take Lily hostage and then to rob Merlotte's. I'm not sure how that impression gathered credibility, but I was glad it did. If the bar patrons assumed that the blonde in question had been Lily Leeds, that was fine with me. She was certainly an outstanding-looking woman, and the strangers might have been following her, or they might have decided to rob the bar and take Lily as a bonus.

Due to this welcome misconception, I escaped from any more questioning than the other patrons got.

In the grand scheme of things, I thought it was about time I got a break.

CHAPTER 6

Sunday morning I woke up worried.

I'd been too sleepy the night before, when I finally got home, to think much about what had happened at the bar. But evidently my subconscious had been chewing it over while I slept. My eyes flew open, and though the room was quiet and sunny, I gasped.

I had that panicky feeling; it hadn't taken me over yet, but it was just around the corner, physically and mentally. You know the feeling? When you think any second your heart's going to start pounding, that your breathing is picking up, that your palms will start sweating.

Sandra Pelt was after me, and I didn't know where she was or what she was plotting.

Victor had it in for Eric and, by extension, me.

I was sure I was the blonde the four thugs had been after, and I didn't know who'd

190

sent them or what they would have done when they got me, though I had a pretty bad feeling about that.

Eric and Pam were on the outs, and I was sure that somehow I was involved in their dispute.

And I had a list of questions. At the top of the list: How had Mr. Cataliades known that I would need help at that particular time in that particular place? And how had he known to send the private investigators from Little Rock? Of course, if he had been the Pelts' lawyer, he might have known that they'd sent Lily and Jack Leeds to investigate their daughter Debbie's disappearance. He wouldn't have had to brief the Leeds as much, and he would have known they could handle themselves in a fight.

Would the four thugs tell the police why they'd come to the bar, and who'd put them up to it? And where they'd gotten the vampire blood — that would be helpful knowledge, also.

What would the things I'd gotten from the secret drawer tell me about my past?

"This is a fine kettle of fish," I said out loud. I pulled the sheet over my head and searched the house mentally. No one was here but me. Maybe Dermot and Claude were all talked out, after their big reveal.

They seemed to have stayed in Monroe. Sighing, I sat up in bed, letting the sheet fall away. There was no hiding from my problems. The best I could do was to try to prioritize my crises and figure out what information I could gather about each one.

The most important problem was the one closest to my heart. And its solution was right to hand.

I gently extracted the pattern envelope and the worn velvet bag from the drawer of the bedside table. In addition to the practical contents (a flashlight, a candle, and matches), the drawer held the strange mementoes of my strange life. But I wasn't interested in anything today but the two new precious items. I carried them into the kitchen and laid them carefully back on the counter well away from the sink as I made my coffee.

While the coffeepot dripped, I almost pushed back the flap of the pattern envelope. But I pulled back my hand. I was scared. Instead I tracked down my address book. I'd charged my cell phone overnight, so I stowed the little cord away neatly — any delay would do — and at last, taking a deep breath, I punched in Mr. Cataliades's number. It rang three times.

"This is Desmond Cataliades," his rich

voice said. "I'm traveling and unavailable at the moment, but if you'd like to leave a message, I may call you back. Or not."

Well, hell. I made a face at the telephone, but at the sound of the tone I dutifully recorded a guarded message that I hoped would convey my urgent need to talk to the lawyer. I crossed Mr. Cataliades — Desmond! — off my mental list and moved on to my second method of approach to the problem of Sandra Pelt.

Sandra was going to keep after me until either I was dead or she was. I had a real, true, personal enemy. It was hard to believe that every member of a family had turned out so rotten (especially since both Debbie and Sandra were adopted), but all the Pelts were selfish, strong willed, and hateful. The girls were fruits of the poisonous tree, I guess. I needed to know where Sandra was, and I knew someone who might be able to help me.

"Hello?" Amelia said briskly.

"How's life in the Big Easy?" I asked.

"Sookie! Gosh, it's good to hear your voice! Things are going great for me, actually."

"Do tell?"

"Bob showed up on my doorstep last week," she said.

After Amelia's mentor, Octavia, had turned Bob back into his skinny Mormonish self, Bob had been so angry with Amelia that he'd taken off like — well, like a scalded cat. As soon as he'd reoriented to being human, Bob had left Bon Temps to track down his family, who'd been in New Orleans during Katrina. Evidently Bob had calmed down about the whole transformation-into-a-cat issue.

"Did he find his folks?"

"Well, he did! His aunt and his uncle, the ones who raised him. They had gotten an apartment in Natchez just big enough for the two of them, and he could tell they didn't have any way to add him to the household, so he traveled around a bit checking on other coven members, and then he wandered back down here. He's got a job cutting hair in a shop three blocks away from where I work! He came in the magic shop, asked after me." Members of Amelia's coven ran the Genuine Magic Shop in the French Quarter. "I was surprised to see him. But real happy." She was practically purring on the last sentence, and I figured Bob had entered the room. "He says hey, Sookie."

"Hey back at him. Listen, Amelia, I hate to interfere in love's young dream, but I got a favor to ask."

"Shoot."

"I need to find out where someone is."

"Telephone book?"

"Ha-ha. Not that simple. Sandra Pelt is out of jail and gunning for me, literally. The bar's been firebombed, and yesterday four drugged-up goons came in to get me, and I think Sandra might be behind both things. I mean, how many enemies can I have?"

I heard Amelia take a long breath. "Don't answer that," I said hastily. "So, she's failed twice, and I'm afraid that soon she'll pick up the pace and send someone here to the house. I'll be alone, and it won't end good for me."

"Why didn't she start there?"

"I finally figured out I should have asked myself that a few days ago. Do you think your wards are still active?"

"Oh . . . sure. They very well could be." Amelia sounded just a shade pleased. She was very proud of her witchy abilities, as well she ought to be.

"Really? I mean, think about it. You haven't been here in . . . gosh, almost three months." Amelia had packed up her car the first week in March.

"True. But I reinforced them before I left."

"They work even when you aren't

around." I wanted to be sure. My life depended on it.

"They will for a while. After all, I was out of the house for hours each day and left it guarded. But I do have to renew them, or they'll fade. You know, I got three days in a row I don't have to work. I think I'll come up there and check out the situation."

"That would be a huge relief, though I hate to put you out."

"Nah, no problem. Maybe me and Bob'll have a road trip. I'll ask a couple of other coven members how they find people. We can take care of the wards and give finding the bitch a shot."

"You think Bob'll be willing to come back here?" Bob had spent almost his whole sojourn in my house in feline form, so I was doubtful.

"I can only ask him. Unless you hear from me, I'm coming."

"Thanks so much." I hadn't realized my muscles were so tense until they began to relax. Amelia said she was coming.

I wondered why I didn't feel safer with my two fairy guys around. They were my kin, and though I felt happy and relaxed when they were in the house, I trusted Amelia more.

On the practical side, I never knew when

Claude and Dermot would actually be under my roof. They were spending more and more nights in Monroe.

I'd have to put Amelia and Bob in the bedroom across the hall from mine, since the guys were occupying the upstairs. The bed in my old room was narrow, but neither Bob nor Amelia were large people.

This was all just make-work for my head. I poured a mug of coffee and picked up the envelope and the bag. I sat down at the kitchen table with the objects in front of me. I had a terrible impulse to open the garbage can and drop them both in it unopened, the knowledge in them unlearned.

But that was not something you did. You opened things that were meant to be opened.

I opened the flap and tipped the envelope. The flouncy-skirted bride in the picture stared at me blandly as a yellowed letter slid out. It felt dusty somehow, as though its years in the attic had soaked into the microscopic crevices in the paper. I sighed and closed my eyes, bracing myself. Then I unfolded the paper and looked down at my grandmother's handwriting.

It was unexpectedly painful to see it: spiky and compressed, poorly spelled and punctuated, but it was hers, my gran's. I had read God knows how many things she'd written in our life together: grocery lists, instructions, recipes, even a few personal notes. There was a bundle of them in my dressing table still.

Sookie, I'm so proud of you graduating from high school. I wish your mom and dad had been here to see you in your cap and gown.
Sookie, please pick up your room, I can't vacuum if I can't see the floor.
Sookie, Jason will pick you up after softball practice, I have to go to a meeting of the Garden Club.

I was sure this letter would be different. I was right. She began formally.

Dear Sookie,
I think you'll find this, if anyone does. There's nowhere else I can leave it, and when I think you're ready I'll tell you where I put it.

Tears welled up in my eyes. She'd been murdered before she thought I was ready. Maybe I never would have been ready.

You know I loved your grandfather more

than anything.

I'd *thought* I'd known that. They'd had a rock-solid marriage . . . I'd assumed. The evidence suggested that might not have been the case.

But I did want chilren so bad, so bad. I felt if I had chilren my life would be perfect. I didn't realize asking God for a perfect life was a stupid thing to do. I got tempted beyond my ability to resist. God was punishing me for my greed, I guess.

He was so beautiful. But I knew when I saw him that he wasn't a real person. He told me later he was part human, but I never saw much humanity in him. Your grandfather had left for Baton Rouge, a long trip then. Later that morning we'd had a storm that knocked down a big pine by the driveway so it was blocked. I was trying to saw up the pine so your grandfather would be able to bring the truck back up the driveway. I took a break to go to the back yard to see if the clothes on the line were dry, and he walked out of the woods. When he helped me move the tree — well, he moved it all by himself — I said Thank

You, of course. I don't know if you know this, but if you say Thank You to one of them you're obligated. I don't know why, that's just good manners.

Claudine had mentioned that in passing when I'd first met her, but I believed she'd told me it was simply a fairy etiquette thing. Mindful of my manners, I'd tried to be sure to never explicitly thank Niall, even when we'd swapped gifts at Christmas. (It had taken every bit of self-control I'd had not to say "Thank you." I'd said, "Oh, you thought of me! I know I'll enjoy it," and clamped my lips together.) But Claude . . . I'd been around him so often, I *knew* I'd thanked him for taking out the garbage or passing me the salt. Crap!

Anyway, I asked him if he wanted a drink and he was thirsty, and I was so lonely and I wanted a baby. Your grandpa and me had been married five years by then and not a sign of a baby on the way. I figured something was wrong, though we didn't find out what until later when a doctor said the mumps had . . . well. Poor Mitchell. Was not his fault, it was the sickness. I just told him it was a miracle we'd had the two, we didn't need the five or six he'd hoped for. He never even looked at me funny about that. He was so sure I'd never been with someone else. It was coals of fire on my head. Bad enough I did it once, but two years later Fintan came back and I did it again, and those weren't the only times. It was so strange. Sometimes I would think I smelled him! I would turn around and it was Mitchell.

But having your dad and Linda was worth the guilt. I loved them so much, and I hope it wasn't my sin that made them both die so young. At least Linda had Hadley, wherever she may be, and at least Corbett had you and Jason. Watching you grow up has been a blessing and a privlege. I love you both more than I can say.

Well, I've been writing for a long time. I love you, honey. Now I have to tell you about your grandfather's friend. He was a dark-headed man, real big, talked real fancy. He said he was sort of like yall's sponsor, like a sort of godfather, but I didn't trust him any farther than I could throw him. He didn't look like a man of God. He dropped by after Corbett and Linda were born. After you two came along, I thought maybe he might come around again. Sure enough, he showed up all of a sudden, once while I was keeping Jason, and once while I was keeping you, when you were both in the cradle. He gave each of you a gift, he said, but if so it wasn't one I could put in the bank account, which would have been useful when you came to live with me.

Then he came by one more time, a few years ago. He gave me this green thing. He said fairys give it to each other when they're in love, and Fintan had given it to him to bring here to me if Fintan died before I did. It's got a magical spell in it, he said. You won't ever need to use it, I hope, he said. But if you do he said to remember that it was a one time thing, not like a lamp, like in the story, with a lot of wishes. He called this thing a cluviel dor, and showed me how to spell it.

So I guess Fintan is dead, though I was scared to ask the man any questions. I haven't seen Fintan since after your dad and Linda were born. He held them both and then he left. He said he couldn't come again ever, that it was too dangerous for me and the kids, that his enemys would follow him here if he kept visiting, even if he came in disguise. I think maybe he was saying he'd come in disguise before, and that worries me. And why would he have enemys? I guess the fairys don't always get along, just like people. To tell you the truth, I'd been feeling worse and worse about your grandpa every single time I saw Fintan, so when he said he was going for good, it was more or less a relief. I still feel plenty guilty, but when I remember raising your daddy and Linda I'm so glad I had them, and raising you and Jason has been a joy to me.

Anyway, this letter is yours now since I'm leaving you the house and the cluviel dor. It may not seem fair that Jason didn't get anything magical, but your grandfather's friend said Fintan had watched both of you, and you were the one it should go to. I guess I hope you won't ever need to know any of this. I always wondered if your problem came from you being a little bit fairy, but then, how come Jason wasn't the same? Or your dad and Linda, for that matter? Maybe you being able to "know things" just happened. I wish I could have cured it so you could have had a normal life, but we have to take what God gives us, and you've been real strong handling it.

Please be careful. I hope you're not mad at me, or think the worse of me. All God's children are sinners. At least my sinning led to life for you and Jason and Hadley.

Adele Hale Stackhouse (Grandmother)

There was so much to think about that I didn't know where to start.

I was simultaneously stunned, startled, curious, and confused. Before I could stop myself, I picked up my other relic, the worn velvet bag. I loosened the drawstring, which crumbled in my fingers. I opened the bag and let the hard thing inside — the cluviel dor, the gift from my fairy grandfather — fall into my palm.

I loved it instantly.

It was a creamy light green, trimmed in gold. It was like one of the snuffboxes at the antiques store, but nothing in Splendide had been this beautiful. I could see no catch, no hinge, nothing; it didn't pop open when I gently pressed and twisted the lid — and there was definitely a lid, trimmed in gold. Hmmm. The round box wasn't ready to yield its secret.

Okeydokey. Maybe I had to do some research. I put the object to one side and sat with my hands folded on the table, staring into space. My head was crowded with thoughts.

Gran had obviously been very emotional when she wrote the letter. If our "godfather" had given Gran more information about this gift, either she'd neglected to mention it or she simply hadn't remembered anything else. I wondered when she'd forced herself to set down this confession. Obviously, it had been written after Aunt Linda died, which had happened when Gran was in her seventies. My birth grandfather's friend — I was pretty sure I recognized the description. Surely the "godfather" was Mr. Cataliades, demon lawyer. I knew it must have cost her plenty to say — *on paper* — that she'd had sex with someone other than her husband. My grandmother had been a strong individual, and she'd also been a devout Christian. Such an admission must have haunted her.

She might have judged herself, but now that I'd gotten over the shock of seeing my grandmother as a woman, I didn't judge her. Who was I to throw stones? The preacher had told me that all sins were equal in the eyes of God, but I couldn't help but feel (for example) that a child molester was worse than a person who cheated on his income tax *or* a lonely woman who'd had unsanctioned sex because she wanted a baby. I was probably wrong, because we also weren't supposed to pick and choose which rules we obeyed, but that was the way I felt.

I shoved my confused thoughts back into a corner of my head and picked up the cluviel dor again. Touching its smoothness was pure pleasure, like the happiness I'd felt when I'd hugged my great-grandfather — but times about two hundred. The cluviel dor was about the size of two stacked Oreo cookies. I rubbed it against my cheek and felt like purring.

Did you have to have a magic word to open it?

"Abracadabra," I said. "Please and thank you."

Nope, didn't work, plus I felt like an idiot. "Open sesame," I whispered. "Presto change-o." Nope.

But thinking of magic gave me an idea. I e-mailed Amelia, and it was a difficult message to phrase. I know e-mail isn't totally secure, but I also had no reason to think anyone considered my few messages of any importance. I wrote, "I hate to ask, but besides doing that research on the blood bond for me, can you find out something about a fae thing? Initials c.d.?" That was as subtle as I could get.

Then I returned to my admiration of the cluviel dor. Did you have to be pure fairy to open it? No, that couldn't be the case. It had been a gift to my grandmother, presumably to use in case of dire need, and she had been completely human.

I wished it hadn't been far away in the attic when she'd been attacked. Whenever I remembered how she'd been discarded on the kitchen floor like offal, soaking in her own blood, I felt both sick and furious. Maybe if she'd had time to fetch the cluviel dor, she could have saved herself.

And with that thought, I'd had enough. I returned the cluviel dor to its velvet bag, and I returned Gran's letter to the pattern envelope. I'd had as much upset as I could handle for a while.

It was necessary to hide these items. Unfortunately, their previous excellent hideaway had been removed to a store in Shreveport.

Maybe I should call Sam. He could put the letter and the cluviel dor in the safe at Merlotte's. But considering the attacks on the bar, that wouldn't be the best place to stow something I valued. I could drive over to Shreveport and use my key to enter Eric's house to find someplace there. In fact, it was highly possible that Eric had a safe, too, and had never had occasion to show it to me. After I'd mulled it over, that didn't seem like a good idea, either.

I wondered if my desire to keep the items here was simply because I didn't want to be parted from the cluviel dor. I shrugged. No matter how the conviction had come into my head, I was sure the house was the safest place, at least for now. Perhaps I could put the smooth green box into the sleeping hole for vampires in my guest bedroom closet . . . but that wasn't much more than a bare box, and what if Eric needed to spend the day there?

After racking my brain, I put the pattern envelope into the box of unexamined paper items from the attic. These would be uninteresting to anyone but me. The cluviel dor was a little more difficult to stow away, at least partly because I kept having to resist an impulse to pull it out of the bag again. That struggle made me feel very — Gollumesque.

"My precioussss," I muttered. Would Dermot and Claude be able to sense the nearness of such a remarkable item? No, of course not. It had been in the attic all the time and they hadn't found it.

What if they'd come to live here in hopes of finding it? What if they knew or suspected

I had such a thing? Or (more likely) what if they were staying here because they were made happy by its proximity? Though I was sure there were holes in that idea, I couldn't shake it. It wasn't my fairy blood that drew them; it was the presence of the cluviel dor.

Now you're just being paranoid, I told myself sternly, and I risked one more glimpse of the creamy green surface. The cluviel dor, I thought, looked like a miniature powder compact. With that idea, the right hiding place came to me. I took the cluviel dor out of its velvet pouch and slid it into the makeup drawer of my dressing table. I opened my box of loose powder and sprinkled just a little over the gleam of creamy green. I added a hair from my brush. Ha! I was pleased with the result. As an afterthought, I stuffed the disintegrating velvet bag into my hose-and-belt drawer. My reason told me the ratty object was just a decaying old bag, but my emotions told me it was something important because my grandmother and my grandfather had touched it.

I had so many thoughts ricocheting in my brain that it shut down for the day. After I'd done a little bit of housework, I watched the college softball world series on ESPN. I love softball, because I played in high school. I loved seeing the strong young women from all over America; I loved watching them play a game as hard as they could, full tilt, nothing held in reserve. I realized while I was watching that I knew two other young women like that: Sandra Pelt and Jannalynn Hopper. There was a lesson there, but I wasn't sure what it was.

CHAPTER 7

I heard my two housemates come in Sunday night, not too late. Hooligans wasn't open on Sunday, and I tried not to wonder what they'd been doing all day. They were still asleep when I made my coffee on Monday morning. I moved around the house as quietly as I could, getting dressed and checking my e-mail. Amelia was on her way, she said, and she added cryptically that she had something important to tell me. I wondered if she had found out information about my "c.d." already.

Tara had sent out a group e-mail with an attached picture of her huge belly, and I reminded myself that the baby shower I was giving her was the next weekend. Yikes! After a moment of panic, I calmed myself. The invitations were sent, I'd bought her gift, and I'd planned the food. I was as ready as I could be, aside from the last-minute flurry of cleaning.

I was working the early shift today. As I put on my makeup, I took out the cluviel dor and held it to my chest. Touching it seemed important, seemed to make it more vital. My skin warmed it quickly. Whatever lay at the heart of that smooth pale greenness seemed to quicken. I felt more alive, too. I took a deep, shaky breath and returned it to the drawer, again dusting it with powder to make it look like it had been there forever. I shut the drawer with something like regret.

My grandmother felt very close to me that day. I thought about her on the drive to work, during my prep work, and in odd moments as I fetched and carried. Andy Bellefleur was eating lunch with Sheriff Dearborn. I was a little surprised Andy wanted to sit down in Merlotte's again after the invasion of two days before.

But my new favorite detective seemed happy enough to be there, joking with his boss and eating a salad with low-fat dressing. Andy was looking slimmer and younger these days. Married life and impending fatherhood agreed with him. I asked him how Halleigh was doing.

"She says her stomach's huge, but it's not," he said with a smile. "I think she's glad school's out. She's making curtains for the baby's room." Halleigh taught at the elementary school.

"Miss Caroline would be so proud," I said. Andy's grandmother, Caroline Bellefleur, had died just weeks before.

"I'm glad she knew before she passed," he said. "Hey, did you know my sister's pregnant, too?"

I tried not to look too astonished. Andy and Portia had had a double wedding in their grandmother's garden, and though it hadn't been a surprise to hear that Andy's wife was pregnant, somehow the older Portia had never struck me as someone who'd welcome motherhood. I told Andy how glad I was, and that was the truth.

"Would you tell Bill?" Andy asked, a little shyly. "I still feel a little weird about calling him."

My neighbor and former flame, Bill Compton, who happened to be a vampire, had finally told the Bellefleurs that he was their ancestor right before Miss Caroline died. Miss Caroline had reacted beautifully to the startling news, but it had been a little harder for Andy, who was both proud and not too fond of the undead. Portia had actually gone out with Bill a few times before he'd figured out the relationship — awkward, huh? She and her husband had sucked

213

up their reservations about their newly acquired living ancestor, and they'd surprised me with their dignity in acknowledging Bill.

"I'm always glad to pass along good news, but he'd be glad to hear from you."

"I, ah, I hear he's got a vampire girlfriend?"

I made myself look cheerful. "Yeah, she's been there for a few weeks," I said. "I haven't talked to him much about it." Like, not ever.

"You've met her."

"Yeah, she seems nice." In fact, I'd been responsible for their reunion, but that wasn't something I wanted to share. "If I see him, I'll tell him for you, Andy. I know he'll want to know when the baby's born. Do you know what you and Halleigh are having?"

"It's a girl," he said, and his smile almost split his face in two. "We're gonna name her Caroline Compton Bellefleur."

"Oh, Andy! That's so nice!" I was ridiculously pleased, because I knew Bill would be.

Andy looked embarrassed. I could tell he was relieved when his cell phone chirped.

"Hey, honey," he said, having glanced at the caller number before he flipped his phone open. "What's up?" He smiled as he listened. "Okay, I'll bring you a milkshake," he said. "See you in a few."

Bud was coming back to the table, and Andy glanced at the check and slapped a ten down. "There's my part," he said. "Keep the change. Bud, I got to go run by the house. Halleigh needs me to put up the curtain rod in the baby's room, and she's dying for a butterscotch milkshake. I won't be but ten minutes." He grinned at us and was out the door.

Bud resumed his seat while he slowly got his own money out of his worn old wallet.

"Halleigh's having one, Portia's having one, Tara's having two, I hear. Sookie, you need to get you one of those little 'uns," he said, and took a drink. "Good iced tea." He set his empty glass down with a little thump.

"I don't need to have a baby just because other women are doing it," I said. "I'll have one when I'm ready."

"Well, you ain't having one at all if you keep dating that deader," Bud said bluntly. "What do you think your gran would say?"

I took the money, turned on my heel, and walked away. I asked Danielle if she'd take Bud his change. I didn't want to talk to Bud anymore.

Stupid, I know. I had to be thicker-skinned

than that. And Bud had only spoken the truth. Of course, he had the perspective that all young women wanted to have children, and he was pointing out to me that I was on the wrong track. As if I didn't know that! What *would* Gran have said?

I would have answered without a pause a few days ago. Now, I wasn't so sure. There'd been so much I hadn't known about her. But my best guess was that she would have told me to go with my heart. And I loved Eric. As I picked up a burger basket and took it to Maxine Fortenberry's table (she was having lunch with Elmer Claire Vaudry), I found myself anticipating the moment of dark when he would wake. I looked forward to seeing him with a kind of desperation. I needed the reassurance of his presence, the assurance that he loved me, too, the passionate connection we felt when we touched each other.

As I waited for an order at the hatch, I watched Sam pull a draft. I wondered if he felt the same way about Jannalynn as I felt about Eric. He'd dated her longer than he'd dated anyone since I'd known him. Maybe I figured he was more serious because he was arranging for nights off so he could see her more often, something he'd never done before. Sam smiled at me when his eyes caught mine. It was sure nice to see him happy.

Though Jannalynn was *not* good enough for him.

I almost clapped a hand over my mouth. I felt as guilty as though I'd said that out loud. Their relationship wasn't any of my business, I told myself sternly. But a softer voice inside me said that Sam was my friend and that Jannalynn was too ruthless and violent to make him happy in the long run.

Jannalynn had killed people, but I had, too. Maybe I judged her as violent because she sometimes seemed to enjoy the killing. The idea that I might be like Jannalynn at heart — how many people did I want dead? — was another downer. Surely the day had to get better?

Pretty much always a fatal thought.

Sandra Pelt strode into the bar. It had been a long time since I'd seen her — and she'd been trying to kill me then, too. She'd been a teenager then, and she still had yet to turn twenty, I figured; but she looked a little older, her body more mature, and she had a cute shag hairdo that contrasted oddly with the snarl on her face. She brought with her an aura of rage. Though her slim body was appropriately dressed in jeans and a tank top, a loose shirt open and flapping, you could see the crazy in her face. She enjoyed dealing out the damage. You couldn't see into her head and miss that. Her movements were jerky with tension, and her eyes roved from one person to another until they found mine. They lit up like Fourth of July fireworks. I could see right inside her brain, and I saw she had a gun tucked in the back of her jeans.

"Uh-oh," I said, very quietly.

"What more do I have to do?" Sandra screamed.

Conversations all over the bar dwindled to silence. From the corner of my eye, I saw Sam reach down under the bar. He wouldn't make it in time.

"I try to burn you up, and the fire goes out." She was still at full volume. "I give those jerks free drugs and sex, and send them to grab you, and they bungle it. I try your house, and the magic won't let me enter. I've tried to kill you over and over, and you *just won't die!*"

I almost felt like apologizing.

At the same time, it was a good thing that Bud Dearborn had heard all this. But he was standing facing Sandra, his table between them, and I knew it would be much better if he were behind her. Sam began to move to his left, but the pass-through was to his right, and I didn't see how he could get across the bar and behind her before she worked herself up to killing me. But that wasn't Sam's plan. While Sandra was focused on me, he passed the wooden bat to Terry Bellefleur, who'd been playing darts with another vet. Terry was a little crazy at times and awfully scarred, but I'd always liked him and gotten along with him well. Terry put his hand on the bat, and I was glad the jukebox was playing because it covered the little sounds.

In fact, the jukebox was playing the old Whitney Houston ballad "I Will Always Love You," which was kind of funny, actually.

"Why are you always sending other people to do your jobs?" I asked, to cover the sound of Terry's quiet advance. "You some kind of *coward?* You think a woman can't do the job right?"

Maybe taunting Sandra hadn't been such a good idea, because her hand darted to her back with shifter speed, and then the gun was out and pointing at me, and then I saw her finger begin to tighten in a moment that seemed to stretch forever. And then I saw the bat swing and connect, and Sandra went down like someone had cut her strings, and there was blood everywhere.

And Terry went crazy. He crouched, screaming, and dropped the bat as if it had burned him. No matter what anyone said (the most popular thing was "SHUT UP, TERRY!"), he howled.

I never thought I'd end up sitting on the floor cradling Terry Bellefleur in my arms, rocking him and murmuring to him. But that was where I was, since he seemed to get worse if anyone else approached him. Even the ambulance people got nervous when Terry shrieked at them. He was still crouched on the balls of his feet, speckled with blood, after Sandra Pelt had gone to the hospital in Clarice.

I was beholden to Terry, who had always been kind to me even when he was having one of his bad spells. He'd come to clear away the debris when an arsonist had set fire to my kitchen. He'd offered me one of his puppies. Now he'd damaged his fragile mind to save my life. As I rocked him and patted him on the back while he wept, I listened to the steady stream of his words as the few people left in Merlotte's did their best to stay a decent distance away.

"I done what he told me," Terry said, "the shining man, I kept track of Sookie and I tried to keep her from harm, no one should hurt Sookie, I tried to watch out for her, and then today that bitch come in here and I knew she was going to kill Sook, I knew it, I never wanted to take blood again in my life but I couldn't let her hurt the gal, I couldn't do it, and I never wanted to kill another person in my whole existence, I never did."

"She's not dead, Terry," I said, kissing him on the head. "You didn't kill anyone."

"Sam passed me the bat," Terry said, sounding a little more alert.

"Sure, because he couldn't get out from behind the bar in time. Thanks so much, Terry, you've been a friend to me always. God bless you for saving my life."

"Sookie? You knew they wanted me to watch out for you? They come to my trailer at night, for months, that big blond one and then the shining one. They always wanted to know about you."

"Sure," I said, thinking, *What?*

"They wanted to know how you were doing and who was you hanging with and who hated you and who loved you. . . ."

"That's okay," I said. "It was okay to tell them."

Eric and my great-grandfather, I guessed. Picking the damaged one, the one easiest to persuade. I'd known Eric had had someone watching me while I dated Bill and while I was on my own later. I'd guessed that my great-grandfather had had some source of knowledge, too. Whether he'd gotten the name from Eric or had discovered Terry on his own, it was very like Niall to use the handiest tool, whether or not the tool snapped during use.

"I met Elvis in your woods one night," Terry said. One of the EMTs had given him a shot, and I thought it was beginning to work. "I knew I was nuts then. He was telling me how much he liked cats. I told him I was a dog person, myself."

The vampire formerly known as Elvis had not translated well because his system had been so saturated with drugs when he'd been brought over by an ardent fan in the Memphis morgue. Bubba, as he preferred to be called now, had a preference for feline blood, luckily for Terry's beloved Catahoula, Annie.

"We got along real well," Terry was saying, and his voice was getting slower and sleepier. "I guess I better go home now."

"We're gonna take you out back to Sam's trailer," I said. "That's where you'll wake up." Didn't want Terry waking up in a panic. God, no.

The police had taken my statement, in a sketchy kind of way, and at least three

people had heard Sandra say she'd firebombed the bar.

Of course, I'd been at the bar much later
than I'd planned, and it was now dark. I
knew that Eric was outside waiting for me,
and I wanted more than anything to get up
and foist the problem of Terry on someone
else, but I simply couldn't. What he'd done
for me had damaged Terry even more, and I
had no way to pay him back. It didn't
bother me that he'd been keeping track of
me — okay, spying on me — for Eric before
Eric was my lover, or for my great-
grandfather. It hadn't done me any harm.
Since I knew Terry, I knew there had to have
been pressure involved, of one kind or another.

Sam and I helped Terry to his feet, and
we began to move, going down the hall that
led to the back of the bar and across the
employee parking lot to Sam's trailer.

"They promised they wouldn't let nothing
happen to my dog," Terry whispered. "And
they promised the dreams would stop."

"Did they keep their promises?" I asked
back, my voice just as quiet.

"Yes," he said gratefully. "No more
dreams, and I got my dog."

That didn't seem to be so much to ask. I
should be angrier at Terry, but I couldn't

scrape up the emotional energy. I was all worn out.

Eric was standing in the shadow of the trees. He stayed back so his presence wouldn't agitate Terry. From the sudden stiffness in Sam's face, I knew he was aware Eric was there, but Sam didn't say anything.

We got Terry settled on Sam's couch, and when he drifted away into the stream of sleep, I hugged Sam. "Thanks," I said.

"For what?"

"For passing Terry the bat."

Sam stepped back. "It was all I could think of to do. I couldn't clear the bar without alerting her. She had to be surprised or it was all over."

"She's that strong?"

"Yeah," he said. "And she's convinced her world would be okay if it weren't for you, sounded like. Fanatics are hard to beat down. They keep coming."

"Are you thinking about the people who are trying to get Merlotte's closed?"

His smile was bitter. "Maybe I am. I can't believe this is happening in our country, and me a veteran. Born and bred in the USA."

"I feel guilty, Sam. Some of this has happened because of me. The firebombing . . . Sandra wouldn't have done that if I hadn't been there. And the fight. Maybe you should let me go. I can work somewhere else, you know."

"Do you want to?"

I couldn't read the expression on his face, but at least it wasn't relief.

"No, of course not."

"Then you have a job. We're a package deal."

He smiled, and somehow it didn't light up his blue eyes the way his smiles usually did, but he meant what he said. Shifter or not, snarly brained or not, I could tell that much.

"Thanks, Sam. I better go see what my better half wants."

"Whatever Eric is to you, Sook, he's not your better half."

I paused, my hand on the doorknob, and couldn't think of anything to say to that. So I just left.

Eric was waiting, but not patiently. He took my face between his big hands and examined it under the harsh glare of the security lights on the corners of the bar. India came out the back way, gave us a startled look, and got in her car and drove off. Sam stayed in the trailer.

"I want you to move in with me," Eric said. "You can stay in one of the upstairs bedrooms if you want. The one we usually use. You don't have to stay down in the dark with me. I don't want you to be alone. I don't want to feel your fear one more time. It makes me crazy to know someone is attacking you, and I'm not there."

We had gotten into the habit of making love in the largest upstairs bedroom. (Waking up in the windowless room downstairs gave me the heebie-jeebies.) Now Eric was offering that room to me permanently. I knew this was a big deal for Eric, a major deal. And it was huge for me, too. But a decision this big couldn't be made at a moment when I was not myself, and tonight I wasn't myself.

"We need to talk," I said. "Do you have time?"

"Tonight, I'm making time," he said. "Are the fairies at your house?"

I called Claude on my cell. When he answered, I could hear the noise of Hooligans in the background. "I'm just checking to see where you are before Eric and I go to the house," I said.

"We're staying at the club tonight," Claude answered. "Have a good time with your vampire hunk, Cousin."

Eric followed me over to my house. He'd brought the car, because as soon as he'd known I was in danger, he'd known it had passed and he could take the time to drive.

I poured myself a glass of wine — unusual for me — and I microwaved some bottled blood for Eric. We sat in the living room. I pulled up my legs onto the couch and swung around with my back against the arm to face him. He angled toward me on the other end.

"Eric, I know you don't ask people to stay in your house lightly. So, I want you to know how . . . touched and flattered I am that you invited me."

Right away, I realized I'd said the wrong thing. That sounded way too impersonal.

Eric's blue eyes narrowed. "Oh, think nothing of it," he said coldly.

"I didn't say that right." I took a deep breath. "Listen, I love you. I . . . feel thrilled that you want us to live together." He looked a little more relaxed. "But before I make up my mind whether to do that, we need to get some stuff straight."

"Stuff?"

"You married me to protect me. You hired Terry Bellefleur to spy on me, and you applied pressure where he couldn't take it, to get him to comply."

Eric said, "That happened before I knew you, Sookie."

227

"Yeah, I get that. But it's the nature of the pressure you applied to a man whose mental state is so wobbly. It's the way you got me to marry you, without knowing what I was doing."

"You wouldn't have done it otherwise," Eric said. As always, practical and to the point.

"You're right, I wouldn't," I said, trying to smile at him. But it wasn't easy. "And Terry wouldn't have told you things about me, if you'd offered him money. I know you see this as the smart way to do business, and I'm sure a lot of people would agree with you."

Eric was trying to follow my thinking, but I could tell he wasn't making any sense of it. I kept struggling upstream. "We're both living with this bond. I'm sure sometimes you would rather I didn't know what you're feeling. Would you be wanting me to live with you if we didn't have the bond? If you didn't feel it every time I was in danger? Or angry? Or afraid?"

"What a strange thing to say, my lover." Eric took a swallow of his drink, set it down on the old coffee table. "Are you saying that if I didn't know you needed me, I wouldn't need you?"

Was that what I was saying? "I don't think

228

so. What I'm trying to say is that I don't think you'd want me to live with you unless you felt like people were out to get me." Was that the same thing? Geez Louise, I hated conversations like this. Not that I'd ever had one before.

"What difference does that make?" he said, more than a trace of impatience in his voice. "If I want you with me, I want you. The circumstances don't matter."

"But they do matter. And we're so different."

"What?"

"Well, there are so many things you take for granted that I don't."

Eric rolled his eyes. A total guy. "Like what?"

I groped around for an example. "Well, like Appius having sex with Alexei. It was not a big deal for you, even though Alexei was thirteen." Eric's maker, Appius Livius Ocella, had become a vampire during the time when Romans ruled much of the world.

"Sookie, it was what you call a done deal long before I even knew I had a brother. In Ocella's time, people were reckoned practically grown at thirteen. They were even married that young. Ocella never understood some of the changes in society that came with the centuries. And Alexei and Ocella are both dead now." Eric shrugged. "There was another side of that coin, you remember? Alexei used his youth, his child-like looks, to disarm all the vampires and humans around him. Even Pam was loath to put him down, though she knew how destructive he was, how insane. And she's the most ruthless vampire I know. He was a drain on all of us, sucking the will and force from us with the depth of his need."

And with that unexpectedly poetic sentence, Eric was done talking about Alexei and Ocella. His whole face turned stony. I recalled my main point: our irreconcilable differences. "What about the fact that you're going to outlive me for, like, forever?"

"We can take care of that easily enough."

I just stared at him.

"What?" Eric said, almost genuinely amazed. "You don't want to live forever? With me?"

"I don't know," I said, finally. I tried to imagine it. The night, forever. Endless. But with Eric!

I said, "You know, Eric, I can't . . ." And then I stopped dead. I'd almost insulted him unforgivably. I knew he felt the wave of doubt emanating from me.

I'd almost said, "I just can't imagine you

sticking around after I start to look old."

Though there were a few more topics I had hoped we'd cover in our rare tête-à-tête, I felt the conversation was teetering on the edge of Disaster Canyon. Maybe it was lucky there was knocking at the back door. I'd heard the car coming, but my attention had been so focused on my companion that I hadn't really registered its meaning.

Amelia Broadway and Bob Jessup were at the back door. Amelia looked the same as ever: healthy and fresh faced, her short brown hair tousled and her skin and eyes clear. Bob, not much taller than Amelia and equally lean, was a small-boned guy who looked kind of like a sexy Mormon missionary. His black-framed glasses managed to look retro instead of geeky. He was wearing jeans, a black-and-white plaid shirt, and tasseled loafers. He'd been a very cute cat, but his attraction as a guy escaped me — or rather it showed itself to me only now and then.

I beamed at them. It felt great to see Amelia, and I felt relieved that my conversation with Eric had been interrupted. We did have to talk about our future, but I had a creepy feeling that finishing that conversation would make both of us unhappy. Postponing it probably wouldn't change that outcome, but both Eric and I had enough on our plates of problems. "Come on in!" I said. "Eric's here, and he'll be glad to see you both."

Of course, that wasn't true. Eric was completely indifferent about ever seeing Amelia again in his life — his long, long life — and Bob didn't even register on Eric's radar.

But Eric smiled (though not a large smile) and told them how glad he was they'd come to visit me — though there was a bit of a question in his voice, since he didn't know why they were here. No matter how long a talk Eric and I had, we never seemed to cover enough ground.

With a huge effort, Amelia repressed a frown. She was not a fan of the Viking. And she was a *very* clear broadcaster, so I got that with as much volume as if she'd yelled out loud. Bob eyed Eric with caution, and as soon as I'd explained the bedroom situation to Amelia (of course, she'd assumed they'd be upstairs), Bob vanished into the room across from mine with their bags. After a few minutes fiddling around in there, he ducked into the hall bathroom. Bob had gotten good at evasiveness while he was a cat.

"Eric," Amelia said, stretching unselfconsciously. "How are things going at Fangtasia? How's the new management?" She couldn't know she'd hit a nerve. And when Eric's eyes narrowed — I suspected that he thought she'd said that on purpose to rile him — Amelia was staring at her toes as she touched them with the palms of her hands. I wondered if I could do that, and then my mind snapped back to the current moment.

"Business is going all right," Eric said. "Victor has opened some new clubs close by."

Amelia understood immediately that this was a bad development, but she was smart enough not to say anything. Honestly, it was like being in the room with someone who was shouting her inmost thoughts. "Victor's the smiley guy who was out in the yard the night of the takeover, right?" she said, straightening and rotating her head from side to side.

"Yes," Eric said, one corner of his mouth going up in a sardonic look. "The smiley guy."

"So, Sook, what troubles do you have now?" Amelia asked me, evidently considering that she'd been polite enough to Eric. She was ready to plunge into whatever problem I described.

"Yes," Eric said, looking at me with hard

eyes. "What troubles do you have now?"

"I was just going to get Amelia to reinforce the wards around the house," I said casually. "Since so much stuff has happened at Merlotte's I was feeling kind of insecure."

"So she called me," Amelia said pointedly.

Eric looked from me to Amelia. He looked mighty displeased. "But now that the bitch has been cornered, Sookie, surely the threat's been removed?"

"What?" Amelia asked. It was her turn to look from face to face. "What happened tonight, Sookie?"

I told her, briefly. "I'd still feel better if you made sure the wards were in place, though."

"That's one of the things I've come to do, Sookie." For some reason, she smiled broadly at Eric.

Bob sidled in then and took up a position beside Amelia but slightly behind her. "Those weren't my kittens," he told me, and Eric gaped. I'd seldom seen him genuinely startled. It was all I could do to keep from laughing. "I mean, Weres can't breed with the animal they turn into. So I don't think those were my kittens. Especially since — think about it! — I was only a cat by magic, not a genetic Were."

Amelia said, "Honey, we've talked about

this. You don't need to be embarrassed. It was a perfectly natural thing to do. I admit I got a little snitty about it, but, you know . . . the whole thing was my fault, anyway."

"Don't worry about it, Bob. Sam already spoke up in your defense." I smiled at Bob, who looked relieved.

Eric decided to ignore this exchange. "Sookie, I need to get back to Fangtasia."

We would never have a chance to say the things we needed to say, at this rate. "Okay, Eric. Tell Pam I said hello, if you two are back to speaking."

"She's a better friend to you than you know," Eric said darkly.

I didn't know how to respond to that, and he turned so quickly my eyes couldn't track him. I heard his car door slam outside, and then he was driving down the driveway. No matter how many times I saw it, I still found it amazing that vamps could move so fast.

I'd hoped to have a chance to talk more to Amelia that night, but she and Bob were ready to turn in after their drive. They'd left New Orleans after a full day's work, Amelia at the Genuine Magic Shop and Bob at the Happy Cutter. After fifteen minutes or so of going to and fro between the bathroom and the kitchen and the car, they became silent in the room across the hall. I'd taken off my shoes, and I padded into the kitchen to lock up.

I was just expelling a sigh of relief at the end of the day when there was a very quiet knock at the back door. I jumped like a frog. Who could be there at this time of night? I looked out across the back porch very cautiously.

Bill. I hadn't seen him since his "sister" Judith had come to see him. I debated for a second, then decided to slip outside to talk to him. Bill was a lot of things to me: neighbor, friend, first lover. I did not fear him.

"Sookie," he said, his cool, smooth voice as relaxing as a massage. "You have guests?"

"Amelia and Bob," I explained. "They just got here from New Orleans. The fairies aren't here tonight. They stay in Monroe most nights, lately."

"Shall we stay out here, so we won't wake your friends?"

It was news to me that our conversation was going to last that long. Apparently, Bill hadn't come over just to borrow a cup of blood. I waved my hand toward the lawn furniture, and we sat in the chairs, already placed at a companionable angle. The warm night with its myriad small sounds closed around us like an envelope. The security light gave the backyard strange patterns of dark and brightness.

When the silence had lasted long enough for me to realize I was sleepy, I said, "How's things going at your house, Bill? Is Judith still staying with you?"

"I'm fully healed from the silver poisoning," he said.

"I, ah, I noticed you looked good," I said. His skin had regained its pale clarity, and even his hair looked more lustrous. "Much better. So Judith's blood worked."

"Yes. But now . . ." He looked off into the night forest.

Uh-oh. "She wants to keep on living with you?"

"Yes," he said, sounding relieved he hadn't had to spell it out. "She does."

"I thought you admired her because she looked so much like your first wife. Judith told me that's why crazy Lorena changed Judith over, to keep you with her. I mean, sorry to bring up bad stuff."

"It's true. Judith does look like my first wife, in many respects. Her face is the same shape, her voice very like my wife's. Her hair is the same color my wife's was when she was a child. And Judith was raised very gently, like my wife."

"So, I would have predicted that would make you happy with Judith," I said.

"But not." He sounded rueful, and he kept his eyes on the trees, carefully averting his gaze from my face. "And in fact, that's why I didn't call Judith when I realized how sick I was. I had to part with her the last time we were together because of her overwhelming obsession with me."

"Oh," I said, my voice very small.

"But you did the right thing, Sookie. She came to me and freely offered her blood. Since you invited her here without my knowledge, I'm at least not guilty of using her. My fault lies in letting her stay after . . . after I healed."

"And why'd you do that?"

"Because I hoped somehow my feelings for her had changed, that I could have a genuine love for her. That would have freed me from . . ." His voice trailed off.

He might have finished the sentence, "loving you." Or maybe, "freed me from the debt I owed her for healing me."

I did feel a little better now that I knew he was glad to be well, even though the price was that he had to deal with Judith. And I could understand how awkward and unpleasant it would be to be saddled with a houseguest who adored you when you didn't return the emotion. Who was the one who'd saddled him? Well, that would be me. Of course, I hadn't known any of the emotional background. Distressed by Bill's condition, I'd reasoned that someone of Bill's bloodline could heal him, and I'd found that there was such a person and tracked her down. I'd further assumed Bill hadn't done that himself from some perverse pride or perhaps even from a suicidal depression. I'd underestimated Bill's desire to live.

"What do you plan to do about Judith?" I asked anxiously, scared to hear his answer.

"He need not do anything," a quiet voice said from the trees.

I came up out of my chair like someone had just shot a few volts through it, and Bill had a big reaction. He turned his head and his eyes widened. That was it, but for a vampire, that indicates major surprise.

"Judith?" I said.

She stepped out of the tree line, far enough for me to recognize her. The security light in the backyard didn't extend that far, and I could only just be sure it was her.

"You keep breaking my heart, Bill," she said.

I eased away from the chair. Maybe I could slink back into the house. Maybe I could avoid witnessing another major scene — because honestly, the day had been chock-full of them.

"No, stay, Miss Stackhouse," Judith said. She was a short, round woman with a sweet face and an abundance of hair, and she carried herself as if she were six feet tall.

Dammit. "You two obviously need to talk," I said cravenly.

"Any conversation with Bill about love has to include you," she said.

Oh . . . *poop.* I so did not want to be present for this. I stared down at my feet.

"Judith, stop," Bill said, his voice as calm as ever. "I came over to talk to my friend, whom I haven't seen for weeks."

"I heard your conversation," Judith said simply. "I followed you here for the express purpose of listening to whatever you had to say to her. I know that you're not making love to this woman. I know that she's claimed by another. And I also know that you want her more than you ever wanted me. I will not have sex with a man who pities me. I will not live with a man who doesn't want me. I'm worth more than that. I'll stop loving you if it takes me the rest of my existence. If you'll remain here a few moments, I'll return to your house and pack my things and be gone."

240

I was impressed. That was a damn fine speech, and I hoped she meant every word. Even as I had the thought, Judith was gone — *whoosh!* — and Bill and I were alone together.

Suddenly he was right in front of me, and he put his cold arms around me. It didn't seem like a betrayal of Eric to let Bill simply hold me for a moment.

"You had sex with her?" I said, trying to sound neutral.

"She had saved me. She seemed to expect it. I felt it was the right thing to do," he said.

As if Judith had sneezed so he'd lent her a handkerchief. I really couldn't think of what to say. Men! Dead or alive, they could be exactly the same.

I stepped back, and he dropped his arms instantly.

"Do you really love me?" I said, out of either insanity or sheer curiosity. "Or have we just been through so much that you think you ought to?"

He smiled. "Only you would say that. I love you. I think you're beautiful and kind and good, and yet you stand up for yourself. You have a lot of understanding and compassion, but you're not a pushover. And to descend a few levels to the carnal, you have a pair of breasts that should win the Miss America Tit Competition, if there were such a thing."

"That's an unusual bunch of compliments." I had a hard time suppressing my own smile.

"You're an unusual woman."

"Good night, Bill," I said. Just then my cell phone rang. I jumped a mile. I'd forgotten it was in my pocket. When I looked at the number, it was a local one I didn't recognize. No call at this hour of the night was a good one. I held up a finger to ask Bill to wait for a moment, and I answered it with a cautious "Hello?"

"Sookie," said Sheriff Dearborn, "I thought you oughta know that Sandra Pelt escaped from the hospital. She snuck out the window while Kenya was talking to Dr. Tonnesen. I don't want you to be worried. If you need us to send a car out to your house, we will. You got someone with you?"

I was so shocked I couldn't reply for a second. Then I said, "Yes, I have someone with me."

Bill's dark eyes were serious now. He stepped closer and put one hand on my shoulder.

"You want me to send a patrol car? I don't think that crazy woman will head out to find you. I think she'll find somewhere to hole up and recover. But it seemed like the right thing, telling you, even though it's the middle of the night."

"Definitely the right thing to do, Sheriff. I don't think I need more help out here. I've got friends here. Good friends." And I met Bill's eyes.

Bud Dearborn said the same things all over again several times, but eventually I got to hang up and think about the implications. I'd thought one line of troubles was closed, but I'd been wrong. While I was explaining to Bill, the weariness that had manifested itself earlier began to sweep over me like a blanket of gray. By the time I'd finished answering his questions, I could barely put two words together.

"Don't worry," Bill said. "Go to bed. I'll watch tonight. I've already fed, and I wasn't busy. It doesn't feel like a good night for work, anyway." Bill had created and maintained a CD called *The Vampire Directory*, which was a catalog of all "living" vampires. It was in popular demand not only among the undead but also among the living, particularly marketing groups. However, the version sold to the public was limited to vampires who'd given their permission to be included, a much shorter list. There were still vampires who didn't want to be known as vampires, odd as that seemed to me. It was easy to forget, in today's vampire-saturated culture, that there were still holdouts, vampires who didn't want to be known to the public in general, vampires who preferred to sleep in the earth or in abandoned buildings rather than in a house or apartment.

And why I was thinking of this . . . Well, it was better than thinking about Sandra Pelt.

"Thanks, Bill," I said gratefully. "I warn you, she's vicious to the nth degree."

"You've seen me fight," he said.

"Yep. But you don't know her. She's completely underhanded and she won't give you any warning."

"I'm a few jumps ahead of her, then, since I know that about her."

Huh? "Okay," I mumbled, putting one foot in front of the other in more or less a straight line. "Night, Bill."

"Night, Sookie," he said quietly. "Lock the doors."

I did, and I went into my room and put on my nightshirt, and then I was in bed and under that gray blanket.

CHAPTER 8

Schools are always more or less the same, aren't they? There's always the smell: a mixture of chalk, school lunches, floor wax, books. The echo of children's voices, the louder voices of teachers. The "art" on the walls and the decorations on each room's door. The little Red Ditch kindergarten was no different.

I held Hunter's hand while Remy trailed behind us. Every time I saw Hunter, he seemed to look a bit more like my cousin Hadley, his dead mother. He had her dark eyes and hair, and his face was losing its baby roundness and growing more oval, like hers.

Poor Hadley. She'd had a tough life, mostly of her own making. In the end she'd found true love, become a vampire, and been killed for jealousy's sake. Hadley's life had been eventful, but short. That was why I was standing in for her, and for a moment

I wondered how she'd have felt about that. This should be her job, taking her son to his first school, the kindergarten he'd be attending in the fall. The purpose of the visit was to help the incoming kindergartners become a little familiar with the idea of school, with the look of the rooms and the desks and the teachers.

Some of the little people going through the building were looking around with curiosity, not fear. Some of them were silent and wide-eyed. That was the way my "nephew" Hunter would look to other people — but in my head Hunter was chattering away. Hunter was telepathic, as I was. This was the most closely guarded secret I held. I wanted Hunter to grow up as normally as possible. The more supes who knew about Hunter, the higher the likelihood someone would snatch him away because telepaths were useful. There was sure to be someone ruthless enough to take such a terrible action. I don't think Remy, his father, had even considered that yet. Remy was worried about Hunter's acceptance among the humans around him. And that was a big deal, too. Kids could be incredibly cruel when they sensed you were different. I knew that all too well.

It's kind of obvious when people are having a mind-to-mind conversation, if you know the cues. Their faces change expression when they look at each other, much as they would if the conversation were out loud. So I was looking away from the child frequently and keeping my smile steady. Hunter was too little to learn how to conceal our communication, so I'd have to do it.

Will all these kids fit in one room? he asked.

"Out loud," I reminded him quietly. "No, you'll be divided into groups, and then you'll hang out with one group all day, Hunter." I didn't know if the Red Ditch kindergarten had the same schedule as the higher grades, but I was sure it would last past lunch, anyway. "Your dad will bring you in the morning, and someone will come get you in the afternoon." *Who?* I wondered, and then remembered Hunter was listening to me. "Your dad will fix that," I said. "Look. This room is the Seal Room. See the big picture of the seal? And that room is the Pony Room."

"Is there a pony?" Hunter was an optimist.

"I don't think so, but I bet there are lots of pictures of ponies in the room." All the doors were open, and the teachers were inside, smiling at the children and their parents, doing their best to seem welcoming and warm. Some of them, of course, had

247

more of a struggle doing this than others.

The Pony Room teacher, Mrs. Gristede, was a nice enough woman, or at least that was what my quick look told me. Hunter nodded.

We ventured into the Puppy Room and met with Miss O'Fallon. We were back in the hall after three minutes.

"Not the Puppy Room," I told Remy, speaking very quietly. "You can designate, right?"

"Yeah, we can. Once. I can say one room I definitely don't want my kid to be in," he said. "Most people use that option in case the teacher is too close to the family, like a relative, or if the families have had some quarrel."

"Not the Puppy Room," Hunter said, looking scared.

Miss O'Fallon looked pretty on the outside, but she was rotten on the inside.

"What's wrong?" Remy asked, his voice also on a confidential level.

"Tell you later," I murmured. "Let's go see something else."

Trailed by Remy, we made visits to the other three rooms. All the other teachers seemed okay, though Mrs. Boyle seemed a little burned-out. Her thoughts were brisk and had an edge of impatience, and her smile was just a bit brittle. I didn't say anything to Remy. If he could turn down only one teacher, Miss O'Fallon was the most dangerous.

We went back to Mrs. Gristede's room because Hunter definitely liked the ponies. There were two other parents there, both towing little girls. I squeezed Hunter's hand gently to remind him of the rules. He looked up at me, and I nodded, trying to encourage the boy. He let go of my hand and went over to a reading area, picking up one of the books and turning the pages.

"Do you like to read, Hunter?" Mrs. Gristede asked.

"I like books. I can't read yet." Hunter put the book back where it belonged, and I gave him a mental pat on the back. He smiled to himself and picked up another book, this one a Dr. Seuss about dogs.

"I can tell Hunter's been read to," the teacher said, smiling at Remy and me.

Remy introduced himself. "I'm Hunter's dad, and this is Hunter's cousin," he said, inclining his head toward me. "Sookie's standing in for Hunter's mom tonight, since she's passed away."

Mrs. Gristede absorbed that. "Well, I'm glad to see both of you," she said. "Hunter seems like a bright little boy."

I noticed the girls were approaching him. They were longtime friends, I could tell, and their parents went to church together. I made a mental note to advise Remy to pick a church and start attending. Hunter was going to need all the backup he could get. The girls began picking up books, too. Hunter smiled at the girl with the dark Dutch-boy bob, giving her that sideways look shy children use to evaluate potential playmates.

She said, "I like this one," and pointed to *Where the Wild Things Are.*

"I never read it," Hunter said doubtfully. It looked a little scary to him.

"Do you play with blocks?" the girl with the light brown ponytail asked.

"Yeah." Hunter walked over to the carpeted play area that was for construction, I decided, because there were all sizes of blocks and puzzles around it. In a minute the three were building something that took on life in their minds.

Remy smiled. He was hoping this was the way every day would go. Of course, it wouldn't. Even now, Hunter was glancing dubiously at the ponytail girl because she was getting angry about the brunette's grabbing all the alphabet blocks.

The other parents looked at me with some

curiosity, and one of the mothers said, "You don't live here?"

"No," I said. "I live over in Bon Temps. But Hunter wanted me to go around with him today, and he's my favorite little cousin." I'd almost called him my nephew, because he called me "Aunt Sookie."

"Remy," the same woman said. "You're Hank Savoy's great-nephew, right?"

Remy nodded. "Yeah, we came up here after Katrina, and we stayed," he said. He shrugged. Nothing you could do about losing everything to Katrina. She was a bitch.

There was a lot of headshaking, and I felt the sympathy roll over Remy. Maybe that goodwill would extend to Hunter.

While they were all bonding, I drifted back to Miss O'Fallon's door.

The young woman was smiling at two children who were wandering around her brightly decorated classroom. One set of parents was staying right beside their little one. Maybe they were picking up on the vibe, or maybe they were just protective.

I drifted close to Miss O'Fallon, and I opened my mouth to speak. I would have said, "You keep those fantasies to yourself. Don't even think of such things when you're in the same room with kids." But I had a second thought. She knew I'd come with

251

Hunter. Would he become a target for her evil imagination if I threatened her? I couldn't be around to protect him. I couldn't stop her. I couldn't think of a way to take her out of the equation. She hadn't yet done anything wrong in the eyes of the law or morality . . . yet. So what if she imagined taping children's mouths shut? She hadn't *done* it. *Haven't all of us fantasized about awful things we haven't done?* she asked herself, because the answer made her feel that she was still . . . okay. She didn't know I could hear her.

Was I any better than Miss O'Fallon? That awful question ran through my mind more quickly than it takes to write the sentences. I thought, *Yeah, I'm not as scary because I'm not in charge of kids. The people I want to hurt are adults and they're killers themselves.* That didn't make me any better — but it made O'Fallon a lot worse.

I'd been staring at her long enough to spook her. "Did you want to ask something about the curriculum?" she asked finally, a little edge to her voice.

"Why did you become a teacher?" I asked.

"I thought it would be a wonderful thing to teach little ones the first things they needed to know to get along in the world," she said, as if she'd pressed the button on a

252

recording. She meant, *I had a teacher who tortured me when no one was looking, and I like the small and helpless.*

"Hmmm," I murmured. The other visitors left the room, and we were alone.

"You need therapy," I said, quietly and quickly. "If you act on what you see in your head, you'll hate yourself. And you'll ruin the lives of other people just the same way yours was ruined. Don't let her win. Get help."

She gaped at me. "I don't know . . . What on earth . . ."

"I'm so serious," I said, answering her next unspoken question. "I'm *so* serious."

"I'll do it," she said, as if the words were ripped from her mouth. "I swear, I'll do it."

"You'd be better off," I said. I gave her some more eye-to-eye. Then I left the Puppy Room.

Maybe I'd frightened her enough, or jolted her enough, that she'd actually do what she'd promised. If not, well, I'd have to think of another tactic.

"My job here is done, Grasshopper," I said to myself, earning a nervous look from a very young father. I smiled at him, and after a bit of hesitation, he smiled back. I rejoined Remy and Hunter, and we completed our kindergarten tour without any further incident. Hunter gave me a questioning look, a very anxious look, and I nodded. *I took care of her,* I said, and I prayed that was true.

It was really too early for supper, but Remy suggested we go to Dairy Queen and treat Hunter to some ice cream, and I agreed. Hunter was half-anxious, half-excited after the school expedition. I tried calming him with a little head-to-head conversation. *Can you take me to school the first day, Aunt Sookie?* he asked, and I had to steel myself to answer.

No, Hunter, that's your daddy's job, I told him. *But when that day comes, you call me when you get home and tell me all about it, okay?*

Hunter gave me a big-eyed soulful look. *But I'm scared.*

I gave him Skeptical. *You may be nervous, but everyone else will feel the same way. This is your chance to make friends, so remember to keep your mouth closed until you've gotten everything straight in your head.*

Or they won't like me?

No! I said, wanting to be absolutely clear. *They won't understand you. There's a big difference.*

You like me?

"You little rascal, you know I like you," I said, smiling at him and brushing his hair back. I glanced over at Remy, standing in line at the counter to order our Blizzards. He waved to me and made a face at Hunter. Remy was making a huge effort to take all this in stride. He was growing into his role as father of an exceptional child.

I figured he might get to relax in twelve years, give or take a few.

You know your dad loves you, and you know he wants what's best for you, I said.

He wants me to be like all the other kids, Hunter said, half-sad, half-resentful.

He wants you to be happy. And he knows that the more people who know about this gift you have, the chances are you won't be happy. I know it's not fair to tell you that you have to keep a secret. But this is the only secret you have to keep. If anyone talks to you about it, tell your dad or call me. If you think someone's weird, you tell your dad. If someone tries to bad-touch you, you tell.

I'd just scared him now. But he swallowed and said, *I know about bad touching.*

You're a smart boy, and you're going to have lots of friends. This is just a thing about you they don't need to know.

Because it's bad? Hunter's face looked pinched and desperate.

255

Heck, no! I said, outraged. *Nothing wrong with you, buddy. But you know what we are is different, and people don't always understand different.* End of lecture. I gave him a kiss on the cheek.

"Hunter, you get us some napkins," I said in the regular way, as Remy picked up the plastic tray with our Blizzards. I'd gotten a chocolate chip one, and my mouth was watering when we'd distributed the napkins and dug into our separate cups of sinful goodness.

A young woman with chin-length black hair came into the restaurant, spotted us, and waved in an uncertain way.

"Look, Sport, it's Erin," Remy said.

"Hey, Erin!" Hunter waved back enthusiastically, his hand moving like a little metronome.

Erin came over, still looking as though she weren't sure of her welcome.

"Hi," she said, looking around the table. "Mr. Hunter, sir, it's good to see you this fine afternoon!" Hunter beamed back at her. He liked being called "Mr. Hunter." Erin had cute round cheeks, and her almond eyes were a rich brown.

"This is my Aunt Sookie!" Hunter said with pride.

"Sookie, this is Erin," Remy said. I could

tell from his thoughts that he liked the young woman more than a little.

"Erin, I've heard so much about you," I said. "It's nice to put a face with the name. Hunter wanted me to come over to go around the kindergarten rooms with him."

"How did that go?" Erin asked, genuinely interested.

Hunter started to tell her all about it, and Remy jumped up to pull over a chair for Erin.

We had a good time after that. Hunter seemed to be really fond of Erin, and Erin returned the feeling. Erin was also *quite* interested in Hunter's dad, and Remy was on the verge of being nuts about her. All in all, it wasn't a bad afternoon to be able to read minds, I figured.

Hunter said, "Miss Erin, Aunt Sookie says she can't go with me to the first day of school. Would you?"

Erin was both startled and pleased. "If your dad says it's okay, and if I can get off work," she said, careful to put some conditions on it in case Remy had some objection . . . or they'd quit dating by late August. "You're so sweet to ask me."

While Remy took Hunter to the men's room, Erin and I were left to regard each other with curiosity.

"How long have you and Remy been seeing each other?" I asked. That seemed safe enough.

"Just a month," she said. "I like Remy, and I think we might have something, but it's too soon to tell. I don't want Hunter to start depending on me in case it doesn't work out. Plus . . ." She hesitated for a long minute. "I understand that Kristen Duchesne thought there was something wrong with Hunter. She told everyone that. But I really care about that little boy." The question was clear in her eyes.

"He's different," I said, "but there's nothing wrong with him. He's not mentally ill, he doesn't have a learning disability, and he's not possessed by the devil." I was smiling, just a little, when I got to the end of the sentence.

"I'd never seen any signs of that," she agreed. She was smiling, too. "I don't think I've seen the whole picture, though."

I wasn't about to tell Hunter's secret. "He needs special love and care," I said. "He's never really had a mom, and I'm sure having someone stable in his life, filling that role, would help."

"And that's not going to be you." She said that as if she were half asking a question.

"No," I said, relieved to get a chance to

set the record straight. "That's not going to be me. Remy seems like a nice guy, but I'm seeing someone else." I scraped up one more spoonful of chocolate and sugar.

Erin looked down at her glass of Pepsi, thinking her own thoughts. Of course, I was thinking them right along with her. She'd never liked Kristen and didn't think much of her mental ability. She did like Remy, more and more. And she loved Hunter. "Okay," she said, having reached an inner conclusion. "Okay."

She looked up at me and nodded. I nodded right back. It seemed we'd arrived at an understanding. When the menfolk came back from their trip to the restroom, I said good-bye to them.

"Oh, wait, Remy, can you step outside for a minute with me, if Erin wouldn't mind keeping an eye on Hunter?"

"I'd love to," she said. I hugged Hunter again and gave him a pat and a smile as I moved toward the door.

Remy followed me, an apprehensive expression on his face. We stood a little away from the door.

"You know Hadley left the rest of her estate to me," I said. This had been weighing on me.

"The lawyer told me." Remy's face wasn't

giving anything away, but of course I have other methods. He was calm through and through.

"You aren't mad?"

"No, I don't want nothing of Hadley's."

"But for Hunter . . . his college. There wasn't much cash, but there was some good jewelry, and I could sell it."

"I got a college fund started for him," Remy said. "One of my great-aunts says she's going to leave what she's got to him since she doesn't have any kids of her own. Hadley put me through hell, and she didn't even care enough about Hunter to plan for him. I don't want it."

"In all fairness, she didn't expect to die young. . . . In fact, she didn't expect to die *ever*," I said. "It's my belief she didn't put Hunter in her will because she didn't want anyone to know about him and come looking for him to use him as a hostage for her good behavior."

"I hope that's the case," Remy said. "I mean, I hope she thought about him. But taking her money, knowing how she turned out, how she earned it . . . that would make me feel sick."

"All right," I said. "If you think it over and change your mind, call me by tomorrow night! You never know when I might

260

go on a spending spree or put that jewelry down on the table at one of the casinos."

He smiled, just a little. "You're a good woman," he said, and returned to his girlfriend and his son.

I started the drive home with a clear conscience and a happier heart.

I'd worked half of the early shift that day (Holly had taken my half and her own shift), so I was free. I thought of brooding over Gran's letter a little more. Mr. Cataliades's visit to us when we were babies, the cluviel dor, the deceptions Gran's lover had practiced on her . . . Because surely when Gran had thought she *smelled* Fintan when she was *seeing* her husband, she was seeing Fintan in disguise. It was hard to absorb.

Amelia and Bob were busy casting spells when I got back. They were walking around the perimeter of the house in opposite directions, chanting and swinging incense like the priests in the Catholic Church.

Some days I realized it was all to the good that I lived out in the country.

I didn't want to break their concentration, so I wandered off into the woods. I wondered where the portal was, if I could recognize it. "A thin place," Dermot had called it. Could I spot a thin place? At least

261

I knew the general direction, and I started east.

It was a warm afternoon, and I began sweating the minute I started to make my way through the woods. The sun broke through the branches in a thousand patterns, and the birds and the bugs made the thousand noises that left the woods anything but silent. It wouldn't be long until evening closed in and the light would fracture and slant, making the footing uncertain. The birds would fall silent, and the night creatures would make their own harmony.

I picked my way through the undergrowth, thinking of the night before. I wondered if Judith had packed all her things and left, as she'd said she would. I wondered if Bill felt lonely now that she was gone. I assumed nothing and no one had popped up in my yard the night before, since I'd slept through the hours of the dark and into the morning.

Then all I had left to wonder about was when Sandra Pelt would try to kill me again. Just as I began to suspect that being alone in the woods wasn't a good idea, I stepped into a tiny clearing about a quarter of a mile, or less, slightly southeast of my back door.

I was pretty sure this was the thin place, this little clearing. For one thing, there was no reason for it to be clear that I could see. There were wild grasses growing thickly, but there were no bushes, nothing above calf-high. No vines stretched across the area, no branches drooped over it.

Before I stepped out of the trees, I gave the ground a very careful examination. The last thing I needed was to be caught in some kind of fairy booby trap. But I couldn't see anything extraordinary, except perhaps . . . a slight wavering in the air. Right in the middle of the clearing. The odd spot — if I was even seeing it right — hovered at the height of my knees. It was the shape of a small and irregular circle, perhaps fifteen inches in diameter. And in just that spot, the air seemed to distort, a little like a heat illusion. Was it actually hot? I wondered.

I knelt in the weeds about an arm's length from the wobbly air. I plucked a long blade of grass and very nervously poked it into the distorted area.

I let go of it, and it vanished. I snatched my fingers back and yipped with surprise.

I'd established something. I wasn't sure what. If I'd doubted Claude's word, here was verification he'd been telling me the truth. Very carefully, I moved a little closer to the wavery patch. "Hi, Niall," I said. "If you're listening, if you're there. I miss you."

Of course, there came no answer.

"I have a lot of troubles, but I expect you do, too," I said, not wanting to sound whiny. "I don't know how Faery fits into this world. Are you all walking around us, but invisible? Or do you have a whole 'nother world, like Atlantis?" This was a pretty weak and one-sided conversation. "Well, I better go back to the house before it gets dark. If you need me, come see me. I do miss you," I said again.

Nothing continued to happen.

Feeling both pleased that I'd found the thin spot and disappointed that nothing had changed as a result, I made my way back through the woods to the house. Bob and Amelia had finished their magical doings in the yard, and Bob had fired up the grill. He and Amelia were going to cook steaks. Though I'd had ice cream with Remy and Hunter, I couldn't turn down grilled steak rubbed with Bob's secret seasoning. Amelia was cutting up potatoes to wrap in foil to go on the grill, too. I was pleased as punch. I volunteered to cook some crookneck squash.

The house felt happier. And safer.

While we ate, Amelia told us funny stories about working in the Genuine Magic Shop, and Bob unbent enough to imitate some of his odder colleagues in the unisex hair salon where he worked. The hairdresser Bob replaced had become so discouraged by the complications of life in post-Katrina New Orleans that she'd loaded up her car and left for Miami. Bob had gotten the job by being the first qualified person to walk in the door after the previous one had walked out. In answer to my question about whether that had been sheer coincidence, Bob just smiled. Every now and then, I saw a flash of what fascinated Amelia about Bob, who otherwise looked like a skinny, rough-haired encyclopedia salesman. I told him about Immanuel and my emergency haircut, and he said Immanuel had done a wonderful job.

"So, the work on the wards is all done?" I asked anxiously, trying to sound casual about the change of topic.

"You bet," Amelia said, looking proud. She cut another bite of steak. "They're even better now. A dragon couldn't get through 'em. No one who means you harm will make it."

"So if a dragon was friendly . . ." I said, half teasing, and she swatted me with her fork.

"No such thing, the way I hear tell,"

Amelia said. "Of course, I've never seen one."

"Of course." I didn't know whether to feel curious or relieved.

Bob said, "Amelia's got a surprise for you."

"Oh?" I tried to sound more relaxed than I felt.

"I found the cure," she said, half-proudly and half-shyly. "I mean, you did ask me to when I left. I kept looking for a way to break the blood bond. I found it."

"How?" I scrambled to conceal how flustered I was.

"First I asked Octavia. She didn't know, because she doesn't specialize in vampire magic, but she e-mailed a couple of her older friends in other covens, and they scouted around. It all took time, and there were some dead ends, but eventually I came up with a spell that doesn't end in the death of one of the . . . bondees."

"I'm stunned," I said, which was the absolute truth.

"Shall I cast it tonight?"

"You mean . . . right now?"

"Yes, after supper." Amelia looked slightly less happy because she wasn't getting the response she'd anticipated. Bob was looking from Amelia to me, and he, too, looked doubtful. He'd assumed I'd be both delighted and effusive, and that wasn't the reaction he was seeing.

"I don't know." I put my fork down. "It wouldn't hurt Eric?"

"As if anything can hurt a vampire that old," she said. "Honestly, Sook, why you're worrying about him . . ."

"I love him," I said. They both stared at me.

"For real?" Amelia said in a small voice.

"I told you that before you left, Amelia."

"I guess I just didn't want to believe you. You sure you'll feel that way when the bond is dissolved?"

"That's what I want to find out."

She nodded. "You need to know. And you need to be free of him."

The sun had just set, and I could feel Eric rising. His presence was with me like a shadow: familiar, irritating, reassuring, intrusive. All those things at once.

"If you're ready, do it now," I said. "Before I lose all courage."

"This is actually a good time of day to do it," she said. "Sunset. End of the day. Endings, in general. It makes sense." Amelia hurried to the bedroom. She returned in a couple of minutes with an envelope and three little jars: jelly jars in a chrome rack, like the kind a waitress in a diner puts on the table at breakfast. The jars were half-full of a mixture of herbs. Amelia was now wearing an apron. I could see that there were objects in one of the pockets.

"All right," she said, and handed the envelope to Bob, who extracted the paper and scanned it quickly, a frown on his narrow face.

"Out in the yard," he suggested, and we three left the kitchen, crossed the back porch, and went down into the yard, smelling the steak all over again as we passed my old grill. Amelia positioned me in one spot, Bob in another, and then positioned the jelly jars, too. Bob and I each had one on the ground behind us, and there was one at the spot where she would stand. We'd form a triangle. I didn't ask any questions. I probably wouldn't have believed the answers, anyway.

She gave me a book of matches and handed one to Bob, too. She kept a third for herself. "When I tell you, set fire to your herbs. Then walk counterclockwise around your jar three times," she said. "Stop at your station again after the third time. Then we'll say some words — Bob, you got 'em in your head? Sookie'll need the paper."

Bob looked at the words again, nodded,

and passed me the paper. I could just read the script by the security light, because the evening was closing in fast now that the sun was down.

"Ready?" Amelia asked sharply. She looked older and colder in the twilight.

I nodded, wondering if I was being truthful.

Bob said, "Yes."

"Then turn and light your fire," Amelia said, and like a robot I did as I was told. I was scared to death, and I wasn't sure why. This was what I needed to do. My match struck and I dropped it in the jelly jar. The herbs flared up with a sharp smell, and then we three were upright again and moving counterclockwise.

Was this a bad thing for a Christian to be doing? Probably. On the other hand, it had never occurred to me to ask the Methodist minister if he had a ritual in place to sever a blood bond between a woman and a vampire.

And when we'd been around three times and stopped again, Amelia pulled a ball of red yarn from her apron. She held one end and passed the ball to Bob. He measured out some and took hold and then passed the ball to me. I did the same and returned the ball to Amelia, because that seemed to be the program. I held the yarn with one hand and gripped the paper with the other. This was busier than I had counted on. Amelia also had a pair of shears, and she extracted those from a pocket, too.

Amelia, who had been chanting the whole time, pointed at me and then at Bob, to indicate that we should join in. I peered down at the paper, picked my way through the words that made no sense to me, and then it was over.

We stood in silence, and the little flames in the jars died out, and the night had set in hard.

"Cut," Amelia said, handing me the shears. "And mean it."

Feeling a little ridiculous and a lot scared, but sure that I needed to do this, I snipped the red yarn.

And I lost Eric.

He wasn't there.

Amelia rolled up the cut yarn and handed it to me. To my surprise, she was smiling; she looked fierce and triumphant. I took the length of yarn automatically from her hand, all my senses stretching out to seek Eric. Nothing.

I felt a rush of panic. It wasn't entirely pure: There was some relief mixed in, which I had expected. And there was grief. As soon as I was sure he was okay, that he hadn't been hurt, I knew I would relax and feel the full measure of the success of the spell.

In the house, my phone rang, and I sprinted for the back door.

"Are you there?" he said. "Are you there, are you all right?"

"Eric," I said, my breath coming out in a great ripping sigh. "Oh, I'm so glad you're all right! You are, aren't you?"

"What have you done?"

"Amelia found a way to break the bond."

There was a long silence. Before, I would have known if Eric was anxious, furious, or thoughtful. Now, I couldn't imagine. Finally, he spoke.

"Sookie, the marriage gives you some protection, but the bond is what is important."

"What?"

"You heard me. I am so angry with you." He really meant it.

"Come here," I said.

"No. If I see Amelia, I'll break her neck." He meant that, too. "She's always wanted you to get rid of me."

"But . . ." I began, not knowing how to end the sentence.

"I'll see you when I've got control of myself," he said. And he hung up.

CHAPTER 9

I should have foreseen this, I told myself for the tenth, or twentieth, time. I'd rushed into something that I should have prepared for. At the least, I should have called Eric and warned him what was about to happen. But I'd been afraid he'd talk me out of it, and I had to know what my true feeling for him was.

Just at the moment, Eric's true feeling for me was anger. He was mighty pissed off. On the one hand, I didn't blame him. We were supposed to be in love, and that meant we were supposed to consult one another, right? On the other hand, I could count the times Eric had consulted me without even using up all my fingers. On one of my hands. So at other moments, I did blame him for his reaction. Of course he wouldn't have let me do it, and I would never have known something I had to know.

So I was hopping from foot to foot mentally when it came to deciding whether I'd done the right thing.

But I was upset and worried pretty much nonstop, no matter which foot I was standing on at the moment.

Bob and Amelia had a consultation in their bedroom, as a result of which they decided to stay another day to "see what happens." I could tell Amelia was worried. She thought she ought to have eased into the idea a little more slowly before encouraging me to take the plunge. Bob thought we were both being silly, but he was smart enough not to say so. However, he couldn't help but think it, and though he wasn't as clear a broadcaster as Amelia, I could hear him.

I did go to work the next day, but I was so distracted and miserable, and business was so light, that Sam told me to go home early. India kindly patted me on the shoulder and told me to take it easy, a concept I had a lot of trouble understanding.

That night, Eric came an hour after sundown. He drove up, so we'd have warning. I'd hoped he would come, and I'd been pretty sure he would have cooled off enough. Right after supper, I'd asked Amelia and Bob if they'd like to go to a movie in Clarice.

"You sure you'll be all right?" Amelia had asked. "Because we're ready to stay with you if you think he's still angry." If she'd been pleased before, it had vanished now.

"I don't know how he feels," I said, and I was still a little giddy at the thought. "But I do think he'll come tonight. It'd probably go better if he didn't have you here to make him madder."

Bob had bristled a little at that, but Amelia had nodded understandingly. "I hope you still think of me as your friend," she said, and for once I didn't see her thoughts coming. "I mean, I think I've screwed you up, but that wasn't my intention. I intended to free you."

"I understand, and I still think of you as one of my best friends," I said as reassuringly as I could manage. If I was weak-willed enough to go along with Amelia's impulses, then it was my problem.

I was sitting alone on my front porch in that gloomy kind of mood where you remember all of your mistakes and none of your good decisions when I saw the headlights of Eric's car zooming up the driveway.

I didn't expect that he would hesitate when he got out of the car.

"Are you still mad?" I said, trying not to cry. Weeping would be craven, and I was

274

forcing some steel into my backbone.

"Do you still love me?" he asked.

"You first." Childish.

"I'm not angry," he said. "At least, not anymore. At least, not right now. I should have encouraged you to find a way to break the bond, and in fact we have a ritual for it. I should have offered it to you. I was afraid that without it we would be parted, whether because you didn't want to be dragged into my troubles or because Victor found out you were vulnerable. If he chooses to ignore the marriage, without the bond I won't know that you are in danger."

"I should have asked you what you thought, or at least warned you what we were going to do," I said. I took a deep breath. "I do love you, all on my own."

And he was up on the porch with me, and then he was picking me up and kissing me, my lips, my neck, my shoulders. He held my feet off the ground and lifted me high enough that his mouth could find my breasts through my bra and T-shirt.

I gave a little shriek and swung my legs until they latched around him. I rubbed against him as hard as I could. Eric loved monkey sex.

He said, "I'm going to tear your clothes."

"Okay."

And he was as good as his word.

After an exciting few minutes, he said, "I'm tearing mine, too."

"Sure," I mumbled, before I bit his earlobe. He growled. There was nothing civilized about sex with Eric.

I heard more ripping, and then there was nothing at all between me and him. He was inside me, deep inside me, and he staggered backward to land on the porch swing, which began rocking back and forth erratically. After a moment of surprise we began working with its motion. It went on and on until I could feel the increased tension, the almost-there feeling of impending release.

"Go *hard*," I said urgently. "Go go go . . ."

"Is . . . this . . . hard . . . enough?"

And I shrieked out loud, my head falling back.

"Come on, Eric," I said, when my aftershocks were still rippling through me. "Come *on!*" And I moved faster than I'd imagined I was able.

"Sookie!" he gasped, and gave me one last huge thrust followed by a sound that I might have thought was primal pain if I hadn't known much better.

It was magnificent, it was exhausting, and it was completely excellent.

We stayed on the swing for at least thirty

minutes, recovering, cooling off, and holding each other. I was so happy and relaxed I didn't want to move, but of course I needed to go inside to clean myself up and to put on some clothes that didn't have the seams ripped out. Eric had only popped the button off his jeans, and he could hold them closed with his belt, which he'd managed to unbuckle before we'd gotten to the tearing stage. His zipper was still workable.

While I arranged myself, he heated up some blood and fixed an ice pack and a glass of iced tea for me. He applied the ice pack himself while I lay on the couch. I thought, *I was right to break the bond.* And it was a relief not to know how Eric was feeling, though simultaneously I was afraid there was something wrong about my relief.

For a few minutes, we talked about little things. He brushed my hair, which was in a terrible tangle, and I brushed his. (Monkeys searched each other for salt crystals, I believed. We groomed each other.) When I'd made his hair all smooth and shiny he draped my legs over his lap. His hand ran up and down them, from the hem of my shorts to my toes, over and over.

"Has Victor said anything to you?" I wasn't looking forward to reopening the conversation about what I'd done, though we'd opened our meeting with a bang.

"Not about the bond, so he doesn't know yet. He would have been on the phone instantly." Eric leaned his head against the back of the couch, his blue eyes at half mast. Postcoital relaxation.

That was a relief. "How's Miriam? Did she recover?"

"She recovered from the drugs Victor gave her, but she's sicker in body. Pam is as close to despair as I've ever seen her."

"Did their relationship come on kind of slowly? Because I didn't have a clue until Immanuel told me about it."

"Pam doesn't often care for anyone as much she cares about Miriam," he said. His head turned slowly, and his eyes met mine. "I only found out when she asked for some time off from the club to visit Miriam in the hospital. And she gave the girl blood, too, which is the only reason Miriam's lasted this long."

"Vampire blood can't cure her?"

"Our blood is good for healing open wounds," Eric said. "For illnesses, it can offer relief, but seldom a cure."

"I wonder why?"

Eric shrugged. "I'm sure one of your scientists would have a theory, but I don't. And since some people go crazy when they take our blood, the risk is considerable. I was happier when the properties of our blood were secret, but I suppose that couldn't be kept quiet for long. Victor certainly isn't concerned about Miriam's survival or the fact that Pam has never asked to create a child before. After all these years of service, Pam deserves to be granted the right."

"Victor's not letting Pam have Miriam out of sheer cussedness?"

Eric nodded. "He has a bullshit excuse about there being enough vampires in my sheriffdom, when actually my numbers are low. The truth is that Victor will block us any way he can for as long as he can, in the hope that I'll do something injudicious enough to warrant being removed as sheriff, or killed."

"Surely Felipe wouldn't let that happen."

Eric hoisted me onto his lap and held me to his cool chest. His shirt was still open. "Felipe would judge in Pam's favor if he were on the spot, but I'm sure he wants to stay out of the situation if he can. It's what I'd do. He's setting up Red Rita in Arkansas and she's never ruled, he knows Victor is sulking about being appointed regent rather than king in Louisiana, and he is busy himself in Las Vegas, which he's running on a skeleton crew since he's sent people out to both his new states. Consolidating this big an empire hasn't been done in hundreds of years — and the last time it was done, the population was only a fraction of what it is today."

"So Felipe's still in complete control of Nevada?"

"Yes. For now."

"That sounds kind of ominous."

"When leaders are spread thin, the sharks gather round to see if they can take a bite."

Unpleasant mental image.

"What sharks? Anyone we know?"

Eric looked away. "Two other monarchs in Zeus. The Queen of Oklahoma, for one. And the King of Arizona." The vampires had split America into four territories, all named after ancient religions. Pretentious, huh? I lived in Amun Territory in the kingdom of Louisiana.

"I wish you were just an average vampire," I said, completely out of the blue. "I wish you weren't a sheriff, or anything."

"You mean you wish I were like Bill."

Ouch. "No, because he's not average, either," I snapped. "He's got the whole database thing going, and he's taught himself all about computers. He's sort of reinvented himself. I guess I mean I wish

280

you were more like . . . Maxwell."

Maxwell was a businessman. He wore suits. He turned up for his duty at the club without enthusiasm, and he flashed his fangs without the drama the tourists had come to see. He was boring, and he had a stick up his ass, though from time to time I'd had a hint that his personal life was exotic. However, not interested in learning more about *that.*

Eric rolled his eyes at me. "Of course, I'm so much like Maxwell. Let me start carrying a pocket calculator with me, and putting people to sleep with things like 'variable annuities,' or whatever the hell it is he talks about."

"I get your point, Mr. Subtle," I said. The ice pack had done all the good it was going to, and I removed it from my yahoo palace and put it on the table.

This was the most relaxed conversation we'd had in forever.

"See, isn't this fun?" I said, trying to get Eric to admit I'd done the right thing, though I'd gone about it wrong.

"Yes, so much fun. Until Victor snatches you up and drains you dry and then says, 'But, Eric, she was no longer bonded to you, so I did not think you still wanted her!' And then he'll turn you against your will, and

I'll have to watch you suffer being bound to him for the rest of your life. And mine."

"You really know how to make a girl feel special," I said.

"I love you," he said, as if he were reminding himself of a painful fact. "And this situation with Pam has to end. If this girl Miriam dies, Pam may decide to leave, and I won't be able to stop her. In fact, I shouldn't. Though she's very useful."

"You're fond of her," I said. "Come on, Eric. You love her. She's your kid."

"Yes, I am very fond of Pam," he said. "I made a great choice. You were my other great choice."

"That's one of the nicest things anyone's ever said to me," I told him, choking up just a little.

"Don't cry!" He waved his hands in front of him as if to ward off my tears.

I swallowed hard. "So, do you have a plan about Victor?" I used Eric's shirttail to dab at my eyes.

Eric looked grim. Well, grimmer. "Every time I make one, I run up against an obstacle so large I have to discard the plan. Victor is very good at self-protection. I may have to openly attack him. If I kill him, if I win, then I'll have to stand trial."

I shivered. "Eric, if you fought with Victor

alone, bare-handed, in an empty room, what do you think the outcome would be?"

"He's very good," Eric said. And that was all he said.

"He might win?" I said, testing the idea out loud.

"Yes," Eric said. He met my eyes. "And what would happen to you and Pam afterward . . ."

"I'm not trying to bypass the fact that you would be dead, which would be the most important thing to me in that scenario," I said. "But I'm wondering why he would be so sure to hurt Pam and me afterward. What would be the point?"

"The point would be the lesson he'd be making to other vampires who might be thinking of trying to overthrow him." Eric's eyes focused on the mantelpiece, crowded with Stackhouse family pictures. He didn't want to look into my face when he said what he was going to tell me next. "Heidi told me that two years ago, when Victor was still a sheriff in Nevada, in Reno . . . a new vampire named Chico talked back to him. Chico's father was dead, but his mother was still living, and in fact had married again and had other children. Victor had her abducted. To correct Chico's manners, he cut out the mother's tongue while Chico watched. He made Chico eat it."

There was so much disturbing about that, that I had a hard time thinking it through. "Vampires can't eat," I said. "What . . . ?"

"Chico was violently ill, and in fact threw up blood," Eric said. He still didn't meet my eyes. "He became too weak to move. While he lay on the floor, his mother bled to death. He couldn't crawl to her to give her blood to save her."

"Heidi volunteered this story?"

"Yes. I had asked her why she was so pleased she'd been sent to Area Five."

Heidi, a vamp who specialized in tracking, had become part of Eric's crew courtesy of Victor. Of course she was supposed to spy on Eric, and because that was not a secret, no one seemed to mind. I didn't know Heidi well, but I knew she had a living child, a drug addict in Reno, so I wasn't at all surprised that she'd taken Victor's lesson to heart. Learning this would indeed cause any vampire with living relatives, or any human loved ones, to fear Victor. But they'd also loathe him and want him dead — and this was the aspect Victor hadn't thought of, I guessed, when he'd taught that lesson.

"Victor's either shortsighted or super

cocky," I concluded out loud, and Eric nodded.

"Maybe both," he said.

"How'd you feel when you heard that story?" I asked.

"I . . . didn't want that to happen to you," he said. He gave me a puzzled face. "What are you looking for, Sookie? What answer shall I give?"

Though I knew it was futile — knew I was barking up the wrong tree — I was looking for moral repugnance. I was looking for "I would *never* be so cruel to a woman and her son."

At the same time I was wanting a thousand-year-old vampire to be upset about the death of a human woman he hadn't known — a death he couldn't have prevented — I knew it was crazy, wrong, and bad that I myself was plotting to kill Victor. His complete absence was what I longed for. I had no doubt that if Pam called to say a safe had fallen on top of Victor, I would dance around with glee.

"That's okay," I said. "Never mind."

Eric gave me a dark look. He couldn't see the depth of my unhappiness — not now, not since the bond was severed. But he certainly knew me well enough to see that I wasn't content. I forced myself to address the problem at hand. "You know who you should talk to," I said. "Remember the night we went to Vampire's Kiss, that server who tipped me off about the fairy blood by just a look and a thought."

Eric nodded.

"I hate to pull him in any further. But I don't see we have another choice. We have to do this with everything we've got, or we're going down."

"Sometimes," Eric said, "you astonish me."

Sometimes — and not always in a good way — I astonished myself.

Eric and I drove to Vampire's Kiss again. The parking lot was crowded, maybe not as much as it had been on our previous visit. We parked out back behind the club. If Victor was actually in the club that night, there'd be no reason for him to check out the employee parking lot, and there'd be no reason for him to remember which car was mine. While we waited, I got a text from Amelia telling me that they were back at the house, and how was I doing?

"Am ok," I texted back. "We're good. C & D there?"

"Yes," she replied. "Sniffing porch, don't know why. Fairies! Got ur keys?"

I told her I did, but that I wasn't sure I'd

be home that night. We were a little closer to Shreveport than Bon Temps, and I'd need to take Eric home unless he flew. But his car would be . . . Oh, well, that was why he always had a daytime guy.

"Did you replace Bobby yet?" I asked. I hated to bring up a sore subject, but I wanted to know.

"Yes," Eric said. "I hired a man two days ago. He came highly recommended."

"By whom?"

There was a silence. I looked over at my honeybun, instantly curious. For the life of me, I couldn't see why that was a critical question.

"By Bubba," Eric said.

I could feel the smile all over my face. "He's back! Where's he staying?"

"Right now, he's staying with me," Eric said. "When he asked after Bobby, I had to tell him what had happened. The next night Bubba brought me this person. He's teachable, I suppose."

"You don't sound too enthusiastic."

"He's a Were," Eric said, and I instantly understood Eric's attitude. The Weres and the vampires really don't get along. You'd think that as the two largest supernatural groups they could form an alliance, but that doesn't happen. They're capable of cooperating on some mutually beneficial project for a short period of time, but after that they revert to distrust and dislike.

"Tell me about him," I said. "Your assistant, that is." We didn't have anything else to do, and lately we hadn't had much time for general conversation.

"He's a black man," Eric said, as if he were saying the new assistant had brown eyes. Eric could remember, vividly, the first black man he ever saw . . . centuries before. "He's a lone wolf, unaffiliated. Alcide has already made overtures to him about joining the Long Tooth pack, but I don't think he's interested, and of course now that he's taken the job with me, they won't be so anxious to have him."

"And this is the guy you hired? A Were, whom you don't trust and have to train? A guy who'll automatically piss off Alcide and the Long Tooth pack?"

"He has an outstanding attribute," Eric said.

"Good! What is it?"

"He can keep his mouth shut. And he hates Victor," Eric said.

That made it a whole different shooting match. "Why?" I asked. "I'm assuming he has a good reason."

"I don't know what it is yet."

"But you're convinced he's not pulling some elaborate double whammy? That Victor didn't cleverly realize you'd hire someone who hated him, so he primed this guy and shot him over to you?"

"I'm convinced," Eric said. "But I want you to sit with him a while tomorrow."

"If I can get some sleep," I said, yawning wide enough for my jaws to be in danger of cracking. It was after two in the morning, and we'd seen signs the bar was closing, but many of the employee cars were still waiting for their owners. "Oh, Eric, there he is!" I hardly recognized the server named Colton because he was wearing long khaki cargo shorts, flip-flops, and a green T-shirt with a pattern I couldn't discern. I kind of missed the loincloth. I started my car after Colton did, and when he pulled out of the parking lot, I waited a discreet moment and followed him. He turned right onto the access road and drove west toward Shreveport. However, he didn't go that far. He exited the interstate at Haughton.

"We're looking pretty damn conspicuous," I said.

"We need to talk to him."

"So, we're giving up on stealth, huh?"

Eric said, "Yes." He didn't sound happy

about it, but we didn't have that many choices.

Colton's car, a Dodge Charger that had seen better days, turned into a narrow drive off a narrow road. He stopped in front of a good-sized trailer. He got out and stood by the car. His hand was down by his side, and I was pretty sure in that hand was a gun.

"Let me get out first," I said, as I pulled up beside the man.

Before Eric could argue, I opened my car door and called, "Colton! It's Sookie Stackhouse. You know who I am! I'm standing up now, and I'm not armed."

"Go slow." His voice was wary, and I couldn't blame him.

"Just so you know, Eric Northman is with me, but he's still in the car."

"Good."

My hands reaching for the sky, I stepped away from the car so he could have a good look at me. The front porch light of the trailer was all he had to see by, but he gave me a thorough scan. While he was trying to pat me down with his eyes, the trailer door opened and a young woman stepped out on the added-on porch.

"Colton, what's going on?" she asked in a nasal voice with a very "country" accent.

"We got some company. Don't worry

about it," he said automatically.

"Who's she?"

"The Stackhouse woman."

"Sookie?" The voice sounded startled.

"Yeah," I said. "Do I know you? I can't see you that well."

"It's Audrina Loomis," she said. "You remember? I went out with your brother for a while in high school."

So did half the girls in Bon Temps, so that didn't really narrow my memory down. "It's been a while," I said carefully.

"He still single?"

"Yeah," I said. "Oh, by the way, can my boyfriend get out now?" Since we were all being just folks here.

"Who's he?"

"His name's Eric; he's a vampire."

"Cool. Sure, let's have a look." Audrina seemed to be a little more reckless than Colton. On the other hand, Colton had warned me about the fairy blood.

Eric got out of my car, and there was a moment of impressed silence while Audrina absorbed Eric's magnificence.

"Well, *okay*," Audrina said, clearing her throat as though it had gone suddenly dry. "You two wanna come in and let us know what you're doing here?"

"You think that's smart?" Colton asked her.

"Hc coulda killed us about six times already." Audrina was not as dumb as she sounded.

When we were all in the trailer and Eric and I were sitting on the couch, which had been covered with an old chenille bedspread and was missing several crucial springs, I got a good look at Audrina. Her roots were dark. The rest of her shoulder-length hair was platinum blond. She was wearing a nightgown that hadn't really been designed for sleeping in. It was red and mostly sheer. She'd been waiting up for Colton with more on her mind than conversation.

Now that I wasn't distracted by a leather loincloth and his startling eyes, Colton was much more of an average guy. Some men just can't radiate sexual attraction unless they take their clothes off, and Colton was such a man. But his eyes were definitely unusual, and he was practically giving me a laser treatment with them now, though not in a sexy way.

"We don't have any blood," Audrina said. "Sorry." She didn't offer me anything to drink. She was doing this on purpose, her brain told me. She didn't want this to seem in any way like a social occasion.

Okay. "Eric and I want to know why you warned us," I said to Colton. And I wanted to know why I'd thought about him when Eric had told me the story of Chico and his mother.

"I heard about you," he said. "Heidi told me."

"You and Heidi are friends?" Eric was intent on Colton, but he spared one of his best smiles for Audrina.

"Yeah," Colton said. "I worked for Felipe at a club in Reno. I knew Heidi from there."

"You moved from Reno to take a low-paying job in Louisiana?" That didn't make any sense.

"Audrina was from here, and she wanted to try living here again," Colton explained. "Her grandma lives in the trailer down the road, and she's pretty frail. Audrina works at Vic's Redneck Roadhouse during the day as a bookkeeper. I work at night at Vampire's Kiss. And the cost of living is a lot cheaper here. But you're right, there's more to the story." He glanced at his girlfriend.

"We came for a reason," Audrina said. "Colton is Chico's brother."

Eric and I both took a second to work that out. "So it was your mom," I said to the young man. "I'm so sorry." Though I hadn't heard any more of the story, the name had been enough to snag in my brain.

"Yeah, it was my mom," Colton said. He gave us an entirely blank stare. "My brother Chico is an asshole who didn't think twice about becoming a vampire. He gave up his life like some lesser asshole would get a tattoo. 'It's cool, let's do it!' And then he kept on being an asshole, talking shit to Victor, not understanding. *Not getting it.*" Colton put his head in his hands and shook it from side to side. "Until that night. Then he got it. But our mom was dead. And Chico wishes he was, but he won't ever be."

"And how come Victor doesn't know who you are, know to be leery of you?"

"Chico had a different dad, so he had a different last name," Audrina said, to give Colton time to recover. "And Chico wasn't a family type guy. He hadn't lived at home for ten years. He only called his mom once every couple of months, never went to see them. But that was enough to give Victor the bright idea of reminding Chico he hadn't signed a contract with the California Angels."

"More like Hell's Angels," Colton said, straightening.

If the comparison bothered Eric, he didn't let on. I was sure it wasn't the worst he'd heard. "So thanks to Victor's employee,"

Eric began, "you knew about my Sookie. And you knew how to warn her when Victor was going to poison us."

Colton looked angry. *Shouldn't have,* he thought.

"Yes, you did what you ought to do," I said, maybe a little huffily. "We're people, too."

"You are," Eric said, reading Colton's expression as accurately as I read his thoughts. "But Pam and I aren't. Colton, I want to thank you for your warning, and I want to reward you. What can I do for you?"

"You can kill Victor," Colton said immediately.

"How interesting. That's exactly what I want to do," Eric said.

CHAPTER 10

As dramatic statements go, Eric's had a high impact. Both Audrina and Colton tensed up. But I'd ridden this pony before.

I puffed out my cheeks in exasperation and looked away.

"You're bored, my lover?" Eric asked, in a voice that could have taught icicles something about chilly.

"We've been saying that for months." That might have been a *slight* exaggeration, but not much. "All we've done is talk smack. If we're going to do something bad, let's go on and do it — not talk it to death! You think he doesn't know he's on our hit list? You think he's not waiting for us to try?" (Apparently, this was a speech I'd kept secret even from myself, for way too long.) "You think he's not doing all this shit to you and Pam to provoke you into something, so he'll be justified in smacking you down? This is a win-win situation for him!"

Eric looked at me as though I'd turned into a nanny goat. Audrina and Colton were openmouthed.

Eric started to say something, then closed his mouth. I had no idea if he was going to yell at me or walk out silently.

"So what's your solution?" he said, his voice quiet and steady. "Do you have a plan?"

"Let's meet with Pam tomorrow night," I said. "She should be in on this." Also, it would give me a time to think of something so that I wouldn't embarrass myself.

"All right," he said. "Colton, Audrina. Are you both sure you want to risk this?"

"Without a doubt," Colton said. "Audie, baby. You don't have to do this."

Audrina snorted. "Too late, buddy! Everyone at work knows we live together. If you rebel, I'm dead anyway. My only chance is to join in so we can do this thing right."

I like a practical woman. I looked at her outside and I looked at her inside. I came up with sincerity. However, I would've been naïve not to see that it would be extremely practical if Audrina went to Victor and turned us in. That would be the most practical course of all. "How do we know you won't be on the phone the minute we're out of the trailer?" I asked, deciding I might as

297

well be blunt.

"How do I know you won't do the same?" Audrina retorted. "Colton done you a good turn in letting you know about the fairy blood. He believed what Heidi said about you. And I guess you want to live through this as bad as we do."

" 'Survival' is my middle name. See you tomorrow night at my house," I said. I'd written directions down on an old grocery list. Since my house was isolated and warded, we'd at least have some warning if anyone was following Eric and Pam or Colton and Audrina.

It had been a very long night, and I was yawning hard enough to crack my jaw. I let Eric drive us to Shreveport, since we were closer to his house than mine. I was so sleepy (and sore) that another bout of sex was out of the question, unless Eric had suddenly developed an interest in necrophilia. He laughed when I said as much.

"No, I like you alive and warm and wiggling," he said, and kissed my neck in his favorite spot, the one that always made me shiver. "I think I could wake you up enough," he said. Confidence is attractive, but I still couldn't summon any energy. I yawned again, and he laughed. "I'm going to find Pam and bring her up to date. I should ask about her friend Miriam, too. In the morning, Sookie, go home when you get up. I'll leave a note for Mustapha about the car."

"Who?"

"My new daytime man's name is Mustapha Khan."

"Seriously?"

Eric nodded. "Plenty of attitude," he said. "Be advised."

" 'Kay. I think I'll stay in the upstairs bedroom since I have to get up," I said. I was standing in the doorway of the largest ground-level bedroom, the one Eric wanted me to move into. The one Eric used had formerly been a walk-out game room downstairs. Eric had gotten some builders to make the wall solid, and he had the protection of a very heavy door that double-locked to bar the stairs. It made me just a wee tad claustrophobic to spend the night in there, though I had done it a few times if I knew I could sleep late. The upstairs bedroom had shutters and heavy curtains installed to make it light-tight for visiting vampires, but I left the shutters open and that made the room tolerable.

After the catastrophic visit of Eric's maker, Appius, and his "son" Alexei, I'd imagined I could still see blood everywhere when I came to Eric's house; and I smelled it, too. But a decorator with a big budget had swapped the carpets and repainted. Now it was hard to tell anything violent had occurred, and the house had a sort of pecan pie smell. That homely fragrance was underlain with the faint dry scent of vampires, a smell not at all unpleasant.

I locked the bedroom door after Eric left (on the theory that *you never knew*) and had a quick shower. I kept a nightgown here, something nicer than my usual Tweety sleep shirt. I thought I heard Pam's voice in the living room as I relaxed on the excellent mattress. I groped around in the night table drawer, found my clock and my box of Kleenex, and placed them close to hand.

That was the last thing I remembered for a few hours. I dreamed about Eric and Pam and Amelia; they were in a house that was on fire, and I had to pull them out or they'd be consumed. Didn't need a shrink to figure out that one. I only questioned why I'd put Amelia in the house. If dreams were more true to life, Amelia would have started the fire herself by some strange accident.

I stumbled out of the house at eight in the morning, having had maybe five hours' sleep. It didn't feel like enough. I stopped at a Hardee's and got a sausage biscuit and a cup of coffee. My day got a little brighter after that. A little.

Aside from a brand-new pickup parked at the front by Eric's car, my house looked sleepy and normal in the warm morning light. It was a dazzlingly clear day. The flowers blooming around the front steps lifted their faces to the morning sunshine. I drove around back, wondering who was visiting and what bed they were in.

Amelia's car and Claude's car were in the graveled area at the back door, leaving just enough room for mine. I found it very strange to walk into my house when there were so many people there already. No one was stirring yet, somewhat to my relief. I started a pot of coffee and went into my room to change clothes.

There was someone in my bed.

"Excuse me?" I said.

Alcide Herveaux sat up. He was bare-chested. The rest of him I couldn't see under the sheet.

"This is pretty fucking weird," I said, riding a rising swell of anger. "Let's have an explanation."

Alcide dropped his slight smile, which was pretty much the wrong expression to be wearing if you're in my bed without asking me first. He looked serious and embarrassed, which was far more appropriate.

"You've broken the bond with Eric," the Shreveport packmaster said. "I've been wrong in my timing on every single occasion we could get together. This time I didn't want to miss my chance." His eyes steady, he waited for my reaction.

I collapsed onto the old flowered chair in the corner. I often toss my discarded clothes on it at night. Alcide had tossed his there, too. I hoped my rear end was mashing wrinkles in his shirt that would never come out.

"So who let you in?" I asked. He must have good intentions toward me or the wards wouldn't have let him in, or so Amelia had told me. But just at the moment I didn't care.

"Your cousin, the fairy. What does he do, exactly?"

"He's a stripper," I said, oversimplifying in the heat of the moment. I was not aware this would be big news until I saw Alcide's face. "So, what, you just decided to sack out here and seduce me when I walked in the door? Home from spending the night at my boyfriend's? After having sex with him that could go in the Guinness Book of Records?"

Oh, God, where had *that* come from?

Alcide was laughing now. He couldn't seem to help it. I relaxed, because as snarly as Were brains are, I could see that he was also laughing at himself.

"It didn't seem like a good idea to me, either," he said frankly. "But Jannalynn thought this would be like a shortcut, and we could draw you into the pack."

Huh. That explained a lot. "You did this on Jannalynn's advice? Jannalynn just wanted me to feel uncomfortable," I said.

"Seriously? What does she have against you? I mean, why would she want to do that? Especially when she must have realized that would mean making me uncomfortable, too."

Him being her boss and all, and pretty much the center of Jannalynn's universe. I understood what he meant, and I agreed with his assessment of Jannalynn. However, in my opinion Alcide wasn't uncomfortable *enough*. I was convinced that he hoped if he sat in my bed and looked rumpled and handsome, I might reconsider. But looking good wasn't all it took with me. I wondered when Alcide had turned into the kind of guy who thought it might.

"She's been dating Sam for a while," I said. "You know that, right? I went to a family wedding with Sam, and I think Jannalynn had expected to go."

"So Sam's not as crazy about Jannalynn as she is about him?"

I held out my hand and wobbled it to and fro. "He likes her a lot. But he's older and more cautious." Why were we sitting in my bedroom talking about this? "So, Alcide, do you think you could get dressed and go home now?" I glanced at my watch. Eric had left me a note to say that Mustapha Khan was supposed to be here at ten, just an hour from now. Since he was a lone wolf, he wouldn't want a meet 'n' greet with Alcide.

"I'd still be glad if you joined me," he said, and he sounded both sincere and self-mocking.

"It's always nice to be wanted. And you're plenty hunky, of course." I tried not to sound like I'd thrown that in as an afterthought. "But I'm going with Eric, bond or no bond. Plus, you went about trying to court me the completely wrong way, thanks to Jannalynn. Who told you we weren't bonded, anyway?"

Alcide slid out of bed and held out a hand for his clothes. I got up and handed them to him, keeping my eyes raised to his. He did have on underwear, kind of a monokini. Manakini? As he shrugged into his shirt, he said, "Your buddy Amelia. She and her boyfriend came into Hair of the Dog last night to have a drink. I was pretty sure I'd met her, so I started talking to them. When she heard my name, she already knew that you and I'd been friendly. She got pretty chatty."

Oversharing was one of Amelia's flaws. I began to have a darker suspicion. "Did Amelia know you were going to do this?" I asked, waving my hand toward the rumpled bed.

"I followed her and her boyfriend back here," Alcide said, which was not exactly a denial. "They consulted with your cousin — the stripper. Claude? He thought me waiting for you in here was a really great idea. In fact, I think he would've joined us for about fifty cents." Alcide paused in zipping up his jeans to raise an eyebrow.

I tried not to let my distaste show. "That Claude! What a kidder!" I said with a ferocious smile. I had never felt less amused. "Alcide, I think Jannalynn was having a big joke at my expense. I think Amelia needs to keep my business quiet, and I think Claude just wanted to see what would happen. He's like that. Besides, you got good-looking Were women hanging all over you, you big ole packmaster, you!" I punched him on a brawny shoulder playfully — more or less — and I saw him flinch just a little. Maybe I *was* stronger with my fairy kin around me.

Alcide said, "I'll drive back to Shreveport, then. But put me on your dance card, Sookie. I want a chance with you, still." He gave me a big white smile.

"Haven't found a shaman for your pack yet?"

He was buckling his belt and his fingers froze. "Do you think that's why I want you?"

"I think that might have something to do with it," I said, my voice dry. Having a pack shaman had gone out of style in modern times, but the Long Tooth pack was trying to find one. Alcide had induced me to take one of the drugs that shamans took to enhance their vision, and it had been both deeply creepy and weirdly empowering. I never wanted to do that again. I had liked it too much.

"We do need a shaman," Alcide admitted. "And you did a great job that night. Obviously you've got the aptitude for the job." Gullibility and poor judgment must be prerequisites. "But you're wrong if you think that's the only reason I'd like us to have a relationship."

"I'm glad to hear that, because otherwise I wouldn't think much of you," I said. This exchange completely slammed the door shut on my good nature. "Let me reemphasize that I don't like the way you went about this, and I'm not nuts about the way you've changed since you became packmaster."

Alcide was genuinely amazed. "I've *had* to change," he said. "I'm not sure what you mean."

"You're way too used to being king of everybody," I said. "But I'm not here to judge you or tell you that you ought to change because that's just *my* opinion. God knows, I've been through plenty of changes myself, and I'm sure some of them haven't done my character any good."

"You don't even like me." He sounded almost dismayed, but with an edge of incredulity that enforced my feeling.

"Not so much anymore."

"Then I've made a fool of myself." Now he was a little angry. Well, join the club.

"An ambush is not the way to my heart. Or any other part of me."

Alcide left without another word. He hadn't been listening until I'd said the same thing in several different ways. Maybe that was key? Saying things three times?

I watched his truck on its way back out to the road to be sure he was really gone. I looked at my watch again. Not yet nine thirty. I changed the sheets on my bed with lightning speed, stuffing the removed bedding into the washing machine and starting it. (I could not imagine Eric's reaction if he climbed into bed with me and found it smelling like Alcide Herveaux.) I opted to use my remaining minutes before Mustapha Khan arrived to do some much-needed grooming rather than wake up Amelia or Claude and lay into them. As I brushed my hair and pulled it into a ponytail, I heard a motorcycle on the driveway.

Mustapha Khan, punctual lone werewolf. He had a small passenger clinging to him. I watched out the front window as he swung off the Harley and sauntered to the front door to knock. His companion stayed on the motorcycle.

I opened the door and looked up. Khan was about six feet tall with his head shaved close, leaving a mosslike burr. He was wearing dark glasses, trying for a "Blade" look, I figured. He was the golden brown of a chocolate chip cookie. When he took off the glasses, I saw that his eyes would be the actual dark chips. And that was the only thing remotely sweet about him. I took a deep breath, inhaled the smell of something wild. I heard my fairy kin come down the stairs behind me.

"Mr. Khan?" I said politely. "Please come in. I'm Sookie Stackhouse, and these two guys are Dermot and Claude." From Claude's avid expression, I was not the only one who'd thought of chocolate chip cookies. Dermot only looked wary.

Mustapha Khan glanced at them and dismissed them, which showed he wasn't as bright as he might be. Or maybe he just didn't think they were pertinent to his errand.

"I'm here to get Eric's car," he said.

"Could you come in for a minute? I made coffee."

"Oh, good," Dermot muttered, and headed for the kitchen. I heard him talking to someone and deduced that Amelia and/or Bob were staggering around. Good. I wanted a word with my buddy Amelia.

"I don't drink coffee," Mustapha said. "I don't take stimulants of any kind."

"Then would you like a glass of water?"

"No, I'd like to head back to Shreveport. I got a long list of things to do for Mr. High and Mighty Dead Guy."

"How come you took the job if you think so little of Eric?"

"He ain't bad, for a vamp," Mustapha said grudgingly. "Bubba's okay, too. The rest of 'em?" He spat. Subtle, but I got his drift.

"Who's your buddy?" I asked, tilting my head at the Harley.

"You want to know a lot," he said.

"Uh-huh." I stared right back at him, not backing down.

"Come here a minute, Warren," Mustapha called, and the small man hopped off the Harley and came over.

Warren proved to be about five foot seven, pale and freckled, and missing a few teeth. But when he took off his goggles, his eyes were clear and steady, and I didn't see any fang marks on his neck.

"Ma'am," he said politely.

I reintroduced myself. Interesting that Mustapha had a real friend, a friend he didn't want anyone (well, me) to know about. While Warren and I were exchanging comments on the weather, the muscular Were was having a hard time reining in his impatience. Claude drifted away, uninterested in Warren and losing hope of interesting Mustapha.

"Warren, how long have you been in Shreveport?"

"Oh my gosh, I been there all my life," Warren said. " 'Cept when I was in the army. Course, I was in the army fifteen years."

Easy to find out about Warren, but Eric

had wanted me to check out Mustapha. So far the Blade wannabe wasn't cooperating. Standing in the doorway was not a good way to have a relaxing conversation. Oh, well. "So you and Mustapha have known each other for a while?"

"Few months," Warren said, glancing at the taller man.

"Twenty Questions over?" Mustapha said.

I touched his arm, which was like touching an oak branch. "KeShawn Johnson," I said thoughtfully, after a little rummage in his head. "Why'd you change your name?"

He stiffened, and his mouth was grim. "I have reinvented myself," he said. "I am not the slave to a bad habit who was named Ke-Shawn. I am Mustapha Khan, and I am my own man. I own myself."

"Okeydokey," I said, doing my best to sound agreeable. "Nice to meet you, Mustapha. You and Warren have a safe trip back to Shreveport."

I'd learned as much as I was going to today. If Mustapha Khan was going to be around Eric for a while, I'd gradually catch enough glimpses into his head to piece him together. Oddly enough, I felt better about Mustapha after I'd met Warren. I was sure Warren had had some very hard times and maybe done some very hard things, but I

311

also thought at his core he was a reliable man. I suspected the same might be true of Mustapha.

I was willing to wait and see.

Bubba liked him, but that wasn't necessarily such a recommendation. After all, Bubba drank cat blood.

I turned away from the door, bracing myself to face my next set of problems. In the kitchen, I found Claude and Dermot cooking. Dermot had found a cylinder of Pillsbury biscuits in the refrigerator, and he'd mastered opening the can and putting them on a baking sheet. The oven had even preheated. Claude was cooking eggs, which was kind of amazing. Amelia was getting out plates and Bob was setting the table.

I hated to interrupt such a domestic scene.

"Amelia," I said. She'd been suspiciously focused on the plates. She looked up as sharply as if she'd heard me pump my shotgun. I met her eyes. Guilty, guilty, guilty. "Claude," I said even more sharply, and he glanced at me over his shoulder and smiled. No guilt there. Dermot and Bob simply looked resigned.

"Amelia, you told my business to a werewolf," I said. "Not just any werewolf, but the packmaster of Shreveport. And I'm sure you did that on purpose."

Amelia flushed red. "Sookie, I thought with the bond broken, maybe you'd want someone else to know about that, and you'd talked about Alcide, so when I met him, I thought . . ."

"You went there on purpose to make sure he knew," I said relentlessly. "Otherwise, why pick that bar out of all other bars?" Bob looked as though he were about to speak, and I raised my index finger and pointed it at him. He subsided. "You told me you were going to the movies in Clarice. Not to a werewolf bar in the opposite direction." Having finished with Amelia, I turned to the other culprit.

"Claude," I said again, and his back stiffened, though he kept on cooking eggs. "You let someone into the house, my house, without me here, and you gave him permission to get in my bed. That's inexcusable. Why would you do such a thing to me?"

Claude carefully moved the frying pan off the burner, turning it off as he did so. "He seemed like a nice guy," Claude said, "and I thought you might like to make love with something with a pulse for once."

I actually felt something snap inside me. "Okay," I said in a very level voice. "Listen up. I'm going to my room. You all eat the food you've cooked, then you pack up and leave. All of you." Amelia started crying, but I wasn't going to soften my stance. I was royally pissed off. I looked at the clock on the wall. "In forty-five minutes, I want this house empty."

I went in my room, shutting the door with exquisite quietness. I lay on my bed with a book and tried to read. After a few minutes there was a knock at the door. I ignored it. I had to be resolute. People staying in my home had done things they knew damn good and well they ought not to do, and they needed to know I wouldn't tolerate such interference, no matter how well intended (Amelia) or simply mischievous (Claude). I buried my face in my hands. It was hard to keep up this level of indignation, especially since I wasn't used to it — but I knew it would be very bad to give in to my craven impulse to throw open the door and allow them all to stay.

When I tried to imagine myself doing that, it felt so wrong and bad that I knew I genuinely wanted them out of the house.

I'd been so happy to see Amelia. I'd been so pleased that she was willing to rush up from New Orleans to do magical repairs on my protection. And I'd been so startled she'd actually found a way to break the bond that I'd let myself be rushed into actually doing it. I should have called Eric first, warned him. No excuse for doing it so brutally, except I'd been sure he'd talk me out of it. That was just as poorly done as letting myself be persuaded to take the shaman's drugs at Alcide's pack meeting.

Those two decisions were my fault. They were mistakes I had made.

But this impulse of Amelia's to try to manipulate my love life had been a bad one. I was an adult woman, and I had earned the right to make my own decisions about who I wanted to be with. I had wanted to remain Amelia's friend forever, but not if she was going to manipulate events in an attempt to try to turn my life into one she liked better.

And Claude had been playing a Claude sort of joke, a sly and naughty trick. I didn't like that, either. No, he needed to go.

When the forty-five minutes were up and I emerged from my room, I was a bit surprised to find that they'd actually done what I'd told them to. My houseguests were gone . . . except for Dermot.

My great-uncle was sitting on the back steps, his bulging sports bag beside him. He didn't try to draw attention to himself in any way, and I guess he'd have sat there until I opened the back door to leave for work if I hadn't happened to go out on the back porch to move the sheets from the washer to the dryer.

"Why are you here?" I asked in the most neutral voice I could summon.

"I'm sorry," he said, words that had been sorely lacking until now.

Though a knot inside me relaxed when he said those magic words, I wasn't totally won over. "Why'd you let Claude do that?" I said. I was holding the door open, obliging him to twist around to talk to me. He stood and turned to face me.

"I didn't think what he was doing was right. I didn't think you could want Alcide when you seem tied to the vampire, and I didn't think the outcome would be good for you or either of them. But Claude is willful and headstrong. I didn't have the necessary energy to argue with him."

"Why not?" It seemed like an obvious question to me, but it surprised Dermot. He looked away, over the flowers and bushes and lawn.

After a thoughtful pause my great-uncle said, "I haven't cared very much about anything since Niall enchanted me. Well, since you and Claude broke the enchantment, more accurately. I can't seem to achieve any sense of purpose, of what I want to be doing with the rest of my life. Claude has a purpose. Even if he didn't, I think he'd be content. Claude is very human in his nature." Then he looked appalled, perhaps realizing that in my clear-the-decks mood I might find his opinion a good reason to tell him to hit the road with the others.

"What's Claude's purpose?" I asked, because that seemed like a pretty interesting point. "Not that I don't want to talk more about you, I do, but I find the idea of Claude with an agenda pretty interesting." Not to say alarming.

"I've already betrayed one friend," he said. After a moment, I realized he meant me. "I don't want to betray another."

Now I was even more worried about Claude's plans. However, that issue would have to wait. "Why do you think you're feeling this inertia?" I said, returning to the topic at hand.

"Because I have no allegiance. Since Niall made sure I was put out of Faery . . . since I roamed around crazy for so long . . . I don't feel part of the sky clan, and the water clan wouldn't have me even though I allied with them. While I was cursed," he added hastily. "But I'm not a human, and I don't feel like one. I can't really pass for a man for more than a few minutes. The other fae

317

at Hooligans, the cluster of them . . . they're only united by chance." Dermot shook his golden head. Though his hair was longer than Jason's, shoulder length to cover up his ears, he'd never looked more like my brother. "I don't feel like a fairy anymore. I feel . . ."

"Like a stranger in a strange land," I said.

He shrugged. "Maybe so."

"You still want to work up in the attic?"

He exhaled a long slow breath. He looked at me sideways. "Yes, very much. Can I . . . just do that?"

I went into the house and got my car keys and my secret stash of money. Gran had been a great believer in keeping a secret stash. Mine had been hidden in the inner zip pocket of my weatherproof winter jacket at the back of my closet. "You can take my car to Home Depot in Clarice," I said. "Here. You can drive, can't you?"

"Oh, yes," he said, looking from the money to the keys eagerly. "Yes, I even have a driver's license."

"How'd you get that?" I asked, absolutely taken aback.

"I went to the government office one day while Claude was busy," he said. "I was able to make them think they were seeing the right papers. I had enough magic for that.

318

Answering the questions on the test was easy. I'd watched Claude, so taking the officer for a drive wasn't too difficult, either."

I wondered if a lot of drivers on the road had done the same thing. It would explain a lot. "Okay. Please be careful, Dermot. Ah, you know about money?"

"Yes, Claude's secretary taught me. I can count it. I know what the coins are, too."

Aren't you the big boy, I thought, but it would have been unkind to say. He really had adapted amazingly well for a driven-insane-by-magic fairy. "Okay," I said. "Have a good time, don't spend all my money, and be back in an hour, 'cause I got to go to work. Sam said I could come in late today, but I don't want to push it."

Dermot said, "You won't regret this, Niece." He opened the kitchen door to toss his gym bag into the house, leaped down the steps, and got in my car, looking at the dashboard carefully.

"I hope not," I said to myself as he buckled up and drove away (slowly, thank God). "I sincerely hope not."

My departed guests had not felt obliged to do the dishes. I couldn't say I was that surprised. I set to work and wiped down the counters afterward. The spotless kitchen made me feel I was making progress.

As I folded the sheets, warm from the dryer, I told myself I was doing okay. I wish I could say I didn't think about Amelia, feel sorry all over again, decide all over again that I'd done the right thing.

Dermot returned within an hour. He was as happy and animated as I'd ever seen him. I hadn't realized how depressed Dermot had been until I saw him actually lit up with purpose. He'd rented a sander and bought paint and plastic sheeting, blue tape and scrapers, brushes and rollers and a paint tray. I had to remind him he needed to eat something before he started work, and I also had to remind him that I needed to leave for work in the not-too-distant future.

Also, there was the summit meeting here at the house. "Dermot, is there any friend you can hang around with tonight?" I asked cautiously. "Eric, Pam, and two humans are coming over after I get off work. We're kind of a planning committee, and we have some work to do. You know how it is with you and vampires."

"I don't have to go anywhere with other people," Dermot said, surprised. "I can be in the woods. That's a happy place for me. The night sky is as good as the day sky, as far as I'm concerned."

I thought about Bubba. "It's possible Eric

may have stationed a vampire in the woods to watch the house at night," I explained. "So could you be in some other woods kind of away from here?" I felt awful about putting so many strictures on him, but he was the one who'd wanted to stay.

"I suppose so," he said, in the voice of one trying hard to be tolerant and helpful. "I love this house," he added. "There's something amazingly homelike about it."

And seeing him smile as he looked around the old place, I was more than ever sure that the unseen presence of the cluviel dor was the reason my two fairy kinsmen had come to stay with me, rather than my own little dash of fairy blood. I was willing to concede that Claude believed that my fairy blood was the attraction. Though I knew he had a mellower side, I was also sure that if he realized I held a valuable fairy artifact, one that could grant his most ardent wish — to be allowed passage into Faery — he'd tear the house apart looking for it. I felt instinctively that I would not like to stand between Claude and the cluviel dor. And though I sensed something warmer and more genuine in Dermot, I wasn't about to confide in him.

"I'm glad you're happy here," I said to my great-uncle. "And good luck with the attic project." I didn't actually need another bedroom up there now that Claude was gone, but I'd made a snap decision to keep Dermot on task. "If you'll excuse me, I'll go get ready for work. You can sand away on the floor." He'd told me that would be his starting point. I had no idea if that was the right order or not, but I was content to leave it to him. After all, considering the state of the attic before he and Claude had helped me clean it out, any work he did would be an improvement. I did check to make sure Dermot had a face mask to wear while he used the sander. I knew that much from home improvement shows.

Jason dropped by on his lunch break while I was putting on my makeup. I came out of my room to find him surveying all of Dermot's Home Depot loot. "What you doing?" he asked his near twin. Jason obviously had very mixed feelings about Dermot, but I'd observed that he was much more relaxed around our great-uncle when Claude wasn't there. Interesting. They clattered up the stairs together to look at the empty attic, Dermot talking all the way.

Though I was running seriously late, I fixed Jason and Dermot some sandwiches, putting the plate on the kitchen table with two glasses of ice and two Cokes while I hurried into my Merlotte's uniform. When I emerged, they were at the table having a lively conversation. I hadn't had enough sleep, I'd had to sweep my house clean of visitors, and I hadn't gotten very far with Mustapha or his buddy. But seeing Jason and Dermot chattering away about grout, spray painters, and weatherproof windows somehow made me feel that the world was on some kind of even keel.

CHAPTER 11

Because Merlotte's was almost empty, my lateness wasn't an issue. In fact, Sam was so preoccupied I wasn't sure he noticed. His abstraction made me feel a little better. I'd wondered if Jannalynn had spun Sam some kind of tale to cover her malice, in case I complained to him about her shoving another man into my bed. Sam didn't seem to have any idea that Jannalynn had done her best to embarrass me by advising her boss to play peek-a-boo with my bedsheets.

Though it was easy to be angry at Jannalynn because I didn't like her, when I thought about it, Alcide should have known better than to take such bad advice. If Alcide had been stupid for giving her idea credence, Jannalynn had been mean for thinking of it in the first place. I understood now that we were enemies. It was my day for unpleasant realizations.

Sam was absorbed in going over the

books. When I discerned from his thoughts that he was trying to figure out how he could manage to pay his bill with our beer distributor, I decided that today he had more problems than he could handle. He didn't need to hear that his girlfriend had embarrassed me.

The more I thought about it, the more I realized that this was between Jannalynn and me, no matter how tempted I might be to inform Sam about his girlfriend's true character. I felt like a smarter and better person after getting my head straight on that, and I hustled food and drinks with a smile and a pleasant word the whole shift. I had some good tip money in consequence.

I worked late to make up my time, and that was okay because Holly was late in turn. It was after six when I went into the office to fetch my purse. Sam was slumped at his desk, looking pretty bleak. "You need to talk about something?" I offered.

"With you? I figure you already know whatever I'm thinking about," he said, but not as if that bothered him. "The bar's in a slump, Sook. This is the worst patch I've ever been through."

I couldn't think of anything to say that wouldn't be completely stale or practically untrue. *Something always turns up. It always seems darkest before the dawn. When God closes a door, he opens a window. All things happen for a reason. Into every life a little rain must fall. What doesn't kill us makes us stronger.* In the end, I just bent and gave him a kiss on the cheek. "You call me if you need me," I said, and went out to the car feeling troubled. I put my subconscious to work on a plan to help Sam.

I loved summer, but sometimes I hated daylight saving time. Though I'd worked late and was going home, it was still glaring sunlight and would be for maybe another hour and a half. Even after darkfall, when Eric and Pam could come to the house, we'd still have to wait for Colton to get off work.

As I got into my car, I noticed there was a chance it would be dark earlier than usual. An ominous mass of dark clouds seethed to the west . . . really dark clouds, moving fast. The day would not end as beautifully and brightly as it had begun. I'd just been remembering my gran saying, "Into every life a little rain must fall." I wondered if I'd been prophetic.

I'm not scared of storms. Jason once had a dog that'd dashed upstairs to hide under Jason's bed every time he heard a crack of thunder. I smiled at the memory. My grandmother hadn't approved of dogs in the house, but she hadn't been able to keep Rocky out. He'd always found a way when the weather turned bad, though that way had less to do with the dog's cleverness than with Jason's soft heart. That was one good thing about my brother; he'd always been kind to animals. *And now he is one,* I thought. *At least once a month.* I didn't know what to think about that. While I'd been looking up at the sky, the clouds had been moving in closer, and I needed to get home and make sure my departed guests had left all the windows closed.

Despite my anxiety, after I looked at my gas gauge I realized I had to fill up the car. While the pump was working, I stepped out from under the awning at the Grabbit Kwik to look up. The sky was ominous, and I wondered if we were under a tornado watch. I wished I'd listened to the Weather Channel that morning.

The wind picked up, and bits of trash whipped across the parking lot. The air was so heavy and damp that the pavement smelled. When the gas pump cut off, I was glad to hang up the nozzle and climb in the car. I saw Tara going by, and she glanced my way and waved. I thought of her impending baby shower and her impending babies, with a little guilt. Though I had put everything in line for the shower, I hadn't thought about it all week, and it was only two days away! Surely I ought to be concentrating on the social event rather than a murder plot?

It was a moment when my life seemed . . . complex. A few drops of rain splashed on my windshield as I pulled out of the parking lot. I hoped I had enough milk for breakfast, because I sure hadn't checked before I left the house. Did I have some bottled blood to offer the vampires? Just in case, I stopped at the Piggly Wiggly and got some. Grabbed up some milk, too. And some bacon. I hadn't had a bacon sandwich in ages, and Terry Bellefleur had brought me some early fresh tomatoes.

I slung my plastic bags into the front seat of the car and dove in after them, because the rain abruptly slammed down in earnest. The back of my T-shirt was soaked, and my ponytail hung sodden on my neck. I reached in the backseat and pulled my umbrella into the front. It was an old one my gran had used to cover her head when she'd come to watch me playing softball, and when I looked at the faded stripes of black and green and cerise, I felt a smile on my face.

I drove home slowly and carefully. The

rain drummed on the car and bounced up from the pavement like tiny jackhammers. My headlights hardly seemed to make a dent in the rain and the gloom. I glanced at the dashboard clock. It was already after seven. Of course I had plenty of time before the Victor Murder Committee met, but it would be a relief just to get to the house. I considered the dash I'd have to make from the car to the house. If Dermot had gone out already, he would have left the door to the back porch locked. I'd be completely exposed to the rain while I fumbled with the keys and my two heavy bags of milk and blood. Not for the first or last time, I thought of spending my savings — the money from Claudine's estate and the lesser sum of Hadley's legacy (Remy hadn't called, so I had to assume he'd meant he truly didn't want her money) — in getting a carport attached to the house.

I was thinking of how I'd situate such a structure, and wondering how much it would take to build it, as I pulled up behind the house. Poor Dermot! By asking him to go out tonight I'd doomed him to a miserable, wet time in the woods. At least, I assumed he'd think it would be miserable. Fairies had a whole different scale than I did. I could lend him my car, and he could drive to Jason's, maybe.

I peered through the windshield, hoping I'd see a light on in the kitchen signaling Dermot's presence.

But the door to the back porch was hanging open over the steps. I couldn't see well enough through the gloom to tell if the house door was open, too.

My first reaction was indignation. *That's so careless of Dermot,* I thought. *Maybe I should have told him he had to leave, too.* But then I thought again. Dermot had never been so careless, and there was no reason to think he would be today. Instead of being irritated, maybe I should be worried.

Maybe I should listen to that alarm bell clanging away in my head.

You know what would be smart? Reversing the car and getting the hell out of here. I yanked my gaze away from that ominous open door. Galvanized, I threw the car into reverse and backed up. I put the car in drive and turned the wheel to rocket down the driveway.

From the woods a sizable young tree crashed down across the gravel, and I slammed on the brakes.

I knew a trap when I saw one.

I turned the car off and threw open my door. While I was scrambling out, a figure lurched from the trees and ran toward me. The only weapon to hand was the quart of milk in its plastic jug, and I grabbed the handles of the plastic bag and swung it high. To my amazement, I connected, and the jug burst, and milk went everywhere. Absurdly, I had a flash of fury at the waste, and then I was scrambling for the trees, my feet slipping on the wet grass. Thank God I'd worn sneakers. I ran for my life. He might be down, but he wouldn't stay down, and maybe there would be more than one. I was sure I'd caught a flicker of movement on the periphery of my vision.

I didn't know if the ambushers intended to kill me, but they weren't going to invite me to play Monopoly.

I was soaking wet within seconds from the rain and the water I knocked off the bushes as I blundered through the woods. If I lived through this, I swore, I'd start running at the high school track again, because my breath was sawing in and out of my lungs. The summer undergrowth was thick, and the vines snaked everywhere. I didn't fall, but it was only a matter of time.

I was trying hard to think — that would be a good thing — but I seemed to be possessed by a rabbit mentality. Run and hide, run and hide. If I was being abducted by

Weres, it was all over, because they could track me through the woods in a jiffy even if they were in human form, though the weather might slow them down.

Couldn't be vampires, the sun hadn't set.

Fairies would have been much more subtle.

Humans, then. I dashed around the edges of the cemetery, since I'd be so easy to spot on the open ground.

I heard noise in the woods behind me, and I headed for the only other sanctuary that might offer me a good hiding place. Bill's house. I didn't have enough time to climb a tree. It seemed I'd leaped out of my car an hour ago. My purse, my phone! Why hadn't I grabbed my phone? I could picture my purse sitting on the car seat. Crap.

Now I was running uphill, so I was close. I paused at the huge old oak, about ten yards from the front porch, and peered around it. There was Bill's house, dark and silent in the pouring rain. When Judith had been in residence, I'd left my copy of Bill's key in his mailbox one day. It had only seemed right. But that night he'd left a message on my answering machine telling me where the spare key was. We'd never said a word to each other about that.

I pelted up onto the porch, found the key

taped under the armrest of the wooden outdoor chair, and unlocked the front door. My hands were so tremulous it was amazing I didn't drop the key and that I got it into the lock correctly the first time. I was about to step in when I thought, *Footprints.* I'd leave wet footprints everywhere I went in the house. I'd advertise my location like a blue light Kmart special. Crouching down by the railing around the porch, I pulled off my clothes and shoes, and dropped them behind the thick azalea bushes surrounding the house. I squeezed out my ponytail. I shook myself briskly like a dog, to rid myself of as much water as I could. Then I stepped into the quiet dimness of the old Compton house. Though I didn't have time to mull it over, it felt decidedly weird to be standing in the foyer naked.

I looked down at my feet. One splash of water. I rubbed my foot over it and took a big step onto the worn runner lying in the hall that led back to the kitchen. I didn't even glance into the living room (which Bill sometimes called the parlor) or venture into the dining room.

Bill had never told me exactly where he slept during the day. I understood that such a piece of knowledge was a huge vampire secret. But I'm reasonably alert, and I'd had a while to figure it out while we were dating. Though I was sure there was more than one such secret place, one lay somewhere off the pantry in the kitchen. He'd remodeled the kitchen and installed a hot tub to create sort of a spa area rather than a place to cook — which he didn't need — but he'd left a small separate room intact. I didn't know if it had been a pantry or a butler's room. I opened the new louvered door and stepped in, shutting it behind me. Today the oddly high shelves contained only a few six-packs of bottled blood and a screwdriver. I knocked on the floor, on the wall. In my panic, and the noise of the storm outside, I couldn't detect any difference in the sound. I said, "Bill, let me in. Wherever you are, let me in," like a character in a grim ghost story.

I didn't hear a thing, naturally, though I listened for a few seconds in utter stillness. We hadn't shared blood in a long time, and it was still daylight, though it wouldn't be for long.

Crapola, I thought. Then I spied a thin line in the boards, right by the doorsill. I looked very carefully and realized the thin line continued around the sides. I didn't have the time to examine any closer. My heart thudding, out of sheer instinct and sheer desperation I dug the screwdriver into the line and levered up. There was a hole, and into it I dove, taking the screwdriver with me and closing the trap behind me. I realized the shelves must be set high to allow the door to swing up. I didn't know where the hinges were hidden and I didn't care.

For a long, long moment I just sat naked in a heap on the packed dirt and panted, trying to catch up with myself. I hadn't moved that fast, that long, since . . . since the last time I'd been running from someone who wanted to kill me.

I thought, *I've got to change my way of life.* It wasn't the first time I'd thought that, the first time I'd resolved to find a safer way to live.

It wasn't any occasion for deep thinking. It was time for praying that whoever it had been knocking trees down across my driveway, that selfsame "whoever" wouldn't find me in this house stark naked and defenseless, hiding in the crawl space with . . . Where *was* Bill? Of course, it was very dark with the hatch shut, and since there weren't any lights on in the house, nothing was coming through the outline of the opening because of the pantry door and the rain-dark day. I patted around in the dark looking for my unwitting host. Maybe he was in another hiding spot? I was surprised at how big a space this was. While I searched, I had time to imagine all sort of bugs. Snakes. When you're buck naked, you don't like the idea of stuff touching areas that rarely meet bare ground. I crawled and patted, and every now and then jumped as I felt (or imagined) tiny feet against my skin.

Finally I located Bill over in a corner. He was still dead, of course. Somewhat more to my astonishment, my fingers informed me that he was naked, too. Certainly that was practical. Why get your clothes dirty? I knew he'd slept that way outside on occasion. I was so relieved to make contact with him that I really didn't mind whether he was clothed.

I tried to figure out how long the whole trip back from Merlotte's had taken, how long I'd dashed through the woods. My best estimate was that I had about thirty or forty-five minutes before Bill woke.

I crouched by him, gripping the screwdriver, listening with every nerve to catch whatever sound I could. It could be that they — the mysterious "they" — wouldn't spot my track here, or my clothes. If my luck was consistent, of *course* they'd spot the clothes and shoes, and they'd know that meant I'd come in the house, and they'd come in, too.

I spared a little disgust for the fact that I'd run to the nearest man for protection. However, I consoled myself, it wasn't so much his muscles I wanted as the shelter of his house. That was okay, right? I wasn't overly concerned with political correctness at the moment. Survival was more at the top of my list. And Bill wasn't exactly at my disposal, assuming he'd be willing . . .

"Sookie?" he murmured.

"Bill, thank God you're awake."

"You're unclothed."

Trust a man to mention that first. "Absolutely, and I'll tell you why —"

"Can't get up yet," he said. "Must be . . . overcast?"

"Right, big storm, dark as hell out there, and there's people —"

" 'Kay, later." And he was out again.

Crap! So I huddled by his corpse and listened. Had I left the front door unlocked? Of course I had. And the second I realized that, I heard a floorboard creak overhead. They were in the house.

". . . no drips," said a voice, probably from the foyer. I started to crawl to the hatch door so I could hear . . . but I paused. There was at least a chance that if they found the hatch and flipped it open, they still wouldn't see Bill and me. We were way back in a corner, and this was a very big space. Maybe it had been sort of a cellar, as close to a cellar as you could get in a place that had such a high water table.

"Yeah, but the door was open. She must have come in here." It was a nasal voice, and it was a little closer than it had been.

"And she flew across the floor, leaving no footprints? Raining as hard as it is out there?" The sarcastic voice was a bit deeper.

"We don't know what she is." Nasal guy.

"Not a vampire, Kelvin. We know that."

Kelvin said, "Maybe she's a werebird or something, Hod."

"Werebird?" The snort of incredulity echoed in the dark house. Hod could really do sarcastic.

"Did you see the ears on that guy? That was pretty incredible. You can't rule out nothing, these days," Kelvin advised his buddy.

Ears? They were talking about Dermot. What had they done to him? I was ashamed. This was the first time I'd thought about what might have befallen my great-uncle.

"Yeah, and? He must be one of those science fiction geeks." Hod didn't sound like he was paying much attention to what he was saying. I heard cabinets open and close.

No way I could have been in any of those places.

"Nah, man, I'm sure they were real. No scars or anything. Maybe I shoulda taken one."

Taken one? I shivered.

Kelvin, who was closer to the pantry than Hod, added, "I'm gonna go upstairs, check out the rooms up there." I heard the sound of his boots diminish, heard the distant creak of the stairs, his muffled footfalls up the carpeted treads. Very faintly, I followed some of his movements on the second floor. I knew when he was directly above me, in the room I figured was the master bedroom, where I'd slept when I was dating Bill.

While Kelvin was gone, Hod wandered to and fro, though he didn't seem very purposeful to me.

"Right . . . there's nobody here," Kelvin announced when he returned to the former kitchen. "Wonder why there's a hot tub in the house?"

"There's a car outside," Hod said thoughtfully. His voice was much closer, right outside the open pantry door. He was thinking about getting back to Shreveport and taking a hot shower, putting on dry clothes, maybe having sex with his wife. Ew. A few too many details along with that. Kelvin was more prosaic. He wanted to get paid, so he wanted to deliver me. To whom? Dammit, he wasn't thinking about that. My heart sank, though I would have sworn it was already down to my toes. My bare toes. I was glad I'd painted my toenails recently. Irrelevant!

A bright line of light suddenly appeared in the thin, thin outline of the hatch or trapdoor or whatever Bill called it. The light had been switched on in the pantry. I held as still as a mouse, tried to breathe shallowly and silently. I thought how bad Bill would feel if they killed me right next to him. Irrelevant!

He would, though.

I heard a creak and realized one of the men was standing right above me. If I could have switched my mind off, I would have. I was so conscious of the life in other people's minds that I had a hard time believing that anyone could ignore a conscious brain, especially one as jittery as mine.

"Just blood in here," Hod said, so close that I jerked in surprise. "The bottled kind. Hey, Kelvin, this house must belong to a vampire!"

"Don't make no difference as long as he's not awake. Or she. Hey, you ever had a female vampire?"

"No, and don't want to. I don't like to hump dead people. Course, some nights, Marge ain't much better."

Kelvin laughed. "You better not let her hear you say that, bro."

Hod laughed, too. "No danger of that."

And he stepped out of the pantry. Didn't switch off the light, wasteful asshole! Evidently the fact that Bill would know someone had been here was not a concern of Hod's. So he was really stupid.

And then Bill woke up. This time he was a little more alert, and the second I felt him move, I crouched on top of him and put my hand over his mouth. His muscles tensed, and I had time to think *Oh, no!* before he smelled me, knew me. "Sookie?" he said, but not at full volume.

"Did you hear something?" said Hod above me.

A long moment of a lively, listening silence. "Shh," I breathed, right into Bill's ear.

A cold hand rose and ran down my leg. I could almost feel Bill's surprise — again — as he realized I was naked . . . again. And I knew the second the fact that he'd heard a voice overhead penetrated his awareness.

Bill was putting it all together. I didn't know what he was coming up with, but he knew that we were in trouble. He also knew there was a bare-naked woman on top of him, and something else twitched. Simultaneously exasperated and amused, I had to clamp my lips shut on a giggle. Irrelevant!

And then Bill went to sleep again.

Would the damn sun never set? His drifting in and out was making me nuts. It was like dating someone with short-term memory loss.

And I'd clean forgotten to listen and be terrified.

"Nah, I don't hear nothing," Kelvin said.

Lying on top of my involuntary host was like lying on top of a cold, hard cushion with hair.

And an erection. For what seemed like the tenth time, Bill had wakened.

I blew out a silent breath. This time Bill was completely awake. He put his arms around me, but he was gentlemanly enough not to move or explore, at least for now. We were both listening; he'd heard Kelvin speak.

Finally, two sets of footsteps crossed the wooden floors, and we heard the front door open and close. I sagged in relief. Bill's arms tightened and he rolled me over so he was on top.

"Is it Christmas?" he asked, pressed

against me. "Are you an early present?"

I laughed, but I still kept it quiet. "I'm sorry to intrude, Bill," I said, very low. "But they were after me." I explained very briefly, being careful to tell him where my clothes were and why they were there. I could feel his chest heave a little, and I knew he was laughing silently. "I'm really worried about Dermot," I said. I'd been talking almost in a whisper, which made the darkness curiously intimate, to say nothing of the large area of skin we were sharing.

"You've been down here a while," he said, his voice at normal level.

"Yes."

"I'm going out to make sure they're gone, since you're not going to let me 'open' early," Bill said, and it took me a minute to understand. I caught myself smiling in the darkness. Bill gently eased away from me, and I saw his whiteness moving silently through the gloom. After a second's listening, he opened the hatch. Harsh electric light flooded down. It was such a contrast that I had to close my eyes to let them adjust. By the time they did, Bill had slithered out into the house.

I didn't hear anything no matter how hard I listened. I got tired of waiting — I felt like I'd crouched on the bare ground forever —

and I hauled myself out of the hatch with a lot less grace and a lot more noise than Bill. I turned off the lights Hod and Kelvin had left on, at least in part because the light made me feel about twice as naked. I peered cautiously out of a window in the dining room. In the dark it was hard to be sure, but I thought the trees weren't tossing in the wind anymore. The rain continued unabated. I saw lightning off to the north. I didn't see kidnappers or bodies or anything that didn't belong in the soaked landscape.

Bill didn't seem to be in any hurry to return to tell me what was happening. The old dining table was covered with a sort of shawl with fringe, and I pulled it off the table and wrapped myself in it. I hoped it wasn't some kind of Compton heirloom. It had holes in it and a large flowery pattern, so I wasn't too terribly concerned.

"Sookie," Bill said at my back, and I shrieked and jumped.

"Would you please not do that?" I said. "I've had enough bad surprises today."

"Sorry," he said. He had a kitchen towel in his hand and he was rubbing his hair. "I came in through the back door." He was still naked, but I felt ridiculous making any kind of thing out of it. I'd seen Bill naked many times before. He was looking me up and down, a sort of puzzled expression on his face. "Sookie, are you wearing my Aunt Edwina's Spanish shawl?" he asked.

"Oh, I'm so sorry," I said. "Really, Bill. It was there, and I was cold and damp and feeling like I wanted to be covered. I do apologize." I thought of unwrapping it and handing it over, but I reconsidered in the same moment.

"Looks better on you than it does on the table," he said. "Besides, it has holes. Are you ready to go over to your house to find out what's happened to your great-uncle? And where are your clothes? Surely . . . Did those men take them off? Have they . . . Are you harmed?"

"No, no," I said hastily. "I told you I had to dump my clothes so they wouldn't see the drips. They're out front behind the bushes. I couldn't leave them in sight, of course."

"Right," Bill said. He looked very thoughtful. "If I didn't know you better, I would think — and pardon me if I offend — that you'd concocted this whole scenario to excuse yourself for wanting to bed me again."

"Oh. You mean, you might almost imagine that I made up this story so I could appear naked and in need of help, the damsel in distress, needing big strong equally naked Vampire Bill to rescue me from the evil kidnappers?"

He nodded, looking a little embarrassed.

"I wish I had enough free time to sit around and think of things like that." I admired the mind that could conceive of such a circuitous way to get what it wanted. "I think just knocking on your door and looking lonesome would probably get me where I wanted to be, if that was my goal. Or I could just say, 'How 'bout it, big boy?' I don't think I need to be naked and in danger to get you lusty. Right?"

"You're absolutely right," he said, and he was smiling a little. "And any time you'd like to try one of those other ploys, I'd be glad to play my part. Shall I apologize again?"

I smiled back. "No need. I don't suppose you have rain slickers?"

Of course he didn't, but he did have an umbrella. In short order he'd fetched my clothes from behind the bushes. While I wrung them out and put them in his dryer, he ran up the stairs to his bedroom, which he'd never slept in, to pull on jeans and a tank top — serious slumming, for Bill.

My clothes were going to take too long to dry, so clad in Aunt Edwina's Spanish shawl and sheltered by Bill's blue umbrella, I climbed into his car. He drove out to Hummingbird Road and over to my house. Putting the car in park, Bill hopped out to remove the tree trunk from the driveway as easily as if it had been a toothpick. We resumed our way to the house, pausing by my poor car, the driver's door still open to the rain. The interior was soaked, but my would-be abductors hadn't done anything to it. The key was still in the ignition, my purse still on the front seat along with the remaining groceries.

Bill eyed the broken plastic of the milk jug, and I wondered which one I'd hit, Hod or Kelvin.

We both pulled up to the back door, but while I was still gathering my grocery bag and my purse, Bill was out and into the house. I had a second's worth of worry about how I was going to dry out my car before I made myself focus on the crisis at hand. I thought about what had happened to the fairy woman Cait, and concern about car upholstery left my head with gratifying speed.

I stepped into my house clumsily. I was having trouble managing my wrapping, the umbrella, my purse, the bag containing the bottled blood, and my bare feet. I could hear Bill moving through the house, and I knew when he found something because he called, "Sookie!" in an urgent voice.

Dermot was unconscious on the attic floor by the sander he'd rented, which was on its side and switched off. He had fallen forward, so I figured he'd had his back to the door with the sander running when they'd come in the house. When he'd realized he wasn't alone and switched off the sander, it had been too late. His hair was clotted with blood, and the wound looked horrible. They'd been carrying at least one weapon, then.

Bill was hunched stiffly over the still figure. Without turning to me he said, "I can't give him my blood," as if I'd demanded it.

"I know," I said, surprised. "He's fae." I circled around to kneel on Dermot's other side. I was in a position to see Bill's face.

"Back away," I said. "Back away. Go downstairs *now.*" The odor of fairy blood, intoxicating to a vampire, must seem as though it were filling the attic to Bill.

"I could just lick it clean," Bill said, his dark eyes fixed on the wound with yearning.

"No, you wouldn't stop. Back off, Bill! Leave!" But his face dipped lower, closer to

Dermot's head. I hauled off and slapped Bill as hard as I could.

"You have to go," I said, though I wanted to apologize so badly it made me shake. The look on Bill's face was awful. Anger, craving, the struggle for self-control . . .

"I'm so hungry," he whispered, his eyes swallowing me. "Feed me, Sookie."

For a second, I was sure Bad Choice time was upon me. The worst choice would have been letting Bill bite Dermot. The next worst would have been letting Bill bite me, because with the intoxicating scent of fairy in the air I wasn't sure he'd be able to stop in time. As all this flashed through my mind, Bill was struggling to master himself. He managed . . . but only by the thinnest of threads.

"I'm going to check to see if they've left," he said, lurching toward the stairs. Even his body was at war with itself. Clearly, his every instinct was telling him to drink blood somehow, some way, from the two tasty, tempting donors at hand, while his mind was telling him to get the hell away before something awful happened. If I'd had a spare person around, I'm not sure I wouldn't have thrown him to Bill, I felt so sad for him.

But he made it down the stairs, and I

heard the door slam behind him. In case he lost his control, I hurried down the stairs to lock both back doors so at least I'd have a little warning if he returned. I glanced through the living room to make sure the front door was locked, as I'd left it. Yes. Before I returned upstairs to Dermot, I went to fetch my shotgun from my front closet.

It was still there, and I let myself savor a moment of relief. I was lucky the men hadn't stolen it. Their search must have been cursory. I'm sure they would have spied something as valuable as the shotgun if they hadn't been looking for something much larger — me.

With the Benelli in my hand I felt much better, and I grabbed the first aid kit to take up with me. I hobbled up the stairs to kneel again by my great-uncle. I was getting pretty damn sick of coping with the huge shawl, which unwound at the most inconvenient moments. I wondered briefly how Indian women coped, but I just couldn't take the time to dress until I'd helped Dermot.

With a wad of sterile wipes, I cleaned away the blood on his head so I could inspect the damage. It looked bad, but I had expected that; head wounds always do. At least this wasn't bleeding much at all anymore. While

I was working on Dermot's head, I was having a fierce inner debate about calling an ambulance. I wasn't sure the ambulance crew would be able to get in without Hod and Kelvin's interference — no, that couldn't be a concern. Bill and I had gotten over here without being stopped.

More important, I wasn't sure how compatible fairy physiology was with human medical techniques — enough that humans and fairies could cross-breed, I knew, which argued that human first aid would be all right, but still . . . Dermot groaned and rolled over to his back. I put a towel under his head just in time. He winced.

"Sookie," he said. "Why are you wearing a tablecloth?"

CHAPTER 12

"You have both your ears," I assured him, feeling a wave of relief so strong I almost fell over. I touched the points lightly so he could be certain.

"Why would I not?" Dermot was confused, and considering the amount of bleeding he'd had, I was sure that was understandable. "Who attacked me?"

I looked down at him and couldn't decide what to do. I had to bite the bullet. I called Claude.

"Claude's phone," said a deep voice I pegged as belonging to Bellenos, the elf.

"Bellenos, it's Sookie. I don't know if you remember me, but I was there the other day with my friend Sam?"

"Yes," he said.

"Here's the deal. Someone attacked Dermot, and he's hurt, and I need to know if there's anything I should or shouldn't do to an injured fairy. Anything besides what you do for a human."

"Who has hurt him?" Bellenos's voice was sharper.

"Two human guys who broke into the house coming for me. I wasn't here, but Dermot was, and there was machinery running, and he couldn't hear too well, and they seem to have hit him on the head. I don't know what with."

"Has the bleeding stopped?" he asked, and I could hear Claude's voice in the background.

"Yes, it's clotted."

There was a buzz of voices while Bellenos consulted with various people, or at least that was what it sounded like.

"I'm coming," Bellenos said at last. "Claude tells me he's not welcome in your home right now, so I'm coming in his stead. It'll be nice to get out of this building. No other humans around besides you? I can't pass."

"No one else besides me, at least now."

"I'll be there soon."

I relayed this information to Dermot, who was simply looking puzzled. He told me a couple of times he didn't understand why he was on the floor, and I began to get worried about him. At least he seemed content to stay there.

"Sookie!" Before it had started raining, Dermot had opened the windows because of the sanding. I could hear Bill clearly.

I trailed over to the window with my fringe swaying.

"How is he?" Bill asked, staying well away. "How can I help?"

"You've been wonderful," I said, meaning it. "One of the fae from Monroe is coming over, Bill, so you better go back to your house. When my clothes get dry, could you just leave them on my back steps sometime when it's not raining? Or if you just put them on your front porch, I can pick 'em up any time."

"I feel I've failed you," he said.

"How come? You gave me a place to hide; you cleared my driveway; you checked out the house so no one could ambush me again."

"I didn't kill them," he said. "I'd like to."

I didn't feel hardly creepy at all at his admission. I was getting used to drastic pronouncements. "Hey, don't worry about it," I assured him. "Someone will, if they keep doing stuff like this."

"Did you form any idea of who had hired them?"

"I'm afraid not." I really regretted that. "They were going to tie me on some vehicle

354

and take me somewhere." I hadn't seen the vehicle in their thoughts, so that part was fuzzy.

"Where was their car parked?"

"I don't know. I never saw one." I hadn't exactly had time to think about it.

Bill stared up at me longingly. "I feel useless, Sookie. I know you need help getting him down the stairs. But I don't dare try to approach him again."

Bill's head turned with a suddenness that made me blink. Then he was gone.

"I'm here," called a voice from the back door. "I am Bellenos the elf, vampire. Tell Sookie I'm here to see my friend Dermot."

"An elf. I haven't seen one of you in over a hundred years," I heard Bill's voice, much fainter.

"And you won't again for another hundred," Bellenos's deep voice responded. "There aren't many of us left."

I went down the stairs again, as fast as I could without breaking my neck. I unlocked the back door and stepped across the porch to unlock the porch door. I could see both the elf and the vampire through the glass.

"Since you're here, I'll be on my way," Bill said. "I can't be of any help." He was out in the yard. The harsh security light mounted on the pole made him look whiter than white, truly alien. The rain was only dripping now, but the air smelled pregnant with moisture. I didn't think it would hold off for long.

"Fairy intoxication?" Bellenos said. He was pale, too, but no one could be more washed out than a vamp. Bellenos's light brown freckles looked like little shadows on his face, and his smooth hair seemed an even darker auburn. "Elves smell different from fairies."

"Yes, you do," Bill said, and I could hear the distaste in his voice. Bellenos's smell seemed to repel at least one vampire. Maybe I could scrape some skin cells from Bellenos to scatter over my great-uncle so I could have vampires over. Oh, gosh, what was I going to do about the meeting with Eric and Pam?

"Are you two through swapping how-de-dos?" I called. "Because Dermot could use some help."

Bill vanished into the woods, and I opened the door for the elf. He smiled at me, and it was hard not to twitch when I saw the long, pointed teeth.

"Come in," I said, though I knew he could enter without being invited.

As I led him through the kitchen, he was looking around him with some curiosity. I

356

hoisted my trailing wrapper to precede him up the stairs, and I hoped Bellenos wasn't getting too much of an eyeful. When we reached the attic, before I could say anything the elf was on his knees beside Dermot. After a quick survey, Bellenos rolled the fairy onto his side to examine the wound. The curiously slanted brown eyes were intent on his wounded friend.

Well, he might have glanced at my bare shoulders a little.

More than a little.

"You need to cover up," Bellenos said bluntly. "That's too much human skin for me."

Okay, I'd totally misread that, to my embarrassment. Just as Bill had been repelled by Bellenos's scent, Bellenos was repelled by the sight of me.

"I'll be glad to put on real clothes now that there's someone to stay with Dermot."

"Good," Bellenos said.

As blunt as Claude could be, Bellenos had him beat. It was actually almost entertaining. I asked Bellenos to carry Dermot down to the guest room on the ground floor, and I preceded them to make sure the room was okay. After a cursory look to make sure the bedspread was pulled up over the sheets, I moved aside for Bellenos, who was carrying

Dermot as easily as he would a child, though Dermot was certainly less maneuverable on the narrow staircase.

While Bellenos settled Dermot on the bed, I zipped into my room to dress. I can't tell you what a relief it was to unwind the fringed and flowered shawl and put on some jeans (not shorts, out of deference to Bellenos's human skin aversion). It was too hot to even think of a long-sleeved shirt, but my offensive shoulders were properly covered with a striped T-shirt.

Dermot was fully conscious when I returned to check on him. Bellenos was kneeling by the bed, stroking Dermot's golden hair and talking to him in a language I didn't know. My great-uncle was alert and lucid. My heart settled into a happier rhythm when Dermot even smiled at me, though it was a shadow of his usual grin.

"They didn't hurt you," he said, obviously relieved. "So far, Niece, it seems living with you is more dangerous than staying with my own kind."

"I'm so sorry," I said, sitting on the edge of the bed and taking his hand. "I don't know how they were able to get into the house with the wards in place. People who mean me harm aren't supposed to be able to enter, whether I'm here or not."

Despite his blood loss, Dermot flushed. "That would be my fault."

"What?" I stared down at him. "Why?"

"It was human magic," he said, not meeting my eyes. "Your little witch friend, she's quite good for a human, but fae magic is much, much better. So I deconstructed her spells, and I intended to put my own around your house as soon as I finished sanding the floor."

I really couldn't think of a thing to say.

There was a sticky little moment of silence.

"We'd better tend to your head," I said briskly. I cleaned it some more and dabbed the wound with Neosporin. I certainly wasn't going to try to sew it up, though it seemed to me that someone should. When I mentioned stitches, both of the fae seemed utterly disgusted by the idea. I put some butterfly bandages on the wound to hold it shut. I figured that was the best I could do.

"Now I'll treat him," Bellenos said, and I was pleased to hear that he intended to do something more active than carry Dermot down the stairs to the bed. Not that that hadn't been a help, but I'd expected a bit more, somehow. "Of course the blood of the one who harmed him would be best, and maybe we can do something about that, but for now . . ."

"What will you do?" I hoped I could watch and learn.

"I will breathe into him," Bellenos said, as if I were a fool not to know that. My amazement startled him. He shrugged, as if I were too ignorant for words. "You can watch if you want." He looked down at Dermot, who nodded, then winced.

Bellenos stretched out on the bed beside Dermot and kissed him.

I'd certainly never thought of curing a head wound that way. If my lack of knowledge of fae ways had been a surprise to him, this was a surprise to me.

After a second I understood that though their mouths were together, the elf was breathing the air in his own lungs into Dermot. After detaching to take in another lungful, Bellenos repeated the procedure.

I tried to imagine a human doctor treating a patient this way. Lawsuit! Though I could tell it wasn't sexual — well, not overtly — this was a little too personal for me. This might be a good time to clean up. I collected the used sterile wipes and bandage wrappers to pitch into the kitchen trash can, and while I was by myself, I took the time to have a snit.

Yeah, fae magic was probably great, *when*

you used it. Amelia's spells might have been human and therefore inferior, but *they'd been in place to protect me.* Until Dermot had removed them . . . and left me with nothing at all. "Jackass," I muttered, and scrubbed the counter with enough pressure to kill any germs by force. That was about as mad as I could get, since Dermot's mistaken sense of superiority had ended with his incurring a severe head injury.

"He's resting and healing. Very soon, he and I have things we must do," Bellenos said. He'd come into the kitchen behind me without my sensing so much as a change in the air. He really enjoyed watching me jump. He laughed, which was weird, because he did it with his mouth wide as if he were panting. His laugh was more a breathy "hee-heehee" than the human guffaw.

"He's able to move?" I was delighted, but surprised.

"Yes," Bellenos said. "Besides, he tells me you have vampires coming later, and he would need to be elsewhere, anyway."

At least Bellenos didn't chide me for expecting vampire guests, and he also didn't ask me to cancel my plans to accommodate Dermot's injury.

I'd considered calling Eric's cell phone to postpone our powwow. But I thought that it was entirely possible that Hod and Kelvin were part and parcel of the same struggle, albeit a clumsy part.

"Wait here for a minute, please," I said politely, and I went to talk to Dermot. He was propped up on the bed, and I spared a second to thank Amelia for making it before she left, though I needed to change the sheets, but I could do that at my leisure — okay, time to stop making housekeeping notes, since Dermot was looking all pale and brave. When I sat by him, he took me in a surprisingly strong embrace. I returned it with interest.

"I'm sorry this happened to you," I said. I bypassed the whole warding issue. "Are you sure you want to go to Monroe? Will they really take care of you? I can cancel the thing for tonight. I'd be glad to nurse you."

Dermot was silent for a moment. I could feel him breathing in my arms, and the smell of his skin surrounded me. Naturally he didn't smell like Jason, though they could have been twins.

"Thanks for not ripping me a new one," he said. "See, I've mastered modern human speech." He managed a real smile. "I'll see you later. Bellenos and I have an errand to complete."

"You need to take it easy. You were hurt

362

pretty bad. How are you feeling?"

"Better by the moment. Bellenos has shared his breath with me, and I'm excited about the hunt."

Okay, I didn't quite understand that, but if he was pleased, I was pleased. Before I could ask him questions, he said, "I failed you about the wards, and I didn't stop the intruders. While I lay there, I feared they'd found you."

"You shouldn't have worried about me," I said, and I was sincere, though I was sure grateful he had. "I hid over at Bill's and they didn't find me."

While Dermot and I were hugging each other, an embrace that was lasting a bit too long, I could hear Bellenos outside. He was circling the house in the rain (which had begun again) and darkness, and his voice rose and fell. I could only catch snatches of what he was saying, but it was in that other language and its meaning was lost on me. Dermot seemed satisfied, and that was reassuring.

"I'll make this up to you," Dermot said, releasing me gently.

"No need," I said. "I'm good, and since you didn't have any permanent damage, we'll just say that was a learning experience." As in, *Don't erase wards without put-*

ting in new ones.

Dermot stood, and he seemed very steady on his feet. His eyes were shining. He looked . . . excited, as if he were going to a birthday party or something.

"Don't you need a raincoat?" I suggested.

Dermot laughed, put his hands on my shoulders, and kissed me. My heart leaped in shock, but I recognized the stance. He was breathing into me.

For a few seconds I thought I'd strangle or suffocate, but somehow I didn't, and then it was over.

He smiled down at me and then he was gone. I heard the back doors slam after him, and I turned to the window to see a blur as he and Bellenos disappeared into the dark woods.

I couldn't think of anything to do after such a crisis. I got the blood off the floor in the attic, I put the shawl in the kitchen sink to soak in some Woolite, and I changed the sheets in the guest bedroom.

After that I showered. I needed to wash the fairy scent off me before Eric and Pam got here. Besides, after being rain soaked, my hair was just a mass of nastiness. I got dressed — again — and sat down for a minute or two in the living room, to watch the Weather Channel gloating over the big storm.

The next thing I knew, I was waking up with sand in my mouth. The Weather Channel was still on, and Eric and Pam were knocking at the front door.

I staggered over to unlock it, as stiff as though someone had kicked me while I slept. I was feeling the result of my desperate run through the rain.

"What's happened?" Eric asked, holding my shoulders and giving me a narrow-eyed look. Pam was sniffing the air, her blond head thrown back dramatically. She gave me a sideways grin. "Ooooh, who's been entertaining . . . Wait . . . An elf, a fairy, and Bill?"

"You been taking tracking lessons from Heidi?" I asked weakly.

"As a matter of fact, I have," she said. "There's an art to drawing in air to sample it, since we no longer need to breathe."

Eric was still waiting, and not patiently.

I remembered I'd bought them some bottled blood, and I went to the kitchen to heat it up with the two vampires trailing behind. While I was taking care of the hospitality portion of the evening, I gave them the *Reader's Digest* version of my adventure.

Someone knocked on the back door.

The air turned electric. Pam glided over to the door onto the porch, unlocked it, went out to the back door. "Yes?" I heard her say.

There was a muffled answer in a deep voice. Bellenos.

"Sookie, you're wanted!" Pam sang out. She seemed very amused by something.

I was curious as I stepped out on the porch, Eric right behind me.

"Oh, she'll be so impressed," Pam was saying, sounding as pleased as I did when someone brought me some fresh produce from his garden. "How very thoughtful." She stepped aside so I could appreciate my presents.

Jesus Christ, Shepherd of Judea.

My great-uncle Dermot and Bellenos were standing in the dripping rain, each holding a severed head.

Let me just say here that normally I have quite a strong stomach, but the rain wasn't the only thing that was dripping, and the heads were face forward so I got a good look at each face. The sight overcame me in a very drastic way. I turned and dashed for my bathroom, slamming the door behind me. I retched and ralphed and panted until I'd recovered a bit of my equilibrium.

Naturally, I needed to brush my teeth and wash my face and comb my hair after losing everything in my stomach . . . though it hadn't been much, because I simply couldn't remember how long it had been since I'd eaten. I'd had the biscuit for breakfast. . . . Oh. No wonder I'd been sick. I hadn't eaten anything since then. I'm a girl who likes her meals, so it hadn't been a weight-loss tactic. I'd just been too busy bumping from crisis to crisis. Go on the Sookie Stackhouse Narrow Avoidance of Death Diet! Run for your life, and miss meals, too! Exercise plus starvation.

Pam and Eric were waiting in the kitchen.

"They left," Pam said, holding up a bottle of blood in a toast. "They were sorry it was too much for your human sensibility. I'm assuming you didn't want to keep the trophies?"

I felt a need to defend myself, but I bit it back. I refused to be ashamed of getting sick after seeing something so horrible. I'd seen a detached vampire head, but it hadn't had the ghastly touches. I took a deep breath. "No, I didn't want to keep the heads. Kelvin and Hod, rest in peace."

"Those were their names? That'll help in finding out who hired them," Pam said, looking pleased.

"Um. Where are they?" I asked, trying not to look too anxious.

"Do you mean your great-uncle and his elf buddy, or do you mean the heads, or do you mean the bodies?" Eric asked.

"Both. All three." I got myself some ice and poured some Diet Coke over it. People had told me for years that carbonated drinks settled your stomach. I was hoping they were right.

"Dermot and Bellenos have left for Monroe. Dermot got to anoint his wound with the blood of his enemies, which is a tradition among the fae. Bellenos, of course, got to take the heads off, which is an elf tradition. They were both very happy in consequence."

"I'm glad for them," I said automatically, and thought, *What the hell am I saying?* "I should tell Bill. I wonder if they found the car?"

"They found four-wheelers," Pam said. "I think they had an excellent time driving them." Pam looked envious.

I was almost able to smile, imagining that. "So, the bodies?"

"They've been dealt with," Eric said. "Though I think the two of them took the heads back to Monroe to show the other fae. But they'll destroy them there."

"Oh," Pam said suddenly, and leaped up. "Dermot left their papers." She returned with two wet wallets and some odds and ends heaped in her hands. I spread a kitchen towel out on the table, and she dumped the items onto it. I tried not to notice the bloodstains on the bits of paper. I opened the leather billfold first and extracted a driver's license. "Hod Mayfield," I said. "From Clarice. He was twenty-four." I pulled out a picture of a woman, presumably the Marge they'd been talking about. She was definitely queen-sized, and she was wearing her dark hair up in a teased style that was what you might call dated. Her smile was open and sweet.

No pictures of children, thank God.

A hunter's license, a few receipts, an insurance card. "That means he had a regular job," I said to the vampires, who never needed hospitalization or life insurance. And Hod had three hundred dollars.

"Gosh," I said. "That seems like a lot." All crisp twenties, too.

"Some of our employees don't have a checking account," Pam said. "They cash their paychecks every time and live on a cash basis."

"Yeah, I know people who do that, too." Terry Bellefleur, for example, who thought banks were run by a Communist cartel. "But this money is all twenties, right from the machine. Might be a payoff."

Kelvin turned out to be a Mayfield, too. Cousin, brother? Kelvin was also from Clarice. He was older, twenty-seven. His billfold did contain pictures of children, three of them. Crap. Without comment, I laid the school shots out with the other items. Kelvin also had a condom, a free drink card for Vic's Redneck Roadhouse, and a card for an auto body shop. A few worn dollar bills, and the same crisp three hundred that Hod had had.

These were guys I could have passed dozens of times when I'd been shopping in Clarice. I might have played softball against their sisters or wives. I might have served them drinks at Merlotte's. What were they doing trying to kidnap me? "I guess they could have taken me up to Clarice through the woods, on the four-wheelers," I said out loud. "But what would they have done with me then? I thought one of them . . . Through his thoughts I caught a glimpse of an idea about a car trunk." It had only been fleeting, but I shuddered. I'd been in a car trunk before, and it hadn't ended well for me. It was a memory I blocked out resolutely.

Possibly Eric was thinking about the same

event because he glanced out the window toward Bill's house. "Who do you think sent them, Sookie?" he asked, and he made a huge effort to keep his voice calm and patient.

"I sure can't question them to find out," I muttered, and Pam laughed.

I gathered my thoughts, such as they were. The fog of my two-hour nap had finally lifted, and I tried to make some sense out of the evening's strange occurrences. "If Kelvin and Hod had been from Shreveport, I'd think that Sandra Pelt had hired them after she escaped from the hospital," I said. "She doesn't mind using up the lives of others, not a bit. I'm sure she hired the guys who came to the bar last Saturday. And I'm also sure she's the one who threw the firebomb at Merlotte's before that."

"We've had eyes looking for her in Shreveport, but no one's spotted her," Eric said.

"So this Sandra's goal," Pam said, pulling her straight pale hair behind her shoulders to braid it, "is to destroy you, your place of work, and anything else that gets in her way."

"That sounds about right. But evidently she's not behind this. I have too many enemies."

"Charming," Pam said.

"How's your friend?" I asked. "I'm sorry I didn't ask before."

Pam gave me a straight look. "She's going to pass soon," she said. "I'm running out of options, and I'm running out of hope that the process can be legal."

Eric's cell phone rang, and he got up to walk into the hall to take it. "Yes?" he said curtly. Then his voice changed. "Your Majesty," he said, and he walked quickly into the living room so I couldn't hear.

I wouldn't have thought so much about it if I hadn't seen Pam's face. She was looking at me, and her expression was clearly one of . . . pity.

"What?" I said, the hair on the back of my neck rising. "What's up? If he said 'Your Majesty,' that's Felipe calling, huh? That should be good . . . right?"

"I can't tell you," she said. "He'd kill me. He doesn't even want you to know there's anything to know, if you can pick up what I'm putting down."

"Pam. *Tell me.*"

"I can't," she repeated. "You need to be looking out for yourself, Sookie."

I looked at her with fierce intensity. I couldn't will her mouth to open, and I didn't have the strength to hold her down on the kitchen table and demand the facts from her.

Where could reason get me? Okay, Pam liked me. The only people she liked better were Eric and her Miriam. If there was something she couldn't tell me, it had to be associated with Eric. If Eric had been human, I would've thought he had some dread disease. If Eric had lost all his assets in the stock market or some such financial calamity, Pam knew that money was not my ruling concern. What was the only thing I valued?

His love.

Eric had someone else.

I stood up without knowing I was standing, the chair clattering to the floor behind me. I wanted to reach into Pam's brain and yank out the details. Now I understood very clearly why Eric had gone for her in this same room the night he'd brought Immanuel over. She'd wanted to tell me then and he'd forbidden her to speak.

Alarmed by the noise of the chair bouncing on the floor, Eric came running into the room, the phone still held to his ear. I was standing with my fists clenched, glaring at him. My heart was lurching around in my chest like a frog on a griddle.

"Excuse me," he said into the phone. "There is a crisis. I'll return your call later."

He snapped his phone shut.

"Pam," he said. "I am very angry with you. I am seriously angry with you. Leave this house now and remain silent."

With a posture I had never seen before, hunched and humbled, Pam scrambled up from her chair and out the back door. I wondered if she'd see Bubba in the woods. Or Bill. Or maybe there'd be fairies. Or some more kidnappers. A homicidal maniac! You never knew what you'd find in my woods.

I didn't say a word. I waited. I felt like my eyes were shooting flames.

"I love you," he said.

I waited.

"My maker, Appius Livius Ocella" — the *dead* Appius Livius Ocella — "was in the process of making a match for me before he died," Eric said. "He mentioned it to me during his stay, but I didn't realize the process had gone as far as it had when he died. I thought I could ignore it. That his death canceled it out."

I waited. I could not read his face, and without the bond, I could only see that he was covering his emotion with a hard face.

"This isn't much done anymore, though it used to be the norm. Makers used to find matches for their children. They'd receive a fee if it was an advantageous union, if each half could supply something the other lacked. It was mostly a business arrangement."

I raised my eyebrows. At the only vampire wedding I'd witnessed, there'd been plenty of evidence of physical passion, though I'd been told the couple wouldn't be spending all their time together.

Eric looked abashed, an expression I'd never thought to see on his face.

"Of course, it has to be consummated," he said.

I waited for the coup de grace. Maybe the ground would open up and swallow him first. It didn't.

"I'd have to put you aside," he admitted. "It's not done, to have a human wife and a vampire wife. Especially if the wife is the Queen of Oklahoma. The vampire wife must be the only one." He looked away, his face stiff with a resentment he'd never expressed before. "I know you've always insisted that you weren't my true wife, so presumably that would not be so difficult for you."

Like *hell*.

He looked at my face as if he were reading a map. "Though I believe it would be," he said softly. "Sookie, I swear to you that since I received the letter, I have done everything I could to stop this. I have pleaded that Ocella's death should cancel the arrangement; I have said that I'm happy where I am; I have even put forward our marriage as a bar. And as my regent, Victor could plead that his wishes supersede those of Ocella, and that I'm too useful to him to leave the state."

"Oh, no." I found myself finally able to speak, though only in a whisper.

"Oh, yes," Eric said bitterly. "I've appealed to Felipe, but I haven't heard from him. Oklahoma is one of the rulers eyeing his throne. He may want to placate her. In the meantime, she calls me every week, offering me a share of her kingdom if I'll come to her."

"So, she's met you face-to-face." My voice was a little stronger.

"Yes," he said. "She was at the summit in Rhodes to make a deal with the King of Tennessee about a prisoner exchange."

Did I remember her? When I was calmer, I might. There'd been several queens there, and not an ugly one among 'em. There were a thousand questions crowding to get out of my head and into my mouth, but I clamped my lips shut. This was not a time to speak, but a time to listen.

I believed this arrangement hadn't been

his idea. And now I understood what Appius had told me when he was about to die. He'd told me I'd never keep Eric. He'd died happy about that, that he'd arranged such an advantageous connection for his beloved son, one that would take Eric away from the lowly human he loved. If he'd been in front of me, I'd have killed Appius again and enjoyed it.

In the middle of this brooding, and while Eric was saying everything all over again, a white face peered in the kitchen window. Eric could see from my face that something was behind him, and he whipped around so quickly I didn't see him move. To my relief, the face was familiar.

"Let him in," I said, and Eric went to the back door.

Bubba was in the kitchen a second later, bending over to kiss my hand. "Hey, pretty lady," he said, beaming at me. Bubba had one of the most recognizable faces in the world, though his heyday had been fifty years before.

"Good to see you," I said, and I meant it. Bubba had some bad habits, because he was a bad vampire; he'd been too soaked in drugs when he'd been brought over, and the spark of life had been almost extinct. Two seconds later, it would have been too

377

late. But a morgue attendant in Memphis, a vampire, had been so overwhelmed at seeing him that he'd brought the King over. Then, vampires had been secret creatures of the night, not on the cover of every other magazine the way they are now. Under the name "Bubba" he'd been passed around from kingdom to kingdom, given simple tasks to do to earn his keep, and every now and then on memorable nights, he wanted to sing. He was very fond of Bill, less attached to Eric, but Bubba understood the protocol well enough to be polite.

"Miss Pam is outside," Bubba said, looking sideways at Eric. "You and Mr. Eric doing okay in here?"

Bless his heart, he suspected Eric was hurting me, and he'd come in to check. Bubba was right; Eric was hurting me but not physically. I felt as though I were standing on the edge of a cliff, narrowly avoiding taking the step off the edge. I was pretty numb, but that wasn't going to last.

At this interesting moment a knock at the front door announced the arrival of (I hoped) Audrina and Colton, our co-conspirators. I went to the door, the two vampires behind me. Feeling absolutely secure in doing so, I opened the front door. Sure enough, the human couple was standing on the front porch waiting, and each of them was gripped by a dripping, grim Pam. Pam's blond straight hair was darker with rain and hanging in rattails. She looked like she could spit nails.

"Please come in," I said politely. "And you, too, Pam." After all, it was my house and she was my friend. "We need to put our heads together." I thought of adding, "Though not literally," when I flashed on the heads of Hod and Kelvin, but Audrina and Colton looked pretty frightened already. It was one thing to talk big in your trailer all alone. It was another thing to meet with desperate and terrifying people in a lonely house out in the woods. As I turned away to lead them to the kitchen, I decided to put out some drinks, a bucket of ice, and maybe a bowl of chips and dip.

It was time to get this assassination party started.

I'd think about other deaths later.

CHAPTER 13

Audrina and Colton obviously couldn't decide what was more amazing: the threat of a sodden and beautiful (but menacing) Pam or the ruin of glory that was Bubba. They'd expected Eric, but Bubba was a complete surprise.

They were entranced. Though I whispered to them on our way through the living room not to call him by his real name, I didn't know if they'd have enough self-control. Luckily for us all, they did. Bubba really, really, didn't like being reminded of his past life. He had to be in a remarkable mood to sing.

Wait. Ha! Finally, I had a real idea.

They all sat around the table. Absorbed in figuring out my scheme, I got out the refreshments and pulled up a chair by Bubba. I had a floaty, surrealistic feeling. I simply couldn't think about the crash and burn I'd just experienced. I had to think about this moment and this purpose.

Pam sat behind Eric so they wouldn't meet each other's eyes. They both looked miserable, and it was a look I'd seldom seen either of them wear. It didn't look good on them. I felt somehow guilty about the breach between them, though it certainly wasn't my fault. Or was it? I ran it through my mind. Nope, it wasn't.

Eric proposed that he infiltrate his vampires into Vampire's Kiss one night in disguise, and that they wait until the club was about to close and the crowds were thin. Then we would attack. And, of course, kill them all.

If Victor hadn't been an employee of Felipe, king of three states, Eric's scheme would have been workable, though there were some definite weak points. But surely killing a bunch of his vampires would piss off Felipe mightily, and I really couldn't blame him.

Audrina had a plan, too, involving discovering Victor's sleeping place and getting him while he was out for the day. Wow, that was fresh and original. However, it was a classic for a reason. Victor would be helpless.

"Except we don't know where he sleeps," I said, trying to slide the objection in there without sounding snooty.

"I do," Audrina said proudly. "He sleeps in a big stone mansion. It's set back from a parish road between Musgrave and Toniton. There's one lone road in, and that's it. There aren't any trees around the house. It's just grass."

"Wow." I was impressed. "How'd you track him down?"

"I know the guy who mows the yard," she said. She grinned at me. "Dusty Kolinchek, remember him?"

"Sure," I said, feeling a stir of interest. Dusty's dad owned a fleet — okay, a small fleet — of lawn tractors and weed eaters, and every summer a group of Bon Temps high school boys earned their walking-around money working for Mr. Kolinchek. Dusty was inheriting the lawn-mowing empire, sounded like.

"He says that the house is almost empty during the day because Victor is paranoid about having anyone come in while he's sleeping. He just has two bodyguards there, Dixie and Dixon Mayhew, and they're some kind of wereanimals."

"I know them," I said. "They're were-panthers. They're good." The Mayhew twins were tough and professional. "They must be strapped for cash to work for a vampire." Now that my sister-in-law was dead and

Calvin Norris had married Tanya Grissom, I didn't see many of the werepanthers with any frequency. Calvin didn't come into the bar much, and Jason seemed to see his former in-laws only at the full moon, when he became one of them . . . in a limited way, since he'd been bitten, not born, as a Were.

"So maybe I could bribe the Mayhews if they're that hard up," Eric said. "You wouldn't need to kill them, then. Less mess. But you humans would have to do the job, since Pam and I will be down for the day."

"We'd have to search the house, because I bet the Mayhews don't know exactly where he sleeps," I said. "Though I'm sure they have to have a pretty good idea." The vampire smell alone should help the twoeys zone in on where Victor slept, but it seemed kind of tacky to say that out loud.

Pam kind of waved her hand. Eric half turned, catching the motion out of the corner of his eye. "What?" he said. "Oh, you can speak."

Pam looked relieved. She said, "I think when he leaves the club in the morning would be a good time. His attention is on whoever he's going to feed on, and we might be able to attack then."

These were all pretty straightforward plans, and maybe that was both their strength and their weakness. They were simple. And that meant they were predictable. Eric's plan was the bloodiest, of course. There would certainly be loss of life. Audrina and Colton's plan was the most human, since it depended on a day attack. Pam's was possibly the best, since it was a night attack but not in a heavily peopled area, though the club exit was so obviously the weakest point that I felt sure whatever vampires Victor used as bodyguards — maybe the toothsome Antonio and Luis? — would be extra vigilant at such a moment.

"I have a plan," I said.

It was like I'd suddenly stood up and unhooked my bra. They all looked at me simultaneously, with a combination of surprise and skepticism. I will say that most of the skepticism came from Audrina and Colton, who hardly knew me. Bubba had been sitting on the high stool beside the counter, sipping a TrueBlood with an unsatisfied air. He looked pleased when I pointed to him and said, "*He's* the way."

I laid out my idea, trying hard to sound confident, and when I was through, they began trying to poke holes in it. And Bubba was reluctant, at least initially.

In the end, Bubba said he would do it if Mr. Bill said it was a good idea. I phoned

Bill. He was over in a flash, and the look he gave me when I let him in told me he was enjoying remembering how I looked wrapped in a tablecloth. Or even before I'd found the tablecloth. With an effort, I swallowed my confusion and explained everything to him. And after a few embellishments had been added, he agreed.

We went over the order of events again and again, trying to allow for every contingency. By three thirty in the morning, we were all in agreement. I was so tired I was asleep on my feet, and Audrina and Colton were barely able to stifle their yawns. Pam, who'd been stepping out of the room to call Immanuel periodically, preceded Eric out the door. She was anxious to get to the hospital. Bill and Bubba had departed for Bill's house, where Bubba would spend the day. I was alone with Eric.

We looked at each other, both at a loss. I tried to put myself in his place, feel what he must feel, but I simply couldn't do it. I couldn't imagine that, say, my grandmother had decided who I should marry and then passed away, fully expecting me to carry out her wishes. I couldn't imagine that I had to follow directions from beyond the grave, leave my home and go to a new place with people I didn't know, have sex with a stranger, simply because someone else had wanted me to.

Even, a little voice said inside me, *if the stranger was beautiful and wealthy and politically astute?*

No, I told myself stoutly. *Not even then.*

"Can you put yourself in my place?" Eric asked, chiming in on my thoughts. We knew each other pretty well, without the bond. He took my hand and held it between his cold ones.

"No, actually, I can't," I said, as evenly as I could manage. "I've been trying. But I'm not used to that sort of long-distance manipulation. Even after death, Appius is controlling you, and I just can't picture myself in that position."

"Americans," Eric said, and I couldn't decide if he said it admiringly or with a mild exasperation.

"Not just Americans, Eric."

"I feel very old."

"You are very old-*fashioned.*" He was ancient-fashioned.

"I can't ignore a signed document," he said, almost angrily. "He made an agreement for me, and I was his to order. He created me."

What could I say, in the face of such conviction? "I'm so glad he's dead," I told

Eric, not caring that my bitterness was written on my face. Eric looked sad, or at least regretful, but there was nothing else to say. Eric didn't mention spending what was left of the night with me, which was smart on his part.

After he left, I began checking all the windows and doors in the house. Since so many people had been in and out that day and night, it seemed a good idea. I wasn't too surprised to see Bill out in the yard when I was locking the kitchen window over the sink.

Though he didn't beckon to me, I took my weary self outside.

"What has Eric done to you?" he said.

I condensed the situation into a few sentences.

"What a dilemma," Bill said, not totally displeased.

"So you'd feel the way Eric does?"

In an eerie echo, Bill took my hand just as Eric had earlier. "Not only did Appius already enter negotiations, so there are presumably legal documents on the table, but also I would have to give my maker's wishes some consideration — as much as I hate to acknowledge that. You have no idea how strong the bond is. The years spent with one's maker are the most important years of a vampire's existence. As loathsome as I found Lorena, I have to admit that she did her best to teach me to be an effective vampire. Looking back on her life now — Judith and I talked about this, of course — Lorena betrayed her own maker, and then had years and years to regret it. The guilt drove her mad, we think."

Well, I was glad Bill and Judith had gotten to talk over fun times in the old days with Mama Lorena — murderess, prostitute, torturer. I couldn't really hold the prostitute part against her, since there hadn't been that many ways for a woman alone to make a living in the old times, even a vampire woman. But the rest — no matter what her circumstances had been, no matter how hard her life before and after her first death, Lorena had been an evil bitch. I pulled my hand away from Bill.

"Good night," I said. "I'm overdue for bed."

"Are you angry with me?"

"Not exactly," I said. "I'm just tired and sad."

"I love you," Bill said helplessly, as if he wished those magic words would heal me. But he knew they wouldn't.

"That's what you all keep saying," I answered. "But it doesn't seem to get me any happier." I didn't know if I had a valid point or if I was simply being self-pitying, but it was too late at night — no, too early in the morning — to have the clarity of mind to decide that. A few minutes later, I crawled into my bed in an empty house, and being alone felt pretty damn good.

I woke up at noon on Friday with two pressing thoughts. The first was, *Did Dermot renew my wards?* And the second was, *Oh my God, the baby shower is tomorrow!*

After some coffee and pulling on my clothes, I called Hooligans. Bellenos answered.

"Hi," I said. "Can I speak to Dermot? Is he better?"

"He's well," Bellenos said. "But he's on his way to your house."

"Oh, good! Listen, maybe you'll know this. . . . Did he renew the wards on the house, or am I unprotected?"

"God forbid you should be with a fairy unprotected," Bellenos said, trying to sound serious.

"No double entendres!"

"Okay, okay," he said, and I could tell he was flashing that sharp-toothed smile. "I myself put wards around your house, and I assure you they will hold."

"Thanks, Bellenos," I said, but I wasn't

389

completely happy that someone I trusted as little as Bellenos had been in charge of my protection.

"You're welcome. Despite your doubts, I don't want anything to happen to you."

"That's good to know," I said, keeping all expression out of my voice.

Bellenos laughed. "If you get too lonely out there in the woods, you can always call me," he said.

"Hmmm," I said. "Thanks." Was the elf coming on to me? That made no sense. More likely he wanted to eat me, and not in the fun way.

Maybe better not to know. I wondered how Dermot was getting here but not enough to call Bellenos again.

Reassured that Dermot was returning, I studied my list of shower preparations. I'd asked Maxine Fortenberry to make the punch, because hers was famous. I was picking up the cake from the bakery. I didn't have to work today or tomorrow, which meant a big loss in tips, but it was turning out real convenient. So my to-do list was like: Today, complete all preparations for the baby shower. Tonight, kill Victor. Tomorrow, guests arrive for shower.

In the meantime, like any incipient hostess, I was going to be all about the cleaning.

My living room was still below par since the attic stuff had been sitting in it, and I started from the top down: dust the pictures, then the furniture, then the baseboards. Then vacuum. I worked my way down the hall, visiting my bedroom, the guest bedroom, and the hall bathroom. I got a squirt bottle of all-purpose cleaner and attacked the kitchen surfaces. I was about to mop the floors when I saw Dermot in the backyard. He'd driven back in a battered Chevy compact.

"Where'd you get the car?" I called from the back porch.

"I bought it," he said proudly.

I hoped he hadn't used fairy enchantment or something. I was scared to ask. "Let me see your head," I said, when he got into the house. I looked at the back of his skull where the gash had been. A thin white line, that was all. "Amazing," I said. "How do you feel?"

"Better than I did yesterday. I'm ready to get back to work." He went into the living room. "You're cleaning," he said. "Is there a special occasion?"

"Yes," I said, smacking myself on the forehead. "I'm so sorry I forgot to tell you. I'm giving Tara Thornton — Tara du Rone — a baby shower tomorrow. She's expecting twins, Claude believes. Oh, she got that confirmed."

"Can I come?" he asked.

"It's all right with me," I said, taken aback. Most human guys would rather have their toenails painted than come to such a party. "You'll be the only man there, but I assume that won't bother you?"

"Sounds great," he said, smiling that beautiful smile.

"You'll have to keep your ears covered and listen to about a million comments about how much you look like Jason," I said. "We'll need to explain you."

"Just tell them I'm your great-uncle," he said.

For one fun moment, I envisioned doing just that. I had to give it up, though with some regret. "You look much too young to be my great-uncle, and everyone here knows my family tree. The human part of it," I added hastily. "But I'll think of something."

While I vacuumed, Dermot looked at the big box of pictures and the smaller one of printed material that I hadn't yet had a chance to go over. He seemed fascinated by the pictures. "We don't use this technology," he said.

I sat beside him when I'd put the vacuum away. I'd tried to arrange the images in chronological order, but it had been a hasty task, and I was sure I'd have to redo it.

The pictures at the front of the box were very old. People sitting in stiff groups, their backs rigid, their faces, too. If the backs were labeled, it was in spidery formal handwriting. Many of the men were bearded or mustached, and they wore hats and ties. The women were confined in long sleeves and skirts, and their posture was amazing.

Gradually as the Stackhouse family rolled along in time, the pictures became less posed, more spontaneous. The clothing morphed along with attitudes. Color began to tint faces and scenery. Dermot seemed genuinely interested, so I explained the background on some of the more recent snapshots. One was of a very old man holding a baby swathed in pink. "That's me and one of my great-grandfathers; he died when I was little bitty," I said. "That's him and his wife when they were in their fifties. And this is my grandmother Adele and her husband."

"No," Dermot said. "That's my brother Fintan."

"No, this is my grandfather, Mitchell. Look at him."

"He *is* your grandfather. Your true grandfather. Fintan."

"How can you tell?"

"He's made himself to look like Adele's husband, but I can tell it's my brother. He was my twin, after all, though we were not identical. Look here at his feet. His feet are smaller than those of the man who married Adele. Fintan was always careless that way."

I spread out all the pictures of Grandmother and Grandfather Stackhouse. Fintan was in about a third of them. I'd suspected from her letter that Fintan had been around more than she'd realized, but this was just creepy. In every picture of Fintan-as-Mitchell, he was smiling broadly.

"She didn't know about this, for sure," I said. Dermot looked dubious. And I had to admit to myself that she had suspected. It was there, in her letter.

"He was playing one of his jokes," Dermot said fondly. "Fintan was a great one for jokes."

"But . . ." I hesitated, not sure how to phrase what I wanted to say. "You get that this was really wrong?" I said. "You understand that he was deceiving her on a couple of different levels?"

"She agreed to be lovers with him," Dermot said. "He was very fond of her. What difference does it make?"

"It makes a lot of difference," I said. "If

she thought she was with one man when she was with another, that's a huge deception."

"But a harmless one, surely? After all, even you agree she loved both men, had sex with both of them willingly. So," he asked again, "what difference does it make?"

I stared at him doubtfully. No matter how she felt about her husband or her lover, I still thought there was a moral issue here. In fact, I knew there was. Dermot didn't seem to be able to discern that. I wondered if my great-grandfather would agree with me or with Dermot. I had a sinking feeling I knew.

"I better get back to work," I said, with a tight smile. "Got to mop the kitchen. You going to get back to work in the attic?"

He nodded enthusiastically. "I love the machinery," he said.

"Please close the attic door, then, because I've dusted down here and I don't want to have to do that again before tomorrow afternoon."

"Sure, Sookie."

Dermot went up the stairs whistling. It was a tune I'd never heard before, which figured.

I gathered up the pictures, keeping separate the ones that Dermot had earmarked as featuring his brother. I was considering building a little fire with them. Up in the attic, the sander started up. I looked at the ceiling as if I could see Dermot through the boards. Then I shook myself and went back to work, but in an abstracted and uneasy mood.

When I was standing on a stepladder hanging the WELCOME BABY sign from the light fixture, I remembered I had to iron my great-grandmother's tablecloth. I hate ironing, but it had to be done, and better today than tomorrow. When the stepladder was put away, I opened the ironing board — there'd been a built-in one in the previous kitchen — and set to work. The tablecloth was not exactly white anymore. It had aged to ivory. I soon had it smooth and beautiful, and touching it reminded me of high occasions in the past. I'd seen pictures including this very piece of cloth today; it had been on the kitchen table or the old sideboard for Thanksgivings and Christmases and wedding showers and anniversaries. I loved my family, and I loved those memories. I only regretted that there were so few of us to recall them.

And I was aware of another truth, another real thing. I realized I really didn't appreciate the fairy sense of fun that had made a lie out of some of those memories.

By three that afternoon, the house was as close to ready as I could get it. The sideboard was draped with the tablecloth, the paper plates and napkins were out, the plastic forks and spoons. I'd polished the silver nut dish and a little tray for the cheese straws, which I'd made and frozen a couple of weeks before. I ran down my checklist. I was as ready as I could possibly be.

If I didn't survive tonight, I was afraid that the baby shower would be a bust. I had to assume that my friends would be too jangled to go ahead with the shower if I got killed. Just in case, I left detailed notes about the location of everything that wasn't already out. I even brought out my present for the babies, matching wicker baskets that could be used as traveling cribs. They were decorated with big gingham bows and packed full of useful stuff. I'd accumulated the items for the gift baskets on sale, bit by bit. Bottles for supplemental feeding, a baby thermometer, a few toys, a few receiving blankets, some picture books, bibs, a package of cloth diapers for use as spit-up rags. It felt strange to think that I might not be around to see the babies grow up.

It also felt strange that paying for the shower hadn't been such a financial hardship, thanks to the money in my savings account.

Suddenly, I had an amazing idea. That made two in two days. As soon as I'd worked it out in my head, I was in my car and on my way to town. It felt weird walking into Merlotte's on my day off. Sam looked surprised but pleased to see me. He was in his office with a stack of bills in front of him. I put another piece of paper on his desk. He looked at it. "What is this?" he said in a low voice.

"You know what it is. Don't you give me that, Sam Merlotte. You need money. I've got money. You put this in your account today. You use it to pull the bar through until times are better."

"I can't take this, Sookie." He didn't meet my eyes.

"The hell you can't, Sam. Look at me."

Finally, he did.

"I'm not kidding. You put it in the bank today," I said. "And if anything might happen to me, you can repay my estate within, say, five years."

"Why would anything happen to you?" Sam's face darkened.

"Nothing will. I'm just saying. It's irresponsible to loan money without making arrangements to pay it back. I'm calling my lawyer and telling him all this, and he'll draw up a paper. But right now, right this minute, you go to the bank."

Sam looked away. I could feel the emotions sweeping over him. Truly, it felt wonderful to do something nice for him. He'd done so many nice things for me. He said, "All right." I could tell it was hard for him, as it would be for almost any man, but he knew it was the sensible thing to do, and he knew it wasn't charity.

"It's a love offering," I said, grinning at him. "Like we took up at church last Sunday." That love offering had been for the missionaries in Uganda, and this one was for Merlotte's Bar.

"I'd believe that," he said, and met my eyes.

I kept my smile, but I began to feel a little self-conscious. "I have to go get ready," I said.

"What for?" His reddish eyebrows drew together.

"Tara's baby shower," I said. "It's an old-fashioned gals-only party, so you didn't get invited."

"I'll try to contain my misery," he said. He didn't move.

"Are you getting up to go to the bank?" I asked sweetly.

"Uh, yeah, getting up right now." He did get out of the chair and call down the hall to let the servers know he was running a quick errand. I got in my car at the same time he got in his truck. I don't know about Sam, but I was feeling really good.

I did stop by my lawyer's to tell him what I'd done. This would be my human, local lawyer, not Mr. Cataliades. Whom, by the way, I hadn't heard from.

I swung by Maxine's house to get the punch, thanked her profusely, left her a list of what I was going to do and had done for the shower arrangements (to her puzzlement), and took the frozen containers back to my house to pop in the little chest freezer on my back porch. I had the ginger ale set out on the counter to mix with the frozen juices.

I was as prepared as I could be for the baby shower.

Now I had to get ready to kill Victor.

CHAPTER 14

Sam called me as I was putting on my makeup.

"Hi," I said. "You got the check to the bank, yes?"

"Yes," he said. "Since you told me like a million times. No problem there. I'm calling to tell you I just got a very weird phone call from your friend Amelia. She said she was calling me because you wouldn't want to talk to her. She said it was about that thing you found. She looked it up. The cluviel dor?" He sounded it out very carefully.

"Yeah?"

"She didn't want to talk over the phone to me about it, but she said to tell you urgently to check your e-mail. She said you were pretty bad about forgetting to do that. She didn't seem to think you'd answer your phone if you knew from your caller ID that it was her on the phone."

"I'll go look at my e-mail right now."

"Sookie?"

"Yeah?"

"You okay?"

Almost certainly not. "Sure, Sam. Thanks for standing in place of the answering machine."

"No problem."

Amelia had certainly figured out how to get my attention. I took the cluviel dor out of the drawer and took it with me to the little desk in the living room where I'd put the computer. Yes, I had a lot of mail.

Most of it was junk, but there was one from Amelia, sure enough, and one from Mr. Cataliades that had come two days before. Color me surprised.

I was so curious I opened his message first. Though he wasn't brief, he was to the point.

Miss Stackhouse,

I got your message on my answering machine. I have been traveling so certain individuals cannot find me. I have many friends, but also many enemies. I am watching you closely, but I hope not intrusively. You're the only person I know who has as many enemies as I. I've done the best I can to keep you a step ahead of that hellspawn Sandra Pelt.

She's not dead yet, though. Beware.

I don't believe you knew that I was a great friend of your grandfather, Fintan. I knew your grandmother, though not well. In fact, I met your father and his sister, and your brother Jason, though he will never remember it since he was quite small. So were you when I first saw you. They were all disappointments except you.

I think you must have found the cluviel dor, since I plucked the term out of Miss Amelia's head when I saw her at the shop. I don't know where your grandmother hid it, I only know she was given one, because I gave it to her. If you have discovered it, I advise you to be very careful about its use. Think once, and twice, and three times before you expend its energy. You can change the world, you know. Any series of events you alter by magic can have unexpected repercussions in history. I'll contact you again when I can, and perhaps stop by to explain more fully. Best wishes for your survival.

Desmond Cataliades, attorney-at-law,
your sponsor

As Pam might say, "Fuck a zombie." Mr.

Cataliades was indeed my sponsor, the dark stranger who'd visited Gran. What did that mean? And he said he had read Amelia's mind. Was he a telepath, too? Wasn't that quite a coincidence? I had a feeling there was a lot to know about this, and though he'd only warned me about Sandra Pelt and using the cluviel dor, I got the distinct impression he was paving the way for a Big Bad Talk. I read over the message two more times hoping to extract some solid piece of information about the cluviel dor from it, but I had to conclude I got zilch.

I opened Amelia's e-mail, not without a deep feeling of misgiving and a residue of indignation. Her brain was open for the picking, apparently. Amelia had a lot of information in her head about me and my doings. Though this wasn't exactly her fault, I resolved not to tell her any more secrets.

Sookie,
I'm sorry for everything. You know I don't think before I act, and I didn't this time. I just wanted you to be as happy as I am with Bob, I guess, and I didn't think about how you'd feel. I was trying to manage your life. Again, sorry.
After we got back home, I did some more research and found the cluviel dor.

I guess one of your fairy kin must have been talking about this? There hadn't been one on the earth for hundreds of years. They're fairy love tokens, and they take a year to make, at least. The cluviel dor gives the beloved one wish. That's why it's so romantic, I guess. The wish has to be personal. It can't be for world peace, or an end to hunger, or something global like that. But on an individual level, apparently this magic is so potent it can really change a life in a drastic way. If someone gives a loved one a cluviel dor, it's really a serious gesture. It's not like flowers or candy. It's more on the level of a diamond necklace or a yacht, if the jewelry or the boat had magical powers. I don't know why you need to know about fairy love tokens, but if you've seen one, you've seen something amazing. I don't think the fae can even make them anymore.

I hope some day you can forgive me, and maybe then I'll hear the story.

Amelia

I ran a finger over the smoothness of this very dangerous object I had, and I shivered.

Warning, warning, and some more warning.

I sat at the desk for a few more minutes, lost in thought. The more I knew about fairy nature, the less I trusted fairies. Period. Including Claude and Dermot. (And especially Niall, my great-grandfather; it seemed I was always on the verge of remembering something about him, something really tricky.) I shook my head impatiently. Not the time to worry about that.

Though I'd put off admitting it as long as I could, I had to face unpleasant facts. Mr. Cataliades, through his friendship with my birth grandfather, had had more to do with my life than I'd ever guessed, and he was only revealing that to me now for reasons I couldn't fathom. When I'd met the demon lawyer, he hadn't quivered an eyelash in recognition.

It was all tied together somehow, and it all added up to a deep misgiving about my fairy kin. I believed that Claude, Dermot, Fintan, and Niall loved me as much as they could (for Claude, this would be quite a small amount, because he loved himself most of all). But I didn't feel that it was a wholesome love. Though that adjective made me wince and think of Wonder Bread, it was the only one that fit.

As a sort of corollary to my increased understanding of fairy nature, I no longer doubted Gran's word. Instead, I believed that Fintan had loved my grandmother Adele more than she'd ever realized, and in fact he'd adored her beyond the bounds of human imagination. He'd been with her much more often than she knew, sometimes taking on the guise of her husband to be in her presence. He'd taken family photos with her; he'd watched her go about her daily business; he'd probably (wince!) had sex with her while disguised as Mitchell. Where had my real grandfather been while all of this was going on? Had he still been present in his body, but unconscious? I hoped not, but I'd never know. I wasn't sure I truly wanted to.

Because of Fintan's devotion, he'd given my grandmother a cluviel dor. Perhaps it could have saved her life, but I didn't believe she'd ever thought of using it. Perhaps her faith had precluded sincere belief in the power of a magical object.

Gran had stowed her letter of confession and the cluviel dor in the concealed drawer years ago to keep them safe from the prying eyes of the two grandchildren she was raising. I was sure that after she'd hidden the items that made her feel so guilty, she'd almost forgotten about them. I figured the relief of unburdening herself was so great, she'd quit worrying about the memory altogether. It must have seemed outlandish, contrasted with the daily difficulties of being a widow raising two grandchildren.

Maybe (I conjectured) from time to time she'd thought, *I really should tell Sookie where those things are.* But of course, she'd always supposed she'd have more time. We always do.

I looked down at the smooth object in my hand. I tried to imagine the things I could do with it. It was supposed to grant one wish, a wish for someone you loved. Since I loved Eric, presumably I could wish Victor would die, which would definitely benefit my loved one. It seemed awful to me, using a love token to kill someone, whether or not it benefited Eric. An idea came to me that made my eyes widen. I could take away Hunter's telepathy! He could grow up normal! I could counteract Hadley's unintentional burdensome gift to her abandoned son.

That seemed like such a fabulous idea. I was delighted for all of thirty seconds. Then, of course, doubt set in. Was it right to change someone's life that much simply because I could? On the other hand, was it right to let Hunter suffer his way through a difficult childhood?

I could change *myself.*

That was so shocking an idea that it almost made me black out. I simply couldn't think about it just now. I had to prepare for Operation Victor.

After thirty minutes, I was ready to go.

I drove to Fangtasia, trying to keep my mind empty and my spirit fierce. (Emptying my mind was maybe too easy. I'd learned so much in the past few days that I hardly knew who I was anymore. And that made me pretty angry, so fierce was easy, too.) I sang along with every song on the radio, and because I have an awful voice I was glad I was alone. Pam can't sing, either. I was thinking about her a lot as I drove, wondering if her Miriam was alive or dead, feeling sorry for my best vampire friend. Pam was so tough and so strong and so ruthless that I hadn't ever considered her more delicate emotions until the past few days. Maybe that was why Eric had chosen Pam when he'd wanted a child; he'd sensed they were kindred spirits.

I didn't doubt Eric loved me, just as I knew Pam loved her ailing Miriam. But I didn't know if Eric loved me enough to defy all his maker's arrangements, enough to forgo the leap in power and status and income he'd gain as consort of the Queen of Oklahoma. Would Eric enjoy being a Sooner? As I navigated through Shreveport, I wondered if Oklahoma vampires wore cowboy boots and knew all the songs from the musical. I wondered why I was thinking such idiotic thoughts when I should be preparing for a very grim evening, an evening I might not survive.

Judging from the parking lot, Fangtasia was jam-packed. I went to the employee entrance and knocked, using a special pattern. Maxwell opened the door, looking positively suave in a beautiful summer-weight tan suit. Dark-skinned vampires undergo an interesting change a few decades after they're turned. If they were a very dark shade in life, they become a light brown, sort of a milk chocolate. Those who were lighter skinned become a sort of creamy ecru. Maxwell Lee hadn't been dead long enough for that, though. He was still one of the darkest men I had ever seen, the color of ebony, and his mustache was as precise as if he'd shaved with a ruler at hand. We'd never been especially fond of each other, but this evening his smile was almost manic in its cheerfulness.

"Miss Stackhouse, we're so glad you stopped by tonight," he said loudly. "Eric will be pleased to see you looking so — so tasty."

I take my compliments where I can get them, and "tasty" wasn't bad. I was wearing a strapless dress in sky blue with a broad white belt and white sandals. (I know white shoes are supposed to make your feet look big, but mine aren't, so I didn't care.) My hair was down. I felt pretty damn good. I held out a foot so Maxwell could admire my self-administered pedicure. Spicy Pink Carnation.

"Fresh as a daisy," Maxwell said. He pulled aside his jacket to show me that he was carrying a gun. I gave him big eyes of admiration. Carrying a firearm was not a vampire norm, and it might be a bit unexpected. Colton and Audrina came in on my heels. Audrina had put up her hair with what looked like chopsticks, and she was carrying a large purse, almost as large as mine. Colton was armed, too, because he was wearing a jacket, and on a sultry evening like this one, humans just didn't wear jackets if they could help it. I introduced them to Maxwell, and after a polite exchange they sauntered down the hall to go out into the club.

I found Eric in his office sitting behind the desk. Pam was sitting on it, and Thalia was on the couch. Oh, boy! I felt more confident when I saw the tiny ancient Greek vampire. Thalia had been turned so long ago that no trace of humanity remained. She was simply a cold killing machine. She'd reluctantly joined the vampires that came out, but she despised humans with a thoroughness and ferocity that had made her a sort of cult figure. One website had offered five thousand dollars to the man or woman who could get a picture of Thalia smiling. No one had ever collected, but they could have tonight. She was smiling now. It was creepy as hell.

"He accepted the invitation," Eric said without preamble. "He was uneasy, but he couldn't resist. I told him he was welcome to bring as many of his own people as he wished so that they could share the experience."

"That was the only way to do it," I said.

"I think you're right," Pam said. "I think he'll bring only a few, because he'll want to show us how confident he is."

Mustapha Khan knocked on the door frame. Eric beckoned him in.

"Bill and Bubba are making a stop in the alley two blocks over," he said, barely glancing at the rest of us.

"What for?" Eric was surprised.

"Ah . . . something about cats."

We all looked away, embarrassed. Bubba's perversion was not anything vampires wanted to talk about.

"But he's cheerful? In a good mood?"

"Yes, Eric. He's happy as a minister on Easter Sunday. Bill took him for a drive in an antique car, then horseback riding, and then to the alley. They should be here right on time. I told Bill I'd call him when Victor arrived."

By then, Fangtasia would be closed to the public. Though the happy and free-spending crowd out on the floor didn't know it, tonight the king of rock 'n' roll would sing again for the Regent of Louisiana. Who could turn down an invitation to such an event?

Not fanboy Victor, that was for sure. The cardboard cutout at Vampire's Kiss had been a big clue. Of course Victor had tried to get Bubba to come to his own club, but I'd known Bubba wouldn't want to go to Vampire's Kiss. He'd want to stay with Bill, and if Bill said Fangtasia was the place to be, that was what Bubba would insist on.

We sat in silence, though Fangtasia is never really silent. We could hear the music from the bar area, and the hum of voices. It was almost as if the customers could sense

413

that tonight was a special night, that they all had cause to celebrate . . . or to have a last hurrah before they perished.

Though I felt it put me one step closer to catastrophe, I'd brought the cluviel dor. It was tucked into my belt behind the huge buckle. It pressed into my flesh insistently.

Mustapha Khan had taken up a stance against the wall. He was deep into his Blade fantasy that night, with dark glasses, a leather jacket, and a great haircut. I wondered where his buddy Warren was. Finally, out of sheer desperation for some conversation, I asked.

"Warren, he's outside the club on the roof of the Bed Bath & Beyond." Mustapha Khan didn't turn his face to me when he spoke.

"What for?"

"He's a shooter."

"We refined your idea a bit," Eric said. "Anyone gets out the door, Warren will take care of them." He'd been slumped back in his chair with his feet on the desk. Pam hadn't looked at me since I'd come in. Suddenly, I wondered why.

"Pam?" I said. I got up and took a step toward her.

She shook her head, her face averted.

I can't read vampire minds, but I didn't

have to. Miriam had died today. Looking at the set of Pam's shoulders I knew better than to say anything. It went against my nature to resume my seat on the couch without offering her comfort, a Kleenex, a few words of solace. But it would be Pam's nature to strike out if I offered those things.

I touched my belt, where the cluviel dor made a hard impression on my stomach. Could I wish Miriam back alive? I wondered if that would satisfy the requirement that the wish be for someone I loved. I was very fond of Pam, but wouldn't that be too indirect?

I felt like I had a bomb strapped to me.

I heard the shimmery sound of the gong. Eric had installed one in the bar, and the bartender rang it fifteen minutes before closing. I didn't even know who'd taken over the bartending duties since Felicia had been killed by Alexei. Maybe I hadn't been interested enough in Eric's business lately. On the other hand, he himself had been abstracted from his normal absorption in his little kingdom by Victor's predations. I realized that lack of conversation about ordinary things was one of our problems. I hoped we'd get to correct it.

I got up and went down the hall to the main area of the bar. I couldn't stand sitting in Eric's office anymore, not with Pam suffering the way she was.

I spotted Colton and Audrina dancing on the tiny floor, arms around each other. Immanuel was sitting at the bar, and I climbed onto the stool next to him. The bartender came to stand across from me. He was a brawny fellow with ringlets cascading down his back, total eye candy. A vampire, of course.

"What can I get you, wife of my sheriff?" he asked ceremoniously.

"You can get me a tonic and lime, please. Sorry I haven't had a chance to meet you before. What's your name?"

"Jock," he said, as if daring me to make a joke. I wouldn't dream of it.

"When did you start work, Jock?"

"I came from Reno when the last bartender died," he said. "I worked for Victor there."

I wondered which way Jock would jump tonight. Interesting to see.

I didn't know Immanuel well — in fact, I barely knew him. But I patted his shoulder and asked him if I could buy him a drink.

He turned and gave my hair a long look, finally nodding his approval. "Sure," he said. "I'd like another beer."

"I'm sorry," I said quietly, after I'd asked

Jock to bring Immanuel a beer. I wondered where Miriam's body was now; at the undertaker's, I assumed.

"Appreciated," he replied. After a moment, he said, "Pam was going to do it tonight, without permission. Turn Miriam, that is. But Mir just . . . breathed out one last time, and then she was gone."

"Your mom and dad . . . ?"

He shook his head. "It was just us."

There was really nothing else to say about that.

"Maybe you should go home?" I suggested. He didn't look like much of a fighter to me.

"I don't think so," he said.

I couldn't make him leave, so I drank my tonic and lime while all the human customers left. The bar grew quiet and relatively empty. Indira, one of Eric's vamps, came in, wearing a full sari. I'd never seen her in traditional clothing before, and the pink and green of the pattern was really fetching. Jock gave her an admiring look. Thalia and Maxwell came out of the back and moved around the club along with the human staff, busy cleaning the place up for the afterparty. I helped, too. This was work I was used to. The tables circling the little dance floor and stage were moved away, and two lines of chairs were arranged instead. Maxwell brought in an elaborate sort of boom box. Bubba's music. After I swept the dance floor and stage, I got out of the way by resuming my stool at the bar.

Heidi, whose specialty was tracking, came in, her hair in narrow braids. Lean and plain, Heidi always carried an air of grief around with her like a cloud. I had no idea what she'd do tonight when the shit hit the fan.

While Jock was cleaning up the supplies on his side of the counter, Colton and Audrina came over. Jock looked surprised to see humans he didn't know. Their presence had to be explained; I didn't want Jock becoming suspicious. I said, "Colton, Audrina, meet Jock. Jock, these two lovely people have agreed to donate in case Victor wants local hospitality. Of course, we're hoping that won't happen on the premises, but Eric doesn't want to fail in his welcome."

"Good idea," Jock said, eyeing Audrina appreciatively. "We can't give the regent less than he expects."

"No." Or less than he deserves.

After forty-five minutes, the place looked pretty good again, and the last of the human employees went out the back door. The only breathers remaining were Colton, Audrina, Immanuel, Mustapha Khan, and me. (I definitely had that conspicuous feeling.) The Shreveport vamps I'd known since I'd started dating Bill had assembled: Pam, Maxwell Lee, Thalia, Indira. I knew all of them to some extent. Victor would be instantly alert if all Eric's vampires were there, or if they were all Eric's heavy hitters. So Eric had called in the little Minden nest: Palomino, Rubio Hermosa, and Parker Coburn, the Katrina exiles. They trailed in looking unhappy but resigned. They stood against the wall, holding hands. It was kind of sweet, but sad, too.

The jukebox cut off. The near silence was instantly oppressive.

Though Fangtasia sits in a busy shopping and dining area of Shreveport, at this hour — even on a weekend — there was not much city sound outside. None of us felt like talking. I didn't know what thoughts occupied other heads, but I was considering the fact that I might die that very night. I was sorry about the baby shower, but I'd gotten things as ready as I could get them. I was sorry I hadn't gotten to have a conference with Mr. Cataliades to get everything straight in my head, all this new information I'd hardly had time to assimilate. I was glad I'd given the money to Sam, and sorry

I couldn't have been frank with him about why it needed to be done this very day. I hoped if I died, Jason would move back into the old house, that he would marry Michele, that they would raise kids there. My mother, Michelle-with-two-*l*s, had been completely different from Jason's Michele-with-one-*l*, at least judging by my childhood memory of her, but they were alike in loving Jason. I was sorry I hadn't told him I loved him the last time we'd spoken.

I was sorry about a lot of things. My mistakes and offenses crowded around me.

Eric drifted over and turned me on the stool so he could put his arms around me. "I wish you didn't have to be here," he said. That was all the conversation we could have with Jock in earshot. I leaned against Eric's cool body, my head resting on his silent chest. I might not ever get to do this again.

Pam came to sit by Immanuel. Thalia scowled, which was her fallback expression, and turned her back on all of us. Indira sat with her eyes shut, the graceful folds of her sari making her look like a statue at Pier 1. Heidi looked from one to the other of us very seriously, and her mouth became set in a grim line. If she was worrying about Victor, I figured she'd go to stand by Jock, but I never saw her speak to him.

Maxwell apparently heard a knock at the back door, inaudible to my human ears. He jetted away and returned to tell Eric that Bill and Bubba had arrived. They were staying in the office until the moment came.

Very soon after that, I heard cars pull in front of the club.

"Showtime," Pam said, and for the first time that evening she smiled.

CHAPTER 15

Luis and Antonio came in first. They were clearly wary. It was like watching a cop show on television; they came inside in a rush, immediately separating to flank the door. I almost smiled, and Immanuel actually grinned, which was not a good idea. Luckily, humans are the last creatures vampires will worry about when they're anticipating trouble. The two handsome vamps, clad in jeans and T-shirts instead of leather loincloths, quickly searched the club, checking out places other vampires could hide. It would have been a severe breach of etiquette to demand body searches, but you could tell they were eyeballing each local vampire for guns or stakes. Maxwell had to give up his gun, which he did without a second's protest. He'd expected it.

After a thorough scan of the premises and a bow to Eric, Luis stuck his head out to give the all-clear.

The rest of Victor's entourage entered in order of expendability: the married human couple he'd been with at Vampire's Kiss (Mark and Mindy), two young vampires whose names I never learned, Ana Lyudmila (who looked much better out of her fantasy bondage gear), and a vampire I'd never seen, an Asian guy with ivory skin and jet-black hair pulled up on his head in a complicated knot. He would have looked great in traditional clothes, but instead he wore jeans and a black vest, no shirt or shoes.

"Akiro," Heidi said in an awed whisper. She'd eased closer to me, and the tension had crept into her, too.

"You know him from Nevada?"

"Oh, yes," she said. "I didn't know Victor had called for him. He's finally replaced Bruno — and Corinna, too. That's how good Akiro's reputation is."

Since he was now officially second-in-command, it was okay for Akiro to be openly armed. He was carrying a sword, like one other Asian vampire I'd met. (Come to think of it, she'd been a bodyguard, too.) Akiro stood in the center of the room, conscious of all the eyes on him, his face cold and hard, and his eyes relentless.

And then Victor made his entrance, resplendent in a white three-piece suit.

"Good God almighty," I said blankly, not daring to meet anyone's eyes. Victor's dark curls were carefully arranged, and his pierced ear sported a big gold hoop earring. His shoes were beautifully black. Victor was a trip. It almost seemed a shame to try to destroy all that beauty, and I wished he weren't so determined to ruin our lives. I set my purse on the bar and unzipped it so I'd have quick access. Immanuel slid off his stool and moved away to the wall, his eyes fixed on the newcomers. Heidi took his place while Victor and his party moved farther into the club.

Though my eyes were fixed on Victor, I felt obliged to speak to Heidi, since I felt she'd perched beside me for a reason. "How's your son?" I asked, like you do, when you know someone had a loved one.

"Eric has offered to let me bring him here," Heidi said, carefully keeping her eyes on the visitors.

"That's very good news," I said, and I meant it. One more on our side.

In the meantime, the reception was moving slowly forward.

"Victor," Eric said. He moved front and center, a careful two yards away from the regent. He was smart enough not to give

Victor a fulsome welcome, since that would be a huge tip that something bad was about to come down. "Welcome to Fangtasia. We're glad to have the chance to entertain you." Eric bowed. Akiro's face remained blank, as if Eric weren't there.

Still standing and flanked by Luis and Antonio, Victor inclined his curly head. "Sheriff, I present my new right hand, Akiro," he said with his flashing smile. "Akiro recently agreed to relocate from Nevada to Louisiana."

Eric said, "I welcome such a well-known vampire as Akiro to Louisiana. I'm sure you'll be a great addition to the regent's staff." Eric could give impassive as well as the next vampire.

Akiro had to acknowledge the greeting of a sheriff, who was higher on the food chain, but you could tell he didn't want to. His bow was a millimeter too shallow.

Vampires.

Great, I thought, very put out. *Finally, Victor replaces his lieutenant and his best fighter. Just at this moment.* "I guess this Akiro is a pretty good fighter, huh?" I whispered to Heidi.

"You could say that," Heidi said dryly, and she drifted forward to greet her regent. All Eric's vampires had to take turns offering obeisance. Jock, the newest member of Eric's staff, was last in line. You could tell he was ready to kiss Victor's ass if he got half a chance.

Mindy, with ill-timed lust, gave Jock a hopeful look. She was so dumb, but that didn't mean she ought to die. I wondered if I could get her to make a trip to the women's room before the time came. No. Unless it was her idea, such a maneuver would be a red flag. I looked at the newcomers and tried to brace myself for what was to come.

This was particularly horrible — this waiting, this planning, knowing I was about to do my best to kill the people in front of me. I was looking into their eyes and hoping they would die in the next hour. Was this how soldiers felt? I wasn't as wired as I thought I'd be; I was suspended in an eerie calm, perhaps because now that Victor had arrived, nothing could stop what was going to happen.

When Victor indicated he was satisfied with his greeting by taking the central chair, Eric told Jock to bring drinks all around. The out-of-town vamps all waited for Luis to drink from a glass he picked from the tray at random. After Luis survived for several minutes, all the newcomers selected glasses and one by one, they all took sips.

The atmosphere grew much easier after that, because the drinks were absolutely kosher: warmed synthetic blood, a premium brand.

"You stick to the letter of the law here at Fangtasia," Victor observed. He smiled at Eric. Mindy was between them, and she was leaning on Victor's shoulder, her own Diet Coke with rum in front of her. Her husband, Mark, on Victor's left, didn't seem to feel well. His color was bad, and he seemed list-less. When I saw the fang marks on his neck, I wondered if Victor had overindulged. Mindy didn't seem worried.

"Yes, Regent," Eric said. He smiled back, just as sincerely, and he didn't elaborate.

"Your beautiful wife?"

"Is present, of course," Eric said. "What would the evening be without her?" Eric waved me forward, and Victor raised his drink to me in appreciation of my appear-ance. I managed to look pleased. "Victor," I said, "we're so glad you could come to-night." I didn't try to summon more than "pleased." Victor wouldn't expect me to be as good at concealing my feelings as Eric was, and I wasn't going to give him cause to think any different.

Of course, Eric hadn't wanted me to be there. He'd made it plain that a frail human should not be around when vampires were fighting. In theory, I agreed. I would much rather have been at home — but I would have worried every second. The clincher in my argument was that Victor would definitely go on the alert if I were conspicuous by my absence, which would have been a clear signal that Eric was about to spring something. Eric couldn't deny that when I'd made the point at our meeting.

Akiro positioned himself behind Victor's chair. Hmmm, awkward. I was trying to think what I could do about that. Pam was behind Eric's chair. When Eric beckoned to me, I smiled and went to join him, my purse over my shoulder.

Colton and Audrina were blending into the background by carrying trays of drinks around the club.

To my astonishment, Heidi went down on one knee by my chair, her posture indicating alert attention. Eric glanced at her but didn't comment. Heidi was taking a stance as though Eric had ordered her to protect me during what might be a touchy visit. I looked down at her, but she didn't meet my eyes. Yep, that was exactly what had happened. At least that was within the scope of "normal" and wouldn't necessarily make the visitors worried.

"Bill," Eric called. "We're ready!"

And Bill emerged from the back hallway, smiling — a totally uncharacteristic broad grin — to stand with his arm outflung toward the hall (tah-DAH!) to announce Bubba's entrance.

And what an entrance it was! It put Victor's in the shade.

"Ohmygosh," I murmured. Bubba was wearing a red jumpsuit that someone had taken a Bedazzler to; he had fake jewels and sequins everywhere, and his hair was styled in an amazing pompadour. He was wearing black boots and big rings. He was smiling that amazing lopsided smile that had made women swoon all over the globe, and he was waving as though there were thousands of us instead of a handful. Bill stood by the boom box Maxwell had set up, and when Bubba leaped onto the tiny stage and thanked us all very much, the lights went down. Bill started the music — "Kentucky Rain."

It was incredible. What can I say?

Victor was totally entranced, or as totally as someone who's perpetually wary can be. Victor leaned forward — Mindy and Mark forgotten, the other vampires forgotten — to absorb the experience. After all, he had Akiro to watch out for him. And Akiro was on the job, no doubt about it. His eyes never fixed on Bubba, but swept the room. Luis and Antonio had positioned themselves by the front door, guarding Akiro's back, and the bodyguard's eyes were doing a 180-degree scan of the rest of the club as he stood behind Victor.

As Bubba bowed to the applause, which was as thunderous as our small crowd could manage, Bill started the music again. This time we heard "In the Ghetto."

Red tears ran down Victor's face. I glanced over my shoulder to see that Luis and Antonio were rapt. The two nameless vampires were standing close to Bill, their hands folded in front of them, watching the show.

Ana Lyudmila was not a music lover, apparently. She was looking bored as she sat on the end of a bench at one of the booths close to the front door. I could see her over Mark's shoulder. Thalia, who was about half Ana Lyudmila's size, sidled up to her and silently offered a tray laden with more drinks. Ana Lyudmila nodded graciously, selected one, and took a big swallow. After a second in which her expression flashed absolute horror, she crumpled. Thalia caught the bottle as it fell from Ana Lyudmila's fingers. The lethal and ancient vampire silently shoved the limp body farther into the booth and turned to look at the stage, standing so as to block the sprawl of Ana Lyudmila's legs. The whole episode took less than thirty seconds. I had no idea what had been in the drink; some form of liquid silver? Was that possible? That little subplan had been contingent on one of the vamps being out of the line of sight of the others, and fortunately for us it had paid off.

One down. We wanted to take out as many as possible before the fighting even started.

Palomino, whose whitish hair and lovely golden skin made her a standout, worked her way close to Antonio by casual increments. She caught Antonio's eye and she smiled, but she was careful not to overdo it.

My purse was on the floor in the tiny space between my chair and Eric's. I dipped my hand down into its open mouth and withdrew a very sharp stake. I pressed it into Eric's waiting hand. After a second of leaning on his shoulder to cover the move, I eased upright to give him room.

Maxwell Lee, who'd been standing by the door back to the offices, took off his suit coat and folded it carefully. I appreciated his clothes care, but it was like a signal he was about to take action. He seemed to realize it, because he settled on the edge of a

431

booth after that.

While Bubba stuck to ballad-type songs he was entrancing, but for his next number he'd picked "Jailhouse Rock," and somehow a tinge of sadness seemed to wash over the performance. Though the transition to vampirism had eased all of his infirmities, he'd still died in poor physical condition, and he still bore the marks of age. Now that he was singing a dancing number, the effect was slightly pathetic. I saw the little audience begin to lose their engrossment in the performance.

Switching the tone was a mistake, but one we couldn't have foreseen.

I could feel Eric's arm tense beside me, and then with the speed of a striking snake he leaned forward to clear Mindy Simpson to his left, his right arm rose up, and he swung in to stake Victor in the chest. As a sneak attack it was perfect. Eric would have hit the mark exactly if Akiro, with equally terrifying speed, hadn't whipped out his sword and brought it down as Eric moved.

Mindy Simpson was doomed to be in the wrong place at the wrong second. Akiro's sword struck her shoulder during its passage to Eric's arm and simply hewed through it, her bones and flesh slowing the lethal blade almost long enough for Eric to escape.

All hell broke loose.

Mindy screamed and died within seconds, and the amount of blood was simply incredible. While she died, a lot of things happened almost simultaneously. As Mark was still gaping, Victor was trying to shove aside Mindy's slumping and bleeding body, Akiro was trying to disentangle his sword, and Eric was ducking and moving forward to evade another slice of the sword. Eric's arm was bleeding, but thanks to Mindy's unintentional block, it was still operative. I stood and lunged backward to get out of the way, knocking my chair aside, and rammed right into Luis, who was launching himself forward to protect his master. I spoiled Luis's trajectory, and we ended up in a heap on the floor. Fortunately for me, he was too intent on the vampire part of the fight to consider me at all dangerous, and he simply used me as a springboard to push off.

Not that that felt exactly good, but it wasn't fatal.

I scrambled up to a crouch and tried to figure out what to do next. In the dimmed lights, it wasn't easy to decide what was happening. A fighting pair close to the club doors proved to be Palomino and Antonio, and a small figure flying through the air must have been Thalia. She meant to land on Akiro's back, but he turned at the last second — so incredibly fast — and instead she hit his chest, and he staggered. His sword was not a weapon for close fighting, not with Thalia doing her best to rip his throat out with her teeth.

Mark Simpson was staggering away from the body of his wife and the fighting vampires, and he was saying, "Oh my God, oh my God," over and over. But he did manage to take cover behind the bar, where he grabbed a bottle and began trying to find someone to hit. I felt I could handle Mark Simpson, and I pushed to my feet.

Colton took care of it before I could get there. He grabbed his own bottle and swung it at the back of Mark Simpson's head, and Mark staggered and went down.

While Thalia was keeping Akiro occupied, Eric and Pam went for Victor. There's no such thing as a fair bar brawl. They double-teamed him.

Maxwell Lee very precisely staked Antonio from the back while he was struggling with Palomino.

I could hear Bubba yelling in an agitated way. I got myself over to the stage and took Bubba's arm.

"Hey, it's okay," I said. So many people

were yelling and screaming that I wasn't sure he'd hear me, but after I repeated myself about twenty more times, he stopped the screaming (thank you, God) and said, "Miss Sookie, I want to get out of here."

"Sure," I said, trying to keep my own voice calm and level when I wanted to scream, too. "You see that door over there?" I pointed to the door that led back to the rest of the club, Eric's office and so on. "You go back there and wait. You did great, just great! Bill will be back there directly, I'm sure."

"Okay," he said forlornly, and I saw his silhouette moving against the faint light coming from the opened door. I finally located Bill, who was picking his way through the combatants with his eyes on the prize. He took Bubba by the arm to steer him to safety, which was Bill's designated job. I was proud to see that Bill had left one of the nameless vampires dead on the floor, already flaking away.

I was so intent on Bubba that I didn't see Audrina staggering toward me, her hands on her throat and blood pouring from a wound, until she actually collided with me, causing me to go down on my knees. I don't know what her goal was — maybe she was trying to go past me to the bar to get a towel to stanch the red flow, maybe she was just trying to get away from her attacker — but she never made it. She went down full-length on the floor a yard past me, and there was nothing I could do for her. I sensed movement behind me as I touched her wrist, and I threw myself away from the body just in time to dodge a blow from the bartender, Jock. He had excellent survival instincts, going after human women instead of vampires. Indira, her sari billowing around her, gripped Jock's heavy arm and swung him with enough force that he cannoned into a wall. A hole appeared in the wall, and Jock reeled back, unsteady on his feet. Indira threw herself down to the floor, reached between his legs, and gripped. Screaming, Jock stomped and kicked, but Indira emasculated him.

I had a new "most horrible thing I've ever seen."

Blood poured from Jock, thick and dark, and he looked down in shock while Indira shrieked in victory. With sudden determination, he swung his clenched fists and smacked her in the side of her head. Indira went flying, and it was her turn to collide with the wall. She lay still on the floor for a second, shaking her head as if there were flies buzzing around it. Jock went for her, but I caught hold of his shoulder long enough to slow him down a bit, and at the moment he reached her Indira revived enough to launch herself upward, throwing a fold of her sari over his face long enough to blind him while she caught the stake I tossed to her and drove it into his heart.

Jock, I hardly knew ye.

I tried to do a quick evaluation.

Jock down, Mark and Mindy Simpson down, Ana Lyudmila down, Antonio down, Unknown Enemy Vamp #1 down. Luis . . . Where'd he gone? I heard a shot outside and figured that answered my question. Sure enough, Luis ran back into the club with a wound in his left shoulder. Mustapha Khan was waiting with a very long knife. Luis put up a furious fight despite the bullet wound, and he had a concealed weapon, too. He drew out his own blade and scored a cut on Mustapha, but Immanuel kicked Luis's knee from the back and Luis crumpled. Rubio took advantage of the moment of weakness to drive in a stake. Though Mustapha said, "Oh, hell," with great disgust, he bowed to Rubio. Surprised, Rubio bowed back.

Palomino was having trouble with Unknown Enemy Vamp #2, who fought like a fiend. Maybe Palomino was not as skilled a fighter, or as old, but she was bloody and weakening. Parker, who was evidently not much of a brawler, kept to Two's back and repeatedly jabbed him with an ice pick, which was not too effective but obviously irritating. Two, a hefty vamp who'd been turned in his thirties, would heal up only to be punctured again. I'm sure it hurt like hell. Parker was apparently too scared to get in close enough to pierce Two's heart. Palomino was too slow from her many wounds to immobilize him. Mustapha, thwarted from the Luis kill, shoved Parker aside and beheaded Two with a dramatic sweep of his blade.

Now Akiro and Victor were the only enemies left standing.

They both knew they were fighting for their lives. Pam's mouth was bloody, but I couldn't tell if the blood was her own or Victor's. I felt the cluviel dor press into my waist and I thought of pulling it out, but the next instant Akiro managed to cut Thalia's arm off. Thalia grabbed it as it fell and hit Akiro with it, and Heidi jumped in behind him and stabbed him through the neck.

Akiro dropped his sword to pluck at his throat, and I nipped in to seize the weapon so he couldn't retrieve it. The sword was long, and not as heavy as I had anticipated. I stepped back to get it farther away from his groping hands, and just then Victor knocked Eric to the wall and pushed Pam down on her back, throwing himself on top of her right in front of me. He bit her neck, his hands locking her shoulders down.

She looked up at me, her face eerily calm. "Do it," she said.

"No." I might cut Pam.

"Do it." She was absolutely compelling. Her own hands flew up to grip Victor by his upper arms, locking him down.

Eric was staggering to his feet, blood dripping from his head, his wounded arm, and his side. He'd bitten Victor at least once, going by his reddened mouth. I looked down at Pam, who was holding on to our enemy with everything she had. She nodded, turned her head to the side. She closed her eyes. I wished I could do the same. I took a breath and swung the sword down.

CHAPTER 16

Pam shoved Victor off and leaped to her feet. I'd been so scared I'd kill Pam that I hadn't been forceful enough. I hadn't cut all the way through Victor, though I'd severed his spinal column. The sword stuck on the bone and I couldn't remove it. Horrified at myself, at the sensation of cutting into Victor, I backpedaled and covered my mouth.

Pam yanked the sword out of the wound and decapitated Victor.

"Surrender," Eric said to the gravely wounded Akiro.

Akiro shook his head. The wound in his throat prevented him from speaking.

"All right, then," Eric said wearily. He grabbed Akiro's head and broke his neck. The audible snap was deeply disgusting. I turned away, my stomach heaving while I told it to sit down and shut up. While Akiro lay helpless, Eric staked him.

And it was over. Victor and all his vampire attendants — and his human attendants, too — were dead. There were enough flaking vampires to change the quality of the air.

I sank down on a chair. Actually, I lost control of my legs and a chair happened to be underneath me.

Thalia was weeping over the pain of her amputated arm, but she was struggling hard against this display of weakness. Indira squatted on the floor looking exhausted but gleeful. Maxwell Lee, Parker, and Rubio had lesser injuries. Pam and Eric were covered in blood, both their own and Victor's. Palomino walked slowly over to Rubio and put her arms around him, drawing Parker into the embrace. Colton was kneeling by the dead Audrina, weeping.

I never wanted to see another battle, large or small, in my life. I looked at my lover, my husband, and he looked like a stranger to me. He and Pam stood facing each other, holding hands and beaming through the blood. Then they simply collapsed into each other, and Pam began laughing in a breathless way. "It's done!" she said. "It's done. We're free."

Until Felipe de Castro comes down on us like a ton of bricks because he wants to know

441

what happened to his regent, I thought, but I didn't say anything. A, I wasn't sure I could. B, we'd already wondered what would happen, but Eric's opinion was that it was better to ask forgiveness than permission.

Mustapha was on his cell phone, which was about as big as a cricket. "Warren, no point in you coming in, man," he said. "The deed is done. Good shot. Yeah, we got him."

Parker said, "Sheriff, we're leaving for home unless you need us." The weedy young man was supporting Palomino, and Rubio was on her other side. They were all pretty battered in one way or another.

"You may go." Eric, smeared with blood, was still very much the ruler. "You answered my call and did your jobs. You'll be rewarded."

Palomino, Rubio, and Parker mutually assisted each other to the back door. From their expressions, I was sure they hoped Eric didn't call them in again for a long, long time, no matter what the reward might be.

Indira crawled over to Thalia to apply Thalia's severed arm to its shoulder with force. She held it there, beaming. Indira was the happiest person in the club.

"Will that work?" I asked Pam, nodding at the shoulder-arm conjunction. Pam was wiping the bloody sword on Akiro's clothing. His throat was almost gone; wounded parts disintegrate more quickly than uninjured parts.

"Sometimes," she said, shrugging. "Since Thalia is so old, there's a chance. It's less painful and time-consuming than regeneration."

"Thalia, can I get you some blood?" I didn't think I'd ever been brave enough to address Thalia directly, but I could sure bring her some bottled blood and be glad to do it. She looked up at me, her eyes full of involuntary tears. It was obvious she was forcing herself to hold still. "Not unless you want to donate yourself," she said in her heavily accented English. "But Eric wouldn't be pleased if I drank from you. Immanuel, give me a mouthful?"

"All right," he said. The skinny hairdresser looked more than a little dazed.

"You sure?" I asked. "You don't quite seem yourself."

"Hell, yes," Immanuel said unconvincingly. "The guy who killed my sister is dead. I'm feeling good."

He didn't look it, but I was sure I didn't, either. I'd said as much as I could, so I sat by while Immanuel crouched awkwardly before Thalia's chair. The height differential was not in their favor. Thalia wrapped her good arm around Immanuel's neck and sank her fangs in without any further discussion. The expression on Immanuel's face went from bleak to blissful.

Thalia was a noisy eater.

Indira squatted beside her in her blood-drenched sari, patiently holding the severed limb to its source. As Thalia drank, I noticed that the arm looked more and more natural. The fingers flexed. I was astonished, but it was only one more extreme event during an evening of them.

Pam looked a little put out once her victory celebration with Eric was over and she saw that Immanuel was offering his blood to someone else. She asked Mustapha if he'd give her a drink, and he shrugged. "Comes with the job," he said, pulling down the neck of his black T-shirt. Pam looked incredibly white against Mustapha, and Mustapha's teeth bared in a grimace when she bit in. He, too, looked happier after a second.

Eric came over to me, beaming. I had never been more undilutedly glad that our bond was broken, because I didn't want to feel what he was feeling, even a little bit. He put his arms around me, kissed me with enthusiasm, and all I could smell was blood. He was wet with it. It was getting all over my dress and my arms and my chest.

After a minute he drew back, frowning. "Sookie?" he said. "You're not rejoicing?"

I tried to think of what to say. I felt like a big fat hypocrite. "Eric, I'm glad we don't have to worry about Victor anymore. And I know this was what we planned. But surrounded by dead people and body parts is not my idea of a good place for a celebration, and I've never been less horny in my life."

His eyes narrowed. He didn't like my raining on his parade. Understandable.

And that was the thing, wasn't it? I found all of this *understandable.* But I still hated it, hated myself, wasn't too fond of anyone else. "You need some blood," I said. "I really am sorry you were wounded, and you go ahead and take some."

"You are being a hypocrite, and I will take blood," he said, and he struck.

It hurt. He didn't make it feel good, an action almost automatic for a vampire. Tears ran down my face without my wanting them to. In an odd way, I felt the pain was merited, justified — but I also understood this was a turning point in our relationship.

Our relationship had been marked by a thousand turning points, seemed like.

Then Bill stood at my shoulder, staring at

Eric's mouth on my throat. His expression was complex: rage, resentment, longing.

I was ready for something simple, and I was ready for the pain to stop. My eyes met Bill's.

"Sheriff," Bill said. His voice had never been smoother. Eric twitched, and I knew he'd heard Bill, knew Eric realized he should stop. But he didn't.

I shook myself free of the lethargy and self-loathing, grabbed hold of Eric's earlobe, and pinched as hard as I could.

He detached with a gasp. His mouth was bloody.

"Bill's gonna take me home," I said. "We'll talk tomorrow night. Maybe."

Eric bent down to kiss me, but I flinched. Not with that bloody mouth.

"Tomorrow," Eric said, his eyes searching my face. He turned away and called, "Listen up, people! We have to start cleaning the club."

They groaned like kids told to pick up their toys. Immanuel went to Colton and helped him up. "You can stay at my place," Immanuel said. "It's not too far."

"I won't sleep," Colton answered. "Audrina's dead."

"We'll get through the night," Immanuel told him.

The two human men left Fangtasia, their shoulders slumped with exhaustion and grief. I wondered how they felt about their vengeance now that it had been accomplished, but I knew I'd never ask them. I might never see them again.

Bill put his arm around me as I stumbled a little, and I found myself glad he was there to help me. I knew I couldn't have driven myself. I found my purse, still with a couple of stakes inside, and I pulled my keys out of an inside pocket.

"Where did Bubba go?" I asked.

"He likes to go hang around the old Civic Auditorium," Bill said. "He used to perform there. He'll dig a hole, sleep in the ground."

I nodded. I was too tired to say anything.

Bill didn't speak again the whole way home, which was a blessing. I stared through the windshield into the black night, wondering how I'd feel tomorrow. That had been a lot of killing, and it had been so fast and bloody — like watching one of those violence-porn movies. I'd seen a few seconds of one of the *Saw* movies when I was at Jason's house. That had been enough for me.

I fully believed that Victor had set this in motion with his own intransigence. If Felipe had put someone else in charge of Louisiana, the whole catastrophe wouldn't have occurred. Maybe I could blame Felipe? No, the buck had to stop here.

"What are you thinking of?" Bill said as we were going down my driveway.

"I'm thinking about blame and guilt and assassination," I said.

He simply nodded. "Me, too. Sookie, you know that Victor did his best to provoke Eric."

We'd parked behind the house, and I turned to him questioningly, my hand on the car door handle.

"Yes," Bill said. "He was doing his best to provoke Eric to act, so that he could kill Eric without having to justify it. It's only because of superior planning that Eric has survived and Victor has not. I know that you love Eric." His voice remained calm and cool as he said this, and only the lines around his eyes told me how much it cost him. "You have to be glad, and maybe tomorrow you will be glad, that this situation has ended the way it has."

I pinched my mouth together for a second while I formed my response. "I'd rather Eric be alive than Victor," I said. "True enough."

"And you know violence was the only way to achieve that result."

I could even see that. I nodded.

"So why the second-guessing?" Bill said. He was calling me on my reaction.

I let go of the door handle and turned to face him. "It was bloody and ghastly, and people suffered," I said, surprised by the anger in my voice.

"Did you think Victor would die without bleeding? Did you think Victor's people wouldn't do their best to prevent his death? Did you think that no one would die?"

His voice was so calm and nonjudgmental that I didn't get angry. "Bill, I never believed any of those things. I'm not naïve. But seeing is always different from planning."

Abruptly, I was tired of this topic. It had happened, it was done, I had to find a way to get over it. "Have you met the Queen of Oklahoma?" I asked him.

"Yes," he said, a definite note of caution in his voice. "Why do you ask?"

"Before he died, Appius sort of gave Eric to her."

This did shock Bill. "You're sure?"

"Yes. He finally told me after Pam did everything but stick her hand up his ass and wiggle her fingers to make him talk."

Bill turned away, but not before I saw the smile he was trying to suppress. "Pam's very determined when she wants Eric to take a particular course of action. Did Eric tell you what he intends to do about this situation?"

"He's trying to get out of it, but evidently Appius signed something. When Appius told me before he died that I'd never keep Eric, I didn't know that was what he meant. I thought he meant Eric wouldn't want to fool with me when I got old and wrinkled, or that we'd quarrel and break up, or that . . . Oh, I don't know. Something would happen to separate us."

"And now something has."

"Well . . . yes."

"You know that he'll have to put you aside if he marries the queen? Eric can certainly feed off humans if he's married to a royal, and he can even have a pet human, but he can't have a wife."

"That's what he gave me to understand."

"Sookie . . . don't do anything rash."

"I already broke the bond."

After a long pause, Bill said, "That's a good thing, because the bond was risky for both of you." Not exactly news.

"I sort of miss having the connection," I confessed, "but at the same time it's a relief."

Bill didn't say anything. Very carefully.

"Have you ever . . . ?" I asked.

"Once, long ago," he said. He didn't want

to talk about it.

"Did it end well?"

"No," he said. His voice was flat and didn't invite me to continue that line of conversation. "Let it go, Sookie. I'm telling you this not as a former lover, but as a friend. Let Eric make up his own mind about this. Don't ask him questions. Though we can't stand each other, I know Eric will try his best to get out of this situation simply because he loves his freedom. Oklahoma is very beautiful, and Eric loves beauty, but he already has that in you."

I must be feeling better if I could appreciate a compliment. I wondered what the queen's real name was. Often the ruler was called by the name of the land she ruled; Bill hadn't meant that the state was beautiful, but that the woman who ruled its night creatures was.

When I didn't respond, Bill continued, "She also has a lot of power. That is, she has territory, minions, real estate, oil money." And we both knew Eric loved power. Not complete power — he'd never wanted to be a king — but he loved being able to call the shots in his own bailiwick.

"I get what power is," I said. "And I get that I don't have it. You want to take the car to your house, or leave it here and go

451

through the woods?"

He handed the keys to me and said, "I'll go through the woods."

There was nothing more to be said.

"Thanks," I told him. I opened the porch door, stepped in, locked it behind me. I unlocked the back door and went in, switching on the kitchen light. There was a quiet emptiness to the house, which I found immediately soothing, and the air conditioners were doing their best to make everything cool.

Though I'd come out of the fight at Fangtasia better than anyone, at least physically, I felt battered and bruised. I'd be sore the next day. I unbuckled the big belt and returned the cluviel dor to my makeup drawer. I pulled off the stained dress, went to the back porch to toss it in the washing machine on cold soak, and got in the shower, turning the water as hot as I could bear it. When I'd scrubbed myself all over, I changed the temperature to cool. I was delightfully clean and fresh when I got out to dry myself.

I wondered if I would start crying or praying or sitting in a corner with my eyes wide open the rest of the night. But none of those reactions set in. I got into bed feeling relieved, as if I'd had a successful surgery or as if a biopsy had turned out well.

I thought, as I curled into a ball and composed myself for sleep, that the fact that I could sleep tonight was almost more frightening than anything else.

CHAPTER 17

All the women in my living room were happy. Some of them were happier than others, true, but none of them were miserable. They were there to give gifts to someone who deserved them, and they were happy that Tara was expecting twins. All the yellow and green and blue and pink tissue paper mounded up in an almost overwhelming way, but Tara was getting a lot of things she needed and wanted.

Dermot was unobtrusively helping with the refreshments and bagging up the torn gift paper to keep the floor clear. Some of my older guests were definitely at the tottering stage, so we didn't need anything on the floor that might cause them to slip. JB's mom and grandmother were here, and his grandmother was seventy-five if she was a day.

When Dermot had come to the back door earlier, I'd let him in and gone back to my coffee without a word. As soon as he was in the door, I felt measurably better. Maybe I hadn't noticed the contrast these past few weeks because I'd been so wrapped up in the blood bond? I'd been under the influence of a lot of supernatural things. I couldn't say it felt better to be just myself, but it certainly made me feel more in touch with reality.

Once my guests had gotten a good look at Dermot and realized how much he looked like Jason, there'd been a lot of raised eyebrows. I'd told them he was a distant cousin from Florida, and I'd heard from a lot of brains that ladies were going to be consulting their family trees to find a Florida connection for my family.

I felt like myself today. I felt like I was doing what I was supposed to be doing, in the community where I lived. I might not even be that same person who'd participated in a slaughter the night before.

I took a sip from my glass cup. Maxine's punch had turned out well, the cake I'd picked up from the bakery was delicious, my cheese straws were crispy and just a little spicy, and the salted pecans were toasted just enough. We played Baby Bingo as Tara opened her gifts, and she glowed and said "Thank you" about a million times.

I felt more and more like the old Sookie Stackhouse as the event progressed. I was around people I understood, doing a good thing.

As a kind of bonus, JB's grandmother told me a lovely story about my grandmother. Taken altogether, it was a good afternoon.

When I went in the kitchen with a tray full of dirty dishes, I thought, *This is happiness. Last night wasn't the real me.*

But it had been. I knew — even as I thought this — that I wasn't going to be able to fool myself. I'd changed in order to survive, and I was paying the price of survival. I had to be willing to change myself forever, or everything I'd made myself do was for nothing.

"Are you all right, Sookie?" Dermot asked, as he brought in more glasses.

"Yes, thanks." I tried to smile at him but felt it was a weak effort.

There was a knock at the back door. I supposed it was a late guest, trying to sneak in unobtrusively.

Mr. Cataliades stood there. He was wearing a suit, as always, but for the first time it seemed somewhat the worse for wear. He seemed not quite as circular as he had been, but he was smiling politely. I was astonished at his presence and not completely sure I wanted to talk to him, but if he was the guy who could answer big questions about my life, I really didn't have a lot of choice. "Come in," I told him, standing back and holding open the door.

"Miss Stackhouse," he said formally. "Thank you for your welcome."

He stared at Dermot, who was washing dishes very carefully, proud to be trusted with Gran's good china. "Young man," he said in acknowledgment.

Dermot turned and froze. "Demon," he said. Then he turned back to the sink, but I could tell he was thinking furiously.

"You're having a social occasion?" Mr. Cataliades asked me. "I can tell there are many women in the house."

I hadn't even noticed the cacophony of feminine voices floating down the hall, but it sounded like there might be sixty women in the living room instead of twenty-five. "Yes," I agreed. "There are. It's a baby shower for a friend of mine."

"Perhaps I could sit at your kitchen table until it's over?" he suggested. "Perhaps a bite to eat?"

Reminded of my manners, I said, "Of course, you can have as much as you like!" I quickly made a ham sandwich and put some chips and pickles out, and prepared a

457

separate plate with party goodies. I even poured him a cup of punch.

Mr. Cataliades's dark eyes glowed at the sight of the food in front of him. It might not be as fancy as he was used to (though for all I knew he ate raw mice), but he dug in with a will. Dermot seemed all right, if not exactly relaxed, at being in the same room with the lawyer, so I left them to make the best of it and returned to the living room. The hostess couldn't be away for long; it wasn't polite.

Tara had opened all the presents. Her shop assistant, McKenna, had written down all the gifts and the givers, and taped the card in with each offering. Everyone was talking about her own labor and delivery — oh, joy — and Tara was fielding questions about her ob-gyn, the hospital where she'd deliver, what names they'd thought of for the babies, whether they knew the sexes of the twins, how far away her due date was, and on and on.

Gradually, the guests began to depart, and when they were all gone I had to fend off sincere offers from Tara and her mother-in-law and Jason's girlfriend, Michele, to help with the dishes. I told them, "No sirree, you just leave them there, that's my job," and I could hear my grandmother's words flow-ing right out of my mouth. It almost made me laugh. If I hadn't had a demon and a fairy in my kitchen, I might have. We got all the gifts loaded into Tara's and her mother-in-law's cars, and Michele told me she and Jason were having a catfish fry the next weekend and they wanted me to come. I said I'd see, that sounded wonderful.

It was a huge relief when all the humans were gone.

I would have thrown myself in the chair and read for thirty minutes or watched an episode of *Jeopardy!* before starting to clean up if I hadn't had the two men waiting in my kitchen. Instead, I had to march back laden with still more plates and cups.

To my surprise, Dermot was gone. I hadn't noticed his car go down the driveway, but I assumed he'd blended in with all the other departing guests. Mr. Cataliades was sitting in the same chair, drinking a cup of coffee. He had put his plate over by the sink. Hadn't washed it, but he'd carried it over.

"So," I said, "they've left. You didn't eat Dermot, did you?"

He beamed at me. "No, dear Miss Stackhouse, I did not. Though I'm sure he would be tasty. The ham sandwich was delicious."

"I'm glad you enjoyed it," I responded automatically. "Listen, Mr. Cataliades, I found a letter from my grandmother. I'm not sure I understand our relationship correctly, or maybe I just don't understand what it means that you are my sponsor."

His beam intensified. "Though I'm in a slight hurry, I'll do everything I can to dispel your confusion."

"Okay." I wondered why he was in a hurry, if he was still being pursued, but I wasn't going to be sidetracked. "Let me sort of repeat this back to you and you can tell me if I got it straight."

He nodded his round head.

"You were good friends with my birth grandfather, Fintan. Dermot's brother."

"Yes, Dermot's twin."

"But you don't seem that fond of Dermot."

He shrugged. "I'm not."

I almost got off on a tangent there, but I stuck to my train of thought. "So, Fintan was still alive when Jason and I were born."

Desmond Cataliades nodded enthusiastically. "Yes, he was."

"My gran said in her letter that you visited my dad and his sister, Fintan's actual children."

"I was here."

"So, did you give them — us — a gift?"

"I tried, but you couldn't all accept it. Not

460

all of you had the essential spark."

That was a phrase Niall had used. "What is the essential spark?"

"What a clever question!" Mr. Cataliades said, regarding me as if I were a monkey who'd opened a hatch to retrieve a banana. "The gift I gave to my dear friend Fintan was that any of his human descendants who possessed the essential spark would be able to read the minds of their fellow humans, as I can."

"So, when it turned out that my dad and aunt Linda didn't have it, you returned when Jason and I were born."

He nodded. "Seeing you wasn't absolutely necessary. After all, the gift had been given. But by visiting Jason and then you, I could know for certain. I was very excited when I held you, though I think your poor grandmother was frightened."

"So only I and —" I choked back Hunter's name. Mr. Cataliades had written Hadley's will, and she hadn't mentioned Hunter. It was possible he didn't know Hadley had had a child. "Only I have had it so far. And you still haven't explained what the spark is."

He gave me an arch look as if to say he sure couldn't get anything by me. "The essential spark isn't easy to pin down in terms

461

of your DNA," he told me. "It's an openness to the other world. Some humans literally can't believe there are creatures in another world besides ours, creatures who have feelings and rights and beliefs and deserve to live their own lives. Humans who are born with the essential spark are born to experience or perform something wonderful, something amazing."

I'd done something pretty amazing the night before, but it surely wasn't wonderful . . . unless you hated vampires.

"Gran had the essential spark," I said suddenly. "So Fintan thought he'd find it in one of us."

"Yes, though of course he never wanted me to give her my gift." Mr. Cataliades looked wistfully at the refrigerator, and I got up to make him another ham sandwich. This time I sliced some fresh tomato and put it on a little plate, and he piled every single bit on the sandwich and still managed to eat it neatly. Now that was supernatural.

When he'd finished half the sandwich, Mr. Cataliades paused to say, "Fintan loved humans, and he especially loved human women, and he even more greatly loved human women with the essential spark. They aren't easy to find. He adored Adele so much that he put the portal in the woods so he could visit her more easily, and I'm afraid he was mischievous enough to . . ."

And it was Mr. Cataliades's turn to stop and look at me uneasily, weighing his words.

"He took my grandfather for a test drive every now and then," I said. "Dermot recognized Fintan in some of the family pictures."

"I'm afraid that was very naughty of him."

"Yes," I said heavily. "It was very naughty."

"He had great hopes when your father was born, and I was here the day after to inspect him, but he was quite normal, though of course attractive and magnetic, as those who are part fae are. Linda, the second child, was, too. And I'm sorry about the cancer; that shouldn't have happened. I blame it on the environment. She should have been perfectly healthy all her life. Your father would have been, if the terrible infighting hadn't broken out among the fairies. Perhaps if Fintan had survived, Linda's health would have stayed with her." Mr. Cataliades shrugged. "Adele tried to reach Fintan to ask if there was anything he could do for Linda, but by then he had passed away."

"I wonder why she didn't use the cluviel dor to cure Aunt Linda's cancer."

"I don't know," he said, with apparent regret. "Knowing Adele, I imagine she didn't think it would be Christian. It's possible that she didn't even remember she had it by that time, or that she regarded it as a romantic love token but nothing more. After all, by the time her daughter's illness became evident, it had been many years since I'd given it to her on Fintan's behalf."

I thought hard, trying to pare down this conversation to learn what I had to know. "Why on earth did you think telepathy would be such a great gift?" I blurted.

For the first time, he looked a bit miffed. "I thought it would give Fintan's descendants an edge over their fellow humans for all of their lives, to know what other people were thinking and planning," he said. "And since I'm nearly all demon, and I had it to give, it seemed a splendid gift to me. It would be wonderful even for a fairy! If your great-grandfather had known that Breandan's henchmen were determined to murder him, he could have squelched the rebellion before it caught hold. Your father could have saved himself and your mother from drowning if he'd known a trap was set for him."

"But those things didn't happen."

"Full-blooded fairies aren't telepathic — though they can sometimes send messages, they can't hear an answer — and your father didn't have the essential spark."

This seemed like a circular kind of conversation.

"So what this all boils down to is this: Since you two were such good buddies, Fintan asked you to give his and Adele's descendants a gift, to stand as their — our — sponsor."

Mr. Cataliades smiled. "Correct."

"You were willing to do this, and you thought telepathy would be a dandy present."

"Correct again. Though it seems I was mistaken."

"You were. And you gave this gift in some mysterious demon way —"

"Not so mysterious," he said indignantly. "Adele and Fintan each drank a thimbleful of my blood."

Okay, I could *not* picture my grandmother doing that. But then, I couldn't have imagined her consorting with a fairy, either. In point of fact, it had become obvious that I'd known my grandmother very well in some respects and not at all in others.

"I put it in wine and told her it was a special vintage," Mr. Cataliades confessed. "And in a way it was so."

"Okay, you lied. No big surprise there," I

said. Though Gran had been plenty smart, and I was sure she'd at least had suspicions. I waved my hands in the air. I could think about that later. "Okeydokey. So after they'd both ingested your blood, any descendants of theirs would be telepathic if they were also born with this essential spark."

"Correct." He smiled so broadly that I felt I'd gotten an A on my test.

"And my grandmother never used the cluviel dor."

"No, it's a one-use thing. A very pretty gift from Fintan to Adele."

"Can I use it to take away the telepathy?"

"No, my dear, it would be like wishing away your spleen or your kidneys. But an interesting thought."

So I couldn't help Hunter with it. Or myself, either. Damn.

"Can I kill someone with it?"

"Yes, of course, if that someone is threatening someone you love. Directly. You couldn't cause the death of your tax assessor . . . unless he was standing over your brother with an ax, say."

"Was it a coincidence that Hadley wound up with the queen?"

"Not really, because she is part fairy, and as you know, part fairy is very attractive to vampires. It was only a matter of time before a vampire came into the bar and saw you."

"He was sent by the queen."

"Do tell." Cataliades didn't look a bit surprised. "The queen never asked me about the gift, and I never told her I was your sponsor. She never paid much attention to the world of the fae unless she wanted to drink fairy blood. She certainly never cared who my friends were or how I spent my time."

"Who's on your trail now?"

"A pertinent question, my dear, but one I can't answer. In fact, I've been able to sense them getting nearer this past half hour, and I must take my departure. I noticed some excellent wards on the house, and I must congratulate you. Who laid them?"

"Bellenos. An elf. He's at the club called Hooligans in Monroe."

"Bellenos." Mr. Cataliades looked thoughtful. "He's my fifth cousin on my mother's side, I think. By the way, on no account let the riffraff gathered at Hooligans know you have a cluviel dor, because they'll kill you for it."

"What do you think I ought to do with it?" I asked curiously. He was standing and straightening the coat of his summer-weight blue suit. Though it was hot outside and he was heavy, he hadn't been sweating when I

467

let him in. "And where is Diantha?" His niece was as different from Mr. Cataliades as you could imagine, and I was kind of fond of her.

"She's far away and safe," he said tersely. "And as for the cluviel dor, I can't advise you. I've already done enough to you, it seems." Just like that, he was out the back door. I caught a glimpse of his heavy body moving at incredible speed across the backyard, and then he was simply lost from sight.

Well, that had been plenty amazing — and now I was out of ham.

What an enlightening conversation — in some ways. Now I knew more about my own background. I knew that my telepathy was a sort of pre-pregnancy baby shower gift from Desmond Cataliades to his friend Fintan the fairy and my grandmother. That was a stunning revelation, in and of itself.

After I'd finished thinking about that, or at least after I'd pondered it as much as I could bear to, I thought about Cataliades's reference to the "riffraff" at Hooligans. He had a low opinion of the gathering of exiles. I wondered more than ever what the fae were doing in Monroe, what they were plotting and planning. It couldn't be anything good. And I thought of Sandra Pelt, still out there somewhere and determined to see me die.

When my head was exhausted, I let my hands take over. I put the leftover food away, transferring it from the pretty serving pieces to Ziploc bags. I washed the epergne and a couple of cut-glass bowls. I glanced out the window as I rinsed them, which was how I came to observe two gray streaks crossing the yard at great speed. I could not identify what I'd seen, and I almost called animal control. But then I realized the creatures were pursuing the half-demon lawyer, and at the speed they were moving, they must already be far away. Besides, it wouldn't be wise to try to lure anything that could move like that into a cage in the back of a pickup truck. I hoped Mr. Cataliades had his running shoes on. I hadn't checked.

Just when I got everything cleaned up and had changed into my cutoffs and a brown tank top, Sam called. There were no bar sounds in the background: no chink of ice in glasses, no juke box, no babble of conversation. He must be in his trailer. But it was Saturday, late in the afternoon, when Merlotte's would be getting busy. Maybe he had a date with Jannalynn?

"Sookie," he said, and his voice sounded funny. My stomach instantly tied up in a knot. "Can you run into town? Come by the trailer. Someone dropped off a package for you at the bar."

"Who?" I asked. I was looking at the living room mirror as I talked to Sam, and I saw that I looked tense and frightened.

"I didn't know him," Sam said. "But it's sure a nice box with a big bow. Maybe you have a secret admirer." Sam emphasized those words, but not in an obvious way.

"I think I know who that might be," I said, putting a smile into my voice. "Sure, Sam, I'll come. Oh, wait! Could you bring it out here? I'm still cleaning up from the party." Out here would be a lot quieter.

"Let me check," Sam said. There was a silence while he covered the receiver with his hand. I could hear a little muffled conversation, nothing specific. "That'll be great," he said, sounding like it would be anything but. "We'll be out in a few minutes."

"Super," I said, genuinely pleased. That gave me a bit of time to plan a welcome. "See you then." After I hung up, I stood for a second organizing my thoughts before I sped to the front closet to retrieve my shotgun. I checked it out to make sure it was ready. Hoping I'd gain an element of surprise, I decided to hide in the woods. I laced up some running shoes and was out the back door, glad I'd put on a dark-colored tank.

It wasn't Sam's truck that came up the driveway, it was Jannalynn's little car. Jannalynn was driving, Sam was in the front seat passenger, and someone else was in the rear seat.

Jannalynn got out first and looked around. She could smell me, knew I was nearby. She could probably smell the gun, too. She smiled, and it was an awful smile. She was hoping I would shoot the person who'd forced them to come out here, shoot her dead.

Of course, the person holding a gun on them, the person in the backseat, was Sandra Pelt. Sandra got out with a rifle in her hand and pointed it at the car, standing a careful distance away. Then Sam emerged. He was mad as hell; I could tell by the set of his shoulders.

Sandra looked older, thinner, and crazier than she had only days before. She'd dyed her hair black, and her fingernails matched. If she'd been anyone else, I'd have pitied her — parents dead, sister dead, mental troubles. But my pity stopped when someone held a rifle on people I cared about.

"Come out, Sookie!" Sandra sang out.

"Come out! I got you now, you piece of shit!"

Sam moved unobtrusively to Sandra's right, trying to turn to face her. Jannalynn, too, began moving around the car. Sandra, afraid she was losing control of the situation, began to scream at them. "Stay still, don't move, or I'll shoot the hell out of you! You, bitch! You don't want to see his head shot off, do you? Your little doggie lover-boy?"

Jannalynn shook her head. She was wearing shorts, too, and a Hair of the Dog T-shirt. Her hands had flour on them. She and Sam had been cooking.

I could let this escalate, or I could take action. I was too far away, but I had to risk it. Without responding to Sandra at all, I stepped out of the woods and fired.

The roar of the Benelli from an unexpected direction took everyone by surprise. I saw red blotches appear on Sandra's left arm and cheek, and she staggered for a moment in shock. But that wouldn't stop a Pelt, no it wouldn't. Sandra swung up her rifle and aimed at me. Sam leaped for her, but Jannalynn got there first. Jannalynn caught hold of the rifle, wrenched it from Sandra's hands, and flung it away, and then the battle was on. I'd never seen two people fight each other as hard, and given my recent experiences that was saying something.

I couldn't find a way to shoot Sandra again, not with Jannalynn struggling with her hand-to-hand. The two women were much the same size, short and sinewy, but Jannalynn was born to battle while Sandra was more used to quick brawls. Sam and I both circled them as they punched and bit and pulled hair and did everything to each other they could possibly do. Real damage was inflicted on both sides, and after a few seconds Jannalynn's side was stained red, and the flow from Sandra's shotgun wounds had accelerated. Sam reached into the struggling duo — it was like putting your hand in a fan — to grasp Sandra's hair and yank, and she screamed like a banshee and spared a fist to punch Sam in the face. He kept his grip on her hair, though I thought she'd broken his nose.

I felt obliged to do my share — after all, this was my fault — so I waited my turn. It was oddly like waiting to jump into the turning rope when I was on the playground in elementary school. When I saw my moment, I surged into the fight zone and gripped the first thing that came to my hands, Sandra's upper left arm. Her momentum seized, she couldn't deliver the punch she was aiming to throw at Jannalynn's face. Instead, Jannalynn cocked one of her own hard little fists and knocked the consciousness right out of Sandra Pelt.

Suddenly I was holding the shoulder of a woman who'd gone completely limp. I let go, and she fell to the ground. Her head sagged oddly. Jannalynn had broken her neck. I didn't know if Sandra was dead or alive.

"Fuck," Jannalynn said pleasantly. "Fuck, fuck, fuckety fuck."

"Amen," Sam said.

I burst into tears. Jannalynn looked disgusted. "I know, I know," I said despairingly, "but I saw a lot of people get killed last night, and this is just one person too many! I'm sorry, y'all." I think Sam would have hugged me if Jannalynn hadn't been right there. I know he thought about it. That was the important thing.

"She isn't completely gone," Jannalynn said after a moment's concentration on the inert Sandra, and before Sam or I could say or do one thing, she knelt by Sandra, clenched her fists, and brought them down on Sandra's skull.

And that was that.

Sam looked across the corpse at me. I

didn't know what to say or do. I'm sure my face reflected that helplessness.

"Well," said Jannalynn brightly, dusting her hands together with the air of one who's finally completed an unpleasant job, "what shall we do with the body?"

Maybe I should install a crematorium in my backyard. "Should we call the sheriff?" I asked, since I felt obliged to at least suggest it.

Sam looked troubled. "More bad news for the bar," he said. "I'm sorry to think about that, but I have to."

"She took you all hostage," I said.

"We say."

I got Sam's point.

Jannalynn said, "I don't think anyone saw us leaving the bar with her. She was sitting low in the backseat."

"Her car's still at my place," Sam said.

"I know somewhere she'll never be found," I heard myself saying, to my own complete surprise.

"Where would that be?" Jannalynn asked. She looked up at me, and I could tell that we were never going to be best friends or paint each other's nails. Aww.

"We'll throw her in the portal," I said.

"What?" Sam was still staring down at the body, looking sick.

"We'll throw her in the fairy portal."

Jannalynn gaped at me. "There are fairies here?"

"Not at the moment. It's hard to explain, but I've got a portal in my woods."

"You're quite the . . ." She couldn't seem to think how to end the sentence. "Quite the surprise," she said finally.

"That's what everyone says."

Since Jannalynn was still bleeding, I stooped over to get Sandra's feet. Sam got her shoulders. He seemed to have gotten over the worst of the shock. He was breathing through his mouth, since his broken nose was clogged. "Where we headed?" he said.

"Okay, it's about a quarter mile that way." I jerked my head in the right direction, since my hands were occupied.

So off we went, slowly and awkwardly. The blood had quit dripping, and she was light, and it went as well as carrying a body through the woods can go. I said, "I think instead of calling this the Stackhouse place, I'll just call it the Body Farm."

"Like that place in Tennessee?" Jannalynn said, to my surprise.

"Right."

"Patricia Cornwell wrote a book called that, didn't she?" Sam said, and I almost smiled. This was a very civilized discussion to be having under the circumstances. Maybe I was still a little numb from the night before, or maybe I was continuing my process of hardening up to survive the world around me, but I found I simply didn't care much about Sandra. The Pelts had had a personal vendetta against me for no very good reason for a very long time, and now it was over.

I finally understood something about the mayhem of the night before. It wasn't the individual deaths I found so appalling but the level of violence, the sheer horror of seeing so much dealt out and received. . . . Just as I found Jannalynn's execution of Sandra the most disturbing thing about today's encounter. Unless I was mistaken, Sam did, too.

We reached the small open space in the trees. I was glad to see the little distortion in the air that betrayed the portal into Faery. I pointed silently, as if the fae could hear me (and for all I knew, they could). After a second or two, Jannalynn and Sam spotted what I was trying to show them. They eyed it curiously, and Jannalynn went so far as to stick her finger in it. Her finger vanished from sight, and with a yelp, she pulled her hand back. She was definitely relieved to see that the finger was still attached.

"Count of three," I said, and Sam nodded. He moved from the end of Sandra's body to the side, and as smoothly as if we had practiced it, we fed the corpse into the magical hole. It wouldn't have worked if she hadn't been so small.

Then we waited.

The corpse didn't get spat back out. No one leaped out with a sword to demand our lives for desecrating the land of the fae. Instead, we heard a snarling and a yapping, and we all stood frozen, our eyes wide and our arms tense, waiting for something to issue from the portal, something that we had to fight.

But nothing came out. The noises continued, and they were graphic enough: rending and tearing, more snarling, and then after some sounds so disturbing I won't even try to describe them, there was silence. I figured there wasn't any Sandra left.

We trudged back through the woods to the car. Its doors were standing open, and the first thing Sam did was shut them to stop the dinging. There were splotches of blood on the ground. I unrolled the garden hose and turned it on. Sam watered down the bloody spots and gave Jannalynn's car a nice rinse while he was at it. In a gut-wrenching moment — *another* gut-wrenching moment — Jannalynn set Sam's broken nose straight, and though he yelled and tears sprang to his eyes, I knew that the nose would heal well.

Sandra's rifle was more of a problem than the body had been. I was not going to use the portal as a garbage disposal, and that was what throwing the rifle in after the body felt like. After some argument, Jannalynn and Sam decided they'd throw it into the woods on their way back to Sam's trailer, and I guess that was what they did.

I was left in my house alone after a truly amazing and horrible two days. Horribly amazing? Amazingly horrible? Both.

I sat in my kitchen, a book open on the table before me. The sun was still lighting up the yard, but the shadows were growing long. I thought of the cluviel dor, which I hadn't had a chance to use in the encounter in the backyard. Should I carry it around with me every minute of the day? I wondered if the gray things after Mr. Cataliades had caught up with him yet, and I wondered if I'd feel sad if they did. I wondered if the vampires had gotten Fangtasia cleaned up by opening time, and I wondered if I would call the bar to find out. There'd be humans there to answer the phone: Mustapha Khan, maybe his buddy Warren.

I wondered if Eric had talked to Felipe yet about the disappearance of the Regent of Louisiana. I wondered if Eric had written to the Queen of Oklahoma.

Maybe the phone would ring when darkness fell. Maybe it wouldn't. I couldn't decide which I wanted.

What I did want to do was something completely normal.

I walked barefoot into the living room with a big icy glass of tea. Time to watch some of my recorded episodes of *Jeopardy!*

Dangerous Creatures for two hundred, anyone?

ABOUT THE AUTHOR

New York Times bestselling author **Charlaine Harris** writes both fantasies and mysteries. She lives in a small town in southern Arkansas with her family.